THE WATCHER

Now you see him, now you die...

A young woman's corpse is found within the grounds of Edinburgh Castle with the message 'More will Die' written on her body in blood. The prophecy is soon fulfilled as more bodies – all young women, all redheads – are found bludgeoned to death, their feet severed. Headstrong lawyer Brodie McLennan teams up with DI Duncan Bancho in an effort to identify the 'Edinburgh Ripper', as he has been dubbed by the media. Unbeknownst to Brodie, the killer's web is spinning ever closer to her teenage sister Connie. When Connie is reported missing, will Brodie's own flesh and blood become the next victim?

THE WATCHER

by

Grace Monroe

Magna Large Print Books
Long Preston, North Yorkshire,
BD23 4ND, England.

British Library Cataloguing in Publication Data.

Monroe, Grace
    The watcher.

    A catalogue record of this book is
    available from the British Library

    ISBN   978-0-7505-3313-3

First published in Great Britain by HarperCollins Publishers 2008

Copyright © Grace Monroe 2008

Cover illustration by arrangement with Arcangel Images

Grace Monroe asserts the moral right to be identified as the author of this work

Published in Large Print 2010 by arrangement with HarperCollins Publishers

Magna Large Print is an imprint of Library Magna Books Ltd.

Printed and bound in Great Britain by
T.J. (International) Ltd., Cornwall, PL28 8RW

Acknowledgments

From Maria:

Once again I find myself indebted to so many people. Principally I would like to thank my girlfriends who encouraged me – Debbie, Helen and Marissa. Jenny Brown you are a star agent and not forgetting the superb team at Avon, Maxine Hitchcock, Keshini Naidoo and Sammia Rafique. Thank you for making this book possible.

From Linda:

Many thanks as always to everyone who has helped so much with this book in so many different ways – Maxine, Keshini and Sammia as always, as well as anyone at Avon who I don't even know but who actually manages to get this on the shelves at the end of the day (if they do want to let me know who they are, I will put them on my Xmas card list, promise). Jenny Brown of Jenny Brown Associates has gone beyond the call of duty, and I get the feeling that a thankful nod in the direction of Stan and Lucy there wouldn't go amiss either! Thanks to all the people whose books I've been ghostwriting as this book has gone along as they've been thrown into a process that they didn't expect – Donna and Jeff have given me huge amounts of support in a tables-turned-sort-of-way. To my Auntie Frances for the lovely words (you don't know how much they meant to me) and to three people who have been particularly amazing for this one – Iain, Norman and Fiona; gold stars all round!

From Maria:

For my Mum and Dad who taught me what it is to be loved.

From Linda:

For Paul – who knows what matters.

Prologue

Edinburgh Castle
Friday 21 December

When Katya Waleski stepped out of the Great Hall at Edinburgh Castle, she had less than fifteen minutes to live.

The castle ramparts were bitter but the chill went deeper than her bones. The north wind whipped and bit her bare shoulders; she shivered – not simply because of the temperature.

Her companion removed his custom-made evening jacket and placed it around her shoulders. Katya lengthened her spine like a cat and purred, more aware of the role she was playing than the man was of the performance he was receiving. Her wine glass was slippery with condensation; it almost fell out of her hand. Her usual poise had deserted her.

Katya gazed into his eyes, showing him white even teeth; for once the smile left her lips. The champagne bubbles tickled her nose, languorously she twirled her curls; it was not often she got paid to enjoy herself. Katya closed her eyes. For a few long seconds she held her breath as she savoured the champagne.

The biting north wind cut through her hair, a country girl. The stars shone in an almost cloudless black sky, the moonlight reflected off the snow, giving the castle battlements an eerie glow. It was difficult to walk on the cobbled stones; they were icy underfoot and the melt-water crept through her satin sandal. It was hard to keep her footing so she held on tightly to the arm of her escort.

She scanned the castle walls, peering into the shadows. Could she feel eyes upon her from somewhere in the distance? Katya was used to being ogled but this surely felt ... different. A lone piper circled the half-moon battery, welcoming late comers to the ceilidh, serenading the lovers who sought intimacy in the ancient nooks and crannies of the castle.

Katya quivered at the caterwaul. You had to have the blood of the Celts in your veins to be stirred by such a noise. The lament merely made the fine hairs at the base of her neck stand on end.

The wind had picked up, and it blew a solitary cloud across the moon, the dense ground cover that hid his static body began to crackle and bend. Branches scratched his cheeks, his jaw tightened and his neck stiffened as the gale began to howl. He could see the clouds rolling in over the River Forth. It was going to snow. He rubbed his leg to ease the paralysing cramp.

The first flake fell.

Didn't that just say it all, though? A snowstorm while he froze his ass off waiting for that bitch.

The Watcher dug himself in deeper; something large scuttled by his ear. They say in Edinburgh you are never more than thirteen feet from a rat. He disciplined his mind to ignore the different types of creepy-crawlies, which might, at this very moment, be crawling their way up his spine or nesting in his ears.

His eyes followed a couple as they left the castle early. The man staggered and leant on the railing of the wooden bridge; clutching on to the rails, the gentleman spewed his guts out. Flaming torches illuminated the massive stone statues of Scotland's guardians – Wallace and Bruce looked down disapprovingly. Were these Protectors judging the drunk, who was now failing to heed the 'don't drink and drive' warnings, or were they judging him? He sniggered at the thought.

The Watcher knows death stalks the castle ramparts.

'The lovers,' he spat out the words, were strolling hand in hand towards the battlements, their heads nestling together like two turtle doves. The man's hand crept underneath the jacket and fondled her tight, high buttocks; he inched the dress up over her hip, and stroked her silky smooth skin. The Watcher held his breath. His tongue crept out of the side of his mouth, like a ravenous dog's, flecks of spit formed at the corner of his mouth. With a life of its own, The Watcher's cock stiffened, uncomfortably; he was forced to shift positions; the bed of leaves rustled beneath his weight

With eyes only for each other, Katya and her beau strolled towards the cannons overlooking Johnston Terrace. *Love is blind* hissed The Watcher. Using his top-of-the-range German night-vision goggles, and aided by the light reflected off the snow, The Watcher had a perfect view. He settled himself down to enjoy the show.

It's freezing but Katya was hot; The Watcher could almost see the sheen of sweat on her skin as he licked his dry lips. She seductively slipped her lover's jacket from her shoulders, mindful of the fact it cost more than she earns in three months, and she handed it back to him.

The Watcher held his breath as she used her lovely white teeth to undo her lover's zip; the jacket is placed on his arm as he leant against the cannon to appreciate his girl. The red silk evening gown slipped easily from her shoulders, revealing full high virgin breasts; her head fell back in ecstasy. A tiny black dragon is tattooed near her nipple; it catches The Watcher's throat when he recognizes it as Mushu, the dragon from Mulan. He shook his head – it would not save her tonight

Her hands reached up to undo her lover's black evening tie. He was more than willing to play ball; the tie lay around his neck as she opened his white pin-tucked evening shirt. The Watcher admired their hardiness – it is seriously cold. He shook his right leg to keep the blood flowing, and placed his free hand inside his trousers.

Raking her long red talons over the expensive evening shirt, his nipples stood to attention. It is not merely a natural reaction to the cold, the man was understandably aroused. He caressed her neck with light tender kisses, moving his mouth down until he found her nipple, her back arched in gratification.

Katya was a bad girl; her sensuous mouth was open wide with pleasure. The Watcher strained to hear her moan, as he stroked himself faster and faster. *Yes, Katya was a very bad girl.*

Her lover could bear no more. The tent pole in his trousers said everything, The Watcher understood as he observed him lay the jacket on the barrel of the siege cannon. Gallantry is not dead, surmised The Watcher; the lover didn't want Katya's back to stick to the icy metal.

The sex did not disappoint The Watcher; Katya's hands quickly undid her lover's trousers as they fell without hindrance to his ankles. Grudgingly, The Watcher conceded his rival was a handsome specimen; no one complained about the cold now – not even The Watcher.

They were good enough to be professional, The Watcher thought as she wrapped her long Eastern European legs around the man's waist. She panted, he could see her breath move in and out of her mouth like exotic smoke, and her back inched along the cannon as her lover thrust himself into her.

It was hard for The Watcher to remain still; he squirmed in the undergrowth, unable to satisfy himself. The moonlight caught the girl's red hair; it seemed to sparkle with excitement, her body shone with sweat, the curves glistening.

The sex was vigorous and uninhibited – in spite of himself, The Watcher felt a reluctant twinge of admiration for her lover. He bit his tongue as the girl slid further along the barrel, blood trickled out of the side of his mouth as a naked Katya finally reached the mouth of the cannon.

Taking out a camera, he caught Katya's final throes of ecstasy, her back bucking in pleasure as she slid off the end. Her lover reached for her as she tumbled over the ramparts.

The Watcher was helpless – he could not stifle his cry: it was not supposed to happen like that. Shock heightened his senses, and he saw in slow motion Katya's body bounce off the volcanic castle rock. Her head cracked open as it hit the first rough edge, marring her once beautiful features. There will be no open coffin for the mourners; like a rag doll she rolled and bounced, each bump shattering another bone. There is no hope for the once lovely Katya.

The police found Katya in a ditch at the foot of the crag and tail structure known as Castle Hill. On her scraped and scuffed body a message could be discerned.

A bloody prophecy:

more will die

Chapter One

Lothian and St Clair W.S. Offices
Saturday 22 December, 8 a.m.

It was the last Saturday before Christmas, I hadn't bought a single present and this year I had sworn it would all be different. I'd even imagined stringing popcorn on a real tree, yet here I was spending another weekend working in the office. And on the front page of the *Evening News* was a photograph that made my heart race and my breath catch in my throat.

Another dead girl had been found.

The story had filled the papers for months, endless column inches, always featuring those painfully ordinary photographs of the murder victim. You've seen them. The school portraits with the stray piece of hair sticking out that makes you ask why someone didn't smooth it down. That picture. The one every parent is forced to buy. When you see it on top of a fireplace a slow smile of nostalgia crosses your lips. But when the same image is on the front page of the *Evening News,* your heart stops, and you look twice. On a second glance you take in more, the bad posture, the shy smile, the timid eyes ... and your imagination takes you to hell.

The hell she suffered in her last moments.

I brought the newspaper over to the window with me. Sipping on the freshly made espresso, with two sugars, I dipped a biscotti whilst I read aloud to Lavender Ironside, official holder of all things to do with power in both the office and my life.

'Reign of terror on city streets.'

'Everyone is running scared. Eddie's trying to impose his own personal curfew. He maybe doesn't have as much sway as he'd like on the entire population of Edinburgh, but he'd lock me up if he could,' she said. As the words came out of her mouth, I could almost hear her regret them. She loved it when Eddie was masterful; Eddie Gibb, my court assistant and Lavender's fiancé. Recently, however, his attentions had been for another reason, and we both knew it.

Lavender's surprise and very much unplanned pregnancy of recent months had ended in a miscarriage. Both she and Eddie had been delighted at the thought of a baby cementing their unlikely love – we all had; and we'd all had to deal with the consequences, which included an even more protective Eddie. I found it hard to talk to Lavender about the baby. We had always looked out for each other but this was one area where I just didn't know what to say. She knew I wasn't the motherly type really, but I had looked forward to being an auntie, even if not by blood – and I always wanted for her what she wanted most. That I couldn't do anything to fix this for her was horrible – for both of us.

'You know the media have named him "The Edinburgh Ripper",' I said, returning to the much easier subject of murder.

The tally of dead girls was rising, and the authorities didn't seem any nearer to catching him. Of course, I had my own explanation for the inept police investigation – DI Duncan Bancho. Duncan Bancho and I had history, none of it was good. In the recent past he had had me arrested and held on suspicion of attempted murder. I wasn't blameless. I tried to get him thrown off the force for corruption.

I cleared my throat and read aloud again, unable to keep the sarcasm out of my voice.

'"We're doing all we can," said DI Duncan Bancho, officer in charge of the investigation for Lothian and Borders police. "We lost valuable time because no one reported that the girls were missing."' I put the paper down.

'"We're doing all we can"?' I banged my head lightly against the window. The news of the girls barely registered at first – the police went through the motions but the media waited until there were enough deaths to get them excited. The death of a prostitute is regarded as an occupational hazard, and the clear-up rate is the lowest of any homicide – so I wasn't buying his PR statement.

The first murder in July had only just made the inside pages of the tabloids, but by the time the second body had been found, three weeks later, rumours were circulating.

'To get Bancho's attention the killer had to send him a text – of course Bancho ignored it,' I snarled.

Lavender was ignoring me – this was a well-rehearsed rant of mine against my least favourite policeman. As I've said, DI Bancho and I go back a long way.

'So what made Bancho sit up and do something? Finally, do something?' I asked myself more than her. 'When the killer put the finger of another victim under his windscreen wiper?' When this occurred, the hunt was on for the body of the third dead girl. It was during the festival so the papers were playing it down. None wanted to spook the wealthy tourists because of three dead whores.

Lavender took her coffee cup and joined me at the window.

'Before you start,' she said, 'I know there are ninety unsolved murders of prostitutes in the UK.'

'Don't believe the crap!' I retorted. 'The bit about "decent women are safe". If a man will murder a prostitute, no woman is safe from him. It didn't keep "decent" women safe from the Yorkshire Ripper, did it? Peter Sutcliffe just moved on from prostitutes to students.'

'Fine.' She saluted me quickly, a parody of a soldier obeying an order. 'Change the subject.'

We stared in silence from the office window to look at Edinburgh Castle. It was a dark winter's morning and I could see police in their luminous jackets climbing on the Castle Rock. Halogen lamps lit what appeared to be a crime scene with an ethereal glow, and a deathly silence hung over Johnston Terrace, the street below the castle façade. Police scurried around in last night's snowfall; they were the first to walk on the pristine surface, and their footprints were like blemishes.

I'd heard a news flash on Radio Forth that another body had been found; they didn't give out any details, and I suppose they were waiting until the family was informed. I often came into the office on a Saturday, as did Lavender – we made the most of the quiet and could run through work much quicker than on weekdays, but today a cold silence fell over us as we watched the depressing scene.

Incongruously, just out of sight on the other side of the rock, Edinburgh's Christmas festivities were gearing up for another fun-packed day. In a few hours skaters would be falling, racing and spinning on the temporary ice-rink in the city's famous Princes Street Gardens. Wurlitzers would boom out hits from twenty years ago and overexcited children clutching candyfloss would be trailing behind the parents on a mission to buy last-minute gifts at the German market. Whatever had happened on the rock, for most life would go on, especially at Christmas.

'You're not in much danger, Lav – Eddie never lets you out of his sight,' I said, patting her on the shoulder, both of us knowing that I was referring to his treatment of her since the miscarriage without me actually saying anything.

'Maybe. But you...' She held my eye, and there was a lot of weight in the stare, 'are too hard on Bancho. These girls are all from Eastern Europe – nobody seems to give a damn about them, so anything Bancho does has to help. Eddie worries about me, Brodie – but I worry about you. Look...'

She led me by the arm to look at the wall behind my desk. I keep it there because I hate seeing pictures of myself. However, clients enjoyed seeing evidence of past victories; it was good for business, so my personal preference was irrelevant.

Lavender tapped the glass of a particularly unflattering photograph; I was standing dressed in my leathers, next to my motorbike, 'The Fat Boy', arms crossed over my chest, looking mean. That wasn't the problem – my helmet hair was bright red and frizzy, as if it had a life of its own. Lavender pulled the picture next to the front page of the article that showed the photographs of the Ripper's victims.

'See what I mean?' She nodded, looking pleased with herself. 'Apart from the fact that you're way too old – you fit his profile. Our man likes redheads.'

'My hair is auburn,' I sniffed.

'Mmmmn. Either way you need a bit of protection – it's time you started speaking to Glasgow Joe.' Lavender walked back to the window as if that was an end to the matter. Even if I didn't want to admit it to her, I could see her point – she was getting married in two days' time and the best man and the matron of honour weren't speaking. In fact, I hadn't spoken to my ex-husband for nearly six months.

I needed to change the subject.

'And what are you doing in the office anyway – two days before you get married and just before Christmas?'

'Unlike you, my presents were all wrapped before the start of November, and in case you hadn't noticed...' She waved her arm around. Lavender's wedding had taken over the offices of Lothian and St Clair – the filing cabinets bursting with contact details for florists, dressmakers and limousines and the million other seemingly vital bits of the bridezilla armoury.

'There's something more happening up at the Castle Rock.'

Lavender pressed her nose to the glass.

'Did you ever doubt it?' Lavender asked, as her voice started to crack. 'Another victim of the Ripper?'

'No, no – it doesn't have to be. Absolutely not,' I said, too hastily. She was getting married in the castle and I didn't want anything to spoil her day. Not even my feud with Joe. 'It's probably a suicide: single people get very lonely at this time of year.'

'Speaking from personal experience?' she quipped.

I turned my head, not willing to let her see just how close she was to the truth on both counts.

Chapter Two

Lothian and St Clair W.S.
Saturday 22 December, 8.30 a.m.

'Do you have a death wish, girl?'

Lord MacGregor shook his head in disgust and threw the weekend paper down on my desk. A silver foil container tipped over, scattering cold chicken and fried rice everywhere.

'That,' he continued, pointing to the offending article, 'is professional suicide.'

Watching him out of the corner of my eye, I refused to turn round. I knew what my grandfather was referring to, and I didn't want to face his anger. Maybe it had been a foolish move on my part; even he'd acknowledged I'd been keeping my nose clean and avoiding trouble until now. Plus I hated disappointing him, which was something I seemed to have a knack for.

'What do you think about this?' He picked up the article again, and threw it down in front of Lavender. She clapped her hands sarcastically.

'Very dramatic,' she said. 'Maybe that's where Brodie gets her antics from.' Looking directly into his eyes she added: 'They do say the apple doesn't fall very far from the tree.'

Using her hand she cleared away the debris of my last night's meal and threw it in the bin.

'Seriously,' said Lord MacGregor, shaking his head in disbelief.

'Seriously, you're a well-matched pair of drama queens!' Lavender snorted and sat down in my seat, opening the offending article out in front of her.

Lawyer Could Force Judges to Declare They Are Masons

'So you asked a judge if he was a Mason.' Lavender rattled the newspaper noisily before placing it down on the desk again. 'I hate to say it ... but His Lordship has a point.'

Lavender had been told by my Grandad to call him by his Christian name, but she refused. He was now known to everyone in the office as His Lordship. Initially, it was her way of getting at him, but now they were allies. He had won her over and he was giving her away when she married Eddie on Christmas Eve.

I kept my back firmly to them; I wasn't turning round to face their torrent of abuse, especially now I had admitted to myself they were right. The case had called six weeks ago in Edinburgh Sheriff Court, but we were still waiting for the judgement to be issued. Anyway, the action on the Castle Rock was revving up, and the rubber-neckers were gathering at the barricade.

'We discussed this.' Lavender inserted her face directly in front of me. 'Are you stupid? It's not just your livelihood on the line.' I could feel her hot breath on my neck. She grabbed my shoulder, and pulled me round to face her; I didn't feel it was a particularly good time to suggest she should perhaps be a little calmer on her wedding day. The consequences of my actions to Scots law were immense. If I was right, the decisions of every judge who was a Mason could be called into question if any party to the case was also a member of the Masonic Lodge.

It all boiled down to the fact that judges are supposed to be impartial, whereas Masons, by their oaths, have sworn to favour their brethren. If the ruling in this case was in my favour, the Edinburgh bar would be eating out of my hand, all bets were off, and lawyers could appeal a decision they didn't like. Their fees would increase, and it would be new Mercedes all round. Of course, if it went against me – which, let's face it, was likely – then the judges would really put the boot in. Lav was afraid that fees would go down but Grandad was pissed because he had ambitions for me to be a judge – and I'd just made that even more unlikely.

Lord MacGregor nodded approvingly at Lav, just wishing he'd had the courage to be so forceful – but my grandfather was too afraid of losing me; our relationship was too new and tentative for him to risk such behaviour.

My grandfather.

We had been reunited for just over two years. Weird is not the word for us lot – we make the Addams family look like the Waltons. Lord MacGregor, Grandfather to me and a retired High Court judge to everyone else, had rescued my birth mother Kailash from his son's clutches. He continued to support her, even after she was charged with the murder of his only child. And if that isn't Jerry Springer enough for you, my mother's a dominatrix: a high-class one, very wealthy, but a dominatrix nonetheless. These are the family members who have the temerity to be annoyed when I make questionable decisions...

I kept up a wall of silence. It was the advice I would give to my clients. Say nothing – you can only hang yourself with your tongue. Lavender was persistent.

'What planet were you on?' she asked, poking me in the back with her finger.

'When is it ever a good idea to ask a policeman if he's a Mason?' she continued.

I shrugged noncommittally.

'Then you have to take it one step beyond the bounds of good taste...'

Lavender rolled her eyes and half turned to face Grandad.

'...and suggest the judge cannot be impartial because he, like the police, is also a Mason!'

This conversation was embarrassing. I had been posturing in court like a little bantam hen and now that the heat of the battle was over I had to agree with them. It's all well and good to have nice legal points, but it didn't have a snowball's chance in hell of winning. I stepped out of range of her finger, and turned to face them.

I caught sight of myself in the wall-sized mirror that Grandad had installed so I could practise my jury speeches. Sticking my left hand on my hip, I walked forward, looking more like one of

Kailash's girls on a very rough day than a lawyer.

'Consider the well-known penalties of the Entered Apprentice who vows to keep Masonic secrets under penalty of having his throat cut, or his tongue torn out and buried in the rough sands of the sea.' I coughed for dramatic effect and held their eyes, just as Grandad had taught me. I could see he was impressed.

Lavender laughed in my face. 'What a pile of crap,' she said. 'You know that's just for effect – them and you – trying to make folk think that they're all mysterious. It's rubbish, Brodie – but it's rubbish that you shouldn't mess with, given how many top people seem to believe in it.'

'Well – why do they say it if they're not going to carry out the threat? Anyway, the Crown Office is issuing a written opinion, and it brought our client one step closer to a "not guilty".'

I walked up to the mirror, not waiting to hear her reply. God, I looked terrible. I started to examine my saggy chin; when did those wrinkles appear? My so-called office assistant approached me. Her eyes were blazing, and holding my gaze she said, 'You're selfish, Brodie – it's going to hurt when you have to think of someone else.'

'That sounds like a threat,' I said.

'No – it's a promise.'

Chapter Three

Girls' Changing Rooms,
The Meadows' Pavilion, Edinburgh
Saturday 22 December, 2 p.m.

It was hard to remain silent and he held his breath as he crouched low on the lid of the toilet seat. The girl in the next cubicle was called Rosie. He had heard another girl call for her and now he held the name to him. She sang a well-worn Christmas song under her breath and The Watcher smiled, imagining the song was for him. Certainly, this was shaping up to be his best Christmas so far.

For three weeks he'd staked out the changing rooms, and now he'd won a prize. Not that his previous visits were wasted – no, he'd put his time to good use. As he stared out through the peephole he'd prepared earlier, he reflected on just how good. Rosie continued singing as she washed her hands. The Watcher was pleased. Hygiene was important to him – too important, some people thought; but, as his mother always said, 'Cleanliness is next to Godliness.'

Standing on her tiptoes, in a pink padded Playboy bra with matching knickers, Rosie leaned over the basin and applied a thick layer of lip gloss. She opened her mouth wide and ran her pink pointy tongue over her teeth. The Watcher shivered. Rosie hurried through to the main changing area. She was running late, so discarded her underwear as she went, throwing it over a railing. She removed her bra and put on a sports version. Bending over, she balanced on one leg, and pushed her foot into her football shorts. They had built-in underwear, so she had not put on her knickers, but he felt an irrational sense of disappointment in the girl. Perhaps her morals were not all they should be. And The Watcher didn't like that; he didn't like that at all.

'For God's sake, get a move on – do you want to miss the kick-off?' A disembodied voice chivvied them all along, but Rosie was the only one he looked at. The voice was likely to be that of a chaperone, given that the whole of Edinburgh was on red alert with all the terrible things that were going on. If truth be told, it was making things difficult – but not impossible – for him.

Rosie refused to leave yet. She stood in the messy, deserted changing room, swivelling around looking for something, for someone. Looking for him perhaps? A smile cracked his face. He was the last person she'd want to find. Holding his breath, he then exhaled as the sound of her boot studs disappeared into the distance. The Watcher noted with regret that she had stopped singing.

Turning, he stared out of the hole he had cut in the thick frosted glass. Rabbit wire on the outside of the pane obscured his vision but he could see well enough. Well enough to note that Rosie kept glancing back at the changing pavilion. A cold chill of fear ran down his spine as she started to run full pelt to the man.

The Watcher knew who he was by reputation,

and he knew that he should be afraid of him – but the path he had chosen did not allow for changes simply because there were obstacles. The big man in a kilt had his arms around Rosie, giving her a pep talk, dispelling her fears. Maybe the big man wasn't that tough – it was good to know that he wasn't infallible.

He had come to see someone else, he'd hidden overnight in the changing rooms and it had finally paid off. He'd waited three weeks to see her. The first week she'd had a knee injury, the second was an away game, but the third time was a trick. The girl was skinny; some people might say she looked undernourished. The Watcher didn't fancy her chances of survival – she would be kicked off the pitch when the game started.

Actually, that could be a problem. The Watcher didn't want her marked. That wasn't part of his plan and his plan had been very carefully con-structed. He was proud of the attention he paid to detail. A feeling of instant calm came over him as he watched her win the toss. This was going to be her lucky day. The girl was skinny and leggy – she might be ungainly but she was fast. Too fast? Would it be a problem? What if she got away from him? That wouldn't do. That wouldn't do at all.

He'd have to recheck his calculations; she couldn't weigh more than five and a half stones. Too much anaesthetic could kill her, too little and she could escape. His plan did not allow for a runaway.

The big bastard was talking to Brodie Mc-Lennan. The Watcher knew who she was – in fact, if he was ever caught, he'd call for her to represent him. He shrugged off that thought – he wasn't going to get caught. He was too clever for that. Patience ran in his blood and his genetic code told him: if at first you don't succeed, try, try again. But he needed to move now – the girls had gone, the game was starting. The Watcher wanted to run but there was no crowd to lose himself in. *Take a deep breath, relax.*

That was why he had waited for her – she was worth waiting for.

He forced himself to walk slowly out of the changing pavilion unseen. A mother stood on guard fifty feet away, leaning against a tree having a sly fag – she smiled at him as he passed.

In these godless times, who takes any notice of a priest?

Chapter Four

The Meadows, Edinburgh
Saturday 22 December, 2 p.m.

There was no escape from the relentless weather. Snow lay on the ground and the driving rain was turning it to slush. My face was numb and the shoes I was wearing were soaking wet. This was, quite undoubtedly, a huge mistake. What the hell was I thinking of when I agreed to spending a Saturday afternoon at a football match? Not even a proper one at that?

It was barely noticeable, but Glasgow Joe

seemed to nod in my direction. Lavender elbowed me in the ribs. 'See,' she hissed, giving him an extravagant wave, 'he's willing to make up.' Ignoring her, I turned my head to the wooden pavilion where a ragtag bunch of girls was snaking out of the dressing rooms. Their legs were already purple by the time they reached the touchline where, jumping up and down, they tried to get warm. They all seemed to shout towards Glasgow Joe, clamouring for his attention. The clever ones gave up and turned to Eddie instead. A wise move if they were trying to get tips – Eddie could educate them on every Scottish football move ever seen, whereas Joe, well, I'd seen Joe play. Even as a boy he was reminiscent of a giant redwood on the pitch, although he was handy to have in defence as long as you didn't expect him to actually run with the ball. Eddie was the soccer coach for this bunch. He'd learnt early on that if he wanted to pretend he was coaching Inter Milan rather than this lot, then he'd have to supply doughnuts to keep their attention.

I dragged my thoughts away from Eddie and Joe to look at the kids on the pitch. To me it seemed obvious – there was one girl who was different, one girl who drew your eyes towards her. Thirteen years old and with the look of Bambi; she could have been made out of pipe cleaners. She appeared to have brought her own valet, Malcolm. He lied about his age. I reckon he was pushing sixty, and he was my mother's 'Girl Friday'. He looked after Kailash, he looked after me, and now it seemed he had another chick under his wing.

Her silver sparkly laces were untied; on cue,

Malcolm came mincing to the rescue. The girl ignored him – but the opposition didn't. Jeering, they laughed and pointed, as a wave of panic came over me. I knew what was going to happen. The Penicuik girls were strong and sturdy – even in a fair fight, Eddie wouldn't stand a chance, and they had the girl with the Lurex laces in their sight.

'God, it's cold; doesn't she feel it?' Lavender shivered as she dragged me round to the other side of the football pitch. They were all there by now – Glasgow Joe, Kailash, Eddie, Malcolm, even Grandad, sitting on his shooting stick drinking hot coffee from a flask. As soon as I sniffed the caffeine I increased my pace. We all stood there, mesmerized, as the girl moved into action. As expected, she was captain of her team – unsurprising, because it was she who supplied the manager, the coach, and the strips, courtesy of Lothian and St Clair. The Penicuik captain towered over her as they tossed the coin, shorts flapping around the waif's thin legs as she watched the coin spin – and won. Placing her boot on top of the ball, she 'sorted' her long hair, it was the most beautiful shade of auburn you could get outside of a bottle. I was only a little jealous. Holding it in place was one over-the-top pink fabric rose; I suspected Malcolm's influence. I caught Kailash's eye and we both shuddered. The girl wasn't going to last two minutes.

We were wrong.

She ran in and out between the legs of the larger girls like a whippet. Taking them by surprise, she made a break and ran down the wing, scoring within the first minute. Grandad

33

was on his feet screaming with pride – and probably heading for a heart attack at this rate. Who would give Lavender away then? The girl was running down the pitch, punching the air in victory; she lifted up her shirt to kiss it, revealing to everyone her thermal vest. Malcolm's doing again, I thought. I could see the Penicuik girls looking, conferring, deciding how to get her. This time there would be no mistakes, no mercy.

My little sister, Connie Coutts, was going down.

Kailash was chewing on gum, her jaws mashing together furiously. I had never seen my immaculate birth mother indulge in anything so common. She caught me watching her out of the corner of my eye. 'It's hellish,' she whispered. 'I hate watching her – I'm a bag of nerves,' she shrugged, as if being here, this whole scene, was the most natural thing in the world, but I knew her history and how much it had taken to get us all here.

Connie was berating her team-mates for not passing the ball, her face red with indignation, exertion and the energy of being a thirteen-year-old. My heart almost stopped as soon as I had the thought and made the connection. Kailash had been thirteen when she had given birth to me. Uncharacteristically, I placed my arm around her.

'It would have been harder to watch me when I was that age.' I squeezed her tightly to me, trying to make light of what had kept us apart since the day I was born and for many, many years afterwards. 'I was shit.'

'And selfish,' butted in Glasgow Joe. 'Always really selfish.' He looked at me. 'With the ball, I mean.' I knew exactly what he meant.

'Deciding to talk now, are you? Well, don't bother sticking your nose in where it's not wanted.' I bridled, instinctively raising my chin. All the mothers were ogling him so we had an audience. He was wearing his kilt. The wind swung it round his legs, and the mums who'd seen the size of his feet were praying the wind would blow it higher.

'Aw ref – are you fucking blind?' Eddie shouted. I turned, following his line of vision, and, surprisingly, my attention was instantly there. Connie was down. Mud spattered her face and was mixed with the blood pouring from her nose. It looked like it must hurt like hell. She clenched her teeth around her mouth guard, keeping the hot tears away. Kailash started to run, but Malcolm placed an arm in front of her chest, barring her. She watched him run onto the pitch instead, healing bag in hand. Kailash remained quiet and a deep furrow creased her brow.

'He spoils her, you know,' I said to Kailash.

'He's allowed to. He raised her. Anyway, look who's talking. I hope you haven't gone overboard with a Christmas present? I've already warned Moses and Joe.'

'Connie has enough stuff without getting more of it in a couple of days,' I said, keeping an eye on what was happening on the pitch as I spoke. Relief washed over me. Connie's Christmas present was a worry. It was too late for eBay and there were only two and a half shopping days left. I suspected that Joe and the crew were well organized, but I wanted to get her something special too. Perhaps now I could just pretend that I was more thoughtful by getting her a chocolate Santa and a bag of satsumas, making sure she didn't get all materialistic. On the pitch, Connie was shrugging Malcolm off, back on her feet with a glint in her eye that suggested revenge was going to be sweet.

I could see Joe standing on the sideline like a silent assassin, giving the ref one of his special looks. I had come to know that look well over the last six months – it was unpleasant, to say the least. It told you in no uncertain terms you had fallen short of the mark, and no one blamed the ref when he succumbed to crowd pressure and pulled out a belated red card.

When I say no one, I'm not being strictly accurate. The girl's father made a move to complain but backed down shamefully quickly when Joe pulled himself up to his full height and squared his shoulders. Glasgow Joe's creed was written all over his face – no one messed with his girls. Kailash, Connie and Lavender are certainly in the gang; I'm not sure about myself these days.

Eddie and Joe ran along the pitch shouting tactics, encouragement – and taunts when necessary. I'd seen managers and coaches receive touchline bans for less in the real world, but the officials here turned a deaf ear in spite of opposition protests. I wondered if Connie knew what was going on. She seemed oblivious, running herself ragged chasing a dirty ball on a muddy field; the enjoyment she was obviously getting was a mystery to me.

'Joe's got the trike,' Lavender said, sidling up to me with the last of the coffee in the top of the thermos flask to warm my frozen fingers. 'Connie and Joe are going Christmas shopping. I wish I'd thought of that... I still don't know what to get her. I want it to be special – the first time that she really has everyone around her.'

I was always touched by the way Lavender had adopted my family as her own. Even Connie, the 'newest' member, was to be her flower girl.

Kailash had kept the existence of my half-sister Connie (then at boarding school in Switzerland) in the dark until she was sure that she and I had a chance of a relationship. I think she was right to do that really – apparently, most mother and adult-child reunions don't have fairy-tale endings. Our bond is not one you'd find in a Disney movie but we rub along – although sometimes it feels more like grating. When Connie was finally brought into the picture, it actually made things easier. I had more of a family now than I'd ever dreamed of, even when I still thought that my adopted parent Mary McLennan was my birth mother and Kailash Coutts was just another pain-in-the-arse client I had to defend.

Joe edged nearer to us as his eyes scanned the skyline. In the distance, the hill of Arthur's Seat was barely visible because of the low-lying cloud. He huddled into us close before pulling a rolled-up newspaper from his pocket. 'Brodie, it's time to stop being so daft,' he said. I raised my eyebrow – in my mind, he was the one to blame and I most certainly hadn't been in on any daftness. 'Seriously, Brodie, there's things going on that ... well, things just don't feel right.' If I'd expected an emotional outpouring, I was disappointed. 'Have you seen this?' he asked, going back to the newspaper. It was the afternoon edition of the one we'd discussed in the office; the dead girl stared out at us from the front page, demanding justice.

'Do you ever have the feeling you're being watched?' Joe asked, staring over his shoulder.

'Joe – you might have red hair but you're not the Ripper's type: your family jewels rule you out,' I replied.

'I'm glad you remember, Brodie, but I wasn't talking about myself. I meant you,' he said. 'Do you ever feel you're being watched?' he asked again. His face was weary and I no longer wanted to laugh. A cold trickle of sweat dribbled down my spine.

A primeval sense of wariness had me on edge. Joe was still scanning the horizon, and he wasn't looking at the weather. I knew better than to laugh at him or dismiss his instincts. He held on to my arms, pinning them down at my side. The cold wind carried his scent to me and, as always, I cursed myself for responding. He noticed me involuntarily pressing up against him but said nothing. If I needed any convincing he was serious, that was it.

Pride comes before a fall, I know, but I shrugged him off. I didn't know how to handle the new Glasgow Joe, the one who could resist me. I stomped round to the other side of the pitch; I didn't need to glance over my shoulder to know Joe was watching me.

My smile fell.

Joe wasn't staring at me – he was scouting the Meadows.

Hunting for the bogeyman.

Chapter Five

Cumberland Street, Edinburgh
Sunday 23 December, 12.30 a.m.

The point of the stiletto blade nicked the underside of my chin. A dewdrop of blood dribbled down my neck. This couldn't be happening. *Please God, don't let this be happening.* Pure panic controlled my body. I wanted to scream but I was shamefully afraid. The knife meandered down my throat, slicing open the cosy grey tee shirt I loved to sleep in. It had once, in happier times, belonged to Joe. Darkness hid the face of my torturer but I knew who it was, and he wanted me dead.

The pain was slicing through me as he traced spirals with the blade. Opening my mouth wide to scream, a disappointing squeak came out. Gripping handfuls of the sheet, I tried to push myself up the bed. *Perhaps if I could sit up, I'd be able to fight back.* He second-guessed me and dug the point of the blade into my carotid artery. It danced as my pulse raced. I imagined a slow smile crossing his face. *How had he gained entry?* I'd recently been robbed and I'd installed new security; they promised me I was as safe as the Bank of Scotland.

I didn't believe them and I hadn't shared their faith. The satisfaction of being right did nothing for me. I-told-you-so doesn't cut it when you're staring death in the face. I refused to expire piti-

39

fully in silence so I shouted for the first person I could think of through the fear – Joe. I knew he wouldn't make it in time but just saying his name made me feel better. At least I'd found the strength to call on him, I reflected as his name rang out through my bedroom. Then my reality shifted. I woke up. Sweat had drenched the tee shirt but otherwise it was undamaged; just another horrible dream and a lingering feeling that the man I needed wasn't there.

I swung my feet over the side of the bed, and my toes landed in leftover pizza. The empty bottles of lager showed me just how much punishment I'd inflicted on my poor body – but I'd live. The phone was ringing in the hall. In an effort to get a good night's sleep, I'd disconnected the one on the bedside table. Last night had obviously been a night of great decisions. I swore under my breath and trampled on the mound of clothes lying in a heap on the floor, smearing tomato sauce and cold mozzarella cheese on the LBD I'd bought last week from Harvey Nicks. Three hundred and fifty pounds I'd paid in the pre-Xmas sale, and now it looked like a window rag. The phone had stopped ringing. I surveyed the bombsite that was my room. My flatmate (and assistant) Louisa had called me Scrooge and then insisted on setting up a fibre-optic Christmas tree; its garish colours threw a macabre glow on the scene and didn't add anything remotely positive.

Stumbling across to the dressing table I picked up a photograph. Why hadn't I just thrown it out? The frame was a plastic snow dome; in the centre of the snowstorm Glasgow Joe had a huge grin on his face as he held me in a bear hug. He smiled like a prizewinner. We were on top of the Empire State building – I should have guessed what was coming when he took me there seven months ago. Bizarrely, Glasgow Joe adores the film *Sleepless in Seattle*.

Naturally, he'd taken me there to propose.

Again.

Being reasonably sane, I said no – on reflection, I did more than just say 'no'. My exact reply went something along the lines of 'when Hell freezes over.' On the picture, I traced the contours of his face with my finger. It was the closest I had intended to get to the real thing, no matter how much Lavender pushed and shoved. It wasn't that I didn't love Joe, or even, God help me, not love him in that way. There were bigger problems this time – Joe wanted a baby. If there was one thing I knew, it was that there was bad blood in me, and that bloodline needed to stop when my candle snuffed.

It wasn't just the need for a baby that had changed him in the past year or so. Joe's paternal streak had been manageable until he met Connie – then he'd fallen hook, line and sinker. Nothing but the best for Connie. He was reliving our childhood, except that now he had money. Eddie and Joe had stepped in to manage the football team when none of the fathers would do it, and there was constant bullying until Lothian and St Clair provided the strips. Naturally, Connie had wanted to be sponsored by Joe's pub, the Rag Doll, but Joe and Eddie didn't feel that gave 'their girls' the appropriate image.

41

The phone started to ring again. Whoever was calling was bloody persistent. Normally it would be annoying, but tonight I needed the diversion.

I knew who it would be. When Lavender got engaged she insisted I employ him full time. He needed a regular wage and I – apparently – needed to get a life. Now that I had someone to share the custodies with, I wasn't on call 24/7. In fact, Eddie did more than his fair share, and, as Lavender made up the work rota, it meant one of two things – either she had gone off Eddie and wanted him out of the house as often as possible or, alternatively, she wanted me to make Eddie a partner. It didn't take a genius to figure out which one she was angling for. Which was just as well, because by the time I reached the telephone my head was beginning to thud.

'Brodie?'

It was a voice I knew well. My heart sank. Trouble was in the offing. No one makes social calls past midnight. I'd expected St Leonards police station, the central holding station for the city, and I'd got Malcolm. I didn't bother to ask him what it was; he was hysterical and not in a mood to listen, preferring to blurt everything out. 'Derek's been arrested and it's all my fault,' he gasped through tears. Dismal Derek is Malcolm's partner. At fifteen years his junior, and although no spring chicken himself, Derek has played Malcolm for a fool. I doubted very much that Malcolm was to blame for Derek's incarceration. Another thing I knew for sure was the last lawyer Derek would ask for would be me.

'What happened?' I asked, thankful he couldn't

see me rolling my eyes, and almost smiling at the irony that all calls would lead to St Leonards after all.

'We had a tiff.' Malcolm sounded embarrassed, which was just as well because I suspected he was underplaying what had gone on. He knew my views on domestic abuse – abusers aren't looking for a marriage licence, they need a dog licence. He started to sob, big heart-rending sobs. I knew what he wanted. He wanted me up there in the cold early hours of the morning holding his hand and telling him everything was going to be all right.

'Hold on. I'm coming,' I told him.

'Brodie, I came out in such a rush I forgot my angina tablets, I phoned Moses and he's picked them up. I said you'd stop and collect them.'

'Okay, keep calm ... I'm coming.'

I owed Malcolm big time; he'd patched me up physically and mentally on more than one occasion. I needed to get to St Leonards quickly but I'd never get a taxi at this time of the night or year. I pulled back the curtains and saw the cobbles shining with ice. Despite that, I still decided to take the Fat Boy. This decision was influenced by the fact I could see exactly where my leathers were. I stumbled around, pulling on my trousers, and accidentally bumped into one of the grotesque decorations Louisa had put in my room – a fat dancing Santa. A nasally sound that was meant to be Elvis singing 'Lonely This Christmas' echoed around the room.

That finally got the attention of the man in my bed. He sat up and scratched his head.

'Please tell me we did?' he said – though it was

clear from the look on his face that he remembered all too well.

Jack Deans was back in town.

Chapter Six

Cumberland Street, Edinburgh
Sunday 23 December, 1 a.m.

'All I knew, Brodie, was that I missed you.'

Jack Deans. Investigative reporter, ex-rugby player, and my booty call, was getting serious.

'I missed you, Brodie.'

'Yeah. You said.'

I was running around like a headless chicken trying to get ready to leave for the police station. As usual I couldn't find anything and I was making another promise to myself to be more organized.

'You're a bloody infuriating woman, do you know that?'

'So people keep telling me.' I pushed my feet into my bike boots.

'You make me so mad but all the time I was in Darfur, I wanted to talk to you, to run stories past you, to get your opinion – even if the only one you ever seem to have is that I should shut up.'

He looked at me, waiting for an answer or encouragement – I couldn't give it to him. The safest way was to continue ignoring him. I rifled through a bag searching for my keys – Malcolm was waiting and I needed to see Moses on my way to St Leonards.

He sat up in bed and a shaft of light came in the window. He was tanned, lean and, in this light, without my contact lenses, did a fair impersonation of George Clooney's less attractive brother playing a war correspondent.

'Brodie – this has been going on too long... Is there any point in me taking all this crap from you – always ending up back in your bed?' I wanted to object to his use of the word 'always' but maybe he had a point. I thought I was safe with Jack; Mr Deans was definitely not the marrying type. Was I wrong? It's sod's law. Whenever you're not looking for commitment they come running – it's the same principle as buses.

'I've spent the last few hours watching you wrestle demons in your sleep, wanting to hold you and make it all better, and knowing there's no point in me even trying. That's not my job is it? That's for Glasgow Joe to do.'

He was trying to look all appealing and sad, but that was never really the type I went for. I liked him rough and uncommitted, and I liked him knowing where the door was as soon as we'd finished having sex. He wasn't playing ball at all.

'Brodie...' he began. Again.

I held my finger up to him. 'Uh! No!' I barked, as if he was a leg-rubbing puppy (which was a pretty accurate description, come to think of it). 'There was never a point when I said I wanted to hear another word from you, Jack.'

'You weren't complaining a couple of hours ago,' he replied, predictably.

'Oh, shut up – that wasn't talking, that was

45

grunting. And you may have noticed you did a hell of a lot more of it than me, so don't go thinking you've waltzed back into town like bloody Casanova.'

'I got a call. A personal one.'

I didn't so much as raise an eyebrow of interest, finding my cuticles much more interesting instead.

'From your Grandad. He had a bit of news for me – namely that you and Joe were definitely over, and if I came back, I might find myself in with a shout.'

'Lovely,' I hissed. 'Did he offer you a dowry as well?'

'The timing was perfect – the Sudanese government was throwing me out anyway. And I got here in time for Christmas.'

He pulled on a red Santa hat that lay on the floor.

'How about we give it a try?'

I slammed the door on my way out.

Chapter Seven

Susie Wong's, George Street, Edinburgh
Sunday 23 December, 1.25 a.m.

I'd ridden the Fat Boy thousands of times – I needed the instant focus that comes over me when I kick-start the engine. I wanted the answers to some questions and the first one was

– how drunk was I when I dragged Jack Deans back to my bed? Sadly, I couldn't have been that bad as I seemed fine to drive – I'd have to just put it down to bad judgement. Again.

I had other things to bother me – I had to get to Malcolm and had been delayed by the festive scenario I'd just left behind in my flat. A chill had settled in my bones; I hoped it could be explained away by the fact that it was minus two degrees. The pavements were slippery and young girls teetered down the street singing Christmas songs.

Following Malcolm's instructions I headed off to meet Moses en route to the police station. The Christmas lights were up in George Street and it was quite a show, classier than the Blackpool illuminations – I didn't like to admit it, but they always made me feel good. Moses Tierney, leader of the Dark Angels gang, and my most important client, had opened a new club there. I walked into Susie Wong's and saw him immediately. As usual he was dressed in full-length black leather coat, leather trousers, black silk shirt and handmade boots. He was leaning on his ebony walking cane surveying the scene when I got there. He raised his cane in salute to me but kept his eyes firmly on the queue. Very few people in Edinburgh know he is the owner; they dismiss the presence of the Dark Angels as the hired muscle, but Moses is shrewd. I'd never underestimate him.

'Have you got Malcolm's pills?'

'They're just coming.'

The burglary skills of the Dark Angels come in handy sometimes.

'Business is good,' I commented, shaking my

hair, trying to get the knots out of it. Moses turned to me and said, 'Appearances can be deceptive,' before turning away. I followed the line of his eyes. A large queue had formed outside the club where two young Dark Angels were out of uniform. The Dark Angels were a brand. They marketed fear in the city, instantly recognizable from their platinum-white hair and ashen skin. Both sexes wore black from head to toe, including nail varnish. Mascara was optional for the men; immaculate grooming was not. They scared lots of people, but I loved them. Moses had looked after me for years – many of them without me knowing it – and, along with Kailash, had saved my life. He wasn't a criminal to me; he was a guardian angel.

'What are you up to?' I asked. Moses didn't reply: too busy directing operations. It was a game that we often played – I had to see if I could figure out his scam, even although we both knew that, as soon as I did, I'd have to leave. It was bound to be illegal. I scrutinized the two Dark Angels. They were beautiful – but that was generally the case. The boy was around seventeen and wore a 1920s evening suit, with tails and a white tie. A battered brown leather suitcase was open on a table. It contained his props. He pulled out two scimitars. To prove the sharpness of the swords, he went up to a man in the crowd. Grasping hold of the man's tie in one slashing movement, he cut it in two. The man's face fell and the crowd stepped back uneasily. They all agreed it was sharp.

'He's going to fix the guy's tie, isn't he?' I was nodding in Moses' face as I asked.

'No.' Moses turned his mouth down and shook

his head.

'That tie is silk, Moses – you can't let them go around destroying customers' clothes. In case it hadn't occurred to you, it's bad for business.' My tone of voice was getting higher. Grandad was coaching me to speak low and slow like Ingrid Bergman, but right now I was doing a fair impression of Betty Boop.

'Do you really think I'd let someone as ugly as that in my club? Anything that happens in the queue will only be to punters that the bouncers won't let in.' Moses laughed, as if I was the one who had lost my marbles. The performance was hypnotic. The magician's assistant had ignored the cold and was wearing a pink tutu. She looked like a malevolent Tinker Bell. It wouldn't be fair to say that all eyes were on her colleague, because she was a beguiling sight. It was true that eyes, particularly male eyes, were on her, but they definitely weren't watching the hands that were picking their pockets. It was just as well they wouldn't miss their wallets until they tried to pay for the taxi home.

'Here.' Moses handed me a bottle of pills, which he'd just been given. I shuddered. The news that I was buying drugs would be all over the 'steamie'; Moses' reputation as the main supplier of ecstasy was well known. I wanted to rattle them and shout 'angina pills', but who would want to believe that?

I'd seen enough. I was tired of the generic Christmas music that was pumping out of the open door of the club and, as usual, Moses' addiction to crime disheartened me. 'There's no need for that petty theft,' I told him. 'You're making

49

enough from your legit businesses.' I moved to put my helmet on.

'How do you know what's enough? Do you have any idea how much it's cost me to put this place together?' he said, shrugging his shoulders as if speaking to a child. 'The fucking smoking ban has made it impossible to turn an honest buck.' We were staring at the hapless smokers as they talked, huddled around an ineffective patio heater. 'Even the brothels have been hit – has Kailash not told you?' He looked into my face, expecting confirmation.

'We don't talk about her business,' I said, tightening my lips to give him a warning look; sadly, subtlety is lost on Moses.

'Illegal brothels are setting up everywhere,' he said, as if hoping I'd be sympathetic He was so wrong, but as usual couldn't read my face, so continued. 'They're bringing in girls from Thailand, Poland, Romania. Sex slaves, Brodie – the bosses don't pay them a penny!'

'What do you want me to say? You want my sympathy? Is that it? All brothels are illegal in Scotland, Moses, not just the new ones – the fact that they get called saunas doesn't give them any legitimacy.' He looked at me blankly; morality wasn't something he could understand.

'You should take an interest, Brodie; after all it's your inheritance. Well, yours *and* Connie's. What have you got her for Christmas?'

He wasn't remotely interested in what I'd bought Connie for Christmas – which was just as well: he was too interested in his own gift. 'I've imported the latest games console from Japan –

it isn't even out here till next autumn.'

'Great. I hope it isn't knocked off,' I said churlishly. He tried to look hurt – and failed miserably. Moses was anxious for me to go, a sure sign he was up to something. I held my breath and watched where he was deliberately not looking. Then I spied them, just around the corner where a smaller queue had formed in front of Blind Bruce and a new member of the gang. I winced as I looked at Bruce – he, and his sightlessness, were kept around as permanent reminders of what happened to Dark Angels who crossed Moses. He had deliberately blinded Bruce after he had questioned the authority of the Dark Angels' leader, cut out his eyes as easily as peeling a banana.

'Who's that?' I pointed to the new guy.

'He's the chemist.' The fact that Bruce was now the one holding the street drugs only emphasized that he was an expendable – probably the most expendable – member of the gang. Moses Tierney has a flair for the dramatic, one that's shared by the rest of the Dark Angels.

'What's his name?' Moses was staring in the opposite direction, which was interesting – maybe he was embarrassed about selling drugs on street corners after all. 'You know,' I continued, 'I'm not going to give up; and if he keeps standing there, I'll be representing both of them, him *and* Blind Bruce, in court tomorrow anyway.' Moses looked disappointed. He was hiding something – we were both sure I didn't want to know, but it had gone too far now.

'If I tell you, will you go?' he asked, and I nodded. 'His name's Cal.' I sniggered and flicked my eyes over the new guy. There was something different about him; for a start I could see the roots of his ginger hair, but he was also wearing a Breitling watch which, from where I was standing, looked authentic. I was surprised to see that he wore handmade brogues, of the type that Grandad wore. Odd.

I had to go. As I opened the throttle along George Street I felt as if strange eyes were upon me. I tried to shake off the uncomfortable feeling and hoped that I was just picking up on the air of panic in the city.

Perhaps I had just outstayed my welcome.

Chapter Eight

George Street, Edinburgh
Sunday 23 December, 1.25 a.m.

He stopped whistling to himself when he saw her – he knew it was her even before she took her helmet off. When she shook her curls free, he felt that she was toying with him but he was still mesmerized. His jaw was tight and his neck stiffened. *He'd show her and then she'd be sorry.*

The Christmas lights shone on her face and The Watcher was pleased that Brodie no longer looked tired or edgy. He hoped this situation would continue. Nothing wrong with a false sense of security – he needed a few more days to bring his plan to fruition. The thought of his plan excited him.

Her long auburn hair spilled around her shoulders in a whirl of tendrils. He cursed the fact that she was wearing her leathers but he could still imagine her body underneath them. He had a very good imagination.

He sniffed the cold night air – just on the periphery he imagined he could smell her. It felt as if she had been talking to that delinquent forever. *What did she see in him?* Didn't they know what time it was? It was way past a good girl's bedtime. A slow smile broke out on his face and reached his eyes. Tapping his fingers on the lamppost he bit his lip to cool his impatience – it was not yet his time.

A pretty girl like Brodie McLennan shouldn't be left alone in a city like this when the Ripper was on the loose. A discreet laugh escaped his lips. Passers-by probably wondered what his private joke was, but it would remain private; that was the whole point of secrets. The Watcher liked secrets.

The Harley growled into life but she didn't drive off. He was torn; it bothered him when she talked to Moses Tierney but at least he knew where she was. The Watcher knew that Tierney wanted her to leave; he kept looking over Brodie's shoulder as if he was expecting someone he didn't want her to see. When she finally did leave, The Watcher would have to find her again and that wasn't always easy. He held his breath as he saw her drive off into the night. Resentment tightened the knot in his stomach – he couldn't follow her yet.

Five minutes passed before Tierney's mystery guest showed up. The Watcher wasn't pleased. The rumble of a bike engine had quickened his pulse for a moment. *She's come back.* But it wasn't

53

Brodie. Glasgow Joe got off his trike and started snooping.

The Watcher disappeared into the shadows to wait.

Chapter Nine

St Leonards Police Station, Edinburgh Sunday 23 December, 1.35 a.m.

St Leonards police station was aglow. The artificial Christmas tree twinkled as its lights flashed on and off – it was enough to cause a punter to have an epileptic fit. As usual my timing was impeccable. I was parking the Fat Boy just as the meat wagon arrived with its cargo of petty criminals, herded up from the city streets. Normally, it's a wonderful opportunity to score new business, but Sergeant Munro was hovering and I knew he would do anything to thwart me. Did that man never sleep?

The lager louts were drunker than usual, filled with Christmas cheer and all manner of illegal substances; there were many well-kent faces in the crowd.

'Brodie, darlin' – you look beautiful! Gies a kiss for ma Christmas!' I could always rely on wee Billy Palmer for an arrest and a compliment; the effect of the latter was shattered seconds later when he threw up in the gutter. The other prisoners laughed and jeered.

'Better out than in, son, that's what I always say,' said Sergeant Munro. Billy Palmer lifted his head and wiped his face on the sleeve of his grubby hoody. Ever the gallant, he blew me a kiss – he used the hand which had L.O.V.E. tattooed on the knuckles.

It was a right rogues' gallery tonight. I'd represented most of these wasters at one time or another over the years. Shuggy McAllister was dragged along by Sergeant Munro – right through the diced carrots and custard or whatever it was that had been in Billy's stomach. Shuggy was a small-time crook who had ideas above his station, and was fussy about his appearance. Lifting his foot, he tried to wipe the sole of his shoe on Billy Palmer's back.

'Palmer – ya dirty wee bastard!' McAllister shouted. 'D'you ken how much these fuckin' boots cost me?' The officers in charge weren't expecting it. McAllister broke free and kicked Billy Palmer full in the face. There was a crack, and then the sound of a jaw breaking carried far into the night. It was always like that; the atmosphere could turn on a five-pence piece. It was always wise to watch your back.

'I'm sorry – I didnae mean it, man!' Billy Palmer screamed his apology through blood-stained teeth as he cowered in the gutter. His eyes held mine, beseeching me to get him out, but he was already on bail so it was Christmas in Saughton Prison for him. I didn't think Santa would bring him anything other than another beating from Shuggy McAllister.

The situation was quickly under control. The

noise had alerted Malcolm who had been inside the station keeping warm. Sergeant Munro had made him a cup of tea. Their association went back years, to the times when Malcolm himself was getting lifted for lewd and libidinous behaviour. Malcolm teetered out on the toes of his patent pumps, watching where he stepped and ignoring the fracas – it was nothing he hadn't seen many times before.

'Honey! You came!' In the best tradition of a drag queen he extended his arms and hugged me, holding on as if he'd never let go. I didn't mind; he smelled a lot better than Billy Palmer.

'Come here,' I said to him gently. 'Let me see what damage that bastard has done this time.' I pulled Malcolm under the nearest streetlamp. Gingerly, I touched his blacked eye. 'What's this – has your mascara run?' I ran my fingertips over his swollen lips; tears of shame filled his eyes.

'I was going to say that you could do with some leeches – but I forgot you married one.' Malcolm is a Beaton, a family known throughout Scottish history as healers. As he himself said many times, 'Life in Glasgow was tough for a pansy'. He went to Amsterdam and honed his skills, patching up people who preferred not to go to a hospital. That's how he met Kailash.

It was hard to tell that he was upset, apart from the tears, because his face had been so frozen by Botox and Restylane fillers. Blowing his nose noisily into an immaculate handkerchief – Malcolm prided himself on his whites – he began to speak. I tried to listen, even though I'd heard it all before.

56

'This guy has no right to hit you,' I said, when he drew breath.

'Brodie, he doesn't mean it. I probably started it anyway and annoyed him with something I said or did.' He tapped me on the shoulder, trying to soothe my anger. The more I looked into his broken face, the angrier I got. He'd tried to patch it up with heavy foundation and concealer, but that just made it worse.

'He's insulting you, Malcolm, not the other way round. Fat bastard that he is – he's never been any good.' I shrugged Malcolm's hand off me; he had to be made to see that this was unacceptable.

'I'm sorry for calling you out, Brodie, but I didn't know who else to turn to. He gets loaded then he loses his temper, that's all. This time the neighbours called the police.' Malcolm kept patting his hand on the left side of his chest, checking his heart to see if it was still beating – perhaps he thought it was broken. Pulling his arm, I led him back into St Leonards.

'Just take a deep breath and relax. I'll check with Sergeant Munro and maybe they'll let me see him.'

Sergeant Munro busied himself with paperwork. It was a game he liked to play with me: how long could he ignore the daft wee lassie? He was the only one enjoying it.

'Sergeant Munro,' I said, smiling – we may have had a longstanding association but neither of us liked it. I even lifted and lowered my lashes very slowly. I'd read in *Cosmopolitan* that men find it irresistible; the journalist who wrote that clearly hadn't come across the good sergeant.

'Miss McLennan.' He stared down at the paper-work. 'Your colleague, one Mr Edward Gibb, has already visited your custodies and you're not getting to see Billy Palmer for another six hours.' He smiled ingratiatingly – he liked to smile at me when he was winning.

'I wanted to check the status of Derek Brown. I–'

He interrupted me, unable to hide his delight; he didn't even have to check his paperwork. 'Derek Brown has asked for another solicitor. In fact, he said – wait a minute, I wrote it down somewhere… I quote: "If that miserable bitch Brodie McLennan comes here, tell her I wouldn't let her represent me if she was the last lawyer in hell."' Sergeant Munro grinned but Dismal Derek's insults were like water off a duck's back to me. However, I needed to get more information so that Malcolm could sleep tonight.

'I take it he's appearing in court tomorrow? Who's his lawyer?' If I found that out then Malcolm could speak to them in the morning.

'Ricky Gordon,' said Munro.

A snort of laughter came out of my nose. It was quite embarrassing, but must have just been nerves. 'Ricky Gordon doesn't do criminal work because of his stutter.'

'Well, he's doing it tomorrow – I'd get there early or God knows what time you'll be out of Court One. I'll get Malcolm a taxi – he needs his bed,' he said.

No man is all bad, even Sergeant Munro, but there were a few that seemed to be devoid of any-thing positive – the Ripper, for one. The atmos-phere in the station was tense; all the officers were working overtime trying to catch the Ripper, yet the people in the cells were the usual suspects. A young Polish police officer shouted that Malcolm's taxi was here. Lothian and Borders police needed foreign nationals as constables to deal with the immigrants – not that I'd ever represented a Polish plumber. I wondered if it was just another PR exercise by the Scottish government.

My nemesis, DI Bancho, appeared, holding the door open for Malcolm. He looked like shit: heading up the investigation into the Ripper murders was taking its toll. I decided it wasn't just Sergeant Munro who could have his fun – baiting Duncan Bancho always made me feel better.

Chapter Ten

St Leonards Police Station, Edinburgh
Sunday 23 December, 2 a.m.

The five dead girls stared at me and I stared back.

Lips were silenced and eyes deadened. They all wanted to know one thing. *Who will speak up for me?*

What could I do? I wasn't their lawyer. The dead don't have lawyers. But though I'd gone into the operations room originally to goad Bancho, the dead girls had silenced me. I felt as if a freezing-cold cloak had been thrown on my back, and I shivered. The silent mouths asked me a new question: *What will you do if he's caught?*

Will you speak for him?

The operations room was a mess. Bancho's cheeks were heavy and drawn, his skin bleached by exhaustion. He walked up to the wall that held the chilling photographs and tapped it reverentially. 'They talk to me too,' he muttered, scratching his head and turning to make some coffee. I didn't bother to deny what he'd said. Waiting for the kettle to boil, he massaged his temples, trying to ease the pressure that was building. All the time he gazed unblinkingly at that wall. The wastepaper basket was overflowing, and an empty box of paracetamol was on the top. If I'd had any I would have given him some of mine. Wonders never cease – me feeling sorry for DI Duncan Bancho.

The desk was littered with crumpled paper that Bancho had discarded. Police reports, details of autopsies, newspaper clippings, buff-coloured folders with spurious leads – everything was laid out for the world to see. If it was an indication of the state of his mind, then no wonder he had headaches. I wanted to help. In spite of my revulsion, I wandered back over to the wall. The families of the victims who could be traced were located in Eastern Europe, Romania, Poland and the Ukraine. A map on the far right contained red dots to indicate the place of origin of the victim. Another map of the city of Edinburgh contained black dots to show where the bodies had been found. To my untrained eye, there seemed to be no obvious link.

For identification purposes, the relatives had been asked to provide a recent photograph. The before shots were more distressing than the after ones. The beautiful faces were arranged in chronological order according to the date of death, not the date they were found. These girls hadn't been reported missing. No one was looking for them – the discovery of the bodies was more a case of luck than judgement. A macabre beauty pageant was lined up on the wall. The girls had taken time to look pretty for their days at weddings, parties, graduations – and they did. I felt old just looking at them. All the victims were redheads, all different shades of red, and haircuts of every description.

Catalina was the first victim, found on 3 July; her hair was a cascade of curls. Florenta, whose body was discovered on 24 July, had her auburn hair cut short into an elfin style that emphasized her eyes; whereas Bianca, whose body was located on 20 August, had hair that fell poker-straight to her waist. Two of the victims had no before photographs. In direct contrast, straight below the glamour shots, the bare, smashed bodies of the murdered girls had been photographed one last time. Blu-Tack held the unnerving, inexcusable gallery to the wall. There wasn't much room left.

'If the Ripper continues with his killing spree, they're going to have to give you a bigger room,' I muttered.

Bancho had written the girl's name and age, if known, where and when the body was found, and the pathologist's estimated time of death. Catalina had lain undiscovered for months. The Ripper, annoyed at being ignored by the police, had cut the index finger from Bianca, the third victim, and placed it under Detective Bancho's windscreen wiper. When Bancho had been given the case months earlier, there had been a fanfare of publicity – he was Lothian and Borders' blue-eyed boy because he'd been seconded to the FBI for six months. He was trained in profiling techniques, but this was his first serial killer.

The two unknown victims were particularly heartrending. Their families didn't even know that they should be grieving. In the last six months, five bodies had been found, in various locations. After the first one, the Ripper made sure to place the bodies where a member of the public would find them. Now, he was becoming increasingly reckless.

'You must have learned something with the FBI,' I said. My shoulders hunched instinctively and it sounded like a criticism. It wasn't the tone I was looking for, but old habits die hard...

'The FBI have unsolved cases too,' he said snippily. 'The Ripper has chosen these girls carefully. At the moment only he knows the reason – but he's marked them with a signature that keeps changing.' DI Bancho turned to look at me. 'He hunts his prey – knows all about them. At the moment he's scouring the brothels of Leith but, as I've said, the bastard keeps changing.'

DI Bancho and I stood in front of the photographs, a heavy silence between us as we stared at the girls.

'What's his signature ... you've said it's changing ... how did it start?'

'With Catalina you can see her body is badly decomposed, but he's cut off her feet and hands to stop her escaping. Then he sewed her eyelids open using heavy black twine. Florenta got the same treatment, but look here.' He tapped an eight-by-ten photograph. 'He tore her tongue out by the root. Finally he cut her throat from ear to ear.'

'What about this one?' An unknown girl, her mouth twisted into an obscene scream, stared at me.

'I told you he varies it slightly ... he's taken the skin off her left knee. And this one...' He pointed to the other unidentified victim. Her breast had been cut open and her heart removed. Bancho coughed. 'The media didn't dub him the Ripper – that's what he calls himself. These aspects of his signature, along with the torn-out tongue, are taken directly from the history books.

'There's also speculation that the original Jack the Ripper was a Mason; he scrawled an incriminating message on the wall at the murder scene. The chief constable at the time rubbed it out and that's why he was never caught. It's no secret there are some pretty powerful Masons in this city. How often have there been calls for public declaration of membership among police and the judiciary? You can see why I am trying to keep this secret – especially after your recent publicity stunt.'

He offered me a Mars bar from a stash of sweeties in his desk and I couldn't resist. I always use food as comfort; it was late and we were both sick and exhausted. A sigh of weariness escaped from his lips as we stared at the dead girls. Christmas was coming but to Bancho and me, the season of goodwill had never felt further away.

'What do they look like to you?' His finger reached out to touch the portrait of Bianca Kowalski, the third body to be found. 'They're all redheads for a start – foreign–'

63

'So far...' he said, interrupting me. I looked back at the gallery of death, recalling the training that Patch, my Professor of Forensics, had given me.

'Good nutrition in childhood has strengthened her bone structure – see the Slavic high cheek-bones – but her mother worked in the fields, I'd guess. Her dress is cheap but she's copied it from something like American *Vogue*. It's bloody sad – she was the prettiest girl in the village, probably dreamed of something more. I bet that all she wanted was to get out, away from the arranged marriage, anything to escape. Jesus, the price was too high.' I said the final words under my voice. I had to admit that it made me sad and the words slipped out as I thought about the girls.

'Tell me something I don't know.' Bancho's shoulders slumped, and he turned away from the girls to place his cup down.

'Okay,' I said. 'I thought the papers had named him the Ripper for no good reason ... but I suppose he is following Jack the Ripper's sig-nature to an extent.'

'The media would have a feeding frenzy over the tongues,' said Bancho, shuddering. 'I mean, they're torn out by the root ... well, it's obviously difficult so he helps the separation along using a serrated knife ... he wants it to look like it's torn out.'

I turned to another part of the wall, on which was a printed, blown-up image of a text message. I'd heard about it at court, but I thought it was an urban myth. Unfortunately, for Bancho, it was not.

**Hi i'm jack c ur still having no luck finding
me
i respect u duncan but ur boys are letting u
down
u have no chance of catching me
warn the whores i will strike again and
again**

'How did that go down in the canteen?' I asked,
turning to face him.

'Depends who you speak to,' he said, scratching
his head. 'Some of the older men are saying that
I sent it to myself.'

'Meaning that they think you're a big-headed
bastard?' I said. It raised a weak smile on his face.

'That, I can handle. Others, including most of
my superiors, think I'm being taken for a ride.
I've overheard whispers as I pass – "He's just like
that detective in charge of the Yorkshire Ripper
murders in the eighties – the fool's being hoaxed
by some prankster." I swear the next one to make
comments like that gets punched, no matter how
many stripes on their shoulders... Fortunately,
they can't pull me off the case because of the fuss
they made about me going on that profiling
course at Quantico.' DI Bancho tightened his
jaw, and rolled his tongue along his lips.

'Maybe both schools of thought are right,' I
said. It was out before I could give it any thought.
Christ, even Bancho needed some sympathy. He
rolled his eyes like he gave a fuck about my
opinion.

Bancho's mobile rang and I strained to eaves-
drop. I could make out parts – the constable on

the other end was excited and shouting loudly. Bancho made noncommittal noises and tried to calm the man down. 'I need you to stay calm, Constable McLeod. We've had tip-offs before... Yes, we've had what we thought were reliable tip-offs before too.' Bancho sighed and punched his 'loudspeaker' option so that I could hear the words he had probably heard many times before. Bancho's ego was such that he felt the need to justify himself, particularly to me, one of his harshest critics.

'But this is the real thing, boss. We can't move on him for a couple of hours because he won't be in place until then – but, after that, it's fucking guaranteed. You'll have your man. The Ripper's yours ... boss.'

'I'll be with you in an hour,' Bancho said, closing his phone. Despite his words to the other man, he rubbed his hands together. How many times has he really been down this road before? I wondered, but I kept my thoughts to myself.

Chapter Eleven

**St Leonards Police Station, Edinburgh
Sunday 23 December, 3 a.m.**

DI Bancho couldn't wait to get rid of me; he practically threw me out of the operations room. I assumed that the detective inspector didn't want to make a phone call to his boss until he heard me clumping up the stairs in my heavy bike boots. I jumped up and down on the bottom step and he thought I'd left. He hadn't even bothered to close the door, although in his defence the office was down in the bowels of St Leonards and it was very late.

I peered in the open door. He was holding his breath. Opening his bottom drawer, he pulled out a can of Arrid Extra-Dry, sprayed each armpit and sighed. Whatever it was he wanted to do, he was putting it off. He looked nervous, his forehead shiny with sweat.

Bancho's eyes kept returning to the phone, as if he was afraid to make the call. Who could have that effect on him – the chief constable? Maybe he had to phone in the details of the search. If I'd had my way he'd be serving a seven-year stretch in Saughton Prison this Christmas, and if Bancho had won, I'd be eating my turkey in Cornton Vale with the rest of the women prisoners. It was no wonder we could barely be civil to each other. We'd both been wrong but neither of us was prepared to forgive and forget. No, I didn't want to admit I owed Duncan Bancho any favours. Maybe we were experiencing something of a truce but there was a long way to go before we buried the hatchet. His fingers trembled as he reached out to make the call. Stress, nerves or drink? I couldn't blame him if he had a tipple off duty; he was under a lot of pressure to deliver the Ripper. His call was answered immediately. It was on loudspeaker so that Bancho could use his computer and what I heard next was one reason why you should never poke your nose in where it doesn't belong.

'Glasgow Joe ... it's me... We've got the bastard. We're gonna get him today at first light.' DI Bancho panted as I held my breath, trying to keep quiet – he played with the cord on the telephone. He waited, presumably for praise; none came. Instead, Joe embarked on his own interrogation.

'What was Brodie doing there? Why didn't she leave with Malcolm? If she was with you – I hope you weren't daft enough to show her the site.' There was more than a hint of a threat in Glasgow Joe's voice. *What website? I was now going to make it my business to know.*

DI Bancho didn't question how he got his information – it was one of the things that made Glasgow Joe unique. 'Do you think I'm stupid?' DI Bancho asked. Joe didn't answer him. Bancho turned from the phone and stared at his computer. I couldn't see what was on the screen.

'Are you on "The Hobbyist" now?' Joe asked, accusingly. 'It was part of our deal you're supposed to keep track of site traffic and note their threads.'

'I've got a WPC on it full time. Remember, I was the one who told you that Brodie was being mentioned.'

Joe was silent.

I wanted to leap out of my hiding place there and then. Why was I on some website and why was it so important that the police were spending scarce resources monitoring it? Not to mention why these two bastards were keeping me in the dark about it. But I would learn more if I kept quiet. It would also have been slightly embarrassing to have been caught spying on Bancho.

'There's no more mention of her – I've just

checked. Nothing since that first mention at the end of July,' Bancho wheedled.

'You shouldn't need reminding – that site is supposed to be checked at least every two hours. These guys have time on their hands right now – most of them have finished their work for Christmas and their wives are too busy shopping to notice they're not there.'

The edge was taken off the detective inspector's high spirits. He stared at his unpolished shoes, it was lucky that he couldn't see his face in them; his skin was flushed with embarrassment. Bancho hesitated before he flipped open the buff-coloured file in front of him.

'I've got the photograph in front of me. It's from the usual source; I think it's enough to go on. Why do you think he posted it to you at the Rag Doll?'

'I dunno. He obviously knows I'm involved – I've been hanging out in every brothel in Leith.'

'Not true – you've been in every slave den in Leith,' DI Bancho said as he walked towards the wall and pinned up another photograph. I couldn't get a clear view of it, but it was obviously a man and it looked professional, not knocked off on a camera phone. The first photograph of the Ripper. I decided to wait until Bancho went to the toilet and sneak in to see the monster. He hesitated, glanced over his shoulder and then put the image back in his pocket. I retreated to the shadows.

'Has Jack Deans been snooping?' Joe's voice was casual, as if he didn't care what the answer was. Bancho didn't look as if he was fooled – and neither was I. But I was surprised.

'He's been in touch – tried to pretend he left Darfur because the Sudanese government was going to throw him out – the truth is that sly bastard couldn't keep away from the biggest domestic news story in years. I hear he's still chasing awards,' said Bancho.

'Vain bastard!' Joe grunted. I could hear he wanted to ask more; maybe he was sniffing around to see if Jack and I were together. The reception was bad and I knew that Joe would have taken this call outside. He couldn't risk anyone knowing he was a police informer. Regardless of the circumstances, that would be the end of his reputation in Edinburgh's criminal underworld – there were no exceptions to this most basic rule, even if he did like to keep a foot in both camps.

I could hear tiredness in his voice; he'd been running around trying to keep me safe. I knew the way his mind worked and felt like a bitch. He would see the threat; every victim would wear my face.

'Are you properly prepared?' Bancho asked.

'Calm down, we'll nail the bastard. Every criminal messes up. It's a myth serial killers are smart – how difficult is it to top a wee Romanian girl?'

'But it's been in the papers, Joe. Apart from this photograph, there have been no ideal leads. The photo could be dodgy. How come this guy has the camera at the exact moment?' Bancho coughed. 'It makes you think.'

Joe was right, the only reason serial killers got away with murder was faulty witness reports.

'You remember our deal?' Joe's voice rang out

70

in the dim room. Most men were too frightened to renege on any deal with him, and Bancho was no exception.

'It's not that easy to just give you five minutes alone with the Ripper – people will notice his injuries.'

'I promise I'll be careful, although I don't feel good about this dawn raid. The Ripper's not dangling on our hook yet – in my opinion your overtime budget isn't going to get cut in the near future.'

'You're filling me with confidence.'

'If you see Brodie – make sure she's safe. The snow's started and if I know her she'll be on the Fat Boy. Don't let–' Glasgow Joe didn't get a chance to finish.

'I'll pick you up at the casino in an hour – and by the way, I'm not a nursemaid.'

Bancho's eyes flickered; it had been a long time since he'd interrupted Joe; he switched the phone off and grabbed his coat. As he left I pushed myself into a corner.

I should have known by now to expect anything of Joe, but even I was stunned by the extent of his collusion and involvement with Bancho, not to mention Bancho's subservient attitude. Who was running this investigation?

I ran up the stairs as if there was no tomorrow. For the dead girls – there wasn't.

Chapter Twelve

Edinburgh's Old Town
Sunday 23 December, 3.30 a.m.

I lifted my face and let the fat snowflakes fall onto it, feeling each one cold and clean upon my skin. I was worn out and felt like crap. I stuck my tongue out to catch a speck; it melted immediately but didn't make me feel any cleaner. The cobbles were covered with a layer of white; it gave the streets an innocence that I'd lost long ago.

There's nothing like confronting death to fire up your will to live. The roads were lethal and I didn't fancy spending Christmas in an intensive care unit. Lavender would kill me if nothing else. Snow lay on the Fat Boy too. He was staying where he was, and I'd have to get a taxi home. Easier said than done – the clubs were emptying and the narrow streets of the Old Town were filled with prime examples of binge Britain. Young girls staggered down the road arm in arm, thinking that there was safety in numbers. It made sense to me in the absence of any other option, so I fell in behind them as they lurched and reeled up St Mary's Street.

The sound of a horn made me jump. My heart raced as I turned and saw Bancho kerb crawling. Putting on my best smile, I hopped in – he'd obviously been bullied into this. As I'd overheard, he was on his way to pick up Joe at the casino to go on the dawn raid. A blast of warm air counteracted the chilliness of his welcome. Glancing at him out of the side of my eye, I put the seat belt on. The wheels skidded as Bancho drove off in the direction of my house; he was obviously in a rush to get rid of me.

We stopped at the top of St Mary's Street, and a shiver that had nothing to do with the temperature ran down my spine.

'What did you think of the City Wall verdict ... did it make you proud?' Bancho asked, exhaling noisily. He watched as I gave my reply.

'No.'

On the corner with the Royal Mile sat the City Wall pub, implicated in one of Edinburgh's most notorious murders. Two young girls, Alice Parks and Jane Derren, had been bound and raped then murdered after they had left the pub. The police had investigated the case for thirty years until advances in DNA techniques allowed them to bring in Andrew Saunders.

'Did you think Alice and Jane got justice?'

'No.'

'You're bloody right. We brought her killer to court; he was a convicted double killer and paedophile – yet he was found not guilty. Nine days of evidence, and thirty years of painstaking detective work down the toilet ... why did the prosecutor close the case without putting the DNA evidence to the jury?'

There was no answer. All I knew was the law must be above suspicion – which was why I'd asked if the judge was a Mason in the earlier case. People make mistakes – there must be no suggestion it's not a mistake.

'You know what the tragedy is, Brodie – we had the evidence to nail him... It just wasn't put forward in court.'

Bancho drove at speed. He couldn't leave the scene of the City Wall fast enough.

'It could happen again, Brodie. When I catch the Ripper there's always a chance he could walk free because of a smartass lawyer – we both know that lawyer could be you. Would you sleep at night? Would you?'

He was looking at the City Wall pub in the rear-view mirror. His eyes showed that the old case still haunted him. 'Nobody cares.' He ran his fingers over his mouth as soon as he spoke; perhaps wishing he could take the words back. 'We couldn't get justice for Alice and Jane and they belonged to the city – what chance does someone like Bianca have?'

His nicotine-stained fingers kept pulling on his hair, and clumps came away in his hand. I hoped for Bancho's sake that this alarming moulting had occurred because he hadn't brushed his hair and not because of a failure to control his stress; otherwise he'd be as bald as a coot come Christmas morning.

'No one cares about these girls,' he said again. 'Not their families, government, no one.' His voice was rising. I could see he wasn't taking me home. That was unfortunate, because I wanted to check out this 'Hobbyist' website as soon as possible.

'The media just think these girls are prostitutes – even if they were that's no excuse – but they were double-crossed, Brodie; told that they were coming to the West to go to college or to model, and then ending up as sex slaves.' Bubbles of spit were forming at the edges of his mouth as he turned into Danube Street and stopped outside Kailash's establishment. He leaned over and opened the door for me to get out. The snow was still falling heavily and I wasn't even home yet. 'Do you know that the American government doesn't have a charter against people trafficking? You'd think Uncle Sam of all administrations would be against slavery – well, they all speak a good game but that's as far as it goes. Bush said in 2002 that there would be zero tolerance and a bill was drafted, but defence contractors objected. The British government is just as bad.'

I thought he was going to leave me alone in the snow; I was bored and just wanted to get home – but no such luck. He got out of the car and grabbed my arm, dragging me to the front door of Kailash's place. I don't choose to frequent my mother's brothel or her casino, but Bancho wasn't giving me any choice in the matter.

It was a while before the door was answered, which gave me plenty of time to inspect the Christmas wreath in front of me. It was extravagant, expensive and unique – just like my mother. I was touching the blue thistles that were intertwined with holly, when Kailash opened the door.

'Well, well, well – to what do I owe the pleasure?' Kailash's tone was sarcastic and acerbic. She wasn't talking to Bancho, she was talking to me. It was a source of great annoyance to her that I had difficulty accepting her choice of profes-

75

sion. I'd hoped that when Connie went to a day school in Edinburgh, Kailash would change her ways. She certainly didn't need the money. Her casino and property developing companies more than paid for her hairdressing bill, which wasn't insignificant. Kailash said that I just didn't understand her – kids were supposed to say that to their parents, but, actually, she was spot on.

My heart sank as she pulled me inside the large Georgian hallway. With one swift kick of her Manolos, she slammed the door shut in DI Bancho's face.

Quality time with Mummy.

Just what I needed from Santa.

Chapter Thirteen

Danube Street Casino, Stockbridge, Edinburgh
Sunday 23 December, 4.10 a.m.

I knew that my scuffed bike boots were leaving dirty marks on the plush red carpet, but I guessed that Bancho's banging on the front door had been much more unsettling for the high rollers. Anything that took their minds off the tables was bad for business, and that made it Joe's business.

The hum of conversation and the shuffle of cards had slowed due to the late hour. It didn't take too long before Glasgow Joe was at my side. He'd approached Kailash with an idea for online gaming; the costs were low, and their profits phenomenal. Against all odds they worked well together.

We weren't really back to chatting – a few minutes spent on a muddy pitch watching Connie couldn't make up for what had happened. Joe's a proud man who didn't take rejection well and that was without him knowing that I'd slept with Jack Deans. Again.

He blamed me. Well, that's always easier. We'd got on great until he wanted more – Joe always wants more.

I pulled a battered black-leather wallet out of my jacket and handed him £500 in fifty-quid notes. I always kept a sizeable quantity of spare cash on me – it made me feel safe. Growing up we never had grubby fivers lying around. Joe crooked his index finger and called over a waitress. He placed the money on her tray, and, after a few moments, she brought back the chips. As I took them, Joe quietly suggested that I try out the poker table, before heading for the front door where Bancho was still creating merry hell. I turned and watched as the door was opened – if the policeman was surprised to see Glasgow Joe in full Highland evening dress, he didn't show it.

'Have you got a warrant?' Joe asked, his tone cool and measured. I wasn't fooled. Despite apparent hostilities, these two were working together, creating a convincing charade to fool the rest of us.

'No. It's a friendly visit – I can get one, though, if that's your last word on it,' replied Bancho.

Their play-acting was pathetic. Joe reached out

into the cold night air and hauled Bancho in off the street. It looked impressive, especially to the punters who were growing a little uneasy. Manhandling the police in front of witnesses was an Oscar-winning bit of theatre.

I wandered through the casino. It was packed with judges, football players, businessmen and wealthy tourists, all desperate to get a last bit of freedom before being shackled to their families for Christmas. I craned my neck looking around for someone – a friend, an acquaintance, but there was no one, so I turned my attention to the tables. I knew that Joe was probably watching me on the surveillance system. The clientele watched me too as I walked around. I contravened every dress code the casino had – my leathers were filthy, still covered in midges from the summer, but the pliable leather clung to my arse in what I'd told myself was a most appealing way. Maybe that would distract them all and I'd walk out of here a millionaire.

Pulling out a chair, I joined the poker table playing Texas Hold 'Em. In for a penny, I thought as I took my jacket off too. I wasn't wearing a bra because I hadn't exactly dressed up when I left the flat, and the only one that wasn't grey was lying on the bedroom floor after Jack had taken it off me, but maybe that was a good thing – more distraction for the saddos around the table.

I kept my face blank as I clasped my cards up from the table. Pocket-Rockets – a couple of aces. I was in good shape. The player across from me, in a bespoke evening suit, white tie, and with the obligatory female companion looking over his

78

shoulder, chucked another grand into the pot. The dealer knew my credit was good at his table, so I decided to play on – thirty minutes with Bancho had reminded me to live for today, but I'd make this my last hand, win or lose. To my surprise, the other player at the table raised too. His toe tapped constantly, he wore a cowboy hat and was difficult to read. In spite of his porky butcher's fingers, he shuffled his chips deftly.

'Two thousand more,' he said, evening off the two stacks of black chips and pushing them into the pot. It was the right bet and it should have scared the third player away. Unfortunately for him, the third player was me and I was just riled.

'I'm in,' I said, pushing one pile of eight black chips into the pot.

'You're bluffing,' the fat cowboy puffed, gulping air as his eyes flicked over me.

'Play and see,' I shrugged. I was sure that Joe would be laughing out loud if he was watching. The fat man looked convinced that all he had to do was push in his remaining chips, and he'd take the hand.

'Yours,' he snorted, flicking his cards over. A pair of sixes.

'You were right,' I told him as I flicked over my two aces. A roar went up as the dealer pushed a mountain of chips my way.

A bit of luck at last – I wondered how long it would hang around for.

Chapter Fourteen

Danube Street Casino, Edinburgh
Sunday 23 December, 4.40 a.m.

Glasgow Joe leaned in to kiss me as he stopped to check that I was all right. The money in my pocket made everything all right. He swept me up and turned me round as I threw the cash in the air. The notes whirled around us like a snowstorm – I was Kailash's daughter. I knew how to put on a good show for the punters.

Bancho came out of the security room. With only an hour to go before his planned raid he was edgy. The smile slid from my face, and I bent down to pick up the notes, carefully collecting them and putting them in the old wallet.

'Get Kailash,' barked Bancho. 'I want to see the dungeons – rumour is that she's got slaves.'

'Arsehole – come back with a warrant,' I hissed.

'What does Kailash want?' Joe turned around to find her. She was leaning against a colonnade, her jet hair curled expensively around her shoulders, and a sheer black Dolce&Gabbana dress clinging to every curve.

'I've never denied owning slaves, Duncan, but there's quite a waiting list. See Malcolm; he'll put your name down.' I was jumping from foot to foot, but Kailash locked eyes with me and it was a look that told me to calm down. 'There are a lot

80

of exhibitionists in tonight – the thrill of being observed by a real policeman means I can push the price up,' she purred. She turned on her heels – he was being given one chance at what he wanted. If he failed to take it, Kailash would shut the doors faster than a Venus flytrap. Everyone concerned knew there was no way Bancho would get a warrant to inspect these premises – the powers that be had no idea who the police would find there or what the tabloids would make of it; they themselves kept Kailash out of the courts because they spent so much time there.

On the other hand, the Ripper's victims seemed to be plucked from the city's disenfranchised community of foreign, probably illegally trafficked prostitutes. Sex slavery. Perhaps, despite their unconventional 'partnership', Bancho didn't trust Joe to check out Kailash's operation with the same dedication he applied to brothels in Leith.

'I'm coming!' Glasgow Joe shouted. 'I hate watching these fucking deviants getting their arses skelped,' he muttered under his breath, and scratched his head as if such behaviour was beyond his comprehension. I knew it was. Joe's sexual taste didn't run along these lines; he was strictly a meat and two veg kind of guy. He grabbed my arm. 'Don't act smart down there – Bancho's been mouthing off to the authorities that Kailash has sex slaves. I've told him he's wrong but she feels insulted. She's ready to knife him, Brodie, so we don't need you shit-stirring as well. I don't think it would be so easy to get Kailash off another murder charge.'

I pulled free. But I went along with their game,

even though they didn't know I was in on it. 'It wasn't so easy for me the first time,' I growled, rather content that we were now back on an even keel and old habits of bitching at each other were to the fore again.

The dungeons were full tonight with 'customers' cramming in one more whipping before the traditions of Christmas demanded that they stay with their families. The dungeons were rooms with bars on them like the type you would see in a Wild West jail. It was a great design. Most fetishists were happy to share their perversion within their private world, and Kailash could check the employees were safe.

'What's the score here?' I asked, pointing to a middle-aged, lumpy woman who was painting liquid latex onto a man. 'And what's with the straws?' The man had thin tubes for breathing protruding from his nose. The dominatrix overheard me and proceeded to demonstrate by putting her thumbs over the bottom of the straws. Her victim, who was in chains, his hands manacled above his head, struggled. She took her boot and jammed the pointed heel into his bare foot. I winced. The man screamed silently, unable to make a noise because of the gag.

'That's enough, Betsy,' Glasgow Joe warned as the male slave passed out.

'This is what I mean, Joe – how can you say she doesn't have more information about foreign sex slaves?' Bancho hissed.

'Because Betsy is married to a solicitor from Melrose – he's a misogynistic bastard according to her, so she comes up once a month and spends his money here in the shops during the day and then helps out here at night, earning a bit of pin money that he knows nothing about. The slaves are quite happy to cooperate with Betsy.' Glasgow Joe sounded tired as he explained matters.

'Anything you need to ask about – ask me,' said Kailash, who was standing behind Bancho long before he had any idea that she was there.

'That girl there looks Eastern European,' he said, squinting his eyes at her. The one he was talking about was a stunning dominatrix who would have been at least six feet tall in her fishnet-stocking soles. Tonight she wore over-the-knee latex boots with seven-inch heels. I winced when I saw the nipple clamps.

'Contessa.' Kailash beckoned the girl, who flicked the black eight-tongued whip over her client's butt before she left the cell. He squealed and I looked twice at him. I thought I recognized him, but it was hard to make out his features. He squirmed in the corner, presenting his naked, flaccid butt – Joe shuddered and I couldn't blame him.

Contessa, gripping the whip, marched over to her employer. 'He wants a word with you,' Kailash inclined her head in DI Bancho's direction, and then started to laugh softly with Joe. I'd met her before – she was notoriously bad-tempered and born for this sort of work. It was unlikely that any attempt at questioning by the police would go down well.

But the Ripper had pulled off what years of community vice work had failed to produce: cooperation. A sex worker from Eastern Europe she may be, but Contessa knew that this time police officers, even ones as smelly, dishevelled and desperate as Bancho, were on her side against a common enemy. They huddled in a corner as I waited for the explosion that never came; instead of kicking the detective's butt (which I was secretly hoping for), Contessa kissed Bancho on both cheeks before returning to her dungeon.

'I'm done here,' Bancho said, walking up the stairs. Turning he faced me, 'And you? You can walk home.'

Silently, I wished them good luck at catching the Ripper.

Chapter Fifteen

Princes Street, Edinburgh
Sunday 23 December, 3 p.m.

The boots bit into my ankles, and it was with throbbing feet that I puttered over to the side, hands flailing wildly as I tried to stay upright on the ice. The Pogues and Kirsty MacColl were singing 'Fairytale of New York', and it rang out around Princes Street Gardens. Connie had dragged me down to Winter Wonderland – the most romantic outdoor ice-skating rink in the world.

I'd found out that ice-skating is a dangerous business as soon as I'd started. I was certain I'd cracked my coccyx from the last fall. Jack was waving a Kielbasa sausage with sauerkraut all wrapped up in a hot-dog bun – the temptation was too much to ignore. Unable to stop, my body slammed off the barriers, every bone rattled. Winded, I reached out and snatched the sausage out of his hand.

'Mind my fingers.' Jack flapped his hands theatrically in the air. 'I got mustard and ketchup – I don't know which you prefer,' I didn't get the chance to find out; the hot dog was teetering on the edge of my lips when a shower of ice came down on top of us. 'Connie!' I screamed as she dug her blades into the ice and came to a sliding stop, shaving the top layer of the rink off and depositing most of it on Jack Deans – the residue ended up on my hot dog.

'Whaaat?' Her eyes widened with innocence as Jack wiped the melting chips of ice from his face. 'When you said a friend was coming Christmas shopping with us, I thought you meant Joe – why is *he* here?' Connie turned her back on Jack, ignoring him completely as she continued whining in my face. *'He's* not coming to Lavender's wedding, is he? Promise me *he's* not coming – cos I don't want Glasgow Joe to be in a mood, I've been looking forward to this wedding for ages.'

'Lavender only set the date six weeks ago,' I told her. (I didn't want to point out that we had all only known her for about five minutes; it might sound like I was surprised at how little time it had taken her to become part of the group. Truth be told, I was – and a little jealous, as I wasn't that sort of person myself.) Taking advantage of her change in mood, I was in the process of escaping, gingerly. I inched along the barrier; luckily, Jack walked beside me – anywhere he was, Connie was sure not to follow.

'Ten quid says that by the end of today she'll be eating out of my hand,' he whispered to me. We both half turned and watched her skating backwards, arms stretched out like the wings of an aeroplane, the point of her tongue poking through her teeth in studied concentration. He'd raised one bet I didn't want to win.

We left the rink. Next on the itinerary was the Edinburgh Ferris Wheel, adjacent to Sir Walter Scott's monument in Princes Street Gardens. The shrine to Scott resembled an illuminated wedding cake – wedding cake always makes me sick, and not just because I hate fruitcake. I was trying to overcome my fear of heights by confronting it. Standing in the queue with jostling, excited teenagers, it felt like one of my dumber ideas. Connie refused to allow Jack to come on with us, hissing that he would unbalance the basket and make it unsafe, cleverly playing on my weaknesses. Her behaviour towards Jack was outrageous really; I was looking forward to getting her on my own to tick her off or bribe her. I hadn't yet decided which tactic would be the most effective.

As soon as the wheel swung into action, I knew my scheme was flawed: fear of heights can be dangerous. I remembered reading on Wikipedia that acrophobics have the urge to throw themselves off high places despite not being suicidal– I'd soon find out if I fell into that category or not. It seemed an especially bad idea when the wheel stopped at the very top; I hadn't noticed that the wind had got up until then. Connie leaned over the edge and the basket swung round and round. I got the same feeling when I watched the part in *Carrie* when she was prom queen one minute, then the next covered in pig's blood. Everything is fine, breathe deeply and just look down, I told myself. I could see the Princes Street shoppers a hundred and fifty feet below me. They swarmed like ants in and out of stores, desperate for a last-minute bargain and oblivious to the drama of me, terrified, playing out above them. Connie was leaning out of her seat and shouting and waving.

'Cal! Cal!' she shouted for some reason, flailing her arms around – a lunatic oblivious to her own safety. A chill ran down my back like an ice cube. I tried to grab Connie and get her to sit down but I was afraid that any sudden movement would send her over the top of the ferris wheel. I had seen too many disaster movies; racing thoughts showed me Connie tumbling through the air until she landed, a broken doll gone from my life forever. I didn't know that there was a feeling around that made you think that your heart could puncture your ribs at any moment – until then. A mouth as dry as a desert river bed meant I couldn't scream her name. If loving a child gave you this much fear, I was glad I had decided to remain childless – Connie was more than enough.

Shuffling along the seat redistributed the weight in the basket, causing Connie to lean out even more. Sensing my discomfort she was playing up. 'Cal – look up! It's me, Connie!' Her voice had risen by several octaves. By this time, other passengers had begun to notice she was in danger of falling. Out of the corner of my eye I could see them pointing with one hand and covering their mouths in disbelief. I'd had enough and lunged and grabbed the back of her coat, breaking two fingernails in the process. Roughly, I hauled her in.

'What the hell are you doing? Do you have a death wish?' As soon as the words were out of my mouth, I realized I sounded just like Grandad.

'Are you blind, Brodie?' She took a deep breath and waited for my answer, which wasn't forthcoming. 'Didn't you see him? Cal?' She nodded expectantly, waiting for recognition as we finally got off the ride. The blank look on my face finally registered with her and she rolled her eyes at me. 'He's a friend of Moses' and if we hurry we'll catch him!' She grabbed my arm and pulled me, leaving Jack to follow. I could tell Connie was getting on his nerves. I wasn't sure if she was intent on getting rid of Jack, or if she truly had a crush on this Cal guy. I thought it best to check it out because there was no way she was dating a Dark Angel. I realized again I was acting like Grandad – he hated me going out with Glasgow Joe, but surely that was different?

Princes Street was still busy. Six Russians from the St Petersburg Brass Band were playing a quick march, which was exactly what Cal did when he saw us coming. I recognized him at this distance; he was the guy selling drugs with Blind Bruce in George Street outside Susie Wong's. Oddly, a woman in her fifties held his arm. It took me a few minutes to work out that she was probably his mother – even Dark Angels have mothers.

The young man was well away by this time, but I had other plans than following a spotty youth anyway. I wanted to relive my childhood through Connie. It was a long shot, but everyone else had bought her a fantastic present and I didn't want to look like Scrooge, so I reckoned that, if I dragged her around Jenners, with Jack behind us still, perhaps I could see what made her eyes light up. Visiting Santa had been a tradition that Mary McLennan and I had. She took me to see him on two separate Saturdays because I refused to believe he would remember what I wanted. Connie was almost as tall as me and wearing about a ton of lip gloss and I doubted I could make her go to the grotto under any circumstances. We wandered around for a little while and I tried to see enthusiasm at every opportunity – but with Kailash and Malcolm there for her every whim, and a whole new 'family' dancing at her feet, Connie was never going to get thrilled about a cuddly toy or a pair of slipper-socks.

Chapter Sixteen

Princes Street, Edinburgh
Sunday 23 December, 3.40 p.m.

The hunched babushka leaned on her walking stick, bundled up against the cold, wearing every article of clothing she owned. Her grey-coated tongue played with her false teeth. Mashing her jaws together, she moved the dentures in and out to pass the time. The Watcher sniffed and got the smell of stale urine on her – he was disgusted, but the old woman was safe from him.

Last-minute Christmas shoppers moved like shoals of fish, endlessly weaving in and out. The windows of department stores were filled with golden tinsel, and expensive dresses that would cost less than half that price in three days' time. The babushka stood in the centre of the pavement, craning her neck, hunting for something, someone – the good citizens of Edinburgh gave her a wide berth but she'd found her mark.

The Watcher giggled to himself: *Who knew that he had so much in common with peasants? Actually, on second thoughts it was an unpleasant idea.*

The old woman reached out and grabbed Brodie McLennan. Clawing on her clothing, she demanded help. The babushka's voice was guttural, low, like a cat ridding itself of a hairball. He shuddered. Her gnarled hands waved a piece of paper in front of Brodie. The Watcher squinted. It was a photograph she was brandishing – it was impossible to tell but he imagined that he knew the face.

Sniggering, as Brodie spoke slowly and deliberately, it was obvious to The Watcher that the hard-hearted bitch was trying to palm the babushka off with enough money for a cup of hot chocolate and no more. Brodie raked through her pockets, coming up with some loose change, which the old woman took and secreted in her bag, but she held on tight to Brodie – this was not an end to the matter. Jack Deans tried to pull Brodie away, but Connie spotted his move; she was having none of it. Suddenly, the old woman's plight became the most important thing in the thirteen-year-old's life. Testily, she slapped Deans's hand and pulled Brodie over to the babushka.

Deans pulled out a well-used wallet and handed Brodie a ten-pound note. 'It's really not going to work, Brodie,' The Watcher heard him say. 'She's oblivious to my charms.' Brodie shrugged her shoulders. 'Fine – you're right. I just think you could try a little harder.'

The Watcher smiled slowly, satisfied that Brodie had been hoodwinked – it made him feel safer. He moved in even closer. He needed crowds – it was easy to get lost in them. An electric shock passed through him as he crept nearer still. Close enough to see that Jack Deans wanted rid of the precocious brat as soon as he could. Connie was obviously cramping his style. He giggled to himself again – in a way, he was about to do Jack Deans a big favour.

The cold damp air was making Brodie's beautiful red hair curl into a rumpled, just-crawled-out-of-bed look. The Watcher licked his lips and flexed his fingers; he was itching to make his move. He could feel his impatience growing. Closing his eyes, he centred himself – *act in haste, repent at leisure*. Another of his mother's maxims. For several long seconds he breathed deeply, consciously relaxing every muscle in his body. The rattling tin broke his state. His eyes flashed open and the Salvation Army officer stepped back. She saw something that gave her pause and caused her heart to race a little; withdrawing the tin she scuttled away.

The Watcher ran, sprinted around the corner –

91

but it was too late. Brodie, Connie, Jack Deans, and the babushka were disappearing in a taxi.

She was getting away from him – again.

Chapter Seventeen

Danube Street Casino, Edinburgh
Sunday 23 December, 5 p.m.

Glasgow Joe opened the front door of the casino to us, looking surprised, to say the least – and he didn't like surprises. He always said he'd never met an assassin who did, which was fair enough. Not that he was in that line of business any more, of course – he'd given that up for me. The fact that I'd brought Jack Deans with me was obviously another source of displeasure. Joe flicked his eyes over his so-called rival, and I could almost hear him thinking that Deans was too bloody smooth by half. In fact, I'd been wondering myself whether Jack hadn't been scrubbing himself up a bit better since he'd returned – maybe it was my imagination, but I thought his hair had fewer grey streaks in it than before.

'What are you looking at?' I said, ignoring the fact that he was Kailash's partner in the casino. In spite of Kailash's protests to the contrary, she was considering dumping the brothel end of her business and concentrating on Internet gambling while still perfecting it in the real world too. The billions-a-year in profit made from online betting was too much for her to resist – she wanted a piece of the pie and had decided to share it with Glasgow Joe. The initial income was set to their quadruple projected forecasts. Joe was going to be rich soon, very rich, but all the money in the world wouldn't solve the problem he was clearly having seeing me with Jack.

'Members only,' he snarled, sticking out his hand in front of my companion. The two men stared, digging into each other. Joe's eyes were stained with insomnia. Jack was the only one who was smiling, and he smiled like the cat that had the cream – in Joe's mind the bastard probably had. I was annoyed at both of them – and myself.

'I told him you wouldn't let him just walk into your casino!' shouted Connie, stirring from the back of the line where she was jumping with glee at the thought of Jack being blackballed. Joe was trying to teach her about good sportsmanship, something he knew little about, so, reluctantly, he stepped aside and let Jack in. It was an up-market establishment, though. How would we explain the smelly old bag lady beside us? 'She's with me,' Connie piped up, as she pushed the crone inside the hallway, obviously having fallen for whatever story she had been fed.

The arrival of our strange party disturbed the gamblers for no more than a few moments before we were shepherded downstairs to the private quarters. Glasgow Joe remained frozen at the front door. He craned his neck to survey his casino. He was acting strangely, as if something was very wrong.

'Joe!'

He turned. Connie stood alone at the top of the stairs, waiting for him to join them. At least she was looking after his interests. Reluctantly, it seemed, he closed the door. What was he up to? Kailash owned two Georgian townhouses in Danube Street. They were adjoining properties linked by a corridor in the basement. Connie was allowed in the casino side, but the girls used the area underneath it for rest and recreation. The kitchen and cellar of the brothel had been transformed into the S&M dungeons that Bancho had been so interested in.

'Hey!' whispered Connie loudly to Joe. 'You need a friend?'

Glasgow Joe shrugged. 'Wouldn't if you'd left me upstairs,' he muttered.

'And miss your chance to get one over on Jack? I've been watching your back all afternoon – if I'd known you were just going to roll over, I'd have saved myself the bother.' Her bottom lip stuck out, a sure sign she was ticked off.

Joe smiled, almost feeling sorry for Jack Deans – he knew just how bloody awkward Connie could be when she set her mind to it. I didn't know whose side to be on – they all had claims on me.

Kailash wandered in and caught Joe's eye. It was early. She wasn't dressed to receive her special clientele. A diva in a white Armani trouser suit, Kailash would never approve of a dressing-down day at work. I couldn't help but squirm as my mother scrutinized my unkempt appearance and my usual biker gear.

Sniffing loudly, Kailash looked pointedly at me, Jack and Connie. Raising her eyebrows, we were

94

left in no doubt that she wanted an explanation, and what Kailash wanted, she generally got.

'Gloria! Get her something to eat!' Kailash ordered the young girl who was making herself beans on toast. 'It's hard to tell under all those clothes, but I suspect the old biddy hasn't had a square meal for some time.' Nodding towards the babushka, Kailash recognized the hungry look in the old woman's eyes. Connie took Gloria's phone and plonked herself on the window seat to play a game, while the rest of us got on with being uncomfortable around each other.

Sitting down at the table, the old woman yammered at Kailash, who held up a beautifully manicured hand and, immediately, the crone fell silent. She slid the photograph across the table to my mother who manoeuvred it with her finger-tips. Breathing deeply, she seemed to be thinking about what to say next.

'Can you help her?' I asked.

'How much has she told you?' Kailash replied.

'Very little – she can't really speak English. She waved that photograph at us, the way she had been waving it at everyone. She was crying and wailing and kept clutching it to her breast. I take it that's her granddaughter and that she's disappeared?'

'Mmmm,' she murmured. 'That's what we need to find out. We need help here. Gloria! Get Contessa!' Kailash ordered. 'She'll be busy, but for once we can interrupt.' Malcolm had been keeping a low profile, embarrassed by his bruises which couldn't be hidden even with thick makeup. But now he emerged to hand Kailash a strong cup of tea, no doubt full of sugar. 'On second thoughts,' she said, 'you go as well, Malcolm – make sure that she hurries.' He shook his head and, muttering, walked out the door.

A silence fell on the room and the smell of burnt toast permeated the air. Gloria had forgotten to take the bread out of the toaster when she'd put it in for a second browning. Joe opened a window, only for Connie to whine: 'Do you want me to catch my death?' She pulled her anorak hood up without breaking stride as she played the game, her thumbs working at double-quick speed.

It didn't take long before Contessa swept into the room, like a Siberian wind rolling along the Road of Bones, pulling her short red silk dressing gown around her. I swear that Jack almost swallowed his tongue trying not to look at her pierced nipples through the fabric. At nineteen, Contessa was a girl of contrasts, from her snow-white skin to her short carbon hair and sky-blue eyes; she was every boy's fantasy of a vampire. And maybe Jack and Joe's too, the way they were drooling.

The babushka ran rosary beads through her fingers, muttering prayers. Beads rattling, she leapt from the seat and threw herself before Contessa, clutching the prostitute's improbably long legs. The supplicant pulled the robe from Contessa's shoulders revealing a tattooed snake; the head of the king cobra nestled at her neck and the tail disappeared down her back. Bending over, Contessa helped the babushka to her feet and Jack helped himself to another look as he tried in vain to figure out exactly where the tail of the snake ended.

Tears of gratitude were diverted down the

wrinkles on the old woman's face as she heard the mother tongue on the girl's lips, while Kailash and I exchanged smiles of self-satisfaction – too soon, too soon.

Chapter Eighteen

Danube Street, Edinburgh
Sunday 23 December, 5.15 p.m.

Contessa was a people person – in her line of work she had to be. Born on the wrong side of the tracks, she had reinvented herself at fourteen. Following that, she'd turned up at Kailash's door when she was seventeen. She hadn't been turned away and Kailash had never regretted her decision.

She stood quietly, listening intently. Her full red mouth was open as she tried to decipher the old woman's jabbering. They all eavesdropped, although they couldn't understand a word; even Connie had laid aside her game. Reaching out, Contessa tucked a stray grey hair back into the babushka's headscarf.

'Her name is Irena Antonescu ... her journey began weeks, maybe months ago ... the old woman has lost track of time.'

Malcolm pulled out a seat from the table and helped the babushka to sit down. Her legs were covered by opaque black stockings, but he, like everyone else, could see the gnarled markings of varicose veins – wiggling his own toes, he looked as if he was guessing how tired her feet must be. Throughout this procedure, she hadn't stopped talking. The wind was building up outside, the windows rattled, momentarily distracting them. Contessa's English wasn't fluent – I'd imagine she'd found it unnecessary to take extra language lessons for her career advancement – and, consequently, she was a frustratingly slow translator. The babushka jabbered on for several long minutes each time, but Contessa gave curt, one-second answers.

'Irena says that the journey cannot stop ... it is a journey to find not her granddaughter. Her daughter, Mihaela.'

Clearly the old woman had had a hard life. I would have guessed any daughter of hers would have been near retiral. I wanted to ask how old she was but Contessa was interrupted by the old woman pulling at her; the girl turned her full attention back to the crone, nodding in silent understanding. 'She says that she wants you to know that her daughter's name means ... gift from God. She is ... was a dancer. She loved to dance since she was a little girl.' Contessa stopped; bending down, she indicated Mihaela had been dancing since she was knee high.

A sudden blast of wind shook the side of the building. A storm was gathering. Business would be slow tonight, so Contessa could spend some time with the old one. Rocking back and forth, the babushka never stopped speaking, not even for a sip of the tea that was growing cold in front of her.

'She is talking about journey again. She is

hoping that will reveal the mystery of the daughter. She was good girl, she kept in touch with her mother who is widow... Irena keeps saying she has to find daughter ... her search for the daughter has brought her to world she does not understand... Mihaela comes from village in countryside ... as you can see, they are peasants.' Contessa's lips curled in distaste. 'The village is called Glod ... is a Romanian word for mud ... no cars in village ... only transport is by horse-drawn cart.' Perhaps Contessa wouldn't spend time with the old woman after all – from what Kailash had told me, she had run many miles to escape a village just like Glod in the first place.

The babushka pulled at Contessa's dressing gown again, anxious for her story to be heard, anxious for any help to find her daughter. 'Babushka says that they are poor people ... but they are still people.' Contessa sighed as she listened to the stream of words from the babushka. 'She says they were tricked by people more educated than them. ... I do not know what she means.' Malcolm handed Contessa tea in a china cup and saucer; she sipped delicately on the hot sweet black brew.

The babushka cleared her throat and was about to begin again; Contessa held up her hand – a full thirty seconds passed before the babushka was given permission to continue. The kitchen was filling up. Girls of all shapes, sizes and hues began to file in – the storm had affected trade and they had some spare time. A semicircle gathered around the kettle waiting for it to boil; normally, the air would be filled with girlish chatter, but tonight there was silence. Out of the corner of their eyes they stared at the battered photograph of Mihaela untouched on the table. More than any other group, these women had reason to fear the Ripper.

Connie removed her anorak. The close proximity of so many bodies had raised the temperature of the room. A cloud of worry passed across Contessa's face as she continued to listen to the babushka. I thought I saw a small bead of sweat run down the side of her face, until I looked again and saw that it was a tear. The old woman reached out and lifted the worn picture from the table; clutching it to her chest, directly over her heart, she began to wail. Her coat was black and worn, and it brought the fresh-faced beauty in the photograph into sharp relief. Mihaela's dreams were reflected in her eyes.

Joe's jaw tightened and he clenched his fist – I knew that he would feel impotent. There was nothing he could do to bring her back, but at least the old woman deserved to be told what was going on in this city.

Glasgow Joe looked carefully into Contessa's face. 'The old woman has to be told what's happening in Edinburgh,' he said. 'The poor old soul can't read or speak English – she has no idea that the Ripper's on the rampage killing girls like Mihaela.'

Fear seemed to quicken in Contessa. Gripping the cup and saucer tightly, she softened her tone and began to speak. The babushka stared into the distance, slowly allowing Contessa's words to sink in. The pendulum clock on the wall ticked loudly, as I watched. The girls were rifling in their handbags, gathering their change to make an offering to the old woman, and Kailash already had a wad of cash waiting. Gloria stood and waited. When Contessa stopped to draw breath, she handed over their offering. Even if Mihaela's body was never found, it was enough to buy a memorial stone to mark the fact that the babushka's daughter had once walked and breathed on this earth.

Rocking back and forth, the old woman keened, the loud shrieking noise no doubt disturbing the few high rollers who were in the casino above – no one moved to quieten her. Holding a fistful of money out to Contessa, the old woman began to speak again. It was a horrible sound, the guttural noise of an animal in difficulty. Contessa suddenly stilled. Her hands joined in prayer, she lifted them to her mouth, as if she was beginning to understand some horror. She struck like lightning. Kicking the money out of the babushka's hands, she grabbed her by the scruff of her neck and dragged her up the steps.

'Put the old woman down, you crazy bitch!' Joe stepped forward as the rest of us looked on in shock at the turnaround. I watched as the old woman hit every step on the way up; she bounced and ricocheted like a black plastic bin bag as Contessa manhandled her to the grand entrance hall. The high rollers gawped; some even placed their cards face down on the table to stare. The red silk robe had slipped from Contessa; the snake was gleaming with the sheen of sweat, the colours of its scales jumped as the muscles on Contessa's back twitched from exertion. Glasgow Joe caught up with them when Contessa was opening up the heavy Georgian front door.

He circled Contessa and her prey crouched low like a hunter; Contessa bent down and took off her left shoe. It was no ordinary shoe – the seven-inch stiletto heel made it an offensive weapon in Contessa's hands.

Firing it, her aim was true; it glanced off Joe's forehead, buying her enough time to open the front door. Using her bare foot, she kicked the old woman out of the house. The babushka rolled down the three steps and landed in the gutter. Contessa gathered phlegm from her throat and spat on the old woman.

'*Vacu draculi!*' she cursed, slamming the casino door.

Chapter Nineteen

Danube Street, Edinburgh
Sunday 23 December, 6.30 p.m.

The Watcher smashed the streetlights and huddled in the dark to wait – he was used to that. All good things come to those who wait. He kicked the shattered plastic into the gutter; he couldn't afford to inadvertently stand on it. He knew he had to be extra vigilant, although the noise from the casino covered any din he made and he made sure to stand at least one hundred yards from the entrance. Kailash's employees were always on the lookout for those who would stalk her doorstep, either as a police informer or a pervert. The Watcher was nothing if not careful.

He placed his gloved hands over his mouth and blew; there was no warmth left in him to thaw his fingers. His lips were frozen. It was even too cold to blow rings with his breath. The wind howled down the street. He felt an icy chill run up the back of his thighs as a gust lifted the flaps of his overcoat. He clenched his teeth and heard his breath hiss: *this feeling had better just be the cold.*

He had arrived at the corner of Danube Street just in time to see Brodie disappear into the high rollers' casino. Joe kept the journo and the old woman on the doorstep longer than the rest of the party, allowing The Watcher time to choose the perfect viewing point. His heart fluttered – things were going according to plan. He felt a surge of pride that he'd tracked her down so quickly.

The feeling of elation was fleeting.

For a few long moments after the party had disappeared, Glasgow Joe remained on the front stoop, staring up and down the street, searching the darkness. The Watcher held his breath. A tingle of excitement ran through his loins – he was unused to being the hunted. He had to fight the urge to run. From inside the casino, a voice called, 'Joe!' Reluctantly, the former assassin turned to answer it, granting The Watcher a stay of execution.

As the door slammed shut, The Watcher allowed himself to think that maybe things were going his way after all; he deserved a break. The snow was falling thick and fast. He was unable to move from his hiding place – the snow formed a virgin perimeter around the casino and his footprints would be obvious as there was no other traffic on the street.

The lamppost was covered in a thick layer of frost. He spat on the end of his glove and traced doodles on the ice with his finger. All the time he whistled softly and pictured how it would be. He felt a familiar stirring – it was never too cold to dampen his ardour for the plan. The Watcher settled himself down, his heart rate slowed as he took himself on a mental journey from the last time. He kept each experience in a separate room in his mind – only he had the key and, when he chose, he unlocked the room and let the exquisite memories unfold.

Years of training had enabled him to recall every minute detail. He sniffed the still night air deeply – underneath the aroma of snow, he imagined fear intermingled with sweat and cheap perfume. Although smell was undoubtedly his favourite sense, he also enjoyed remembering the tiny whimpers that escaped from deep within their bodies. His memories came flooding into his mind – perhaps, after all, the taste of salty skin was his favourite.

There was no sign of life. All was quiet, except for the sound of the wind rushing down the Georgian street, rattling windowpanes, rustling through the bare trees that lined the Water of Leith and provided his cover.

Kailash's girls opened the shutters – obviously the kitchen must have been too hot. In the darkness, the light from the basement of the casino reminded him of watching a drive-in movie. The girls had come to enjoy a coffee break – The Watcher could see them in their underwear. His hand went to his trousers as he felt himself stir to life. He unzipped his fly as the red silk gown fell off the girl he watched; he stroked himself and stared at her. Now he envisioned what it would be like if she wrapped those long bare legs around him. He stroked himself faster still. He grunted loudly in his head, but stopped himself just before he ejaculated: *he who lives without discipline lives without honour.*

He stood chewing his lips. It seemed like an hour, but in reality it was only a matter of minutes before the front door swung open and the girl kicked the old woman down the steps.

The Watcher heard every word.

'*Vacu draculi!*'

The Watcher whispered it under his breath, interpreting Contessa's words. He sniggered and repeated the words – 'You are the devil's cow!' So, that's the way it was. It was no surprise to him; there was no evil that his mind could not conceive of. He had little or no faith in his fellow man. The Watcher knew the score from these shouted words. He had heard the old babushka's story increasingly often in recent years – a worthless daughter had suddenly become the family's greatest asset for the price her body bought in Bucharest. The girl would be taken out of the country to work in a brothel. After she had paid off the initial money outlaid to her family, her new owners would take rent from her and send any remaining pennies home to the family. The babushka had travelled to Scotland to slap the wretched girl for withholding the money.

She picked herself up out of the gutter and

105

brushed the snow from her coat. As she retied her headscarf, The Watcher noticed a ribbon of blood running down her face from a cut above her eye. Slowly, she lifted her hands and wiped it away. For a few long seconds, she stared at her bloody palms and fingers. A little surprised, The Watcher opened his eyes wider as he waited for her to seek absolution. Reaching into her deep pockets, she pulled out a string of rosary beads. Limping slowly along Danube Street, she passed close to The Watcher's hiding place; he heard her prayers.

He guessed that she was praying for herself.

Chapter Twenty

Court Meeting, Lothian and St Clair W.S.
Monday 24 December, 7.30 a.m.

By virtue of rising at the crack of dawn, I'd finally made good my promise to check out the mysterious website Joe and Bancho had been discussing, and I had only one word to go on: 'Hobbyist'.

I don't know what I was expecting – disgruntled legal clients bad-mouthing myself and others of my illustrious profession perhaps?

It took a lot of Googling, but the only Hobbyist I could find appeared to be an American-based 'adult' site where men with bizarre and violent tendencies got their rocks off discussing the adventures they'd enjoyed with prostitutes – sometimes very young and not always willing prostitutes. I comforted myself that, as usual when men discuss their fetishes, at least 50 per cent of it could probably be dismissed as fantasy and wishful thinking.

It certainly wasn't my reading of choice, and I was about to give up and log off when I caught sight of my name. One of the dirty old fuckers had been trying to get in touch with a 'Brodie McLennan'. Okay, it's not a common name, but I reasoned there must be at least a few Brodie McLennans in the States or on the worldwide web. I checked the date of the entry. Six months ago. Before I could read any more – not that I really wanted to, having established that I clearly wasn't the vice girl he was looking for – Lavender staggered into my office labouring under the weight of a tray of coffees and a basket of muffins.

'I don't pay you enough to turn up to work on your wedding day!' I shouted to her, while quickly closing down my web access. She held a handful of napkins between her teeth – it was bliss: for once she was unable to answer me.

At Lothian and St Clair, we're family. It's a small court practice and if it's a day when the court is sitting, at least one of us has to be there. My well-publicized fights with the Law Society and the Edinburgh Bar Association meant we had difficulty getting solicitors to work for us, so our choices were limited.

Eddie was nervous about the wedding ceremony, so he came in for me to hold his hand. Lavender didn't trust us to appear on time for the ceremony, so she had everything arranged.

I pulled the plastic lid off a takeaway coffee cup. 'I asked for a skinny latte!' I said, grabbing a bran and molasses breakfast muffin. I dropped it like a hot potato as Lavender smacked the back of my hand.

'The dress is a size ten. I told you at the time you'd never stick to that diet – you lost twenty pounds on that bloody Atkins Diet, which, by the way, we all had to suffer for with your cranky cravings for carbs, and now you look as if you've put on thirty. Skimmed milk isn't going to cut it, Brodie.'

'Well, this won't make much difference either, then.' I grabbed the muffin out of the basket, making sure to take a big bite before she could snatch it and give it to someone else. I wandered over to the outsize mirror. Breathing on it, I pulled my sleeve over my hand, and rubbed.

'Bloody hand prints – again,' I said.

'Better than bum prints!' She laughed. Lavender's natural curiosity had led her to develop skills that would have given Sherlock Holmes a run for his money. She had been unable to settle until she'd uncovered the origin of the strange body prints I periodically found on the mirror. Apparently, a security guard and a cleaner were having an affair – and they were rather partial to watching themselves. It was bad enough that illicit sex was taking place in my office whilst I wasn't getting any, but these two?

'There's nothing on at court today,' Lavender told me. 'A few custodies that Danny can cover – you and Eddie have a deferred sentence each. Get your arse into court early – ask the fiscals to call your cases first. I want you in and out of court – you *will* be at the Sheraton no later than ten thirty a.m., Brodie!' she ordered. Lavender ran the office like a border collie herding a flock of sheep – I met Eddie's eyes and held them. We were having our heels nipped – if we knew what was good for us, we'd obey her commands to the letter.

'What are you doing here, anyway?' I asked Lavender. 'Don't you know it's bad luck for the bride to see the groom on the morning of the wedding?'

'I know what you two would get up to if I was stupid enough to leave you to your own devices – I'd be left standing at the altar while you acted like this was just any working day,' she replied.

There was one cup of coffee remaining on the tray. Eddie, Lavender, Danny the agency lawyer and Louisa the trainee were all sipping away in companionable silence watching the winter sun struggle to rise above the Castle Rock. The door creaked open – Grandad was here. At first it irritated me, him hanging about the office controlling things, demanding to see me rehearse my jury speeches – but I couldn't deny that I had improved under his tutelage; so much so that the challenge had gone out of defence work. Maybe it was having Connie in my life, but suddenly I wanted the streets of Edinburgh to be safe so she could go out without the fear of being attacked by some little shit I had got off.

Grandad kissed me good morning, smelling of expensive gentlemen's cologne, the type that was probably in vogue in the 1940s. His eyes glittered and he clapped his hands excitedly; he couldn't wait to get down to business. He had made it clear that the only thing better than walking Lavender down the aisle would have been to have me on his arm – under the strict proviso that he approved of my choice of groom, of course. Everyone knew that would never happen.

'Did Joe phone you yet?' Grandad asked.

'No.' I narrowed my eyes, suspicious of his motives. It was no secret that Grandad liked Joe, but not enough for me to marry him – again. 'Have you heard the news this morning?'

'Er, yes,' I answered. 'Why?'

'Not the stuff on the radio or TV – the real stuff. According to Joe, they've caught the Ripper – it was too late to catch the morning edition of the papers and they're trying to keep the media circus in check until after the indictment hearing.'

'Why did he call you?' Eddie Gibb asked Grandad. 'No disrespect, Your Lordship, but you're hardly bosom buddies.'

'No offence taken, Eddie,' Grandad beamed, his ancient yellow teeth glinting. 'DI Bancho asked for my phone number – quite rightly Joe wasn't prepared to give it to him without checking with me first.'

I looked at him quizzically – he really was muscling in on my life. I coughed, inviting him to explain further. Lifting an eyebrow, he turned and faced me. His look told me he wasn't used to being questioned, silently or otherwise, but on this one occasion he would do what I wanted. Arrogant old bastard.

'This case has to be handled correctly. Bancho cannot allow trial by media – if the press isn't tightly reined in, then the case could be dropped if the defence demands a mistrial.'

'So Bancho has finally succeeded,' Danny whistled through his teeth.

'Don't be so sure. After all, it's Bancho we're talking about – I'm willing to take a bet he's got the wrong man, and that he won't care too much as long as he gets a conviction,' I said.

'Don't be so hard on him. Bancho's a better cop than you give him credit for – if he was such a dunderheid, Brodie, Lothian and Borders police wouldn't have sent him to Quantico on that profiling course,' Eddie said.

'Profiling my arse – how hard can it be if they sent Bancho? What are they going to say? That the perp is single, Caucasian, a white-collar worker approaching forty who lives with his mother?' I said, looking around for support. I didn't find it in their eyes. 'I take it back – he lives with his redheaded mother.' I smiled and sarcastically threw a tenner on the table. 'Put your money where your mouth is,' I told them.

Danny McCabe laid a ten-pound note on the desk, as did Lav. 'I'll bet it's a woman,' she said. 'Only a woman is smart enough to have escaped detection for so long.'

'I hate to disagree with you, darlin' – but serial killers are overwhelmingly male and of European descent,' said Eddie, throwing in another tenner. 'But my money's on Bancho.'

'Eddie's right ... it's a man and he's white, he hates women and he's pretty much killing in his own ethnic group, but Bancho has made a mistake if he tries to impose archetypes on this guy – you need to be open. The Ripper is a thrill

111

seeker because he's playing with the media and he's targeting prostitutes, so he could be on a mission to exterminate certain types from society,' I said. 'The red hair thing is creepy. I think he does live with his redheaded mother.'

'You've more money than sense, the lot of you,' Grandad sounded off, but he was right. We weren't exactly model profilers. 'And you have other things to be thinking of today,' he emphasized, looking at Lavender. She sniffed in the background and pointed to her watch. It was 8.45 a.m. and she wanted us to be the first lawyers at the Sheriff Court. Eddie threw my court gown to me. I caught it and lifted the two files Lavender had laid out. I was going to walk to court with Eddie, then I had to meet Kailash, Lavender, Connie and Malcolm at the Sheraton hotel. I was already imagining myself in the spa, lying back in the Jacuzzi, quaffing champagne. I knew that Kailash had other ideas though. Malcolm was a fabulous stylist and my mother wanted us to look our best. She didn't have any formal photographs of Connie and me together, and this was her chance. I was halfway out of the door when the phone rang. Lavender's face fell; reluctantly she raised her arm and curled her index finger. I took the receiver from her.

'Hello?'

'Brodie McLennan?' I knew it wasn't St Leonards; as far as I knew they didn't employ any policemen with American accents. 'Adie Foster here.'

I may never have met Adie Foster – but, like everyone else in the country, I'd heard of him.

Chapter Twenty-One

Lothian and St Clair W.S.
Monday 24 December, 8.45 a.m.

'Ms McLennan – Lucas Baroc suggested I call you.'

I wanted to whistle. Lucas Baroc had, a few years ago, won the European Footballer of the Year award and was playing out the twilight years of his career in Edinburgh. He may have been at the end of his professional life, but he was still in a class above the 'talent' we generally put on a pitch – not only was he the leading goal scorer in the Premier League, he was also (and more importantly) drop-dead gorgeous. I'd got him off a drink-driving charge earlier in the year. Baroc had originally appeared, and pleaded not guilty to the charge. A date was set for his trial, but he was playing in Europe and 'forgot' to turn up at court for an intermediate hearing. The sheriff issued a warrant for his arrest but didn't discharge his original trial.

As soon as Baroc was back in the country I arranged for him to appear, but it was after the trial date. New dates were fixed for the trial but I decided to attack the competency of the charge. I appealed to the High Court on the basis that the original trial had not been discharged, therefore when it was not called in court on the appointed day it had fallen – the Appeal Court

113

found, in our favour, that Baroc could not be tried for the charge of drink-driving.

The case brought me a lot of publicity, not only because it involved Baroc, but because, potentially, it affected thousands of criminal cases in Scotland – it also led to the accusation that I set guilty people free. And Adie Foster fitted into all of this because he owed me for keeping his star striker's licence.

'Lucas Baroc recommended me,' I repeated loudly for Eddie's benefit. He had been as sick as a pig when I had appeared for Baroc, who played for an 'enemy' team. Eddie's greatest love, behind Lavender, was Hibs football team. He would have made sure Baroc had gone down if he'd been representing him.

'That's correct. Lucas – he was very pleased with the result of his trial. Your name was bandied about quite a few dressing rooms – in the nicest possible way, of course,' Adie Foster laughed.

'Well, we can certainly schedule an appointment after Christmas, Mr Foster,' I said.

'Oh no, that wouldn't do at all, Ms McLennan,' he said calmly. 'I need to see you today.' His voice was low and brooked no opposition. His tone said that Adie Foster was a man who was used to getting what he wanted – he had married a rich woman, turned her millions into their current fortune, and clearly thought that everyone else should jump when he said so. Her family came from oil money He was one of the first investors in the North Sea fields. Most of his money now came from oil reserves in Tatarstan in Russia and he had businesses all over the old communist countries of

114

the Eastern bloc. His construction company was rebuilding Bosnia, which was why he had so many football players in his team from that part of the world. I looked across and saw Lavender's face. She was giving me the evil eye; I turned my back on her. There was no way I could take on a new case today – unless...

'Unfortunately, Mr Foster, I'm matron of honour at a wedding this afternoon,' I started to say. Lavender poked me in the back and hissed, 'Unfortunately?'

Coughing, I began again. 'I am totally committed to this wedding – you have to understand that, if I did agree to meet with you, it would be at great personal sacrifice.'

Lavender stood on my foot. I placed my hand over the receiver. 'You're on my toes,' I whispered. 'It hurts.'

'I know,' she replied, 'and I haven't even started yet.'

'I understand. If there's anything I can do for you – please don't hesitate to ask, Ms McLennan. This matter is very close to my heart,' he drawled. I thought there was a great deal an American billionaire could do for me; however, there was one thing in particular that only Adie Foster could do for me, and was the reason for me sacrificing my toes to Lavender.

'Well, now you happen to mention it...' A smirk crossed my face as I anticipated Connie's face on Christmas morning if this worked out. 'I have a thirteen-year-old sister who is football mad – the ideal present for her would be to run out onto the turf at Easter Road as a mascot for Hibs. I was bidding in the Hibs' auction but I was unsuccessful.'

'I take it you would settle for her being our mascot on New Year's Day when my team meets them?' he clarified.

'Yes,' I said, wincing, knowing full well that this would be difficult. The team mascot would already have been picked so some other kid would have to be bumped for Connie to take the place. Still, it was our first Christmas together, and I wanted to get her something she'd always remember.

'Consider it done. I'll get my secretary to courier you the details. Now, as to how you may help me, Ms McLennan. I've just been advised by a ... friend ... in the force that my son Thomas is appearing at Edinburgh Sheriff Court this morning. I don't have any details of the charges. My son has never been in trouble with the police before. He's a second-year mathematics student at Yale but his course allows him to study at a foreign university for a year. He chose Edinburgh. Naturally, his mother and I will both be there this morning.'

'If he's appearing from custody then he won't be coming up from the cells until noon – they might be earlier today, though; everyone wants finished for Christmas,' I told him as Lavender shoved a note in front of me. *I'm getting married this afternoon – or had you forgotten?* 'It'll be fine,' I mouthed back at her. It would be an in-and-out job and I'd get there to the wedding in plenty of time. Of course I wouldn't make it to the Sheraton, which was where my dress was, and there was the added difficulty that Malcolm wouldn't be there to do my hair, but I liked the natural look, even if Kailash and Lavender didn't, and someone else could always pick up my frock.

There was, of course, another difficulty. Thomas Foster was an adult and therefore entitled to choose his own lawyer. No matter how much Mr Foster wanted me to represent his son, it was down to Thomas, not his dad. Actually, the best case scenario would be that Thomas had already instructed someone else, leaving me to buzz off to the Sheraton at the prearranged time having bagged the best Christmas present ever. I still believed in Christmas miracles – when I had to.

Chapter Twenty-Two

Custody Cells, Edinburgh Sheriff Court
Monday 24 December, 9.55 a.m.

Thomas Foster sat huddled on a bench in the corner of a solitary cell. He had been separated off from the other inmates – in deference to his father's position, I assumed.

The noise in the cells is always jarring – small-time criminals shouting out to their lawyers, friends or enemies, an undercurrent of violence that could spill out at any moment – yet Thomas maintained his poise and wore a hawk-like look of self-control.

The walls of the cell were white, flecked through with every colour under the sun and some suspicious brown marks, which I couldn't imagine were anything other than shit. It wouldn't have

117

come from Thomas Foster. He had the kind of movie-star good looks only rich, well-nourished Americans can possess; they didn't make maths students like that when I was at Edinburgh University, I thought to myself.

Sergeant Davidson and I stared in at him through the tiny peephole in the thick steel door. I thought he was unaware of our presence until he stood up, walked to the door, and stared straight at me.

I stepped back.

The air was warm; smelly with the fug of fear. A trickle of sweat ran down the side of my face. Nothing was as it seemed. I'd assumed Thomas Foster was up on some student prank. Sergeant Davidson was a man of few words, and he also took it for granted that I knew all about Foster. Who else would turn up to represent a billionaire's son knowing fuck-all about the case? Actually, quite a few probably – the nature of the work is such that we're often called upon to improvise. It wouldn't be the first time Eddie had a trial file then got caught up in court, or the trial was heard early and I had to go into court knowing nothing but the client's name. It's not comfortable. The choice is that, if a lawyer isn't there to represent a client, the lawyer gets found in contempt of court.

'Open it up,' I said to Sergeant Davidson. He didn't ask me why no one had been to see my client last night; he didn't ask why our names were not against his as he came in. This was a breach of procedure and I was surprised that he didn't pick up on it.

'I said I didn't want a lawyer,' came Foster's

voice. He had a soft Californian drawl that I recognized from Hollywood, not real life.

In fact, he was a dead ringer for Leonardo DiCaprio, which was strangely unnerving.

I walked past him and sat down, careful to wrap my gown around me. You needed to be vigilant. A fair percentage of my clients carried nasty diseases that they weren't afraid to share. Looking at Thomas Foster's unblemished tan skin and bright blue eyes, I was willing to bet he was clear, but old habits die hard. As I reached into my briefcase for a pen and pad, I had time to reflect – it was unusual for me to see a prisoner in the police cell and not out in the agents' area.

'Brodie McLennan,' I said, holding out my hand – which he didn't take.

'Ms McLennan, whilst I do not wish to appear rude, I do not require the services of a lawyer. There has been a mistake, which will soon be cleared up.' His voice was soft and a bit seductive. A random thought flew through my head – was I too old for him? Maybe, but he seemed so polished that he was more grown-up than me, and he was a looker.

'Well, you might not require my help but I need yours,' I told him. 'Your father has agreed that my little sister can be the football mascot at the Ne'erday match – on the condition I came here to see you today.' I scratched my head before putting on my most winning smile and said: 'Now, I'm a busy woman – contrary to what people in here will say, I don't need to press-gang clients, so why don't you just sit down and tell me what the score is so that I can decide if you need my help or not?'

His eyes opened. He smiled. 'She really likes soccer that much?'

I nodded.

'Well there's no accounting for taste,' he said as he half turned and swept the bench with his fingers before he sat down. Leaning on his knees he stared at his Italian handmade shoes. 'They've taken my belt and laces,' he said, mostly to himself, before placing his hand in his waistband and holding it out. 'The belt I can understand – but what the hell can anyone do with a pair of laces?' he asked.

'You'd be surprised,' I said, 'but that's protocol for any prisoner. They assume that they all want to attempt suicide – why would they think that about you?'

'Why not? Do you think being brought up in a wealthy family stops pain? Maybe the guys here *have* got it right,' he said.

I flinched. God, that was a bit quick, I thought. I didn't sign up for psychobabble, just a quick present for Connie; I needed to come clean otherwise we'd get nowhere. 'I don't know what you've been charged with unless you tell me. I won't find out until the papers are served on you later this morning. I have a wedding to go to, and much as Connie would love to be a mascot, I really can't let my best friend down by wasting my time here when I should be throwing confetti.'

I think he understood about a quarter of what I said. 'Only one per cent of people in the world have an IQ over one hundred and thirty-five – Einstein's was just over a hundred and sixty – mine is

120

a hundred and eighty. What's yours?' he asked.

'I don't need to prove myself – I certainly didn't graduate from charm school,' I told him. 'But you will get out of here faster if I stand up for you in court, because I'm going to beg and plead with the prosecutor to take my cases first on account of the wedding. Every other lawyer will be doing that too, though, as they'll all want off for Christmas, and you, my friend, will be left sitting until last. So what I say is, use that genius IQ of yours – you can sack me once you're out. How does that sound?'

I watched him intently. A tiny frown appeared between his eyes. Fuck it. I wasn't going to sit and read his emotions – I had better things to do with my time. I got up and moved towards the door.

'I behaved like a dork,' he said, behind me. 'I'm not proud of it – but I didn't kill her.'

My throat tightened and I stopped stock-still. There was no way this was an in-and-out job. Christ – given what Grandad had said, there was only one murderer up today.

The Ripper.

I looked at Thomas Foster and knew that DI Bancho had made another bloody mistake – on top of that I had placed a tenner on the profile; the only thing I'd got right was that he was white. Thomas wouldn't hit middle age for at least another twenty years, and, from what I'd seen in the glossy mags, his mother wasn't even a redhead.

Throwing myself down on the bench, I held his eyes, searching for lies.

'Tell me about it,' I commanded.

'I went to a ball in Edinburgh Castle on Friday night. My partner was a girl called Katya Waleski.

121

It was our first date. I spent some time in Bosnia during the summer holidays – the family firm has reconstruction contracts, and when I have any time off, I travel. I was a token employee, I know that – my presence made no difference so I spent a lot of time moving around Eastern Europe. I picked up a smattering of the languages.' He didn't seem ashamed by this – in fact, he seemed downright cocky still.

'Due to your genius IQ?'

'Sorry about that ... but, yes, I do pick up languages easily; when I get the chance, I like to practice.' He stared at his perfectly manicured hands and picked at the nails which were getting jailhouse-grubby already.

'Okay – you don't need to explain why you took a girl to a dance, but you do need to tell me what happened.' He placed the chess piece in his pocket as I spoke and began to pick imaginary fluff off his trousers.

'It's a bit embarrassing, ma'am,' he mumbled, without lifting his head.

'I'm a big girl – I've heard worse.' I didn't want to add that I'd probably *done* worse. The naiveté of youth makes them think that they invented sex. And if he called me 'ma'am' again, he wouldn't be able to perform for quite some time. It was bad enough that I was already thinking he was part of a younger generation and I was past it. He looked at me as if to check I wouldn't be offended. On another occasion I'm sure that his manners would have been charming, but right now I had things to do and they were only slowing me up.

'It was hot ... crowded in the Great Hall ... a

122

band was playing ceilidh music. Frankly ma'am, the noise was getting on my nerves. An old man played the squeeze-box – it sounded as if he was in pain. I mean, that's not music, is it?' he asked.

I ignored his point. He paused and I didn't fill the empty space; instead I sat on the edge of my seat looking expectantly at him. DI Bancho must have at least something on him or he wouldn't be here.

'Katya and I went out for some fresh air,' he said.

I didn't mean to raise my eyebrow – it just popped up. He had definitely told me a lie there. I knew how cold it had been on Friday night; surely, it would have been more comfortable to have a snogging session inside where it was warm? Maybe I *was* getting old.

'The wind got up and there was a bright moon. I wanted to show Katya Edinburgh at night. We went to the battlements ... and she looked so pretty in the moonlight.' He swallowed hard, fumbling with his fingers. He increased the pace of his speech almost as if he needed to hurry through the next part of the story or he wouldn't be able to tell me it. 'I gave her my jacket...' He seemed to have a lump in his throat. He swallowed hard, but I knew he'd stalled.

'Yes?' I encouraged, nodding my head, urging him on.

'She wasn't cold; in fact she was burning up,' he said.

Bloody hell. I was careful not to roll my eyes, but it seemed like he'd been reading 1970s porn for his research.

'I was covered in goose bumps, but the next thing I knew was she was slipping out of her dress – it was just a little silky thing so it wasn't much in the way of warmth anyway...'

'You didn't try to stop her?' I couldn't keep the sarcasm out of my voice, wondering what world he lived in.

'No – in fact when she started getting naked, I sort of forgot about the cold. She was so beautiful – we kissed and she lay back naked against one of those huge old cannons.'

'A siege cannon,' I said, as if it added anything to his tale. I was getting a bit embarrassed by all of this and needed him to cut to the chase.

'The lining of the jacket might have been slippery or it could have been the ice, but, as we were making love – she fell.' His head fell into his lap. He gulped for breath as he tried to stop himself sobbing.

It was all a good performance. He looked up red-eyed and held my gaze. 'I couldn't stop her. I reached out to grab her but I was too slow. She tumbled down those rocks and ... and ... she was still alive as she hit them the first few times ... but by the time she reached the bottom, I knew she was dead. I panicked. I ran away. The police picked me up yesterday. I didn't want my parents to know.' He finished his tale in a rush – he'd better not think that it was all over. I had plenty of questions to ask.

'Does your father know you've been charged with murder?' I asked, because if Adie Foster had withheld that information from me then I had a good mind to resign from acting immediately.

Even as I let this thought run through my head, I knew I was being dishonest to myself really. There was no way I was going to pass up this trial. I hated to admit it, but I'd have chewed Lavender's leg off to get it, never mind miss her wedding.

Chapter Twenty-Three

Edinburgh Sheriff Court
Monday 24 December, 11.45 a.m.

'Happy the bride the sun shines on,' Jack whispered in my ear as I went outside from the custody cells. I looked up and saw an anaemic winter sun trying to break through the heavy cloud cover.

'It's hardly splitting the pavements,' I said. I didn't want to think of the wedding. My stomach was knotted – I hoped it was only the fact I feared I might miss Lavender and Eddie's big day rather than anything to do with Thomas Foster. The Sheriff Court was normally deserted at this time of day and year, but my client had changed all of that. The media swarmed around outside like maggots on a cadaver, all hungry for a piece of the action, including (or should that be especially?) Jack Deans.

'I've got to go,' I said, pushing Jack away. I didn't want to confirm to Adie Foster that his only son had been charged with murder, but somehow it seemed more honest than hanging around the press pack.

Foster and his wife McKenzie stood at the front door of the court. They were unmolested by the reporters despite the fact that everything they did usually made the news. There was at least a ten-foot no-go area around them that had nothing to do with Adie Foster's stinking cigar, but everything to do with the sumo wrestler they employed as a bodyguard.

'Mr and Mrs Foster?' I held out my hand as I approached them. McKenzie Foster proved to me there was definitely a point when you could be too thin. Looking as if she had just sucked on a lemon, she turned her back to avoid touching me. I didn't take it personally. As far as McKenzie Foster was concerned I was part of the problem, not the solution. Her son belonged in a country club, and in the society pages, featured with a succession of models, heiresses and talentless daughters of ageing rock stars. He did not belong in a criminal court. By contrast, her husband shook my hand until I was afraid he'd cracked several small bones.

'There is no way I can make this any easier,' I began. 'The procurator fiscal has charged Thomas with murder.' I cleared my throat so there would be no mistake about what I was going to say. 'The more demoralizing news is that it's a holding charge. They think that Thomas is responsible for the deaths of those other girls.'

'What do you mean, Miss McLennan? What "other girls" are you referring to?' McKenzie Foster hissed at me, but her Texas drawl made it seem almost ladylike. I was sure that I had laid it straight on the table but no matter how offensive I thought

McKenzie Foster was, she was a mother and there are some things mothers just refuse to hear.

'The police seem convinced that Thomas is ... well, that he's the Ripper.'

The phrase had an effect. McKenzie Foster fell back against her husband – which I suspected was the warmest contact they'd had in years.

'I don't care what they're saying, what they're claiming, and I certainly don't care for what you are saying or your tone. This is absolutely preposterous,' she said as she got more and more indignant. Her entire body language changed, she straightened her back, and her eyes blazed at the accusations. 'Of course Thomas is totally innocent. He did not kill this girl or any other – how ludicrous! This needs to end here. I will stand up in court and tell the judge myself.'

McKenzie Foster wiped her brow with a very clean white handkerchief; all of this stress looked as if it had brought on a hot flush.

'Mrs Foster – the proceedings today are in private.'

She looked at me blankly.

'You won't be allowed in court. Only the accused and his representative can be present at the calling of the indictment. I understand how difficult this is for you...'

She interrupted me. 'Do you? Do you really, Miss McLennan? Do you have a brilliant son who is innocent yet has been charged with murder? This ridiculous scandal will haunt him for the rest of his life.'

'I have to go and speak to the fiscal. I'll see if there is any chance of bail, but it's unlikely.'

'Do you mean that he might not get home with us today, that he may spend Christmas in prison?' McKenzie Foster went white beneath her spray-on tan. 'We can obviously post any amount of money for bail. Adie has already spoken to the bank. One million, two million pounds... Whatever it takes.'

I took a deep breath. 'In Scotland, money does not buy the freedom of the accused. Bail is conditional. In rare circumstances, bail will be granted for murder but I have to tell you that, in Thomas's case, I'm not hopeful.'

'This is entirely your fault,' McKenzie Foster spat at her husband, poking him in the chest. Suddenly, my shoes seemed very interesting. I stared at the ground trying to give Thomas's parents a moment of privacy. As the eyes of the press bored into us, a sneaky voice whispered in my head: Why had he alerted his bankers that a huge sum of bail money might be necessary? 'If you hadn't insisted on coming to this godforsaken place, then Thomas would be safe. Why couldn't you buy an American football team?' she whined.

'The NFL is sewn up, honey – you know that there are very few teams to buy, besides revenue from soccer and its worldwide rights make it a very viable business proposition.' They were unbelievable – their son was up for murder and they were having a business meeting. I excused myself – this 'chat' was going to keep on running but someone had to take care of their son, and I'd drawn the short straw. I didn't have a hope of getting their boy home for Christmas, and with his pretty looks I was sure he'd be filling some old lag's stocking before Boxing Day.

I went back inside to find that Sheriff Agatha Lochan was sitting on the bench. I'd appeared before her many times, and she always seemed to bend for the prosecution, but she was meticulous, fair, and ran a tight court. However, she was a fearsome sight with dyed red hair, backcombed into a style that wouldn't have looked out of place on the set of *The Mikado*. Thick white face powder, to prevent a shiny nose, clung in desperation to her heavy facial hair. I couldn't help thinking a wee bit of shine couldn't look as bad as that.

I moved over and sat in the well of the court at a table; at the head of it, directly underneath the sheriff, sat her clerk. Davie Hooper was known as the snake; his yellow bloodshot eyes watched me warily, and the smell of stale drink was off-putting. I nodded at him but he stared right through me – he may still have been drunk.

Seated opposite me was the only friendly face in the room, even if he was on the opposite side of the case here. Frank Pearson was the procurator fiscal. He'd lost the toss on the holiday rota but I knew he had New Year off. We were in the habit of hitting the drink at Hogmanay and Lavender had organized tickets for the party in Princes Street. Last year Frank had been forced to take a duvet day – it had been hard to convince his bosses he was suffering from the winter vomiting bug; to try it on two years in a row would be impossible.

The rustlings of paper fell silent as the police officers escorted Thomas into the court; the officials craned their necks to look at the boy who was being touted as the Ripper. His mother was actually right – it was ludicrous. When he stood in the dock, I knew that any trial involving Thomas Foster would be a media circus. I wondered if *Hello* magazine would bid for the rights. He looked like a Calvin Klein underwear model in spite of stress, dirt, and sweat – maybe Sheriff Lochan would fall for his halo effect.

Most of us don't like to think of people as being mixed: they are either good or bad. A study showed if we think a person is attractive, then we think their other traits must be equally attractive. Genetics had just improved Thomas Foster's chance of getting bail.

'HMA against Thomas Barthlomew Foster.' The sheriff clerk's voice was low and rough, honed by a daily diet of a bottle of generic whisky and sixty fags.

'Are you Thomas Bartholomew Foster?'

This was my cue. I leapt to my feet and nodded respectfully at Sheriff Lochan. I placed my hands on my black court gown, stood to my full height, and spoke clearly.

'M'lady, I appear on behalf of the accused who makes no plea or declaration at this stage – the defence seeks to apply for bail.'

Sheriff Lochan looked at the fiscal and said, 'I take it the Crown opposes any motion for bail?' Christ, she was going to do Frank's work for him. He didn't even bother to stand and simply threw me a look that said what I already knew – not a chance. I hadn't bothered to sit back down. Frank needed to say nothing.

'M'lady, Mr Foster is twenty-one years of age. He has no previous conviction. He would be willing to hand in his passport and report every day to a police station. He lives with his parents in Edinburgh. It is extremely unlikely that Mr Foster would abscond.'

My heart was pounding. Appearing in court is always a fight. I don't like to lose. The acid in my stomach crept upwards, filling my mouth; it burned as I forced it back down. I glanced back at Thomas Foster. He looked frightened. His baby blue eyes were wide, unblinking; as a student of body language, I noted that he held his own hand for comfort. His hands were joined as if in prayer in front of his genitals – for protection. His lips were pursed. I suspect he was clenching his arse too – I couldn't blame him.

Sheriff Lochan put on her half-moon reading spectacles. They slipped to the end of her bony nose and whatever she was going to say to me was put on hold as the courtroom door creaked open. We all turned to see the intruder.

Bancho.

Leaning against the wall, he remained at the rear of the court. It was against policy that he should be there, but he'd come to ensure Thomas went down.

Sheriff Lochan cleared her throat: 'Do you have anything further to add?'

When you're asked that question in court, you know you haven't done enough. Habit makes you scramble around for something else to say. Inevitably it's irrelevant and often downright stupid, but it was a habit I couldn't break. 'I'd just like to emphasize, M'lady, that Mr Foster will hand in his passport and report to the police.'

It is always important in these situations that your client knows you said something, no matter how lame. It is surprising how many lawyers keep quiet in these situations because they are afraid of the wrath of the bench.

Sheriff Lochan drew herself up, placed her glasses on the bench, and looked at me like a cobra about to strike. 'The problem, Miss McLennan, is not that your client would escape – but that he would kill again,' she hissed at me, and I had her. She had played right into my hands. My pen had been poised and I scribbled her words. I could now appeal to the High Court against her decision to refuse bail. Whatever happened to the principle of Scots law, innocent until proven guilty?

Bancho had no idea what had just happened. I could only assume he hadn't been listening, as it had been pretty clear – he was punching the air in celebration. The snake was irritated. Sheriff Lochan stared uneasily into space – no one likes to be appealed and I suspected that she knew exactly what was going to happen as soon as the words were out of her mouth. More worryingly for me, professionally and personally, was that Frank's mouth curled in displeasure.

I barely noticed that, in the background, my client howled like a baby as he was led away. And me? Did I think he was guilty or not? I tried not to care – I was a lawyer, not a person. Wasn't I?

Chapter Twenty-Four

The Witchery by Edinburgh Castle
Monday 24 December, 1 p.m.

'I can feel you're mad at me,' Jack Deans said as he handed me a glass of cold, pink champagne. We were standing in his suite at The Witchery, looking down the Royal Mile at the last-minute Christmas shoppers scurrying back and forth. The pedestrians who still had free hands scampered like rats in and out of the shops, desperate to buy anything. I knew what they felt like; apart from Connie, I hadn't bought a single gift – let alone wrapped one.

'I just asked, was the Ripper case worth ruining Lavender's wedding for?' he said.

'I'm not angry at you,' I lied. 'When I took the case I didn't know he was charged with murder or that Bancho was using this charge as a holding device to pin the rest of the murders on Thomas Foster.'

'Brodie, try to convince yourself all you want. Just don't drag me into your delusion. You've a sixth sense when it comes to situations like this and you knew the Ripper had been arrested. Unless it was something serious, no PC Plod was going to keep Adie Foster's son in custody on Christmas Eve.'

'You've a bloody cheek!' I told him. 'Just for

once I'd like you to hang around with me for who I am – not because you can get the inside scoop on some trial,' I said.

Attack is the best form of defence, and Jack interrupted me by kissing my neck; it's usually a winner and my train of thought was lost.

'I'm your stalker because of who you are. You're Brodie McLennan, the lawyer who would do anything to win,' he said.

I dug my elbow into his stomach, pushing him away from my erogenous zones.

'You make me sound delightful – besides, I haven't ruined Lavender's wedding plans. I just couldn't make it to the Sheraton.'

'Lavender trusts you as far as she can throw you. She called me up, and told me to haul ass down to the Sheraton to collect your dress.' He looked at me suspiciously. 'How did she know I had a suite here?' He smiled, and drawled, 'Brodie – have I been the subject of gossip?' Jack held my face and stroked it. 'People believe you – that's why you are so good in front of juries.'

Lavender understood me well enough to make contingency plans. I told her Jack had a suite at The Witchery, an eerie restaurant with rooms, located near to the Witches' Well at the entrance to Edinburgh Castle. In case she ever needs to find me, Lavender makes it her business to know the ins and outs of my sex life: generally, there's not much to know.

The wedding was taking place at 4 p.m. in St Margaret's Chapel, the oldest building in Edinburgh Castle. In the worst-case scenario, I would have been stuck in court until 3.30 p.m., but as long as I had my dress I could run up the road, and still be on time. I switched my mind to the wedding. I was starting to get in the mood but Jack Deans had other ideas.

He refilled his glass, and said, 'It's not just some trial ... it's the trial of the century – at least that will be my headline.'

Wandering over to the mullion-paned window, I stared down at the Witches' Well, tapping my glass on the old window. I pointed out a ten-inch by six-inch black and gold sign that hung on the wall.

'That is a pretty pathetic plaque. After all, it commemorates the fact that over three hundred women were burnt as witches on Castle Hill during the sixteenth century.'

I half turned to face him. 'And another thing. Everyone believes the Witch Trials at Salem were bad – but no one was burned.'

'That's misleading, Brodie. You always push it too far. In America the punishment for witchcraft was hanging – women were burnt in Europe because being a witch was heresy. Nineteen people were hung in Salem.'

I poked my empty glass into his chest; it was my way of asking for a refill.

'People are already saying hanging is too good for Thomas Foster,' I said.

Jack poured me some more of the chilled champagne. He didn't agree with me.

'As a matter of fact, people are saying they are surprised. No one thought he was a serial-killer type.'

'Perhaps,' I said. 'But I'll bet they're denying

knowing him... No one wants to be best mates with a serial killer. It's bad for your image.' Even as I said the words, I questioned them – Thomas Foster had been a fixture of the glossy society pages for some time, generally pictured with talentless hangers-on. They could all make a quick buck if he was found guilty.

Room service knocked on the door of the 'Old Library suite.' A young waiter rolled in a trolley covered with the finest starched linen and topped with more champagne and the largest seafood platter I had seen outside of Maine.

'Why Mr Deans, I do believe you are trying to seduce me!' I purred, using my best Scarlett O'Hara voice.

'Tax deductible … you haven't forgotten I'm only interested in the Ripper case.' Rhett Butler fashion, he raised an eyebrow before pulling out my chair.

It's never a good idea to eat seafood with someone you hardly know. I tucked into the mountain before me with gusto, juice from the fresh Loch Fyne oysters running down my chin. It wasn't so much that I knew Jack Deans well, I just didn't care whether my table manners sickened him or not. I needn't have worried; his face was down at the trough. I reached under the table and grabbed him by the bollocks. His eyes opened wide with anticipation and, squeezing his stomach, I said: 'I thought there was supposed to be a famine on in Darfur?'

'Not in the hotels frequented by foreign correspondents with large expense accounts and fuck-all to do.'

Jack wiggled his fingers in the bowl of lemon-scented water beside his plate.

The lobster claws clanked noisily off the side of my plate. I'd lost my appetite and my head was beginning to hurt. I would have to start drinking again before the hangover took effect.

Jack had told me earlier that seventy children under five die every day in Darfur, and the thrill I got from envisaging Connie running out onto the pitch on New Year's Day paled into insignificance.

'You can't save the world – there's no point in being maudlin. Lavender deserves to have a good day.' Jack poured me more drink.

'It's the same the world over – children and women trafficked for sex,' I said.

'In every continent I've been in it's the same ... even Bosnia. But the governments will not even pay lip service to it. America doesn't have a law against people trafficking because their defence contractors say it's unenforceable in foreign lands.'

'Is that unreasonable?' I asked.

'It is if the slave traders are American citizens.' Jack grabbed me, pulling me over to the window again. His greasy finger marked the glass. 'See that?' He poked at the window. 'That is the most Masonic street in the world.'

'Jack, that's bullshit! Masons are not sex slavers,' I scoffed.

'If you don't believe that Masons are a force, why did you stir up the hornets' nest by demanding to know if the judge was a member of any secret society?' Jack said.

'Doh ... to get my client off.'

'You should know better. If you want to get

Thomas Foster off, use the fact that he's a "Bonesman",' he said.

'Pardon?' I said, walking away from the window to refill my glass. He had reignited my interest in this conversation. I was open to any ideas about how to get a 'not guilty' for Thomas Foster, but with Jack it didn't do to show you were too interested. Besides, I needed to get ready for the wedding.

I pushed open a panel of books in the library wall, and it swung open revealing a bathroom. It was a suite we had stayed in before. The claw-foot bathtub was approximately one hundred years old, I remembered – I remembered that it was big enough for two as well but I didn't want any distraction. I closed the door on Jack's face, secretly pleased to see the look of disappointment. He shouted to me loud enough so I could hear him clearly above the roar of the water and through the books.

'The society of Skull and Bones was started at Yale in the nineteenth century.'

My ears pricked up. Thomas Foster told me he had been forced back to America to go to college; he was at Edinburgh University on exchange. The Molton Brown pomegranate bath gel was foaming into mounds of soapy suds. I lay back and allowed the hot water to relax my neck; the contrast with the champagne bubbles going up my nose was divine.

'It was founded by Russell – a Boston opium trader. Russell and Co. was led by an old sea captain named Warren Delano the Second, the former American vice-consul in Canton and grandfather of Franklin Delano Roosevelt, the thirty-second president of the United States. Not that we can talk – Russell and Co. were the second biggest drug dealer in the world. The Scots firm Jardine Matheson were the biggest,' he said.

'If Thomas Foster is a Bonesman, it doesn't seem to be doing him much good,' I shouted back, jumping out of the bath, soapsuds clinging to my skin dripping water all over the floor. I made straight for Jack's razor; rubbing my hairy legs, I knew the real reason I hadn't let him join me – still, there was always tonight!

'Wait and see. Adie Foster is a Bonesman and Thomas was born to be one.' *Nepotism, I knew all about that.*

I remained silent, so Jack was forced to speak. He abhorred a void.

'The Skull and Bones Society is not some two-bit club. President George Bush and presidential candidate John Kerry were both members – their influence makes the Enlightenment Society look like a joke.'

'But not in Scotland,' I shouted back. 'Here the Enlightenment Society holds sway and it wouldn't have any interest in Thomas Foster.'

The Enlightenment Society, formed in the eighteenth century, was a secret brotherhood of lawyers, recruited as first-year students at Edinburgh University. Until recently, over 90 per cent of judges were alleged to be members.

'They're linked. Edinburgh New Town was built and designed by Masons – the Masons who built Castle Street went directly to work on the White House; the cornerstone of the Statue of

139

Liberty was laid by a Scottish Mason – need I go on?' he asked.

'Can I stop you?' I whispered.

'Okay, you think this investigation is going to be based on reason, reliable evidence. It's not. If you don't believe me, ask your grandfather. Why did the police contact him when they arrested Thomas Foster? More to the point, I'd ask why he didn't tell you Thomas was the Ripper?'

At that moment, I stopped shaving my legs.

Chapter Twenty-Five

St Margaret's Chapel, Edinburgh Castle
Monday 24 December, 3.30 p.m.

Step we gaily on we go
Heel for heel and toe for toe,
Arm in arm and row and row
All for Lavender's wedding

A piper played 'Mairi's Wedding', and Connie sang in her clear high voice, changing the words to suit the occasion. She skipped along excitedly in the late afternoon air; sometimes she ran back to squeeze my arm and whisper it was Christmas Eve. It was already dark and Edinburgh Castle was floodlit, eerie in the freezing fog. The bridal party marched across the bridge between the statues of Bruce and Wallace, through to the inner entrance. The uphill route to St Margaret's Chapel was hazardous, the icy, uneven cobbles threatening to trip us up. We chatted and laughed as Dark Angels carrying flaming torches lit the bride's way. Lavender held on to Grandad's arm as they marched through the portcullis, as much to steady her nerves as to keep her balance.

Eddie and Glasgow Joe in full Highland regalia were waiting at the altar. As a special concession to Eddie, Joe had agreed to matching kilts in Hibs' tartan, predictably a fairly vivid green, toned down by black Prince Charlie jackets and waistcoats both with silver buttons. Full sporrans, brogues and traditional cream socks complete with skean-dhu daggers and green flashes completed their ensembles. Lavender was already ten minutes late; late enough to keep Eddie on his toes. Malcolm held on to my arm, probably afraid of slipping in his new, leather-soled shoes, but he kept bringing out his hanky and sniffing; there had been no last-minute reconciliation with Derek.

St Margaret's Chapel is high on a mound within the inner castle. Joe had left the Norman church to check if the bride was en route. He didn't see us. He wandered over to the battlements. Edinburgh was partially hidden from him, like a fairy city concealed in the mist. He looked jumpy to me. He was swallowing too hard – from what I could remember, that was pretty much the only sign that Joe was afraid. He seemed to be searching the ramparts – I don't know why. I might have to believe in Thomas Foster's innocence, but Joe could rest easy and believe the story the police were putting out.

In truth, I felt as if someone was walking over

my grave. Maybe, we were both just remembering the tacky Las Vegas wedding chapel where we tied the knot. Sniffing the wind, I could smell that snow was coming, but there seemed to be something else out there, something that made my skin crawl. The Boxing Day sale signs were already up in the department stores on Princes Street – everything looked normal. But it didn't feel normal, and I had no idea what was causing me to feel that way.

Joe spotted us and waved. 'You look gorgeous!' he shouted at us. 'Eddie's here, he sent me out to check he hadn't been stood up.'

In an effort to include everyone in her happy day, Lavender had asked Patch to be the celebrant. When Joe saw him, it just looked as if his day had been made even more macabre – Patch had carried out the autopsies on the Ripper's victims and the nuptials were now feeling just a bit too closely allied to death.

Joe continued to search the night sky. He scrutinized the faces of the bridal party as well. He seemed to be the only one bothering. Moses was too busy ensuring no one set light to Lavender's train to have much else on his mind. The Dark Angels formed a guard around her; not such a fabulous plan as hot wax seemed to be dripping everywhere. It certainly landed on my arm as I marched through to the church, sending me rushing into the chapel like a scalded cat.

The Norman church was small, and serene; people had been baptized, married and buried there for nearly a thousand years.

Huge candles lit the tiny chapel; flowers filled

the altar and Eddie Gibb smiled from ear to ear as his bride walked towards him. William Wallace had worshipped here, as had The Bruce, but the look on Lavender's face said only one man was her hero.

The size of the chapel dictated that the Dark Angels remain outside; it was no bad idea. Their presence inside would have given Joe the willies even more. He was appalled when Eddie had told him he'd already seen Lavender today. That was considered so unlucky that no Scottish girl would allow it – but Lavender was from London after all and they were a different breed down there.

Patch stood waiting at the altar and, as Lavender walked towards Eddie, Elvis crooned that he couldn't help falling in love with someone or other. The pathologist claimed that he was Elvis's biggest fan, attending conventions, and even standing at the gates of Graceland on his hero's birthday. Joe often said that he didn't know what unnerved him most: Patch's fondness for the dead or the fact that a member of a strict, Scottish, Presbyterian congregation could risk eternal hell and damnation for Elvis.

I looked across at Connie who, despite her previous excitement and delight at being a bridesmaid, was now fidgeting and, regardless of the romance of the occasion, already beginning to look bored. Fleetingly, I remembered my own awkwardness as a young teenager at adult events. No matter how much I'd looked forward to them, I'd felt out of my depth and lacking in confidence. As the only child present, being still, quiet and behaving 'like a grown-up' observer was as alien to her as it would be to a Labrador puppy. Both were used to being the centre of attention.

I turned my attention back to Lavender and Eddie, facing each other, holding hands, ready to recite their vows. She looked absolutely beautiful – and a damn sight thinner than I'd ever seen her in the past. Give him his due, Eddie didn't look too bad either – clean and, from what I could tell, sober. Joe watched me out of the corner of his eye, no doubt for any sign that I remembered our wedding day. Marry in haste, repent at leisure was the theme of that excursion into marital bliss. It was Joe who'd backtracked the quickest. Divorce in haste was the mistake he'd made. There was no way that I would come back to him, as I told him then – from my vantage point, he'd cast me aside, even if he claimed that it was for my own good. For more than two decades, Joe and I had laughed and loved and hated one another. It was a pattern and passion that looked set for life, and I refused to be tabloid fodder for marrying and divorcing the same guy over and over.

Perhaps Jack represented an escape route from that fate. Perhaps that was his attraction. When Jack was in my bed, Joe couldn't be. And the temptation was removed. But despite the highs and lows, it was difficult to imagine my life without Glasgow Joe somewhere at the heart of it.

Looking at the assembled cast, I realized that, even though he liked Joe in theory, my Grandad would probably cut his eyes out rather than watch me be with him. He would never think Joe was good enough for me, and I guess he still thought that old families had certain standards to maintain. Assassins didn't come into that – even if paedophiles did. The old man allowed a tear to fall unashamedly from his eye as the vows got underway and Eddie's voice cracked with emotion. In accordance with the ancient tradition of the Celts he and Lavender spoke in unison.

'I pledge to you that yours will be the name I cry aloud in the night, and the eyes into which I smile in the morning.
'I pledge to you the first bite from my meat and the first drink from my cup.
'I pledge to you my living and my dying each equally in your care.
'I shall be a shield for your back and you for mine.
'I shall not slander you, nor you me.
'I shall honour you above all others and when we quarrel we shall do so in private, and tell no strangers of our grievances.'

Joe placed the gold Celtic knot rings on Patch's Bible. With a trembling hand, Eddie placed one on the third finger of Lavender's left hand; she steadied his hand and firmly placed a ring on him. Eddie kissed his bride, then 'Amazing Grace' filled the night air as Mr and Mrs Gibb walked out through the torchlight arch held by the Dark Angels. Lavender shouted 'catch' and her bouquet spun through the air. I don't know whether it was a reflex or perhaps Lavender had aimed it directly at me, but I had to catch it to avoid serious injury. I didn't want anyone to get ideas.

The Dark Angels were feeling the cold. Edinburgh Castle is a draughty place to be, even in

August when the tourists flock there, but on a Christmas Eve that seemed to deny global warming, it was beyond bitter. Moses' lips seemed to be turning blue as he kept an eye on his crew, and the piper led the procession smartly back down through the cobbled roads of the inner courtyard before he had a death on his hands. Marching quickly down the hill, Grandad admonished us all to plant our feet firmly to avoid sliding. We concentrated on this instruction, and striding through the portcullis, in our absorption, no one noticed that Connie wasn't with us. No one that is, except Joe who, just as he had before the ceremony, had patrolled the battlements and chapel surrounds after it.

Whatever he was looking for, he instead found Connie, huddled in the doorway, lip trembling, but trying to hold back the sobs of self-pity and confusion to which only a thirteen-year-old can succumb.

'What's wrong, darlin'?' he asked anxiously.

He told me later that night that Connie couldn't quite explain, other than that she felt anxious, left out, in the way, ignored, and at the same time guilty about not feeling happy.

Joe didn't know what to do except envelop her in a comforting bear hug and assure her we all loved her.

Clearly, once Christmas was out of the way, I should schedule a sisterly chat about how to deal with the natural, but nonetheless unpleasant, effect that blossoming hormones have on mood swings.

Fortunately, by the time Connie and Joe had

caught up with us at the bottom of the hill, her spirits were restored – and we had a wedding to celebrate.

Chapter Twenty-Six

Edinburgh Castle
Monday 24 December, 3.30 p.m.

The fog hung in dense pockets like ectoplasm. It covered his tracks, muffling any sound he might be careless enough to make – even his breath was concealed in the cold night air. The freezing mist was harsh on his lungs. He stuck his nose deep into his scarf in case he coughed. It was extremely unpalatable; the material was wet with snot and condensation but he couldn't take any chances.

The night-vision goggles showed the groom's party arriving, denting his hopes. He should be filled with triumph. His plan was working, but instead of a tingle of excitement, his muscles constricted, causing him to momentarily double in pain – the bastard was still looking for him.

Glasgow Joe's kilt moved the air around him as he turned from side to side, watching his back. The big man cased the joint as though he were looking for a sniper. The Glaswegian was light on his feet, despite his size, but The Watcher was quick. Too quick for him. Thomas Foster was in jail and that was enough for the present. Anything else was the icing on the cake.

147

The Lewis bridal song called out to him as a small clear voice sang and eased his fears. It was all worth it. The excitement now began to flow through his limbs. He struggled to remain where he was. He wanted to see them and he wanted to smell them but, most of all, he desired to touch them.

I want never gets his mother had admonished. Well, he was fed up being the good boy. He wanted a taste of the action himself, and what a delicious dish it was. The flickering flames held by those juvenile delinquents called attention to the bridal party. His girls, as he had come to think of them, were particularly appetizing today.

Unusually, they were dressed identically in red duchesse satin cut on the bias, which shimmered as they walked. In deference to the weather, they wore short cream fur stoles over their shoulders. The Watcher rubbed the front of his trousers, satisfied with the throb, feeling the blood pump back into his loins. A slow smile crossed his face and he nodded to himself as he stared at them, stroking methodically with his right hand.

Connie's hair fell in long, loose ringlets. Her eyes were wide with delight as she hopped and skipped trying to get attention. He watched as her bottom lip jutted out. Would she be happy if she knew he was watching? He thought so – in fact he knew she would be. Brodie was a different kettle of fish altogether. Her scarlet dress clung to her curves; some would say that it was too tight but The Watcher felt it was just right.

His body temperature was rising. She was here. It was all worth it. He was doing it for her and, one day soon, she'd know it.

Fuck it.

They were going in just when he was starting to enjoy himself. The Dark Angels remained on guard by the door of St Margaret's Chapel; he felt himself wither inside as she disappeared. His heart couldn't take the strain, he would have to bring it to a climax soon, perhaps sooner than he would have liked, sooner than was safe or sensible. With Thomas Foster in jail, the only reason to hurry was his need. It was growing every day. Every day he found it harder to stand in embalmed silence and watch her.

The chill settled into his bones. He sniffed back the snot that had formed on the end of his nose, and waited. He was no longer so good at waiting.

To those inside it was no doubt a short, happy service; to The Watcher it seemed interminable. His patience was growing shorter, and that wasn't a good sign for anyone. He closed his eyes to dream. Pictures came into his mind that made it difficult for him to swallow – they made him ashamed but he didn't open his eyes until he heard the skirl of pipes. Uncoiling, he stared through the binoculars he had fixed on her and observed the antics. Digging his nails into his skin as she caught the bouquet – *she would be no one's bride.*

They were making it easy for him. There was one person in the party who was not enjoying herself, one person who would have a better time with him. Connie. His eyes scanned her body again and made the calculations; he was absolutely certain he had it right. Initially, she would have to be drugged, but then she would be happy.

149

She stood alone in the mist as the grown-ups disappeared down the hill, lingering behind to see if anyone missed her. They didn't. Rubbing his hands together The Watcher grabbed his bag – he always carried his tools with him – ready to take her. He hated the idea that she would think she was unloved, unwanted.

He would take better care of her. Standing alone in the dark, she huddled into the stone doorway. The Watcher could sense her fear as he moved closer, readying himself to make a move. Clutching his bag of tools to his chest, he inched forward in the fog, anxious not to alert her, not to scare her into running.

Clenching his body tight, The Watcher savoured the thrill. He had anticipated this for so long. Everything was leading up to this moment.

Was that a sob?

His heart warmed at the sound of the girl. He recognized it as a moment of happiness; she would think he was a hero. The Watcher could taste her fear, it was sweet to him. The unexpected noise on the cobbles made him stop and scuttle for cover by the side of a cannon. Peering over the top, he saw the bastard. For a few seconds his heart stopped. Glasgow Joe scooped Connie up in his arms – regrettably he didn't give her a row. The Watcher bit his tongue so hard that blood mixed with saliva, dribbling out of the corner of his mouth. Joe put the frightened little girl down, clutching her to him. Did he know that evil was so close by?

Grasping his tool bag tighter to his chest, The Watcher turned. He didn't look over his shoulder, walking away to live and win another day.

Chapter Twenty-Seven

Kailash's home, Ravelston Dykes, Edinburgh
Tuesday 25 December, 3 p.m.

'Happy Christmas.'

Kailash and I kissed, and held each other for longer than usual. We had travelled a short, hard road together but maybe our relationship would turn out all right. Connie bundled her way in, shoving a present in my face, the first of many from my mother.

'I'm sorry...' I started. Kailash shrugged. It was of no importance that I wasn't bearing gifts. Smiling, she put her arms around her girls and walked us into the living room – I wondered if she had been on the sherry. Truthfully, I could only guess at what her childhood Christmases had been like. This time, she had certainly tried her best to create the ideal, festive, family scene. It was like a greetings card photo-shoot in its perfection – the only thing it lacked was Bing Crosby crooning by the fireplace.

The eight-foot tree was real and it filled the room with the scent of the forest. The baubles hanging from the branches were not colour-coordinated or newly bought. They represented Kailash and Connie's life together. You know the sort of thing, salt-dough Santas, made by Connie aged three. But there was one that caught the back of my throat. I fought the tears and looked out of the French windows. There was no escape. Kailash took it off the tree and handed it to me. It looked the oldest decoration; shiny, glittery and dented. In the middle was a picture of me, aged seven, without my front teeth. 'I've had this for over twenty years,' she told me. 'Your grandfather got the photo from Mary.' She took it back and put it on its branch.

'Happy Christmas!' Grandad handed me a glass of buck's fizz which I shied away from. 'Hair of the dog,' he insisted and, God knows, I needed it. My liver was complaining, and I was praying that Kailash had forgotten to put the turkey in the oven so that dinner would be delayed until at least 8 p.m. No such luck. She was on the ball since it was our first Christmas dinner as a family – the bird had been stuffed and in the oven since 8 a.m.

Connie called us through to her games room. She'd linked the television to her computer, and she was showing us photographs from the wedding. Kailash looked amazing; it's hard having a mother who belongs on the cover of *FHM*. I wished I'd stuck to the Atkins Diet.

Moses beamed out at us from the TV screen, a microphone in his hand. It was the wedding video and he was singing 'My Way.'

'That boy is the world's worst Sinatra impersonator,' Grandad smiled, still enjoying the performance.

'I tried to tell him that he couldn't sing; he'd have none of it because the Dark Angels – and other people – say he's fantastic,' I said, looking at

152

my grandfather accusingly. Grandad shuffled uncomfortably. Cruelly, he encouraged Moses to sing, purely because it made him howl with laughter.

'Dinner!' Kailash shouted, as she staggered into the dining room under the weight of a 14lb bird.

Connie insisted we pull our crackers, I'm sure they were expensive but those cheap paper hats never fit my oversized head. A yellow one sat perfectly on Kailash's black hair, Connie was fine, and even Jack managed not to look ridiculous. As I glanced around the table there was one other person who had to rip his hat at the seam to make it fit: Grandad. My heart sank a little when I remembered who had given me the genetics of Humpty Dumpty.

'Just a little bit for me thanks,' said the surprise guest – a surprise to me at least. Grandad had invited Jack Deans because he was still matchmaking, although he'd whispered to me that Jack had nowhere else to go. He was a sly old bugger.

Kailash can't cook. It was the driest turkey I'd ever tasted, but I bravely fought my way through the food mountain in front of me. The roast potatoes were hard and soggy at the same time – a feat I didn't think was possible. I chewed and chewed my way through the main course and managed to keep it down. Connie's eyes were wide with excitement – she insisted on lighting the Christmas pudding so we all had to have some to show willing. I'm not keen on it at the best of times, but with the mother of all hangovers I was positively gagging at the thought.

There was quite an art to it. Connie's head was

bent close to Kailash's as she heated a large silver spoon over a candle, then, striking a match, the alcohol became a mass of blue flame which Connie poured over the pudding. The fire lit her face. Kailash pulled back Connie's hair in case she set fire to herself. The tenderness of the action stopped me. Kailash did look like a mother, she just didn't look like mine. Again, it was hard to believe she had been Connie's age when she had given birth to me. I've never given her enough credit for the way she loves me. Logically, it wasn't my fault, but I would have been hard-pushed to blame her if she'd held the circumstance of my delivery against me.

'I'm proud of you,' Grandad said, tapping my hand with a cracked blue leather box. 'You've kept your nose clean ... except for that one incident ... and it wouldn't be you if you weren't irritating someone. I have to face facts, you're never going to be an angel, but you'll always be mine.' He stopped, and I prayed he wasn't going to get emotional or start crying – or both. 'This belonged to your grandmother,' he started up again. 'I thought you might like it. I kept it especially, hoping that one day there would be someone who would appreciate it.'

I smiled but my heart sank. Could I pull it off? A present from my deceased grandmother, some ghastly earrings or a hellish diamond brooch, no doubt, either of which I would be forced to wear. Locking a smile ear to ear, I opened the box, readying myself to squeal with delight.

'What is it?' I asked, holding a key up between my thumb and forefinger.

154

'It's a key,' Grandad replied, reaching out, covering my fingers and the key with both his hands.

'Uh-huh – I can see that.'

'Come and see, come and see!' Connie shrieked.

'So you're all in on it except me?' I asked.

Kailash opened the front door. Grandad covered my eyes with his hand and Connie led me into the driveway. They didn't give me time to get my coat and the wind whipped round my legs. I'd worn a skirt in honour of the fact it was Christmas Day and I was regretting it. The snow was melting and the slush around the front door had formed a grey crust that seeped into my light shoes.

'Open your eyes now!' Connie shouted. Although my eyes had been shut for a relatively small amount of time, it was still difficult to adjust to the light. The floodlights on the garage door were on and I had to blink several times, sure that alcohol poisoning had blinded me.

'What is it?' I asked again.

'It's a car, stupid.' Connie slapped my head. 'And not just any car – it's a metallic blue 1954 Chevrolet Corvette Convertible,' she shouted, jumping into the driver's seat, her learned words ringing in my ears.

'I think we should let Brodie sit in her present first, don't you?' Kailash leaned into the car and manhandled Connie out of it.

'Grandad! Promise me that I can have one just like that? Did Granny have two?' asked Connie, innocently.

'No, darling, she only had one,' he answered. 'She was a remarkable lady even to have owned that. I think that Brodie gets her taste for out-

155

landish motor vehicles from her.'

'Am I like her too?' Connie asked. This was getting onto difficult ground. Connie was my half-sister, although I didn't think the penny had dropped yet with her. I didn't know who her father was and perhaps Kailash didn't either.

'Stop stealing my thunder,' I interrupted, trying to change the subject. 'You can sit in the passenger seat if you promise to be quiet.' I turned to Grandad. 'It's absolutely beautiful.' I kissed him on the cheek as he whispered, 'Maybe now you'll stop driving that damned motorbike – you know I hate you driving that thing, it's awfully dangerous. I couldn't bear to lose you, Brodie.'

The top was down and the beige leather seats sent a chill straight through to my bones as soon as I sat down. The sensation didn't go away as the seats warmed up. It wasn't a good feeling and I couldn't help but wonder how much of it was truly to do with the car. The vibration from my mobile phone buzzed on my hip. I answered it, thinking it would be the blushing bride calling to wish us all a Happy Christmas.

'Brodie?' an American voice asked.

Adie Foster. This was my personal mobile – how did he get the number? I swivelled in the seat and caught Grandad's eye. He looked away. I'd have to have a word with him about this.

It didn't seem appropriate to wish Adie Foster Happy Christmas, not with his son languishing in Saughton Prison. Still, if it was a consolation to him, Thomas had probably had a more edible Christmas dinner than I'd had.

'I've just had word through from the chief

constable, Brodie. It was good of him to keep me up to date,' he said, as I marvelled yet again at how the old boy network operated. His next words were even more dramatic. 'The Ripper has struck again. DI Bancho is with the body now – they must be made to see that Thomas can't be the Ripper, Brodie. Go over there and get my son out of jail, immediately.'

'It's not as easy as that, Mr Foster.'

'Make it that easy: you're supposed to be the best. DI Bancho is at St Giles' Cathedral. And Brodie? It's the Ripper's work ... a girl has been found.' The phone went dead.

'Happy Christmas, Brodie,' I whispered.

Chapter Twenty-Eight

St Giles' Cathedral, Edinburgh
Tuesday 25 December, 6.30 p.m.

It wasn't far to St Giles' Cathedral. The roads were empty, it was Christmas night, and most people were still sleeping off the effects of lunch. Jack and I drove in silence. He had insisted on accompanying me.

My stomach knotted at the thought of what lay before me. Bitter bile jumped from belly to throat and back again. Would I be able to control myself? It was bad enough vomiting in front of Patch and a lone detective as I had once done at an autopsy, but this was a crime scene and it would be heaving with people. If I knew about it, someone eager to make a fast buck would have tipped off the media. A shadow crossed my mind: Jack was the media. Maybe his motives for coming weren't so altruistic. Mentally I kicked myself; I was dumping that bastard as soon as possible.

I parked the car outside the High Court and, from the shadows, we observed the action. St Giles' was floodlit. In Parliament Square, directly in front of the cathedral entrance, there was a life-size Nativity scene. Less than twenty-four hours ago this place had been packed with worshippers at the Christmas Eve Watch Night service. Had the dead girl heard them sing 'Away in a Manger'?

A chill ran down my spine and my teeth chattered. I couldn't stop shivering.

'Do you want my coat?' Jack asked.

'No.' I couldn't tell him my trembling had nothing to do with the cold. We had no right to be there, and if I was to follow Adie Foster's instruction, then I had to blag my way in. I couldn't think of anything more macabre than sneaking into what was essentially a grave. But I wasn't doing it for Adie Foster. Thomas was innocent and I had to prove it. I knew that when Bancho thinks you're guilty, all evidence to the contrary is disregarded. It was up to me to play detective for my client.

In the blackness I spied DI Bancho, deep in conversation with Joe. What was he doing here? The Ripper was in jail. Joe's head was bent towards the policeman. If any of the regulars from his pub, the Rag Doll, saw him now, his business would be in trouble. No self-respecting crook could freely discuss his dealings with a

158

man who was so friendly with the cops, regardless of his motives or reputation.

The crime-scene boys were still inside. Around the corner in Parliament Square I spied Patch's twenty-year-old Volvo. It was time to come out of the shadows and declare our presence but I decided not to park beside Patch.

All heads turned as I roared up with Jack in the Corvette. I got out of the car like a finishing school graduate, opening the door and swinging my legs out, knees locked together. I climbed over the black heavy chain barrier and spat on the Heart of Midlothian, a brass heart set into the cobbles of the Royal Mile outside St Giles' Cathedral. Superstition decrees that you must spit on it to ward off the evil eye. I was taking no chances – I needed every piece of luck I could get to pass through the police cordon.

'Duncan, Joe!' I shouted, waving as if I was expected. Joe turned his back on me. He was swearing, and not under his breath. Marching confidently towards them, we weren't stopped by the constables on duty.

'You're like a bad penny, Brodie – anybody ever tell you that?' Bancho said. 'Who the hell told you about this? I only found out myself half an hour ago.'

'Adie Foster. It seems you have a leak – probably the chief constable from what Foster said – but it might not be the best thing for your career to mention it.'

'When I want advice from you on anything, I'll ask for it.' As usual, Bancho and I were squaring up to one another – who knows what would have happened next if Joe hadn't intervened.

'Nice set of wheels,' he whistled.

'A Christmas present,' I said.

'I didn't know hacks earned that much.' Joe's jaw tightened and he started to bristle as he looked Jack up and down.

'Don't look at me – the glory belongs to old MacGregor... I don't need to buy her toys.'

'Adie Foster said the Ripper went on a killing spree last night... You'd be the chief constable's second-best pal if you let me see the crime scene,' I said.

'Don't!' Glasgow Joe intervened, holding DI Bancho by the shoulders and fixing his eyes upon him. 'Don't let her in there.' He shook his head as if his words were not enough.

'I never took you for a grass, Joe – mind you, neither did the rest of Leith.' I was trying to rile him. It worked.

'Okay, suit yourself, Brodie. Let her in ... and I hope you're sick, because if you're not, you've got a stronger stomach than anybody here except Patch.'

'I'm not ten,' I snarled.

'Well stop bloody acting like it. Girls are being murdered here. All of them redheads. How do I know Connie's not next?' Joe was definitely pissed off; but I could see through the charade.

I walked past him and whispered a silent prayer for the victim. I hadn't seen the Ripper's handi-work first hand. The photographs were bad enough, and I was in no rush. My footsteps echoed as I walked up the aisle; my pace was funereal, the bad feeling I had earlier just kept getting worse.

'Jack, this is someone's daughter ... don't write this up more sensationally than need be.'

He looked annoyed for a second, but then he shrugged his shoulders. He was what he was, a journalist, and stories like this were his bread and butter.

'It's not unusual for mothers of murder victims to die early of a broken heart.'

He sighed: 'I've written stories about them.'

'I know ... it's one of the few times I believe what I read.'

'Where's Bancho ... we won't get in without him.' I turned and looked around the large, dark cathedral, tattered, limp flags hung from the roof. It seemed to me they were flying at half-mast out of respect for the girl.

St Giles' has a long, cold aisle. I stared into its gloomy recesses. Where was Bancho?

I was in no hurry; obviously neither was he. *Why?* Of course this could be embarrassing for him. My client was safely locked up in Saughton Prison, so Thomas Foster was in no position to quench his thirst for blood. Egg on the face again for Duncan Bancho. I couldn't say I was sorry; now he would start looking for the real Ripper.

Then I saw Bancho enter. I think he'd just taken a fag break and from the grim smile on his face he was enjoying keeping me waiting. He walked past at a double-quick march and cursorily waved his hand in our direction.

'He stays here,' Bancho said, pointing at Jack, and I went off to face my demons alone. My heart was beating rapidly, adrenalin pumped

161

through my body, all my senses were on red alert. We had reached the entrance to the Thistle Chapel and my heart sank.

'Stand at the door – you can see all you need to from there and you won't contaminate the scene,' Bancho barked.

What he said was important because I could be a suspect if my fingerprints were found at the scene. Fingerprint evidence had recently been called into question, and it wasn't as reliable as we all thought. The Scottish government had been forced to pay compensation to a young police-woman, Shirley McKie, whose fingerprints had supposedly been found at a crime scene. The legal world was still reeling from the findings of the in-vestigation ... our fingerprints are not unique after all.

Without a glance, DI Bancho turned and headed back to the entrance of the cathedral, leaving me alone and saddened. It wasn't just the tragedy of another murder. It was the contrast. I love the Thistle Chapel. When I was in the High Court I would often go in and just look at the angels, and now they had been defiled.

The most important thing for Thomas Foster was that I could establish the time of death as occurring when he was in police custody. Estimating this is not an exact science and leaves room for error. Having said that, I didn't need to know anything about forensics to work out that Thomas was still in trouble. A body can't smell this awful without having being dead for days – I couldn't understand why the girl hadn't been discovered before now.

The arc lights displayed the body in a shallow grave. I was some distance away but I could see all too clearly her mutilated form. I had to ignore the smell but the heat from the lamps was adding to the stench and I tried not to breathe particles of dead girl. My temperature was increasing; it seemed hotter than hell in here. Small droplets of sweat appeared on my upper lip and the cold stone pillars of the ante-chapel brought me only a few short moments of relief. A shiny aluminium instrument tray stood upright on the Knights of the Thistle stalls, an ornate wooden, canopied seat reserved for members of the Order of the Thistle, the senior order of chivalry in Scotland. I caught my reflection, a pale, queasy woman stared back at me – I had aged ten years since I came in here.

I recognized the victim.

Mihaela's eyes were sewn open using black industrial-strength thread ... presumably so that she wouldn't miss a moment of the delights the Ripper had in store for her. Her black mouth was gaping, screaming screams that no one answered. The body had been undressed for the assault and then the clothes carefully arranged – post mortem, I'd guess, but I'd wait on Patch's confirmation for that. Singing celestial bodies carved into the relief looked down and wept. If I saw the babushka tonight I would be able to tell her that her daughter slept with the angels – unfortunately, that bitch of a 'mother' surely shared some of the blame.

Chapter Twenty-Nine

Cumberland Street, Edinburgh
Tuesday 25 December, 11.45 p.m.

'Happy Christmas, Brodie.'

'If I'd known it was you, I wouldn't have answered the door,' I snapped.

Glasgow Joe lay back against the railings and smiled apologetically. 'Happy Christmas, darlin'.' He smelled of whisky.

'You're repeating yourself. Is that old age or drink?' I snapped.

'Brodie ... it's the season of goodwill ... peace to all men. Are you inviting me in?' He stepped forward. The light shone directly on him and I saw lines on his face that weren't there before. He looked exhausted. I couldn't turn him away, really; we'd shared too much.

'What are you? A stranger? Do you need an invite to come into my house? Before you'd have walked straight through.' I turned my back on him and walked into the hallway.

'Before what, Brodie? I can't assume anything about you now,' he slurred. I dreaded to think how much he must have consumed to get into this state but I was just relieved I hadn't picked up the tab. Mind you, Joe could go into any pub in certain parts of Edinburgh and have them queuing up to buy him alcohol.

164

'You need some coffee.' He dutifully followed me into the kitchen, banging off the walls in the hall; he was swinging more than an IKEA wardrobe. I switched the kettle on, not wanting to wait for the espresso machine to heat up. He needed strong black coffee inside him immediately. Joe opened the fridge and rooted around looking for food. It was well stocked since my flatmate Louisa had come to stay. There was no doubt about it, she looked after her men well and I knew she considered Joe to be one of her men. That was why she always encouraged Jack, I guessed.

Joe found a leg of turkey left over from the Christmas dinner that Louisa had cooked for her parents; she was determined to prove her independence to everyone, as if there was a shred of doubt left. I sometimes worried her father would hear about her antics but she seemed to think whatever he thought of her behaviour was his problem.

Whenever I'm in a confined space with Joe, I'm so aware of his size – he seems to fill the room. Tonight, the kitchen smelled like a distillery.

I tried to encourage him to sit but he continued to stand, smiling like an imbecile.

'You hurt me, Brodie McLennan.' He waved the turkey leg reproachfully in my direction. '...Did ... don't try to deny it.'

I pushed and shoved in an effort to get him safely into a chair. He was determined to stand, in spite of this fact; he would slide a few steps down the kitchen worktop before regaining his balance. Tired out, I sat down and drank my coffee.

'You hurt me, Brodie McLennan.'

'I heard you the first time – you're like a stuck CD.' Joe wandered over, placed his hand on my hair and rested on it: the weight was crushing.

'But I'm not kidding. You did. I saw it in your eyes. You thought I was selling people out – that's not the case, Brodie. How could you ever think that about me?' He slumped heavily on the chair next to me, his kilt lifting well up his thigh. I knew Joe was a true Scotsman, so I pulled it down. 'Don't go trying to take advantage of me when I'm drunk,' he laughed, breathing a fine mist of Islay malt on me. 'Oh go on then – you know I'd let you.' His voice was suddenly serious.

I backed away – I knew that him being drunk gave me the perfect chance to find out exactly what his relationship with DI Bancho was; maybe he wouldn't clam up.

'What have you been doing with Duncan Bancho anyway?' I asked. 'You know I hate him.'

'You know what your problem is? You hate too many folk. Duncan's not that bad. He's trying his best to save those lassies.'

'What's that got to do with you?' I poured more coffee into his cup.

'His investigation is being hampered outside and inside the force. Half his colleagues are desperate to see him fall on his face ... and no one on the streets will speak to him, so I go round the brothels and see what I can find out,' he told me.

'Hard job but someone's got to do it sort of thing?'

'When did you get bitter like this, Brodie? I've never had to pay for sex in my life. Not

166

financially anyway…' He stared at me as he made the last comment. 'I'm not so hard up that I'd take a freebie from some poor Polish lassie just to make myself feel better.'

He was in a huff. Pushing his chair back from the table, shakily, he got to his feet.

'Sit down and behave, Joe. What did you come to say? Apart from Happy Christmas – again.'

He waited a few moments before answering, and his eyes cleared as he spoke. 'I'm frightened for you, Brodie, and for Connie. It's probably just my imagination, but I wanted to catch the bastard to keep you both safe ... then I got to know some of the girls that Duncan was talking to.' I couldn't keep the look out of my eye. 'No – not in that way. These girls, they're not like Kailash's girls; they've been sold in a market like bloody slaves.' He stood up and walked over to get himself a glass of water; evidently he'd decided it was time to sober up.

'Did you know Bancho and I went to Bucharest a couple of months back?'

I felt numb; I really didn't know anything about him any more. I shook my head.

'I heard a rumour that the Ripper attacked a girl ... but she survived. Brodie, somewhere out there is a girl who can nail the bastard; she's seen his face. Well. Bancho I needed to find her but she just disappeared ... we thought she might have gone back to Bucharest ... so we followed up that lead, unofficially of course.'

'Did you find her?'

'No, I'm still searching.'

All the colour drained from his face. He looked guilty. Something had happened in Romania.

167

'There's something you're not telling me.'

'Yeah ... I was offered a thirteen-year-old red-head for twelve hundred pounds. But that's not the saddest thing... I wouldn't have been her first owner.' He hit his big fist off the table. 'The government is doing fuck-all about it.' He shook his head in disbelief, unshed tears filled his eyes.

'And what did you do?'

'Kailash and me bought her.'

The surprise showed in my eyes – just how close was he to my mother?

'Her name is Angelika – we bought her pal as well. Took them out to a charity who keep them safe, send them to school. That's the tip of the iceberg though, Brodie; there are bloody thousands of children being trafficked as sex slaves into Britain alone.' He placed his head in his hands. 'With all this going on in the world, is it wrong for me to worry so much about you and Connie?'

I heard the front door opening; voices told me it was Louisa and a beau. They also hit the wall several times before falling in the kitchen door. I had warned her about binge drinking – her small body couldn't take it; her bones were brittle and I didn't want her snapping a thigh bone. She was far too good in court to be languishing at home. It turned out that Louisa was sober but Chris Mattel, one of the young advocates she was seeing, was not.

'Happy Christmas, Joe,' she said, climbing into his lap. She threw her arms around his neck and kissed him. 'We've got company, Brodie,' she told me. 'Room for another one in here?' She jumped off Joe's lap, shrugging her shoulders, and grabbing Martel's hand and a bottle of Dom Perignon out of the fridge. She ran as fast as her little legs would carry her – which wasn't very fast – and bumped into Jack as he came in the door.

'This is embarrassing...' he said.

The nosy wee minx lingered in the doorway to see if there would be blood. Suddenly sober, Joe stood up. 'Not at all, Jack, I was just leaving.' He almost seemed resigned.

'I'll see you out,' I said, feeling guilty and not knowing why. After all, he'd been the one to divorce me years ago. I didn't want to be the sort of bride who appears in tabloid papers getting married for the fifth time to the same man, although, secretly, I suspected that could be Joe and me. The night air was cold and starry. 'How are you getting home?' I asked. He hit his thigh. 'Shanks's pony – the walk will do me good, give me a chance to sober up, and think. I don't know what possessed me coming here.'

'You know perfectly well what was on your mind,' I said. I couldn't deny the electricity. Joe was cute when he was drunk, and cute isn't a word that could often be used to describe him. I felt a pull in my stomach.

'I only came to give you your Christmas present. I've bought you one since I got a paper round when I was twelve – did you think I would forget this year?' He pulled out a small red box from Hamilton & Inches, jewellers with a royal warrant. *Oh God, what if it was a ring?* I needn't have flattered myself. Nestling on the velvet was a platinum locket. Joe struggled with his big fingers to open it.

'The photograph was Connie's idea.'

Joe, Connie, and Greyfriars Bobby in the middle, grinned out at me.

'She says you're Bobby,' he laughed.

'Thanks. I seem to recall you said I was like Greyfriars Bobby too.'

'Not any more. Bobby was faithful to the man he loved, remember. The one man. Goodnight, Brodie.'

With that, be left me standing on the doorstep. Aching for him.

Chapter Thirty

Pathology Department, Edinburgh Royal Infirmary Wednesday 26 December, 2 p.m.

I didn't have to be here; post-mortems were not necessarily part of my job description. God knows I hate them. So why was I following the putrid stench of death? I'd like to say it was because I'm a masochist, but the truth is more unpalatable: I'm a smart-arse. If I wasn't there, some detail could be missed or ignored; in other words I was here because I need to win. I could be honest with myself – my need to solve the case was probably greater than my need for justice. The matter of possibly finding some evidence to show that Thomas didn't kill Katya was a bonus. Did I think I was indispensable? Well, Lavender constantly reminds me that the human-sized fridges in Patch's department are filled with indispensable workaholics like me.

I clumped along the corridor in my bike boots. The only way to salvage this miserable excuse for a Boxing Day would be to ride the Fat Boy down to North Berwick, somewhere clean where I could feel the wind in my hair; somewhere I could smell salt, not decomposing flesh.

Patch had called at eight that morning, more or less as a professional courtesy – and to wish me 'Happy Christmas'. He had been asked if he would come in on a public holiday and perform two autopsies. My client was only charged with the murder of the girl who fell from the castle battlements.

Money talks and Adie Foster, through the good offices of the chief constable, had persuaded the Crown Office to have the autopsy on a public holiday. Patch likes nothing better than to delve around in cadavers so he didn't object.

Pushing the swing doors open I clung to one nugget of information – the temperature in the Thistle Chapel was cold enough to have prevented the body decaying too badly. In spite of the smell, I hoped that meant that the brain hadn't turned to mush, or that when Patch touched the hair it wouldn't come away in tufts bringing bits of scalp with it. I'd seen this before and it always turned my stomach.

Patch was already at work, and sounds of Elvis singing 'Suspicious Minds' echoed around the sterile room; dressed in green scrubs and white wellies, the pathologist pulled his mask down.

'No rest for the wicked – get over here,' he said. 'Let's see what we've got. Technically, Thomas Foster isn't charged with this murder, so I just started before you got here.' Patch's baby-blue eyes were wide with curiosity and, dare I say it, delight. Sometimes, I just couldn't understand why I was so fond of him.

Bancho was there, of course. 'What have you found?' he said.

Mihaela's naked body was laid out on the cold metal gurney. The sight of it wiped the smile off my face. I recognized her from the babushka's photograph – just. Her skin, which had been creamy white, was now grayish-green, and the freckles on her face were gone. Cruelly, her eyes were open – and looked like black pools of pain. Her long red hair was spread out, the ends hanging over the edge of the gurney, knotted together and stained black with blood. Most pathologists cover the cadavers with a crisp white linen sheet, but, even with the dead, Patch's bedside manner is lacking. I suppose if the body had been covered, the mess might have shocked me more.

'These purple bruises...' He pointed to marks on her face and neck, and then looked at me. It was his way of keeping my mind off my heaving stomach.

'Those marks indicate she was alive at that point?' I ventured.

'Correct – she has a cocktail of drugs inside her including benzodiazepine. It's a hypnotic that would have allowed him to torture her for up to five hours. It relaxed her muscles so she couldn't fight back – but she would have felt everything.'

'And that's the same as the other victims?' Bancho asked, and Patch nodded at him.

My eyes scanned down the body at all the purple bruises. 'She was alive while all that was done.' Patch nodded again.

'Her throat was cut – and her tongue has been pulled out by the root. It's taken some doing ... so again he's used a serrated knife, but his intention is to make it look torn,' Patch said, barely looking up as he took scrapings from beneath Mihaela's nails. Her hands were manicured, the red polish was chipped, and, as the pathologist handled the fingers, the skin became baggy. After a period of time, skin slips in the direction of gravity – Patch calls it 'de-gloving' and it was what was happening now. 'The skin was removed from her left knee, as if she had been kneeling on it too long,' he told us.

'It's your fucking sicko client's signature, Brodie,' muttered Bancho. 'He takes young red-headed girls, drugs them, strips them ... fillets them...' He stopped to hold his breath and control his heaving stomach, and, shaking his head, looked over again to Patch who was following his own strict procedure. His routine ensured that he missed nothing; now he was collecting samples of hair. A clump came away on a two-inch-square piece of scalp. It looked like a ghastly divot of grass. Undisturbed, he said: 'It's nasty the way he sews their eyes ... she'll go to her grave that way – the skin's too delicate to remove his handiwork.'

I didn't comment on the purple bruising round her sockets. Patch placed her hair on an instrument tray; his gloved hands were covered in what

173

closely resembled faecal matter, as he walked decisively up to the bloodied stumps that passed as ankles.

'He hacked the feet off, ante mortem.' He pointed to some more purple bruising.

'What about DNA?' I asked.

'We have DNA samples but they are no good without a suspect.'

Bancho said, smugly looking towards me, 'But now we have Thomas Foster – everything has changed.'

Patch snorted and walked over to a gurney that was covered by a sheet. Bancho followed him, so I fell into step – this was Patch's domain and even the police didn't take liberties here. Bancho waited for Patch to reveal to me what was under the sheet. With the flourish of a magician he pulled it off. Luckily, he didn't shout 'abracadabra'. I was expecting another dead girl, but what I got was a pig. It's incredible how big they are – the surprise was clear on my face.

'Pig skin is the closest you can get to human skin. I've been experimenting on what kind of knife made the marks.

'I have a whole collection here, everything from bread knives to military issue. But I can't find anything that comes close and that's extremely unusual.'

He poked about the dead sow, indicating markings on the skin. I felt sick. I dreaded that one day I'd end up on Patch's table, naked and vulnerable, with pathology assistants laughing at my body, just like anyone else's. Sometimes I cursed myself that I spent so much of my living

174

time with Patch. I had no doubt that he would do my autopsy himself if he outlived me. His strict Wee Free upbringing means he believes the body is a shell, and he would be the one to carve up my shell if he could. He'd see it as his duty – both to me and God. Perhaps that's why I get upset when I'm in here; I look to see the soul of the deceased and it's just not there.

'Come over here,' said Patch, walking to a side table near Mihaela's body. He picked up a pair of feet and waved them about like a bargain hunter in a shoe shop.

'Can anybody spot what's wrong?' he asked. 'Simple question. Simple answer.'

Bancho looked blank. The condition his stomach was in he couldn't risk getting any closer. His reaction stoked my courage. I moved towards Patch. I stopped short of touching the feet, ignoring the smell as best I could. I got in close.

He was right. It was simple.

'Two left feet,' I said. 'They're two left feet.'

This was no eureka moment.

Somewhere out there was a dead girl we hadn't found yet.

Chapter Thirty-One

Pathology Department,
Edinburgh Royal Infirmary
Wednesday 26 December, 2.45 p.m.

The coffee was strong and black, just the way I liked it. Patch had been worried about the look of Duncan Bancho and he'd taken his tea break early to allow the detective inspector to get his shit together, although Patch phrased it slightly differently.

Elvis's *Home for the Holidays* CD crooned in the background in Patch's messy office. Reports were littered across the table, forensic textbooks, one on entomology – that one gave me the creeps when I borrowed it and I'd never look at a fly in the same way again.

DI Bancho's face turned a shade of grey as we returned to the lab. We went back to the gurney where Katya Waleski had been laid out by the pathology assistant, standing exactly where we were before. Patch was at the head of the cadaver within reach of his microphone; Bancho was about ten feet away, standing opposite me. Katya, unsurprisingly, remained where she was. Her eyes were closed. Her face and body were battered, but at least she had both feet.

'Katya Waleski, twenty-two years of age, found at the bottom of the Castle Rock.' Patch spoke in a monotone into his microphone. It might have been inappropriate but I chose to interrupt. 'Thomas Foster doesn't deny he was with her when she fell off the battlements at the castle.'

Bancho's anger or an improvement in his hangover allowed him to creep closer. He looked at Katya then pointed his finger at me, as he shouted: 'It was freezing cold! Who the fuck has sex in the middle of a snowstorm?'

'More vigorous men than you, Duncan,' I told him. 'And, anyway, the snow hadn't started then.'

'If I may interrupt...' Thankfully Patch had switched off the microphone when the childish bickering had started. The look he gave me suggested that I had presumed too much on our friendship. He was right. If it had been any other pathologist I would have bitten my tongue.

'The toxicology reports show that the young woman had consumed a cocktail of drugs. The main drug in her system was ecstasy. But it's a higher strength than normal, and it's already been responsible for at least one fatal overdose in the city.'

'Did she have any benzodiazepine?' Bancho asked, turning to look at me.

'No.'

Bancho's face fell. He quickly rearranged his features and stared straight through me. Katya's toxicology report was different to the Ripper victims' – and my next thought was Moses. He was the biggest supplier of ecstasy in Edinburgh. He might not have sold her the tablet himself, but he was probably responsible. The potency of the drug on the street had increased and he had a new chemist. Guilt by association made me want to fight harder for Thomas; I was too lenient on Moses and the Dark Angels at the best of times.

'Ecstasy increases your temperature,' I said, 'so when Katya Waleski was out on the battlements she wouldn't have felt cold in the same way as we would. We don't know, I haven't asked, because at the time I saw him in the cells of the Sheriff Court, I had no idea drugs were involved. But if Thomas had taken the drug too, which is likely, he wouldn't react in the same way either.' I was anxious to distinguish Katya from Mihaela; if I could do that, then Thomas had a chance of being released from Saughton Prison before the trial.

'Thomas Foster has admitted he was there when the girl fell,' Bancho said as our eyes locked. 'He ran away. He's only admitting something because we received a tip-off and a photograph from an anonymous witness who claims to have seen the whole thing. That's the only reason Thomas Foster was identified and has confessed to anything. If he was innocent, why did he leg it?'

Katya lay on her cold slab, impervious to the arguments raging over her naked body. How quickly one becomes immune to the dead. Throwing my hands in the air I asked Bancho: 'What are you going to charge him with? Being a coward?'

'No ... but he is going down for the murders of all these girls.' He tapped his breast pocket where he carried photographs of the victims around with him. The strain was affecting his judgement. Patch was ignoring us and quietly, patiently, proceeding with his work, humming along with Elvis to 'Silent Night'.

'Your client did tell you the girl was a prostitute?' Patch asked as he rolled Katya onto her side, revealing a network of healed crisscross whip marks. 'This sort of pattern is indicative of girls who work the sado-masochistic market. Are you sure Kailash doesn't know her?' Momentarily, I was lost for words; my mouth opened and closed like a fish. Even although I knew full well what my mother did for a living, I was a little surprised at his blunt tone. It was an emotional conflict from out of the blue – I wanted to defend Kailash but I know what she is. Patch went on: 'Before you say anything, I think you should be aware these marks did not come from abuse in the accepted sense – she is too well cared for. Her teeth are lovely, her hands are manicured. No doubt about it, she was a whore, and a high-end one at that, and these marks are likely to be from her job rather than anything else.'

Bancho clenched his lips together in what passed for a smile.

'Before you look too smug, Duncan, there's a problem with your case,' Patch, said.

'She doesn't have red hair!' I exclaimed, feeling a surge of relief.

'Never heard of wigs, Brodie?' Bancho asked. Katya had short dark locks and her pubic hair matched the top of her head, but the DI walked to the table where her clothes were lying and picked up a plastic evidence bag. Inside was a curly long auburn wig. 'She was a prostitute who wore a red wig. Hardly rocket science – but, unfortunately for her, she fooled your client into thinking she was his type. Are you blind, stupid, or just greedy for his father's money?'

Patch scratched the purple port-wine stain on his face which gave him his name; he was a man of infinite patience, which was why he was so good at his job – but that patience was running out.

'If I may be allowed to speak in my own lab – the colour of her hair was not the problem I was referring to.' His voice was raised and it silenced us. 'The girl died of natural causes.' He held his hand up, no doubt to stop DI Bancho saying that my client had pushed her, and continued: 'She died of an acute myocardial infarction.'

'Shit, Patch,' I said. 'She was only twenty-two – how likely is that?'

'In layman's terms, a massive heart attack induced by ecstasy killed her outright,' he said in reply.

'A heart attack would make you lose your balance and fall.' I looked Patch directly in the eye, nodding, asking for him to agree with me.

'I don't believe it for a second,' said Bancho. If white foam had started gushing out of his mouth, I wouldn't have been surprised. 'Thomas Foster is the Ripper. I know it. Look at that – how do you explain that?' He seemed to have completely recovered from his hangover induced aversion to cadavers – quite against protocol he was tapping Katya's naked breast. 'How do you explain that then, Professor?' he asked again.

Beneath the grime and bruising, something was written in red.

'It's red lipstick – probably her own, although I'm waiting for confirmation.' Patch held Bancho's eyes.

'Not the material – the content! Tell her what it

says!' He leant on the mortuary slab but Patch didn't follow anyone's orders. Stubbornly, he turned his back and walked away. I read it myself. It was difficult but I spoke aloud once I had deciphered the words.

'More will die?'

Shaken, but unbowed, I whispered to Bancho defiantly: 'What are you going to do – charge Thomas with vandalism or desecration?' I picked up my gear, waved to Patch and moved away.

'Where was her bag found?' I shouted at Bancho. He didn't answer me, so I knew it was beside her body at the bottom of the rocks. This day was over – I had a Fat Boy waiting for a ride. I should have guessed that Bancho wouldn't leave it there. I heard his footsteps charging after me. It was pointless to walk faster; he was running and I wasn't going to start a race. He grabbed me by my shoulder, pulling me round to face him. I was glad that I had a leather jacket on.

'Police brutality?' I shrugged him away. He pushed me against the wall.

'I know we've had our differences, Brodie...' he said, his eyes locked into mine.

'That's the understatement of the year,' I replied.

He sighed and leaned against the wall beside me, sliding down until he sat on the ground. 'Please ... don't do it ... don't have him released. I know in my gut that he's the Ripper, Brodie. More girls will die if you get him out.'

I joined him on the floor, placing my helmet between my legs. 'You have to understand, Duncan, that my job is not to decide who is guilty or innocent. I only go on the facts – and the fact is that you have nothing to pin Thomas Foster to those other deaths, and in the case of Katya Waleski, it looks like whoever gave us the tip-off witnessed a nasty accident.'

'He's the Ripper – I know it, and when I get the DNA results I'll prove it!' He held his head in his hands.

'You've made this personal, Duncan. Stand back from it and it'll be easier.'

He tapped his breast pocket again. 'Of course it's fucking personal, Brodie. I never understand people who say it's not.'

'You're too close. You're not the first cop to make a mistake. What about Wearside Jack? The inspector made the same mistake you're making now.' Bancho said nothing, but I could tell he was listening – it was, after all, his greatest fear. 'Remember the seventies? The Yorkshire Ripper case? The detective in charge was like you – blind. He had the real killer questioned several times and released because he didn't have a Wearside accent. Turned out Wearside Jack was a hoaxer – thirteen women were murdered because of that mistake. The inspector had to take early retirement; he was disgraced; he died young. Do you want that to happen to you?' I picked up my helmet and walked away. Without turning, I whispered: 'Release Thomas Foster.'

I saw Bancho's reflection in the glass. Still sitting on the floor he held his arm up in defiance and gave me the finger.

It was better than seeing his tears.

Chapter Thirty-Two

Cumberland Street, Edinburgh
Wednesday 26 December, 4 p.m.

The smell of an autopsy always stayed in my hair and nostrils for the rest of the day but I was too exhausted to shower. My half of the house, the half Louisa doesn't stray into, was cold and lonely when I returned. Her half of the house is immaculate, even anal. I go there sometimes to think – or to breathe. Today I didn't want to think. It was all too tiring and depressing. I popped a couple of paracetamol, hoping they would shift the pounding in my head. Switching on the heater, I raked through my drawers searching for my favourite red flannelette pyjamas. I flopped onto the bed with an almost empty selection box – only the caramel was left; not my favourite but it would do. The wind howled against the window as I pulled the duvet up around my ears and dipped a piece of chocolate into a mug of hot steaming tea. It would go some way to restoring my spirits.

Switching the television on, I was careful to keep it on mute. I didn't want the Ripper case invading my bedroom any more than I could help it. The news channel was on and, sure enough, footage of me speaking to Adie Foster on Christmas Eve was being played. It seemed a lifetime ago. The picture switched to St Giles' where a reporter was stand-

183

ing on the pavement doing a piece to camera. I turned it over and broke off two bits of chocolate to dip in my mug. I kept *The Simpsons* on mute while I dialled 1571 to get my messages; a computer-generated voice answered me. *You have no new messages.* No surprise. *And one saved message.* My fingers stopped fumbling around for chocolate. That was strange. I pressed to hear the message.

Saved message ... message received ... twenty-sixth December, at two fifteen p.m.

Connie's clear voice spoke out at me. A smile crossed my lips.

'*Hi – it's me. You're probably out in the Corvette – that car is to die for, anyway, I told the girls on the football team what I'm doing on New Year's Day and they are sooooooo green. I said that we could take some of them to the match – we can, can't we? I mean there's no point in doing something as fabby as this if your friends don't see you. You could take me in the convertible! Mum or Malcolm could give the girls a lift. Oh, by the way, I also said you'd take them for pizza – bye! Love you!*'

Connie was presenting me with a *fait accompli* – she'd arranged everything so that if I changed her plans I'd be the wicked big sister. I didn't mind. She'd cheered me up. At least someone wanted to spend time with me – oh God, I was getting maudlin. I needed more chocolate. I had to accept that I also needed to go to Saughton Prison to see Thomas Foster in light of the autopsy findings.

Maybe a shower would wash the dread away. I tried hot water, and then I switched to cold, even using neon yellow carbolic soap – disgusting

184

doesn't come close. I use it because Mary McLennan did. She always told me that it kept scabies and ringworm at bay: the estate where I grew up might have been riddled with it, but Mary McLennan would never have allowed anything like that near me. She was proud and she adored me. The shower gave me time to think. The saved phone message was a mystery. I had definitely checked the answering machine and cleared it before I went out. It left only one possibility. Louisa. Louisa must be listening to my calls. I was vaguely surprised, not because I've imbued my trainee with any principles or moral fibre, simply I'd thought she was too smart to get caught. Louisa's brain is as huge and agile as her body is small and brittle. I was disappointed in her lack of ingenuity; still, I'd have to say something so that she didn't get caught out again in a similar situation with somebody else. Wrapping a fresh towel around me, and placing the damp one on my head, I walked back down the hallway.

Fear ran up and down my spine as I moved towards my room.

In the hall mirror, I could see that my bedroom door was open. Louisa wouldn't be as stupid as that. Quickly, I mentally retraced my steps before taking the shower – yes, I'd definitely closed the door. The umbrella stand in the hall provided the only weapon I had. I threw the wet towel from my head onto the floor – it unbalanced me. The real reason I've never bothered about security is that I've always thought that I can take care of myself. I picked up an old hockey stick left over from the days when I played at university. Brandishing it, I leaned against the open door; jumping into the centre of the room, I covered all bases.

Where was he?

The bed had been made. Very well.

Lying out on the duvet was my favourite little black dress – now miraculously with all the pizza stains sponged off, Jimmy Choos placed neatly beside it and a pearl clutch bag. I certainly hadn't laid it all out.

He knew I was going out tonight. It was exactly the outfit I would have chosen to wear to the WS Library with Grandad.

On top of the outfit the intruder had left a message. Dropping the hockey stick, I stooped to pick it up.

Active evil is better than passive good

The telephone rang, cutting into the silence, and I jumped. Holding the note in my hand I picked it up. Silence. A crackling line. I knew he was there and my skin crawled. I wished that I had my clothes on. Perhaps he could see me? Tightening my jaw, I promised myself that I wouldn't let him know that he frightened me.

I picked up the hockey stick again.

'Brodie, Brodie – where are you?'

His voice had a high, singsong quality to it.

'You're not very original,' I told him. 'The message? The William Blake quote? Spooky guy stuff. Very disappointing.'

A note of irritation entered his voice. 'Originality means being brave enough to go beyond what is acceptable. Did you like the outfit

I chose for you?'

'Is there a reason for this phone call?' Sighing, I did my best to sound bored and to hide the shaking in my knees.

A sharp intake of breath. Maybe he was disappointed that I wouldn't play ball.

'It's a warning, Brodie. It's in both our interests for Thomas Foster to stay in jail. Don't go to the fiscal and have him released or I won't answer for the consequences.'

The line went dead.

My heart could start racing now – he had gone and I didn't have to hide it.

Chapter Thirty-Three

Saughton Prison, Edinburgh
Wednesday 26 December, 5.30 p.m.

The sleet was driving into the helmet visor and I was steaming up. Visibility was low and the bike was chugging. He'd been built for the black tops of California, not the Western Approach Road in a Scottish winter. The incessant rain had soaked through the leathers and my thighs were sticking to them like sausage meat to clingfilm. It wasn't comfortable; it wasn't even safe, so why in hell was I doing it? Maybe I was a masochist after all, or perhaps driving the Fat Boy in conditions like this kept my mind off the real problem.

Thomas Foster was innocent, and I was being

stalked by the real Ripper. He'd threatened me – I knew in my bones that it wasn't an idle threat. His voice chilled me more than the obscene weather conditions. *Active evil is better than passive good.* What the fuck did that mean? Whatever it was, it didn't sound good.

I walked into the visiting room in Saughton Prison as if I was straddling a horse. Water ran down the crack of my arse but, luckily, my leathers are black so I escaped the incontinence jokes. I joined the prisoners' families at one of the tables. The agents' room where I would normally have seen Thomas was shut; no other criminal lawyer was visiting their client on Boxing Day. The guard hadn't even been sure whether it was allowed, but had decided to chance it rather than go to the bother of checking with anyone else who would be in a similarly bad mood.

The girlfriends were there in force, most of them aged fifteen, with babies on their laps; teenagers in skimpy outfits that would not have looked out of place on a Rag Doll lap dancer. Naturally, they weren't wearing tights or stockings so their legs were covered in the Glaswegian tartan of mottled blue. Celtic tattoos on the ankle were *de rigueur.* Mothers of prisoners were also waiting to see their sons – the fathers were curiously absent as they had probably been for most, if not all, of their lives. I had more in common with the mothers than the girlfriends – we waited expectantly for the guards to open the doors and allow the prisoners in.

I bit my nails. I could hear them coming, young boys, barely men, still excited by Christmas.

Most of them thrived inside. Their dreams and expectations are pretty limited to start with; doing time simply narrows them down more. Many of them are used to being physically and sexually abused, so there are no surprises there.

Thomas wasn't from that mould. My bread-and-butter clients have habits, and they steal to fund those habits, but it's easy to find junk in the joint. If the government was serious about stopping drugs, prisons would be clean – how hard could it be? CCTV cameras, cops and guards ... but prisons are a microcosm of the streets – and they weren't like any streets that Thomas Foster had walked down before.

The doors opened and the wave swept in. It was like watching an Internet porn show – I guessed. This display of nubile tonsil hockey had nothing to do with sex and everything to do with passing speed, coke and heroin. Naturally, some of the girls had been searched so they hide the drugs in their anus. I was almost relieved that the Ripper's phone call had put me off food.

Thomas Foster wandered in last. He was a Yale WASP out of his league. As a remand prisoner he was allowed to wear his own clothes and he looked – well, he looked great actually. I don't think Calvin Klein will be using this particular prison hall in his next catalogue, but Foster could have been signed up if he did.

'Dinnae haud yer breath.' A prison guard leaned on my shoulder and whispered this sage advice in my ear. He'd obviously had garlic bread for lunch. 'Very popular that chap – look at him – you'd think it was the Queen. You might wait a long time for him.' The pudgy finger of the guard trembled so much as he pointed at Thomas that the swallow tattoo on his hand looked as if it was flying. Thomas had been called over to meet a mother and he was warmly shaking hands with Mags McIntosh, the matriarch of one of the largest criminal families in Scotland. Her son, Dino, wasn't one of my clients. I knew him merely by reputation. But if Thomas was under Dino's protection, Adie must have paid someone very well.

'That laddie would get a biscuit at anybody's door – he worked all Christmas Day making scrolls.' The guard, still staring at Thomas, stuck his tongue round his gums, presumably trying to dislodge some of the aforementioned garlic bread. He walked over to another table and brought back a rolled-up piece of thick paper. 'Here, see the laddie's work.' I unfurled the page. The calligraphy wouldn't have shamed a Japanese master. The ivy and Christmas roses looked so lifelike that I was tempted to scratch and sniff. The words, sadly, weren't of quite the same standard.

Plenty of love, tons of kisses,
Hope some day you'll be my missus.

'And that's no' the end o' his talents,' the guard said proudly. 'After the queue had died down for the scrolls last night, they invited him in to play poker. Poker! And him a new laddie – that's some honour, y'ken. Mind you, I bet they wish they hadnae bothered – the wee bugger won every hand. I was convinced he was cheating, I watched verra closely to see if he was counting cards but he had me fooled.'

Personally, I didn't think that was the hardest task on earth.

'You see, miss, he fits right in here.'

'Oh, his mother will be proud.' I couldn't help myself but he didn't get the sarcasm anyway.

'Aye, she should be. We'd taken bets on how long it would be before he started greeting his eyes oot – who could blame him? No one won the pot. He's made o' strong stuff that one. Of course...' he dropped his voice to a whisper, 'nobody here knows the police suspect he's the Ripper – otherwise he'd be dog meat.'

'At last,' I said to Thomas as he strolled up, leisurely.

'Sorry to have kept you, ma'am – these people have been kind enough to make me one of their own. They're so kind.' He leaned in close and I exchanged the smell of garlic breath for that of Clive Christian cologne. As I looked around the meeting room in Saughton, I was hard-pressed to recognize the kind people drawing Thomas Foster to their collective bosom; they all looked like they'd stab him for a packet of fags, but his soft American drawl was hypnotic – maybe they'd fallen for that too. I sat back in my chair refusing to be drawn in, but it was hard work. 'Like I said, ma'am,' he continued, 'some of these men are fine, fine people ... but I do want out of here. Do you know what I mean?'

I ignored him. I thought I'd told him to stop calling me ma'am. It made me feel old.

'Did you know that Katya Waleski was a prostitute?' I snapped.

191

'Do I look as if I have to pay for sex?' he quickly replied.

I wanted to ask him what a man who pays for sex does look like; unfortunately, thanks to close association with Kailash, I knew, and, by and large, they did not resemble Thomas Foster.

The voice of the Ripper ran round in my head – *it was in my best interest for Thomas Foster to stay in jail.* Or what, I wondered? I had no idea, but professionally, I knew that I couldn't let Foster linger in jail. There was a little voice in my head that was telling me to save my own backside and let him rot, but I didn't see how keeping him in there would actually help or protect me. Anyway, I was used to ignoring that little voice. The sooner the real Ripper was caught, the better for every woman – including me.

'Katya Waleski died from a heart attack,' I told him, and watched his face to see any reaction. Relief. Relief flooded through his eyes. 'I thought she died from the fall,' he muttered. 'From the castle walls?'

'Under normal circumstances that wouldn't help,' I told him. 'But her heart failed – that's why she fell.'

'So ... there's no way they can blame me for that, right?'

He wasn't exactly heartbroken, but why should he be? Some quick screw had almost had him done as a serial killer – I couldn't really expect him to be weeping and wailing over her. 'She was a young healthy woman – the heart attack was caused by the cocktail of drugs she'd taken. Did you supply them?'

He looked insulted at the question. 'No, of course not,' he said, shaking his head and looking down at his hands. 'It was stupid, ma'am. We met in a bar. Susie Wong's, I think it's called. I asked around as to where I could get some gear – and we bought it from some blind guy. They looked suspicious, the guy and the other one with him, but – you know, dealers generally do.'

Moses. My suspicions had been confirmed. Katya Waleski had been killed by the new improved ecstasy provided by Cal, Moses' chemist.

'Is something the matter?' Foster asked me.

'No,' I said hastily. 'I was just wondering how quickly we can get you released.' I knew that Cal had supplied the drugs but if he was ever arrested it would be covered under client confidentiality. There was no way I could go to the police, so I was out of that one, even if the weight of Katya Waleski's death felt pretty heavy on my shoulders. 'Just one more thing, Thomas,' I added. 'There was a message written on Katya's chest. Whoever did it used the victim's own lipstick – any idea how it got there?'

His pink tongue appeared between his lasered white American teeth. He appeared to be thinking and it looked like hard work. He shrugged his shoulders. 'I can't help you, ma'am. Maybe it could have been written by the police as a joke, or maybe by the person who found the body? Anyway, I've got to go.'

With that, he got up. Half turning he asked me: 'I don't wish to tell you how to do your job, ma'am, but did you ask the police where they found her handbag – and if her lipstick was still in it?'

It shouldn't have taken a genius to figure out that question.

Chapter Thirty-Four

The Signet Library Edinburgh
Wednesday 26 December, 8.30 p.m.

I was late but I had nothing else to wear except that bloody outfit picked for me by the Ripper. I searched. Everything in my wardrobe was now lying on the floor. I even rummaged through the piles of clothes that had been left in heaps for God knows how many days. I couldn't wear my leathers and that wasn't because they were too wet – the problem with my attire came from the fact that I was Grandad's partner at a function in the Signet Library to honour his legal career. He was being inducted into the legal equivalent of the Hall of Fame. Naturally, the event was being held in a swanky place. Although it's a working library, the Signet has been described as Edinburgh's best-kept secret for events and nights out, located in Parliament Square, just off the Royal Mile. You have to walk past St Giles' Cathedral to get in, which brought the Ripper's handiwork to mind again, but I had to put that out of my mind. The library had been completed in 1822 – George IV described it as Europe's finest drawing room. King George knew a thing or two, I'd imagine, and he'd probably have warned me that turning up in a tatty frock was a no-no. In spite of the fact it made my skin crawl, I put on the black dress. I promised myself that I would burn it when I got home.

The function was in the Upper Library. Luckily it was a drinks reception for four hundred of his closest friends and no one noticed that I was late. Grandad was talking to the lord justice clerk of the Court of Session when I walked in, so I stayed out of his way: I didn't care for the company he was keeping. The lord justice clerk is Scotland's second-highest judge; he is in charge of a group of judges known as the Second Division. I'd had an appeal before him last month and the old bastard threw it out with an unnecessarily cutting judgement. Obviously, I would never cast aspersions on his legitimacy out loud; not least because to speak against a judge is called 'murmuring': it's a criminal offence. No wonder they think they're God Almighty.

Still, it was nice to see them fawning over Grandad. My heart sank as he waved me over. I overheard him as I got closer, and he sounded like a boastful mother at a parent and toddler group. 'Yes! Yes! She's a chip off the old block!'

I didn't like the sound of that – just exactly which block was I chipped from? My prostitute mother? My paedophile father? Neither passed the functioning test, which was why I had given up on parenthood before I'd even started. I was pretty sure that Grandad meant that I was like him though – if that was any better, given the type of son he'd fathered.

'Brodie!' Grandad exclaimed, as he reached out

and pulled me into the company, making sure to keep hold of my back in case I ran. Like slugs to lettuce, the senior members of the bench, all old men, crawled towards us. Nodding acknowledgement to one another, no one nodded in my direction. I noted that they were drinking whisky, probably the finest single malt, whereas I had been palmed off with cheap cava masquerading as champagne.

'Ah, Miss McLennan!' Lord Port Soy, the justice clerk, smiled showing his tombstone teeth. He managed to make my name sound like a disease. After the day I'd had, I wasn't taking any shit.

Grandad leaned across and whispered a warning in my ear. 'Play nice,' he hissed. His grip on my back seemed to tighten. Lord Port Soy leaned into me, glancing over both shoulders before he spoke again. The cadre of slugs shuffled closer until we were huddled together like a rugby scrum. It wasn't pleasant – where was the salt when you needed it?

'You're representing Adie Foster's son.' Lord Port Soy seemed to be leading the cross-examination. I didn't reply because it wasn't a question. 'I was across at Yale in '52. I knew his grandfather.' Grandad pinched me, so I nodded at the lord justice clerk, feigning interest in what he was saying. I was not naive enough to think Hector McHale, as he was formerly known before he became a judge and assumed his new title, was merely passing the time of day with me. Whatever his game was, I wasn't interested in playing ball.

'We were all very pleased that you're the defence agent,' he said, looking around the cluster of men, who nodded their agreement alongside some gruff mumblings. 'Now in the past, even the recent past...' The lord justice clerk raised his shaggy white eyebrow and I knew that he was referring to the case last month. I also understood he wanted a favour from me and that he wouldn't have given me such a shitty decision if he'd ever believed he would be in this position. Was it possible? Was I going to have the last laugh? 'Well, let's just say that we've had our differences, my dear, but I think you may have misunderstood the aims of our society.'

The penny dropped and my heart sank – he was talking as head of the Enlightenment Society not as a member of the judiciary. 'We are mainly a charitable organization, upholding society,' he said, as they all nodded and murmured. 'Sometimes it is difficult – justice is not always what it seems and we must intervene. With young Thomas Foster there are difficulties with his case that must be ironed out. At the moment, my dear, it really doesn't suit us for Thomas Foster to be released on bail. The public are quite happy that the Ripper is behind bars. If he were to be released the effects on the city would be catastrophic.' The muttering increased in volume. 'The terrible media campaign behind all of this has been successful in whipping up hysteria. We can't allow that to get even worse, can we?'

'Girls are dead!' I told him. 'I was at a crime scene last night in the Thistle Chapel – a hundred yards from here as the crow flies.' I stopped to get my breath and tried to keep my voice down, mindful of where I was. 'At the autopsy today, a foot found in the chapel was discovered to not even belong to the victim lying in the morgue. Do you understand? We have at least one other victim who we haven't even found yet.'

Grandad's hand had tightened still further on my back. Whilst he was concentrating on controlling me, I reached down and filched the whisky glass from his hand. I needed a proper drink.

'Please don't misunderstand me – no one's saying it's not regrettable, my dear.' The lord justice clerk tried to placate me; his liver-spotted hands were open in conciliation.

'Not regrettable? You've lived longer than three of the victims put together,' I said. 'What you really mean is that they're not the same as us ... so they don't count.' My jaw tightened. I knew I was snarling – I don't make good decisions in this state.

'Did anyone hear me say that these girls don't matter?' the lord justice clerk said as he rounded on me, trying to keep his voice down but furious at being pulled up. 'There are difficulties with this case; I can say no more at present.' He had stopped smiling.

'Yes! The main one being that Thomas Foster is innocent! You want me to keep him in Saughton until after the Hogmanay party so that the tourists will still come, don't you? Who in their right mind would come to a city where a homicidal maniac is preying on foreign girls?'

'Foreign prostitutes,' interjected Lord Munro of Caithness.

'Jesus Christ,' I sighed, exhausted by their attitudes.

Lord McKenzie of Alvie, an elder in the Church of Scotland, clearly irritated by my blasphemy, turned to Grandad and said – as if I wasn't even there: 'I thought you could control her? Just tell her to keep the boy in Saughton – we don't want anything else in the press.' They shuffled off.

Grandad still held me as we watched them disperse into the crowd. A damp, cold feeling crept over my skin – I had ruined his party, but I wasn't apologizing.

Thomas Foster was innocent and I knew that better than anyone, thanks to my anonymous caller. I didn't want to share today's break-in with Grandad. He'd worry, and I failed to see what use an octogenarian could be to me. There was always Glasgow Joe though.

The voice on the phone hadn't laid down specific threats. What could he do? I was on guard. I didn't trust Bancho and I believed bringing in the police could only make things worse. I was on my own with this one.

Chapter Thirty-Five

Cumberland Street, Edinburgh
Thursday. 27 December, 3 a.m.

The phone rang. Fear made me leave it unanswered. I'd been dreaming an anxious dream. Something important to me was lost but I didn't know what it was. And now, for a few long seconds, my eyes declined to open while my wits tried to understand the sound that I had just heard – it didn't belong in my dream. Pure panic raced through my veins. Bent into a foetal position I held my knees while sweat ran down my back, gathering in the downy hair at the base of my spine. The swelling in my neck made it hard to breathe, even harder to swallow. Then, in a split second, my eyes opened wide in terror. Blinking, I adjusted to the blackout conditions in the room. Senses on red alert, I watched the now-quiet phone. The illuminated clock on the table showed me it was 3 a.m.: the devil's hour. It was minus four outside, and not much warmer in my bed. I reached out – it was definitely empty. Ashamedly, I longed for the smell of whisky and stale fags.

The phone rang again. I watched it suspiciously, willing it to stop. If I could stop it, I wouldn't have to deal with whatever someone wanted to tell me. A heavy black stone weighed on my chest, crushing the wind out of my lungs as I lay down again. I didn't want to talk to Adie Foster. I didn't want to have to deal with Thomas Foster at this time of the morning. And I certainly didn't want to deal with whatever tragedy had befallen Thomas Foster in Saughton Prison.

'Are you going to answer that bloody phone? Some people are trying to sleep!' shouted Chris Martel from Louisa's room. Floorboards creaked as small feet ran heavily, flat-footed, along the hall. The bedroom door squeaked and a shaft of light landed on the worn rug. I didn't look up; there was no danger to me in this house and the only person running to me would be Louisa.

The phone stopped ringing but I still couldn't move. Clutching the covers up to my chin I stared at the one in my room. I knew it would begin again. A clenching pain in the gut told me so. A figure approached the side of the bed and soft fingers smelling of calendula stroked my hair. Like a cat, I didn't uncurl, but I inched towards my handler, grateful for human contact.

'Brodie, honey, why didn't you answer the phone?' Louisa's voice was soft and cajoling, but she couldn't hide the edge of worry that had crept in. The phone line came directly into my bedroom; calls that disturbed my sleep were always welcome as they meant more work. I worried if three nights in a row passed without a call from the emergency services – it was a sign I was losing my touch. The call that heralded the end of sleep tonight was different. I don't know how I knew but a silent scream in my head told me to stop all the clocks.

Frantically, Louisa pushed my shoulder at the sound of the ringing phone, but her slight weight couldn't move me. I had enough sense still in me to take long, slow, deep breaths. It didn't work. I held my breath until the ringing wasn't there.

The phone had stopped and I gulped the cold night air down like a newly caught fish. For a few long seconds the darkness was silent, and then the attack began again from another direction.

'Your mobile? Where is it? Where is it, Brodie?' Louisa, affected by the atmosphere, manhandled me. Intending to cause pain, her long fingernails scraped and pinched me. I refused to respond. I was petrified by fear – this went way beyond anything Adie Foster could inflict on me, yet I had no idea why that was. Exasperated, Louisa's sigh echoed around the corners of the room. A soft hand smacked me across the cheek – it stung. Nonetheless, I refused to answer her.

The old cast-iron radiators rumbled thunderously into life as Louisa searched amongst the heaps of clothes on the floor. She didn't miss a beat. Delving into the dirty knickers pile, my private mobile was still calling to her, but things were in such a mess she couldn't locate it from the sound.

'Fucking get a grip, Brodie! What's wrong with you? Where is your mobile?' Her gaze locked on to me; inadvertently my eyes darted to the leather trousers hanging over a chair. It was the only clue she needed, and she ran over the mounds of tee shirts, trousers and jumpers that lay on the floor. 'Tomorrow you're tidying this shithole up.'

The mobile still rang.

Louisa answered.

'Hello? Brodie can't come to the phone right now.'

I grabbed it out of her hands. 'Hello?'

There was no sound, just laboured breathing. I fancied that I could hear heartbeats in the darkness. I knew what my fear had been – that this was the Ripper. And I knew now, immediately, that he was far from the worst thing that could happen to me.

'What's happened to Connie?' I asked suddenly, as if the words had nothing to do with me. I laid my hand on the left side of my chest; breathing deeply, I swallowed the air to bring myself back to the present. I couldn't slow the beats down.

'For Christ's sake, speak to me,' I pleaded.

Kailash spoke softly. 'Brodie – she's gone. He's taken her.'

Chapter Thirty-Six

Kailash's home,
Ravelston Dykes, Edinburgh
Thursday 27 December, 4.05 a.m.

'Tell me it's not true. Please God, Jesus, tell me it's not true,' I whispered to myself. But it didn't take a genius to work out that something was seriously wrong. Fear poisoned my body as I approached Kailash's house, Four Winds. Connie and I had connected in a way I neither knew nor understood; our lives were inextricably linked. I needed her, and, somehow, she needed me. This was odd for me, new ground, and I didn't really know how I felt, or how I should feel.

The clock in the car glowed 4:05 a.m. In spite of the pounding behind my eyes, I counted two police squad cars, Glasgow Joe's racing motorbike, and Malcolm's Mini crowded into the driveway. Louisa had insisted that I was in no fit state to drive; she had snivelled her way up through the deserted streets running every red light we encountered.

Falling out of the car, I stumbled up the gravel driveway. The seconds were ticking away. The doorbell was loud enough to wake the neighbourhood, but no one answered. I kept my finger on the bell as Louisa tried to calm me. Shrugging her off, I kicked the door. I welcomed the pain shooting up through my toes because it spurred me to kick harder. Running shoes don't really make a good battering ram.

Footsteps in the hallway calmed me momentarily; a WPC opened the door. She stared out suspiciously, not knowing who I was. I was in no mood to be polite. I pushed the half-open door back against the hallway wall and the young policewoman jumped out of the way to avoid being injured. An unnatural silence pervaded every corner in the house. I strained to listen for sounds of Connie, even though I knew they wouldn't come. If she didn't come rushing to greet me at the door, her habit was to sit in her games room playing computer games on the Internet, shouting and chatting with kids in America and Europe. All I could hear were muffled voices. I followed them and they led me to the drawing room. The WPC, who I assumed was the family liaison officer, was on my heels. Over her objections, I shut my eyes and opened the door. I knew that I couldn't cope with Kailash's pain – I'd never really seen her vulnerable – but I certainly wasn't prepared for Joe's.

Sitting in the corner, the big man's head was in his hands. He didn't look up. His shoulders heaved with silent sobs. In the room, people were almost mourning. Inside, my stomach was cramping over the idea that I might never see Connie again. I thought I might be sick.

I tried to distract myself by staring at the stain on my trainers. It had been caused by Connie dropping hair dye on them. We had been in the sitting room a few months ago, eating Mackie's ice cream and chocolate flakes whilst watching My Super Sweet Sixteen on MTV. After a period of silence she'd told me: 'Malcolm says you're a slob.' 'He's right,' I'd answered. Connie had lifted a brush and tried to pull it through my tangled hair. 'That hurts!' I'd squealed as she lifted half my scalp off. 'Suffer for beauty – that's what Malcolm always says,' she retorted. 'And what else does Malcolm say?' I'd asked, but she'd missed the sarcasm in my voice. 'He says if you're not going to rinse your hair in vinegar, you need a semi-permanent. Hair without dye is like a face without makeup.' I could have pointed out that I didn't choose to take style advice from a man that made Quentin Crisp look like a member of the Amish, but by then she was already brandishing a home-dye kit. How much harm could it do, I'd asked myself? It cost me £140 to rectify the damage – and that didn't include the cost of repainting the bathroom wall.

I couldn't distract myself any longer – I had to face Kailash.

'She's gone – our Connie is gone,' she said, breaking down as soon as she saw me. 'I went in to check on her when I came in from work – I got in a bit earlier than usual, but it was still nearly three. Her bed was empty – the window was open, Brodie. Someone came in her own window!' Kailash wiped her silent tears. I expected that she thought it was a punishment on her. I said nothing. She told me that Malcolm had been babysitting, that Derek had come round as they were back together. They didn't hear a thing, Kailash said, and I couldn't help a voice in my head from saying that they were probably too busy having reunion sex downstairs to hear my sister cry out for help.

'They're both crying in the kitchen – Malcolm is blaming himself,' Kailash said. I stopped myself from saying that he bloody well should.

'It might be ransom,' I said, clutching at straws. 'Someone's read the papers, what's going on, known you from other ... coverage ... and thought the best way to get a bit of easy cash was to take Connie. You'd pay out anything just to get her back – it could be as simple as that.' I felt like falling to the floor and howling like a wounded animal, but I knew that I couldn't. Connie needed me, and I imagined I heard her crying out, begging me to find her.

Malcolm and Kailash had known each other since shortly after I was born. He was her 'dresser' in the brothels of Amsterdam. He patched her up when vicious clients went over the top, and he was with her when she finally decided that if any pain was to be inflicted, she would be the one wielding the whip. He was like a live-in retainer and, when Connie came along, it was the natural order of things that the care of the baby fell mainly to Malcolm; Kailash simply had no idea how to be maternal. She'd been robbed of that chance with me. Tonight an emergency doctor had made a house call to sedate him – she was as dear to him as anyone could be, and I knew that, even as I was blaming him for her disappearance.

Malcolm was saying nothing now; as I looked at his half-drugged body sitting on the couch, I didn't know that someone could age so quickly. He shuffled over to me and pulled me into his arms. I couldn't breathe. I didn't mind that when I opened my wet eyes, Kailash had left the room.

Old habits die hard: even in his drug-induced state, Malcolm was presiding over the residence. To be fair, Dismal Derek was in the kitchen making cups of tea that no one would have the will to drink. Malcolm led me through the hallway; his long fingers gripping my wrist – we both needed that hold. He pulled me up the stairs. The door to Kailash's room was open. Turning left, we walked down the upper landing, past a smiling photograph of Connie on her first birthday, bald as a coot with a lace bonnet to disguise her hairlessness. Malcolm stood in front of it, his thin blue lips quivering as he traced her face with his finger. Unshed tears cracked his voice. 'I thought her hair would never grow. She just had a few wispy curls at the back for ever such a long time. I was always touching her head – Kailash said that's what was keeping her bald. I even tried sacro-cranial massage – I put her down in her cot one night when she was eighteen months old and it all just sprouted. It hasn't stopped since. She's got such bonny red hair – don't you think?'

I didn't answer him. How could I? Red hair, bonny or not, meant something different to me now. It was a lure, a necessity for the Ripper, not just a beautiful aspect of my sister. How could I share this with Kailash and Malcolm? How could

I make them even more panicky?

We were at the entrance to Connie's room.

'Maybe this is a ransom grab,' I said again to a new audience, praying that it was. It was the only possibility that meant Connie was still alive. You don't pay for a dead child. Malcolm ignored my comment. 'Glasgow Joe's a nut job; he's lost it. I don't think he'll be any help.'

'How is she?' I whispered, inclining my head towards Kailash's room.

'She's strong – Kailash is always strong for her girls.' He squeezed me hard. From inside the room, I heard a voice, female and harsh. It didn't sound like Kailash, who usually had a lilt like melted chocolate. 'Malcolm, your only job is to make sure that the police are well fed – they can't find Connie if they're thinking about their bellies. Stop gossiping and get that sorted. Please.'

'Derek's taking care of that,' he answered. 'I'm here for you and Brodie.' Malcolm wasn't able to stand up to Kailash. He capitulated, going off to join Derek in the kitchen. I grabbed his arm to stop him collapsing. The place was falling to pieces – now was not the time to do my grieving too. Kailash came to the doorway. I locked eyes with hers. They were not the red-rimmed, swollen eyes of mothers I'd seen on TV. She was a survivor; she had fought so many battles in the past. She would not beg the bastard to return her child. She would send out the Dark Angels to scour the sewers and bring Connie home.

So soon after Connie's abduction, Kailash was dressed and barking orders. This was her coping mechanism, pretending she still held the reins over

208

her own life. Obviously, she didn't – Connie's life, and so her own, was in the hands of the Ripper.

'We're going to get through this,' I told her, emptily. 'I'll find her – I promise.'

'You better find her fast then: she was taken just before midnight from what I can tell.' She glowered at Malcolm, who had obviously admitted that was when he'd last checked on my little sister. Kailash didn't need to tell me any more – children who are abducted and then murdered rarely survive longer than one hundred and eighty minutes.

It might already be too late.

Chapter Thirty-Seven

Kailash's home, Ravelston Dykes, Edinburgh
Thursday 27 December, 9.30 am.

'You *know* the fucking bikes! Don't give me any shit! You can take them all – just one fucking condition. I need the cash, all of it, in readies this afternoon.' Glasgow Joe paced the kitchen floor, screaming into a mobile. Alone for a second, he paused, leaned his head against the fridge and shut his puffy, red-rimmed eyes. Eyes still closed, he switched the mobile off and slipped it into his leather trousers. He raised his clenched fist and banged it in vain against the door.

'Knocking shit out of the fridge won't help,' I told him. 'There's nothing you can do – except pace this house and pray.'

He narrowed his eyes at me. 'This morning ... I said my first fucking prayers since you left me. I'm not losing her, Brodie. There's always something I can do, even if it's only to have the money ready to pay the fucker when he calls.'

'Is that what you were doing – selling your bikes?' I asked.

He shrugged. 'It's more like giving them away, the way that bastard's taking advantage of the situation, but I'm not complaining. I need to be ready for the phone call.'

'You really think it's ransom? You really think he'll call?' I asked, not sure I believed my own idea any more.

'I need to believe the bastard will – so does Bancho. He's got the phones tapped and everything.'

'Bancho's waiting for a phone call because you had him up against the wall, threatening him. He just did it to keep you off his back. Bancho's in charge of the Ripper investigation, Joe – do you really think he could take on child abduction as well?' I asked, inhaling deeply and exhaling slowly. 'Listen, Joe, you need to get a grip. We need you. Connie and I need you – time is running out for her,' I said, but his fear was running rampant in his usually disciplined body. The Ripper had attacked Glasgow Joe where he hurt.

'Where is she?' he whispered, banging his fist off the fridge again. I could see the rage rise within him. 'Is she dead, Brodie, is she dead?' he cried, shaking me, unaware that his size and strength was likely to break my collarbone. 'Is she alive? How could Malcolm let someone take her? Christ, if he didn't look like a fucking corpse already, I'd kill him.'

I moved over to him, and took him in my arms, cradling him like an infant just as Bancho came in. 'Sorry to interrupt,' he sniffed. 'I heard it's on Radio Forth. I don't know where they are getting their information, but they're quick off the mark.' He stared at his shoes, embarrassed because he knew I would assume the leak came from within the police force.

'I'm warning you.' He took a deep breath before he continued: 'It's not going to be easy under the media's scrutiny – they're detailing the family history.' He looked directly at me. 'All of you are being scrutinized. Of course Kailash's business interests will keep the tabloids going for days ... but you don't get away scot free.'

Derek handed DI Bancho a cup of tea and then disappeared into the background. Bancho leant in conspiratorially, 'They're already saying a member of the family did it – Kailash's murder case just became news again. Of course, there was some suggestion that it might be the Ripper because she's got red hair.' Joe looked shocked. 'I'm sorry, I didn't mean to blurt it out like that,' said Bancho. 'I assumed you'd made the same connection.'

Joe ranted at Bancho's insensitivity: 'How can they say it's the Ripper? Thomas Foster is linked to the other murders – this doesn't follow the m.o. of the other murders. This is child abduction and we're going to get her back.' Bancho and I locked eyes over his shoulder.

'It's not just about the headlines – there's some

211

pretty sordid stuff about Ms Coutts's occupation, really not fit to read over the breakfast table,' Bancho advised, going all moral on us all of a sudden.

Kailash was upstairs in Connie's bedroom. She wanted to be on hand to answer every question the technicians had. They were taking Connie's laptop away for further examination. The fingerprint guys had already dusted the scene, the authorities already had records of Kailash's fingerprints on file, which might speed things up as in cases like this the usual suspect was the mother anyway. It was a subject everyone was tiptoeing around. The newspapers lay untouched on the table. Connie smiled out from them all braces and dimples, dressed in her team strip. As captain of the football team, she held the shield they won for coming top of the league.

'I want you to meet a colleague – Detective Inspector Smith; she works child abductions.' Bancho turned around to introduce a middle-aged woman with thinning hair who had just arrived. She held a bacon roll in one hand and a cup of tea in the other. A fine smear of grease lined the outside of her mouth, like lip gloss. Kailash appeared downstairs and, pouring an espresso, shut her eyes against the pain as she spied Connie's photograph in the newspaper.

'You okay, Ms Coutts?' DI Smith's mouth was full of bacon.

'Yes, but Connie's not is she? Shift your arse and find her rather than standing there bloody chomping!' I wasn't the only one surprised – I'd never really seen Kailash lose it before and the detective choked on her butty. She placed the cup on the granite counter top and, taking out a black notebook, said: 'Ms Coutts – I've worked fifteen child abduction cases.'

'And? What exactly does that mean?' Kailash snapped.

'It means I find children who have been snatched.'

'Does it? Do you find them? Or do you just coordinate looking for them?'

'Usually,' Smith said.

'How many of them have you found alive, Detective Smith?' Kailash asked.

She had asked the question, the question that detectives always tried to avoid.

'None,' she said, looking down at her notebook.

I could see that Kailash had made her mind up not to act like other mothers of abducted children, sobbing in front of a media circus, begging for their child to be returned. Kailash Coutts did not beg. DI Smith slumped, diminished in Kailash's presence, but trying to rally. I could see the fear in her eyes; she was probably a good woman who had stuck with this job longer than was ideal for her health.

'Ms Coutts, what colour, size and make of pyjamas was Connie wearing?' Detective Inspector Smith asked the question as if she was asking for more sugar in her tea. I watched as Kailash's jaw tightened. 'I don't know – I left for work yesterday before she went to bed. Malcolm!' she shouted. Malcolm scurried into the kitchen. Sizing up the situation, he took the detective inspector's elbow and led her away. Kailash

213

already knew she wouldn't be winning any prizes as mother of the year – it seemed pointless to rub her face in it. Placing her untouched espresso cup on the table, she half turned and left the kitchen. Joe and I followed her, along the hall, up the stairs to Connie's bedroom. It was a typical thirteen-year-old's space. On the wall were digital print-outs of the wedding that seemed like a lifetime ago. 'Eddie? Lavender?' I whispered.

'I phoned them about half seven this morning,' said Joe. 'I know it's a bastard disturbing their honeymoon, but it would have killed Lav to see that front page or to have heard it on the radio. They're leaving Gleneagles right away – I'm ex-pecting them to walk through that door any min-ute.' He finished speaking and silence took over.

'What about Grandad?' I had thought of more people to worry about. 'At his age a shock like this could kill him.'

'I phoned Jack – he's with him now. We didn't want to give the old man the news over the phone.' Things must be bad if Joe was willingly contacting Jack. As an afterthought, Joe added: 'Moses wanted to come up, but I said that the house was crawling with police so it'd be easier if he stayed where he was. He's not happy about it. He feels he's to blame – he knew Malcolm was having domestic troubles.' Joe raised his eyebrows.

Kailash shook her head: 'Didn't we all?'

I was breathing hard. Everyone felt that Con-nie's abduction was their fault. Kailash was being punished for being a bad mother. Malcolm had sinned by being self-obsessed. Glasgow Joe felt obligated to protect anyone he loved – the list was very short and in his opinion it should have been well within his capabilities.

But they were all wrong.

They'd stupidly ignored putting my name on the list.

'You're hiding something – tell me!' Joe demanded as the thought went through my mind and showed on my face. 'Now, Brodie!'

Shit. How could I tell him this?

Chapter Thirty-Eight

Kailash's home, Ravelston Dykes, Edinburgh
Thursday 27 December, 10.15 a.m.

Last autumn's leaves and the odd plastic bag blown in from the nearby bus stop crunched underfoot as we walked through the garden, away from the prying ears of Bancho. 'Is this private enough for you?' Glasgow Joe's breathing was short and shallow. Kailash, never good in the morning or in the cold, eyed me suspiciously.

'I didn't want to worry you.' I leaned against a large elm tree and stole a cigarette from Kailash's packet. Crouching over her cupped hands I tried to light it in the gusty wind. It was minus one, but the wind-chill factor made it feel like minus ten. When the second match failed, Joe's hand covered the matches – there would be no cigarette until I had confessed.

'Admit it – you thought you could handle whaever it was on your own,' he accused. It was the truth, but a guilty conscience wouldn't let me admit it.

'It was on Boxing Day – it's all connected with Thomas Foster,' I said.

'You mean the Ripper?' Kailash brought Indian prayer beads out of her pocket and ran them feverishly through her fingers.

'No – not unless he's acting with someone else. There's another guy,' I told them.

'I knew it!' said Joe. 'I've felt the bastard watching us. I swear he was stalking us at Lavender's wedding.' His fist clenched and unclenched as he mentally pummelled whomever he had felt; it was his way of taking pain and burying it down deep. I clamped my jaws together so closely that my molars hurt.

'On Boxing Day, I went to the autopsies in the morning.' Kailash reached out and squeezed my hand. Her fingers were cold, the knuckles white and bloodless. A vein in her temple pounded furiously and her skin beneath the makeup was ashen.

'The girl who'd been battered against the Castle Rock – Katya – died of a heart attack; it was nothing to do with the Ripper. The second autopsy was the girl whose photograph the babushka showed us in the casino.'

Kailash blessed herself, a curious religious mixture in which she tried to embrace both sides of her bloodline. 'The feet had been hacked off – one of them didn't belong to the body so there's a girl out there they haven't found yet.'

Quiet tears ran down Kailash's cheeks, she

moved the Mala through her fingers at an ever-increasing speed, and Glasgow Joe put his arms around her, pulling her close to his chest.

'That's not the full story. The victim who died at the rock–' said Joe.

'Katya Waleski,' I interrupted. It was important to me that the murdered girls retained an identity; then we knew what we were facing – a human butcher who stole lives.

'Yeah, Katya Waleski. She had stuff written on her chest – what was it again?' Joe spoke to me over Kailash's head.

'It was in red lipstick,' I said. 'It said, "More will die".'

'What makes you so sure Thomas Foster didn't write it?' Kailash probed. She needed answers.

'The handbag with all her makeup in it was found at the bottom of the crags beside her body. I spoke to Bancho. Even he's having difficulty pinning this on Thomas ... it seems that she put her dress and bag on the cannon.'

'But what would make her do that?' Joe was sticking to Bancho's line that Thomas Foster was the Ripper.

'Oh for God's sake, Joe... It was bloody freezing. The girl had to earn some money and no doubt the bastard wasn't offering to put his jacket on the cannon for her. Use your head, it was probably her one good dress and handbag, she couldn't throw it in the snow... Katya expected to be very busy over Christmas and New Year.' Kailash spoke from experience.

'That explains it ... and it gives my client a way out. You know that Bancho was sent a photograph of Katya and Thomas Foster...? The photograph didn't show him writing any messages on her body,' I said, taking the cigarette out of the palm of my hand. I fished around in Kailash's pocket for the matches. It was vital to avoid Joe's stare. I knew he would see the fear. With closed eyes I inhaled the smoke deep into my lungs. The nicotine found the spot and hurriedly raced through my bloodstream, at last reaching my brain and central nervous system. Like a miracle, it instantly calmed every ragged, uptight nerve ending it passed. Joe reached out and stroked my chin. He knew me, knew that I was still hiding something. I didn't immediately respond so he moved on to his next tactic.

'There's more, Brodie. You'd better tell us *all* your secrets.' Joe's face was set; he wanted answers.

'I'm not the only one with secrets, Joe. Why don't you tell us about the Hobbyist's website?' I nodded in Kailash's direction.

'Brodie, I know all about the Hobbyists – and Moses said he tried to tell you in George Street when you collected Malcolm's pills but you didn't want to know about my business. So please, answer Joe's question.'

'Yeah, spit it out – we'll all feel better for it,' he said, removing his hand.

'After the autopsy I got back to Cumberland Street about four. I'd meant to take the Fat Boy out for a ride.'

'We know. We know you hate autopsies; just get on with it.' Joe's breath was still short, shallow and now his face was reddening – only I would

218

defy him when he was reaching this point. I was thinking that Connie would too, but he never got mad with her as far as I knew. Connie was loved unconditionally.

'Well ... I went into my room.'

'I'll bet it was fucking difficult to tell if anyone had broken in there,' Joe commented. He was right. Maybe if my room had been tidier I would have spotted the signs. Joe disapproved of my untidiness, which got worse if I was drinking too much.

'Okay, now is not the time,' I said. Kailash stared at me with a coldness in her eye that I had never seen before. 'I lounged on my bed, checked my phone messages and found a saved message from Connie. But I'd never heard it before.' I closed my eyes again. The world had stopped. She was gone and the moment I realized that again, there was an instantaneous change in my priorities. They both leaned towards me hopefully. 'It was lovely, it was nothing, just a chat – you know how she is. The point was that I checked my messages before I went to the autopsies: there were no new messages. Connie had phoned whilst I was with Patch, but before I got home, someone else had listened to the message and saved it.'

'Louisa,' Joe said. It was well known that she crossed all social boundaries but she didn't cross this one, I was sure of it.

'I thought so too, but then I went to have a shower.' I took a deep breath before continuing. 'When I came out, my clothes for the evening were laid on the bed: black dress, handbag, shoes, even clean stockings, knickers and bra. It

219

was appropriate for Grandad's WS function so I think he ... he ... knew where I was going. Then he phoned. His voice was pretty unremarkable. He said that it was in both our interests that Thomas Foster stayed in prison. I thought he was threatening me.'

I couldn't hold it together. My face was wet with tears, snot ran down my nose. I didn't care. Nothing mattered. I wiped the mess on the back of my sleeve but it made little difference.

'Because of the holidays, I haven't done anything to get him released anyway, so he's still in Saughton Prison. I did everything he asked, everything this man asked, even if I didn't mean to.'

'Tell me that you didn't wear the outfit he laid out for you?' Kailash had pulled away from Joe. There was a mixture of fear and confusion on her face. She lit another cigarette and stared through me, waiting for an answer. I couldn't see the significance of it but I couldn't lie. She would know.

'I'd nothing else clean to wear and it was what I'd intended to put on anyway,' I told her.

'You imbecile! He's watching you! He knows your every move. Wherever you are, he's there too. Now, because you wore the outfit he chose for you, he thinks that he owns you. You're the key in this, Brodie – Connie's just caught up in his net.'

Chapter Thirty-Nine

Kailash's home, Ravelston Dykes, Edinburgh
Thursday 27 December, 10.15 a.m.

The east wind blew his hair into his eyes, making it difficult to watch them, but not impossible; the yew-tree hedge concealing him swung back and forth, threatening to reveal his presence. *That wouldn't do at all.*

Dark grey clouds hung over the Forth road and rail bridges; the wind was pushing the rain cloud towards him. He knew it was going to chuck it down – soon. He sniffed the wind. It was cold enough for snow and the thought depressed him; snow was his enemy. He was too easy to track in the snow and shortly they would be looking for him. A shiver ran down his back. It had nothing to do with the inclement weather and everything to do with his fear of being caught; *misunderstood – all his life he had been misunderstood.*

Burying deeper into the hedge, he was grateful for the tactics learned when he passed himself off as an animal-rights activist. They had taught him well; the week's course in covert observation in an urban setting had proved particularly useful in this case. Pulling his collar up to protect himself against the cold, he lifted his shoulders to his ears and dropped them; he did this five times in an

221

effort to relieve the stiffness in his neck.

He tried not to breathe through his mouth. The cold air hurt his lungs, and his chest was weakened by asthma.

Then Brodie walked into the garden. His jaw fell open. She was looking pale and drawn but she still excited him. He hoped she would see he had done it for her. Sure, Connie was nice enough, but the real woman he wanted, sought to please, was Brodie. Shifting from foot to foot, the rotting vegetation beneath him, crisp with ice, crackled and snapped like cereal. Forcing himself to ignore the bone-chilling cold, he twisted his neck to get a better view. His body responded to Brodie and showed him just how pleased he was to see her.

Fingering the sharp, serrated blade that he always carried, he dug the point of the knife into the pad of his frozen index finger to see if he could still feel pain. A fat globule of blood appeared satisfyingly red and vibrant against the white skin. Something brushed against his skin; a black house cat with white paws. He looked at the red collar: 'Loki'.

'Loki! Here puss-puss.' The wind carried the voice of a tired householder shouting in the distance, anxious to retrieve a beloved pet before the snow started.

The Watcher had now decided it would definitely snow. He couldn't afford to risk discovery by the searching owner. He picked up the cat. Loki squirmed in The Watcher's grip, he was not a 'cat' person, whatever that meant, and they say animals know. Loki was anxious to be away, not to answer the call of her owner, just to be away

222

from him. He smiled as he took the knife to her throat. *Curiosity killed the cat.*

The warm blood steamed lightly in the air as it stained the icy ground. The Watcher was forced to shift positions to avoid contamination and, irritated, he threw the body of the lifeless animal on the ground. It bounced noisily with the force, which was always one of his problems – he did not know his own strength.

Brodie, Kailash and Glasgow Joe huddled in the garden. Everything was quiet, but for the noise of the wind clattering through the silver birch trees, and the constant inharmonic rattling from a dozen or so hollow bamboo tubes passing as wind chimes. *Feng Shui had a lot to answer for.*

He could hear nothing of their conversation. High walls and dense ground cover protected him, gave him a sense of security. He crunched his way, inch by inch, over the carpet of rotting vegetation; ever closer to Brodie.

The big bastard, Glasgow Joe, looked like shit; he must be missing the girl. The Watcher didn't think they were that close; the football games he was sure were just a ruse to get back into Brodie's life. Who knew? Not The Watcher – he might have changed his plan if he'd known. Covering his mouth, he sniggered at the thought of having got one up on Glasgow Joe.

I knew it wouldn't last, whispered The Watcher as Brodie lit up a cigarette; he inhaled deeply, trying to catch a whiff of her second-hand smoke. She was a bad girl; there was something so sensuous, so phallic about a woman smoking a cigarette. He moved his hand down to his trousers and rubbed himself; he felt his hard-on swell to life. Brodie's head was back; her eyes were closed in pleasure as she exhaled. The Watcher knew that was how it would be when they were together.

He envisioned the post-coital cigarette and his hand moved faster. He recalled how she had looked in the outfit he had chosen for her, the black dress clinging to her firm high tits. He closed his eyes and rubbed himself faster still. Now he imagined touching those fine black lace-topped stockings, as Brodie wrapped her legs around his back. His hands holding her six-inch stiletto heels, lifting her legs up, up to the ceiling, and then spreadeagling them while she shrieked; at first she would be afraid and then the pleasure could begin.

He could almost smell her auburn hair spread out on the pillow below him, her arms and legs tied tight to the bedstead. He groaned loudly, his breath frothed as it escaped through lips pursed into a smile. He stopped before it was too late and, opening his eyes, he could see again. Sweat trickled down his cheek, a stray snowflake fell and he felt himself slowly shrink in his trousers.

The second hand on his watch seemed to have stopped; time dragged by as the three of them huddled, whispering in the cold. He could see from their eyes that Brodie had told them about his little visit. He stood gnawing his bottom lip for what seemed like an hour; in truth it was a matter of minutes.

He ground his teeth together. He wanted Brodie to leave Glasgow Joe's company so he could have her to himself; he had enjoyed these past months being her shadow, her destiny. The wind gusted, black bins rolled around gardens and his cover swayed ever more violently. Each long second he stayed he risked discovery; he knew he would have to go. He couldn't wait until he saw her again. *Their next date, he'd forgotten how many they'd had; now it was time to move their relationship up to another stage.*

'Loki ... Loki!' The annoying cat owner shouted, not walking but running. *Funny how we always sense when something is wrong, seriously wrong.* The woman fell and her support hose was torn, revealing a bulging blue varicose vein; a skinned bleeding knee did not stop her. Neither did the shards of black gravel sticking to her wounds. On hands and knees she searched, scrambling in the undergrowth, impervious to the cold. *Searching for her fuckin' cat. God she's fond of it – was fond of it.*

In front of him the woman lurched and tripped up again; her neat court shoes and tight Harris Tweed skirt were not suited to this task. The Watcher almost broke cover to help her. The heel of her right shoe had broken off; she tossed the other one aside.

Her broad feet had bunions and corns and they flattened the grass beneath them. She was a heavy-set woman, a spinster by her looks. Maybe the cat was all she had. 'Loki ... Loki!' Her voice was growing hoarse now. The air became eerily still as she crawled to the correct bush. The Watcher held his breath as the elderly woman moved slowly, commando-style, through the bushes.

Her screams rent the air, frightening the ravens nesting in nearby trees. They echoed her grief as

225

they rose noisily into the air. The cat was about the size of a baby, a furry black baby. The woman cradled the dead animal to her breast, not caring that her expensive white silk blouse was now stained red with blood. It looked like her heart was bleeding; The Watcher was a sensitive enough man to concede it was.

Reluctantly, The Watcher gathered together his bits and pieces, and left the yew-tree hedge, counting the seconds until the next time. He knew there would be a next time for him and Brodie.

Chapter Forty

Kailash's home, Ravelston Dykes, Edinburgh
Thursday 27 December, 11.45 a.m.

If Connie wasn't dead she would be alone, upset, and praying to be found. And I wasn't doing anything to find her. Kailash had already established that DI Smith's track record was abysmal: fifteen cases and not one child found alive. We couldn't leave this to the police – but I didn't know where to start. So I was staring out of an upstairs window at morbid sightseers coming to lay floral tributes and tacky teddies at Kailash's front gate. I wanted to open the window and throw cold water on them, but Kailash had warned Joe to keep me under a tight rein. She had misplaced one daughter; she wasn't

226

going to allow it to happen again any time soon.

Connie went to an exclusive private girls' school in the area. Despite it being holiday time, her classmates started arriving to leave her flowers. There was a life-sized photograph of Connie in her football kit. A message was painted on it saying, *Connie – we love you now and forever.* Beneath the poster, the pile of condolences was already gathering in size.

Malcolm came out; he wanted to beg them to go away but he was too polite. Derek held his arm as Malcolm defiantly pinned a missing poster to the tree as if she were a lost cat. A photograph of a smiling Connie taken on her thirteenth birthday beamed out.

The truth was so simple. Connie was gone because I thought I could handle things. I wasn't much of a sister. Glasgow Joe put his arm round my waist and pulled me close. I didn't object for a moment – I needed the comfort.

'Look at that brave old bugger,' Joe nodded at Malcolm who was pushing his way through the media snake pit. Cameras stalked him as he tottered along the road putting up posters on every tree. Reporters had told him that if it was on television the kidnapper might see the pain Malcolm was in, feel ashamed, and let her go. But all Malcolm could think about was Connie's pain.

'I've got to go.' I kissed Joe on the cheek and took the stairs two at a time, not stopping to put my coat on. The snow was dusting the air; too light to be taken seriously. As I ran out of the front door, I kept my head down, looking neither to my right nor left. Pushing through the reporters, I ignored the flashbulbs and cameras. I had one aim in mind, but Malcolm was moving remarkably fast for an old man in carpet slippers who had enough tranquilizers in his system to slay an elephant. Out of breath, I finally reached them. Derek, his long-term partner, was still holding on to Malcolm's right elbow. My eyes locked with Derek's and in a few long, wordless seconds, hatchets were buried, love and sympathy exchanged. He recognized a need in me to do something. He stepped aside and I took Malcolm's elbow. We marched up the streets and avenues with our posters. Derek walked a pace behind, carrying tacks and a hammer, followed by the press.

Malcolm held the poster to his heart. He said in a whisper: 'I didn't tuck her in.' As we walked back home, I heard the children singing; the strains of 'Abide With Me' carried on the wind.

'Usually, I love that hymn – they played it at Mother Teresa's funeral – but I wish they'd shut the fuck up,' Derek said, opening a fresh packet of hankies and handing one to Malcolm. His tears had disintegrated the others.

'Malcolm!' The girls from Connie's class all rushed towards him. He put his arms out, glad to be needed. Patting their heads he whispered: 'It's going to be all right. She's still alive. I know my Connie, I've had a bond with her since the day she was born. I would know if something really bad had happened. But say your prayers and I promise next Thursday you'll all be round for chocolate brownies as usual.'

'Malcolm.' One of the mothers was in tears as she reached out to touch him. 'We're thinking of you ... all.'

'Thank you. Connie needs all the prayers she can get at the moment.' The woman's hand patted his back in a gesture of comfort as he passed. I thought how strange we were, an odd family. I wouldn't have blamed the neighbours for fearing that Kailash's presence would bring the price of property down, yet Malcolm and Connie were loved in the community. But in the midst of this terror, they showed how much Kailash was included.

Kailash was upstairs sleeping, having surrendered to exhaustion. Glasgow Joe felt it was safe to come out and comfort the girls from the football team. Most of them lived in Leith and their mothers lived off less than a nanny was paid in Ravelston Dykes. He wandered amongst them with a bag of jam-filled doughnuts; Lavender and Eddie had stopped off for provisions on the way down from Gleneagles that morning. Everybody felt they needed to do something. The girls clamoured around Joe, and I didn't blame them. His sheer physical presence made everything around him seem that bit safer. He looked uncomfortable as they all tried to hug him, but I could see that they needed some sort of reassurance. Eddie was vomiting in the toilet but Lavender assured us that as soon as he had finished he would be out to see the team. He had been in there for ten minutes and we could all hear him crying. He tried to save us from his grief but failed to notice that the window in the downstairs lavatory was open.

Connie's abduction was growing news. TV

crews, reporters from red-tops and broadsheets made themselves at home on the grass verge outside Four Winds. They were reclining on shooting sticks and garden chairs, drinking instant coffee out of flasks. Bitching about the weather, I could hear them freely offering their professional opinion.

'Who's that?' asked a reporter from one of the big national dailies, pointing at Joe.

'Him?' Another stranger pointed at Joe.

'Yeah, him – the big guy fondling all the kids.' The reporter's voice was disturbing.

'He's the manager of Connie's football team.'

'Has he been checked out?' I heard the first guy asking. 'I'd be terrified to touch kids like that. I was in Soham – that Ian Huntley was so fucking helpful, always hanging around us, trying to ingratiate himself. Were you there?' The reporter stopped to pick his nose and consider the scene.

'Nope. I usually do politics,' replied the second guy. 'But it's Christmas and I'm on call, so... Huntley was unusual though. Funny how it always used to be poor kids that got abducted. Nowadays, it's rich kids ... like Connie.'

Examining the snot on the end of his index finger, the seasoned crime hack wiped it down his trouser leg. 'It'll be someone she knows, always is. Her mother's a whore.' He glanced at the house. 'She must be good – she's obviously paid well; nice job if you can get it. They're dodgy, definitely dodgy.' They all nodded their heads in agreement. Engrossed in their gossip, they didn't see him coming and I wasn't going to warn the bastards. Glasgow Joe pushed his way through like a steam train heading for a collision. He grabbed them and they started to argue, shouting for help. DI Bancho sent the constable at the front door inside for a cup of tea, then turned and followed him into the house, as Joe banged their heads together. His large hands grabbed the scruffs by the collar. He dragged them to the road. Booting them up the arse, they fell into the gutter, cameras still clicking.

'Fuck off – if your papers want the story, they'll have to send someone else. If I catch any of you bastards up here again, I'll give you something to worry about. Now, piss off!' Glasgow Joe straightened himself up. The reporters did not look back. I knew Joe had played right into their hands. His photograph would be on the front page alongside Connie's. So what, it felt good to see him smack those ghouls who wouldn't leave us alone.'

'Connie's kidnap is news ... they think she belongs to them,' I said, as a CNN van drove up the road. 'We've got to find her, Joe.'

Time wasn't on our side.

Chapter Forty-One

Cumberland Street, Edinburgh
Thursday 27 December, 8.23 p.m.

'Brodie! Did you get my earlier messages? For fuck's sake, pick up ... I'm dying here, it's on the news. They keep showing her face.' Moses broke down and I listened to his sobbing on the message. 'Kailash has ordered me to find her ... but I don't know where to start ... I've beaten up three known paedophiles but they don't know anything about her.' He sniffed loudly. 'Please, for Christ's sake, let me come to you ... let's see what we can do.'

All afternoon Joe and I had searched the dives of Leith looking for any signs of the girl who had seen the Ripper's face, the one who'd escaped. But it appeared she was terrified and had disappeared into the underbelly of society. Everyone claimed to have heard of her but no one knew her name, what she looked like, or where she worked. I was starting to despair that she was an urban myth.

The answering machine clicked off. Moses left the message hours ago. I had retired to my room, to think, to see if I could locate or feel Connie's presence. My bedroom was silent. I lay on the bed in the darkness and listened to nothing. It wasn't constructive to mentally replay Connie's last message, which was burned into my brain. I had erased it at the time, taking her voice for granted. The Ripper's voice slithered through my mind, haunting me. I did replay our conversation to understand him better, but all I understood was – I was to blame. I had underestimated him. And now he had shown me what he could do to me.

Who could hate me so much that he would want to take my little sister? I searched my memory banks. Was it someone I'd represented? Someone who had seen me on TV? Someone I'd hurt in some way?

I turned over and groaned. My body ached, my head was pounding, and bile from a nervous gut kept coming back – all the symptoms of a hangover and I swear I hadn't touched a drop.

I rolled to the edge of the bed, flung my legs over and fell out. I hit the wooden floor hard. Staggering to a sitting position, I pulled on the nearest pair of jeans. They smelt of smoke; the hem was frayed and encrusted with mud. I gave up looking for a clean pair of socks; I didn't even bother to sniff the ones I was shoving my feet into. If I'd stayed at Kailash's house, I might have made an effort to keep myself together for her sake, but we had decided that Connie's abduction was a ransom case. Convincing ourselves that she didn't fit the Ripper's profile didn't take very long. In which case, it was agreed that we'd split up; I came back to Cumberland Street to wait for the ransom call. The Ripper had contacted me before and he might do so again, looking for money. Together we all had the capital to pay a substantial amount.

A wave of nausea hit me as I stood up. I had to go out there and face them. Lavender, Glasgow Joe and Louisa were waiting in the kitchen whilst Grandad, Eddie and Jack were staying with Kailash. Jack was fielding any press questions, acting as the family spokesman and trying to head off any intrusion into Kailash's business affairs. DI Smith was staying with Kailash, and Bancho was moving between both houses.

I heard Connie's voice scream at me as I opened the door from my room. The house smelled of freshly brewed coffee; a quick glance in the kitchen showed it was empty. I wandered down into the drawing room; the whole crew were there, sitting in semi-darkness – watching

233

Connie play her last game on the TV. The rerun of her first goal was on. I couldn't help the smile that cracked my cheeks as she did a victory slide along the turf, strip over her head, showing the world a pink thermal vest that Malcolm had insisted she wore.

Moses was sitting on the settee and he noticed me first – I suspect he had been waiting for me to emerge from my self-imposed exile and had been there shortly after his emotional phone message. Placing his hand on the back of the settee he vaulted over it, landing at my feet.

'Aw doll, what are we going to do?' His tears had started before he even hit the floor. Sweeping me up into his arms he cried into my neck. Moses and Kailash had a special closeness. Both had been abused by my father. And he'd known Connie long before I knew of her existence.

'We're going to find her, Moses; that's what she wants.' I gripped his hair and pulled his face round so that I could see into his eyes. I was speaking to myself as much as to him – which was just as well because he didn't appear to have heard a word. He pointed to the television. 'She wanted me to come for Christmas – you all went; I said I was too busy. Too busy at fucking Susie Wong's – what good is it now?' He threw his hands in the air, railing at the futility of it all. I suddenly remembered that I was angry with him for having sold the drugs to my client.

'You know that I'm acting for Thomas Foster?'

'Aye, the Ripper.' Moses' eyes glazed over. Nothing mattered to him except Connie. My dilemma with Foster wouldn't even register.

234

'The girl he was with died of a heart attack caused by drugs – he says he bought them from you.' I watched his face. Not a flicker. He'd been accused of worse.

'I don't sell drugs, doll, and I certainly don't force anyone to take them. He shrugged his shoulders; his eyes were fixed over my shoulder, watching Connie running rings around the Penicuik girls. To get anywhere, I'd have to humour him.

'If she'd been a boy, a scout would have signed her.' Moses inhaled and exhaled deeply. 'That's one fucking great dummy she's just done – look, she left the defender standing. What a girl.' Connie beamed out at us, a living, breathing spirit, proud of her talent. Waiting on the applause, she ran to the home support. I saw us huddled together, beaming back at her.

'Obviously, you're not a drug pusher, Moses,' I wheedled. 'You're a businessman, right? But maybe Blind Bruce or the new guy might remember them?'

'Bruce is too fond of sampling the product – you can't rely on him for anything.' Being the most dispensable member, Moses sanctioned the use of Bruce in drugs testing. Whenever a new batch was made, Bruce tried it. This human testing was supposed to make it safe for the streets; in fact, Moses, in his new role as businessman, even referred to it as his unique selling point. So if it was safe, how could it have killed Katya Waleski? Unless it was a batch Bruce did not test, or, more likely, Bruce had developed an unnaturally high tolerance level.

'You can speak to Blind Bruce if you like, but

235

that daft bastard is not giving evidence. No way. Cal's not in Edinburgh at the minute – he's gone tae his mother's for Christmas.'

'So you'll make sure I can speak to Bruce?'

'Is that no' just what I said?' Moses was back staring at the TV screen. I followed his eyes. I sat down next to Lavender; she squeezed my hand, never taking her eyes from the screen.

'I hope he's got other talents – he's a shite cameraman.' Onscreen, Eddie was playing with his new no-brainer camcorder, taking in views of Arthur's Seat or, when he got particularly excited, dropping the lens; all you saw were shoes jumping up and down with lots of noise off camera.

On the flat-screen TV, Connie lay stock-still; her face contorted with pain, holding her breath so she wouldn't cry. Unusually, her face was smeared with mud. Her ponytail, which Malcolm had dressed with the ridiculous neon pink fabric rose, lay across her cheek. The images came and went, herky-jerky, as Eddie ran across the field to her. We saw the sky, pedestrians, Arthur's Seat, and the whole panoply of the Meadows. What the hell was Eddie doing with the camcorder? He certainly hadn't found a new calling. Connie had been hacked by a defender and was lying injured. We all froze, just staring at the screen. Malcolm ran on and soothed her, spraying instant freeze on her ankle, then helped her to her feet. She waved to Kailash to show she was okay – if only this were so easy.

'Press hold! Rewind it!' I said suddenly.

Lavender took charge. 'Eddie! Pause it!'

The picture was frozen on the changing rooms.

'I can see something. Look at the shadow behind the window – it looks like someone's in there,' I said.

'It could be one of the girls – maybe she went to the toilet in the middle of the game?' Lavender said.

'At this point in the game, all the players were on the pitch. That's a stranger in the toilets,' said Joe.

'It needn't be anything suspicious – there are no toilets up at that end of the Meadows. I know myself that if I was desperate for a pee, I'd nip in.' Lavender didn't want me to build up my hopes, but Joe was on my tag team.

'You might want to spend a penny there, but you couldn't. I lock the changing rooms,' he said. The remote was now in his hands.

'Fast forward it to the end of the game, Joe,' I said.

'What have you seen?' he asked.

I didn't answer him immediately; I wasn't sure – it was just a vague, unsettling feeling. 'Stop! There – look!' I pressed my finger against the flat screen. 'Is there any way anyone can make this image bigger?'

Lavender pressed the zoom button on the camcorder.

'Stop! Pause it!'

We all stared at the screen – at the man leaving the girls' changing rooms.

'What the hell was a priest doing there?' I asked.

Chapter Forty-Two

Cumberland Street, Edinburgh
Friday 28 December, 3.15 a.m.

I didn't know which was worse – waiting for the phone to ring or it actually ringing.

I'd been expecting his call. I lay fully dressed underneath the duvet, just waiting. We'd split up into teams. Lavender and Jack had gone to the office to enhance the image of the priest; Joe and Moses had just returned from another fruitless trip to the brothels and pubs to hunt down the only person who could identify the Ripper. And I waited by the phone. A sense of helplessness and the sound of my racing heart must have lulled me into a dreamless sleep sometime after midnight. Then it came, the jolting ring, jarring me to the bone, shocking me back into a living nightmare.

Desperation magnifies your senses. He was coming, and there was nothing I could do about it. I could feel him creep around inside my head, there was no escape; my heart knew that. He was inside me, a parasite, one of those worms that can only live inside a human eye. But as sure as a drumbeat he was coming, bringing more evil to my doorstep.

Don't answer it.

I pulled the duvet over my head but the phone rang again. God help me, I whispered, as I picked up the phone.

His breathing was hard, hot and heavy – oppressive. The panting echoed off the corners of the room, darkness amplifying the rasping quality of the sound, jangling my nerves. Panic set in. I knocked a glass of water over. It smashed on the wooden floorboards as I struggled to find the lamp. He held his breath, listening to my terror. I fought to regain my composure.

He invaded my darkness and pinpricks of sweat broke out on my skin as the wave of nausea swelled. I did not cry out. Like a good girl I listened. I knew how he could punish me. I held my breath, afraid to inflame the monster, but he said nothing. I could sense him enjoying my fear. For Connie's sake – get a fucking grip, I told myself. For once, heeding my conscience, I sat bolt upright in bed, fumbling again for the bedside light. This time I found it and my eyes struggled to adjust.

'You'll suffer.'

He sounded different – disguised.

This time he was whispering. It was difficult to make out whether it was even a man or a woman; there were no recognizable characteristics. Bancho was monitoring my calls; knowing that he was listening gave me strength.

'What the hell are you talking about?' Surprisingly, I sounded much stronger than I felt. 'Why do you want me to suffer?' I demanded.

'You're going to suffer.' The Ripper inhaled deeply, as if I exhausted him, and then he gently put the receiver down. I held the phone in my hand and stared at it. I wanted him back – he was my only link to Connie.

Suffer? Suffer for what, for God's sake?

When the shit hits the fan, I feel an overwhelming urge to laugh. There's nothing I can do to stop it. I've tried. That was how they found me, rolling around in bed laughing hysterically. I saw Bancho and Joe wedge in the doorway, both trying to be heroes, to save the day. Well, it was too bloody late for that. I stopped laughing.

'We're trying to trace the call, but...' Bancho's eyes were hooded with concern at my apparent hysteria. Leaning across the bed I dialled 1471 and threw the phone at him – just in case. They watched me in disbelief, probably thinking I must have completely lost it if I thought things were that simple. 'For Christ's sake, Brodie,' said Bancho, 'let me do my job. If he was stupid enough to call from a non-payphone, do you really think he'd have left his number? Do you think he's a fucking amateur?' said Bancho. An automated voice told him that the caller rang at three nineteen – and then gave Bancho the number. His eyes almost popped as he got straight on to Fettes police HQ asking them to trace the number. 'Why are you calling headquarters?' Joe asked. 'Why not just ring back and tell the bastard we're coming for him?'

'Because I don't want him to know that we know and I need backup. DI Smith needs to be told. Connie's abduction is her case,' said Bancho. 'And, like her...' he nodded in my direction, 'shut up and let me do my job.'

'Come on, Bancho,' I said. 'He's not stupid. If he's left the number, it's on purpose.'

'Do you want a cup of tea?' Joe asked, as if that

240

would somehow make this all right. We were at an impasse until the information on the caller came through. I didn't feel like joining the others in the kitchen. Perhaps if I just lay here maybe I would hear Connie's voice again.

Switching the light off, Joe told me to get some sleep. I lay shaking and chilled; maybe the tea would have done me good after all. Recognizing that I was in a state of shock, I clasped my knees, trying to ward off the cold feeling stealing into my bones. It was hard to breathe; the air was stale and hot under the covers.

I tried to put it all out of my mind, to relax, but no sooner had I started the process than Joe came rushing in.

'Fettes have just called with the details of that number, Brodie – can you fucking believe it? It came from your Grandad's house!'

Chapter Forty-Three

Cumberland Street, Edinburgh
Friday 28 December, 4.05 a.m.

A watchful silence surrounded me as Bancho, Joe and the others tiptoed around, whispering conspiratorially, making plans, treating me as if I'd already suffered a death. When they asked how I was feeling, I said: 'Do you think the Ripper wants to be caught? Sometimes they do, you know. Either he wants to be caught or he thinks

I'm a fuckwit. I wouldn't argue the toss with him,' I said, completely spaced out with guilt.

They murmured niceties, seeking to assure me that I wasn't guilty, that it was lack of sleep making me shoulder blame for something I wasn't responsible for. They didn't use the word paranoid.

Naturally, the first thing I wanted to do was speak to Grandad to confirm that he wasn't harmed, but his phone wasn't being picked up. Bancho had told me not to do it, but he couldn't stop me trying. It didn't matter. There was no one there. Or no one answering. Or no one able to answer. Glasgow Joe called the service provider. They listened in on the line but there was nothing wrong – it was just off the hook. In spite of this information, I ground my teeth and kept trying. Maybe he was en route to Kailash. I didn't really believe that; just as quickly as I was putting a family together, one by one I was losing them again.

I wanted to know what was going on. Bancho had already radioed and asked for backup; he was heading for the door of the flat with Joe when I stopped him. 'There's no way you're leaving here without me,' I told him. 'It's my family – you don't have the right to stop me.'

'It's precisely because its your family that I don't want you there,' said Bancho, softly. His face was right next to mine. He smelled of stale smoke and anchovy pizza; he wore a stubble that was twelve hours past designer and a shirt that looked as if he'd slept in it. Still, I wasn't picky. If I had to hold on to his ankle there was no way he was leaving without dragging me along. He must have sensed my resolve and decided that, after less than four hours' sleep, he didn't have the strength to fight me off. Something shifted in his eyes. Pity? I didn't care what his emotion was as long as he took me to Grandad's side.

I tried to get in the front seat, but Bancho pushed me into the back and Joe piled in beside me. Bancho's car would be useful I guessed, in case we needed to run any red lights. The streets were deserted, the black-topped roads icy, and the cobbles treacherous. I prayed the constable in the front had been through his advanced driving course: even that was no guarantee we would get there safely. Joe's knuckles were white. We were both piss-poor passengers.

Driving up the hill to Princes Street, the same old tinsel-covered Christmas trees were displayed in windows, and fairy lights flashed down on me mockingly – this was the holiday period. Life went on, but I wanted it to stop. In George Street they were gearing up for the big Hogmanay street party and I could see drunken stragglers leaving Susie Wong's. Clenching my fist, I gestured helplessly and stared down at my shoes – I was wearing the same trainers that Connie had dropped the hair dye on.

The driver tried to make small talk, but we'd retired into stubborn silence, fighting the worst-case scenarios in our minds. The Ripper had a talent for surprise. Why did he abduct Connie? Why had he phoned me from Grandad's phone? 'Why' questions were on an endless loop. Grandad and Connie were related to me, ergo I was to blame. I heard the rasping whisper, 'I'll make you suffer.' Steeling myself, I lifted my chin and put

243

my shoulders back; pumping up ready for a fight – for my family's sake I had to be fit for the ring.

Bancho's driver sped down Hanover Street, flying straight through the lights, no siren on. Princes Street was still lit up like Blackpool illuminations, the Ferris Wheel glowed in the dark and I heard Connie's belly laugh again. Speeding up the Mound, we turned right past the seventy-foot Christmas tree that the residents of Norway give to Edinburgh every year. We screeched to a halt outside Ramsay Gardens – two other squad cars blocked the street and DI Bancho spoke into the radio, co-coordinating their assault. Wariness prevailed. My grandfather was a very important man, the police didn't have a search warrant, and there had been no threat to his life. It was a dangerous move for DI Bancho's career to kick in Lord MacGregor's door as if he was on a drug raid.

Sitting helplessly in the back I had to wait for Bancho to let me out. Suddenly, it hit me: I was scared shitless. What would I find? I didn't know. All I did know was I had to be the first one in, the first one to find Grandad.

DI Bancho climbed the outside staircase, avoiding the carefully potted containers filled with winter-flowering primula. Caution slowed him sufficiently for me to catch up and I pulled him by the shoulder and turned him round. Using crude sign language I motioned that this was up to me. Glasgow Joe locked eyes with Bancho; he had my back. We knew the risks.

I rang the bell.

No answer. Keeping my finger on it, I kicked the door in frustration. Soundlessly, a meaty hand

244

pushed me aside. Leaning on the balcony railing, Joe kicked the door. Nothing for him either. Tilting out precariously over the railing to gain more leverage, he wobbled. Holding on to the railing tighter, he used his foot on the Yale lock and the door burst open as if it was made of cheap cardboard. Inhaling as if going into a blazing fire, I stepped into the darkness.

The narrow hallway was tastefully decorated with pen and ink sketches of old Edinburgh, all hung in a row and framed in black. A small Waterford crystal chandelier hung at the far end. I made no sound. Creeping along in the dark until I got to Grandad's bedroom, I knew that someone was there. Joe pushed me behind him and gingerly opened the door. A figure lay slumped on the bed. Joe switched the light on. I heard a sigh of relief coming. from Joe. 'It's all right, Brodie ... your grandpa is sleeping like a log.'

'Hey, ya daft old bugger!' said Joe to the sleeping form. Grandad didn't stir. 'Come on now. You'd better put your teeth in – you've got company.'

Grandad was slow to rouse, but he was coming round. I wandered over to the bed. I didn't fall over any piles of discarded clothing. His suit was hung on a trouser press, and handmade brogues, shiny to within an inch of their lives, were in shoetrees. It was the first time I'd ever been in Grandad's bedroom. I took the opportunity to nose around; it smelt a bit of old man with a vague bouquet of expensive cologne – not enough of it. On the walnut bedside table was a brown tablet bottle: Ambien 200 mg prescribed for Jack Deans. Well, that bloody explained it.

Grandad didn't take tablets as a rule and these sleeping tablets were hard stuff. No wonder the poor old bugger was out cold. I gave the bottle to Joe. Shaking his head and swearing, he helped Grandad to a sitting position.

'That fucker Deans is an idiot – he could have killed him.' Half turning to me, Joe spoke again. 'There's a word for people like him.'

'Pusher?' I added helpfully.

'No, junkie. Have you never noticed he can give you a pill to pop for any occasion? He's as bad as bloody Moses. The old boy could sell these tablets for a pound a go.'

'He could if he could get out of his bed.'

Bancho and the boys were staying respectfully in the hallway. 'Bancho! The old boy's fine!' Joe shouted.

'I'll have less of the "old boy" thank you very much.' Grandad had slipped in his teeth before he spoke.

The lights went on in the hallway.

Detective Inspector Smith shouted: 'I think you'd better come and see this!'

Screaming echoed round the flat. It took me a few moments to realize I was the screamer. Bloody footprints made by a trainer marked the carpet. There was one set into the drawing room, another leading back out to the front door – and freedom. DI Bancho was trying to protect the crime scene but, in the confusion, I wandered across the bloody path blindly.

Standing in the doorway, apart from the footprints, everything seemed normal, except for a nagging raspy whisper in my head. It was as if the

Ripper was talking to me. *Pay attention – or you'll suffer even more.* Adrenalin pumped through my veins, improving my senses; breathing in through my nose I fancied I could smell him and he smelled – familiar. I knew him, just as he knew me; all I had to do was remember.

You haven't gone to all this trouble just to make a mess on the shag pile – have you?

I heard his laugh and oddly, I thought of it as educated. Stepping into his shoes I took an inventory. Oxblood Chesterfield settee – where it should be. Winged armchair exactly in the place I had last seen it– I hadn't sat on it for it was Grandad's favoured chair. My graduation photograph, in pride of place on the Chippendale table. I was grateful the Ripper had not stood on the seventeenth-century Aubusson rug; obviously he had enough taste to know it was irreplaceable. *How considerate!*

Screwing up my eyes, I saw what was bothering me – the telescope used to spy on the pedestrians in Princes Street. It was fixed into position rather than free on its swivel as usual. I looked through it like it was an old fairground attraction, What the Butler Saw. I hope for his sake he did not see what I saw.

Connie.

I don't know whether I screamed again before I fainted.

Chapter Forty-Four

Edinburgh Castle
Friday 28 December, 5.15 a.m.

The gatehouse entrance to the castle was floodlit and covered in snow. The snow was stained like a frozen red waterfall; there was so much blood. I didn't think one little body could hold so much fluid. The telescope had been well positioned so that I could see a mutilated young girl.

I had to hold Connie.

As I came to, all I could see were anxious faces crowding me. Joe's eyes streamed; his worst fears had come to pass. He crushed me to his heart, more for his sake than mine. I couldn't breathe. My world had changed in an instant. For Connie's sake I had to be a survivor. I couldn't bear the thought of her body lying in the snow, cold and alone for one second more than she needed to be.

Fighting Glasgow Joe off was easy; his heart had been taken. Grandad didn't stop to collect his coat or dressing gown. He held my hand and walked up Castle Hill in his pyjamas and I'm sure that none of us could bear to think of Lavender's wedding. I heard Connie sing clear and true in my head, her version of the Lewis wedding song. Somehow, together, we stumbled through the gatehouse and on up through the portcullis.

Detective Inspector Smith, the detective in

charge of the abduction, was somewhere close by. I wasn't conscious of her but she must have smoothed our passage. Joe told me that Bancho had already received a tip-off by the time we'd roused Grandad – certainly, the castle had been cordoned off as a crime scene although no one tried to bar our way. DI Smith led the way; we pushed past the yellow tape. Clearly, no one thought that we were mere onlookers. Grief had already etched its signature on our faces. Grandad seemed to have lost inches. He slumped beside me sunken in pain; the only reason he could keep going was that he wouldn't let me face this alone. Although the Ripper had not stabbed Grandad tonight, I was sure this would kill him. It was just another score I had to settle with the bastard.

Uniformed officers crawled over the castle like termites. We walked up the cobbled road, past substantial black signposts with gold lettering directing us to less gory locations – we ignored them. A young Lothian and Borders officer, who looked all of seventeen, stood guard anxiously at the makeshift barricade, clearly conscious of the fact that his every move was being recorded and then analysed live on news channels. DI Smith pushed us past the youngster, and I was aware I was making headlines. At this very second probably, across the bottom of TV screens, would be running a headline – *Family visit last resting place of Connie Coutts in grim attempt to identify body parts.*

Inside a makeshift white tent, crime-scene technicians swarmed, their latex-gloved fingers probing every square inch of cobbled stone, gathering and preserving forensic samples. Everything and anything was now considered evidence – I watched as a discarded chewing-gum wrapper, probably left by a thoughtless tourist, was now sealed and sent to a crime lab. Flashes lit the pre-dawn sky as crime-scene photographers took pictures from every conceivable angle. Fingerprint powder covered any surface on which the Ripper might have left a print, and some where he could not. The cannons had not seen as much action since the seventeenth century.

I knew that the human body contained about ten pints of blood. I just didn't know that it could spread so far. We encountered the red snow long before we could see the body. A shiver ran through me, though it had nothing to do with the cold. This place was a blood bath.

DI Bancho put his arm in front of me, barring the way. He looked me in the eye and said: 'Do you think you can handle it?' I tried to push past him without answering; he was stronger than he looked. 'Think about it carefully, Brodie – this isn't a stranger…' His voice trailed off.

'Let her pass, Duncan. If I can bear it, she can bear it – we owe it to Connie.' Glasgow Joe's voice sounded from over my shoulder. I looked to my right and he was there; he seemed smaller too. I was scared. I was really scared, but I had to go on. Walking between Joe and Grandad, gripping their hands, I got my first sight of the body. I was still too far away to do more than note the position. Her naked corpse was grotesquely draped over a cannon; her back lay along the barrel of the mas-sive gun with arms falling limply to the side and legs spreadeagled. I was close enough to see that her feet had been hacked off. She was tied by her ankles and wrists to the cannon so that there was no danger of her falling off. Focusing on her limbs, I could tell she had been bound post mortem – there were no purple bruises on her skin.

I wanted to run to her, to take her in my arms, give her some dignity, but I couldn't interfere with the crime scene; contamination might mean a court case would fall because of lack of evidence. My head knew this, but all my practice at murder scenes involving strangers could never prepare me for this.

Inching forward, I strained my neck to see. I'm sure Joe's eyes were closed because it felt as if I was leading a blind man. There was something wrong. Deviating from his m.o., the Ripper had shorn her hair, her beautiful hair. A picture of Malcolm brushing and de-tugging her ponytail before catching it up in that bloody silly neon rose flashed before my eyes. A whimper caught in my throat and I ran to her.

It was hard to see in the darkness. As I drew closer, I was drawn to the thorn bush tied to her hand; the Ripper was developing, telling us a story ... it was changing. The body had been hit with a blunt instrument; battered like a veal escalope. Perhaps Patch had been successful with his pig experiments and would be able to tell us definitively which blunt instrument had bludgeoned her to death.

I'd never known such grief, but I couldn't look away. Not only had the Ripper shorn her hair but, as the first light of dawn cracked over the castle, I saw what had been concerning me about the thorn bush.

Eyes.

Her eyes hung on branches of thorns in a grotesque parody of a Christmas tree bauble.

Duncan Bancho looked over my shoulder.

I turned to face him.

Reaching between his legs, I grabbed his balls and squeezed until my fingers hurt.

'You bastard,' I whispered, 'you knew it wasn't Connie, but you had to prolong it, didn't you?' I twisted his balls once more. 'Maybe you'll think twice about fucking with my head again, Bancho, or I'll rip those off next time.' I let go. Walking away, clenching and unclenching my fingers, I tried to bring the circulation back. In other circumstances, what I had done would have felt good. I was honest enough to concede maybe I was my mother's daughter after all, but in the circumstances I wouldn't break out the champagne just yet – guilt ate at my stomach. When I looked at that poor dead girl, all I felt was relief: relief that we still had some hope ... and that's when I received the text.

It shd hve bn u

Chapter Forty-Five

Castle Hill, Edinburgh
Friday 28 December, 7.35 a.m.

'Brodie!' came the voice behind me.

I kept on walking. If I never saw that man again it would be too soon.

'Brodie...! We need to talk.'

Bancho lurched after me, clearly in pain. I sighed in resignation as I motioned to Joe that he and Grandad, who was still in shock, should go on ahead. I needed to speak to Bancho on my own.

Now that the ball-clenching moment had passed, I regretted my action. It was violent, childish and criminal. I could still be charged with police assault, although I knew that there was no way Bancho's pride would allow him to admit what I'd done. All I could say in mitigation was that I'd been under a great deal of strain.

Glasgow Joe didn't argue with me. We were both worried about Grandad's health. Someone needed to walk him back to Ramsay Gardens and make sure that he got into warm clothes. I slowed up and watched them walk down past the Whisky Centre. I stood motionless until they had disappeared around the corner.

Bancho grabbed me by the arm, not in an arresting sort of way; it was more that he didn't want me to run off. I looked bad but he was worse and I couldn't meet his eye. Small specks of yellow vomit from when the pain had been too much lined his lips. I did that to him and I didn't feel proud. Joe was right – he was doing his best.

'I'm sorry, Duncan – it was unforgivable for me to do that ... even to a low-life bastard like you. All I can say is that you bring out the worst in me.'

'Are you serious...? I'd rather think you had a bad case of PMT.' He shook his head: 'What kind of animal do you think I am? I didn't know the girl wasn't Connie.'

Should I believe him? Bancho held out his hand for me to shake.

I stared at it.

'I care about the victims... I'm not the one who's trying to get their killer off.'

He stuck his hand out again.

'We both know we're never going to be bosom buddies, or even polite acquaintances, Brodie, but at least we can try not to hurt each other physically or mentally... Anyone who would mislead you like that is an animal, and that's not me.'

He squirmed. Obviously his balls still hurt. I took his hand, hoping that it hadn't been anywhere on a soothing mission.

'I have it from a reliable source that people pay good money to have their testicles enlarged.'

Grabbing a non-existent crease in his trousers, Bancho adjusted himself. 'Believe me when I say, I'm not one of those people. The most you'll get out of me is a cup of coffee – and you're bloody lucky to be getting that.'

He tried to force a smile and failed.

'We need to work together, Brodie ... the most

important thing is that we end this.'

'Thomas Foster is in jail. The case is closed – in your opinion.'

'Yes well ... the case has just taken a new twist. Look up at the castle ... the bloody snow proves that. Come back with me and look at the evidence again ... you know Thomas Foster better than me.'

'Yes, I do ... and he's innocent... He's still in jail, for God's sake.'

We drove in silence to the coffee box at the Meadows; my stomach growled and I became conscious that the last time I could remember eating was Christmas Day. I knew that I must have nibbled something since then, but I couldn't get my memory to work properly. The light was struggling. Only just past the winter solstice, the sun was far away in the southern hemisphere – it felt like it.

Driving to St Leonards was a long journey. Bancho had admonished me not to eat in his car and, in spite of the earlier burying of the hatchet, I was sure he was saying it just to be mean. I'd been in his office and this guy was no clean freak; if anything he was a bigger slob than me.

I didn't eat anyway. How could I? Connie was still missing and now another dead girl had turned up – was she next?

Chapter Forty-Six

St Leonards Police Station, Edinburgh
Friday 28 December, 8.10 a.m.

A grey dawn was breaking over the Salisbury Crags. Arthur's Seat looked bleak, and ancient. In the seventeeth century, men thought the earth was made 6,000 years before. After examining the crags, they realized that the earth could be as much as a million years old. I wondered if Bancho would have such an epiphany – I wasn't holding out too much hope.

I wanted to know what progress Lothian and Borders police had made. DI Bancho led me into a quiet station and, unusually, Desk Sergeant Munro was not on duty.

It was still the season of goodwill and the St Leonards Christmas tree perfectly illustrated the fact that police stations simply don't do festive gaiety with any aplomb. Six feet of scanty green tinsel branches, it had been bought years before and badly stored. Cheap supermarket baubles hung from its limbs, while the tree itself was contained in a cardboard box covered with wrapping paper. In silence, we headed down into the bowels of the station, along a semi-dark corridor. The station operated a green policy – lights only came on when a room was in use. It was disconcerting to walk into the black room knowing what its walls

256

depicted. There was a certain amount of theatre as the lights came on; the once pretty faces in Bancho's chilling beauty pageant stared out at me.

Katya Waleski had been added.

'You'll need to take her down.' I tapped the picture with my finger, noting how dirty my nail was.

'Why?'

'Oh come on! You were at the fucking autopsy – she died of natural causes.'

'A girl of Katya Waleski's age does not just die of a heart attack.' His eyes narrowed to slits as he held my eyes.

'Granted, but it was drug-induced heart failure. You can't pin it on Thomas Foster – do you have anything personal against him?'

'Yes. He's a murdering little bastard who thinks he can get away with anything. And when the results come back from the crime lab, I'll have all the evidence I need.'

'Hello, Bancho? Reality check here. Thomas Foster is in Saughton – although he shouldn't be. I'm going to petition the court... Crown Office will have drop the case.'

'He's also charged with breach of the peace.'

'You know that's not going to keep him locked up. Anything constitutes a breach of the peace. If you so much as look at me the wrong way, I'll say it's a breach of the peace. Face facts, Bancho: Thomas Foster will be released. He's not the Ripper.'

'I *know* that he is. What about the theory that there's two of them? This new killing – is it a copycat or are there two?'

'Bancho, you saw yourself that the m.o. keeps changing.'

The Ripper's modus operandi had altered but there were elements that remained constant, the peculiar knife marks in particular and the ripping out of the tongue.

He stared at the dead girls and I followed his eyes to a new picture. Connie. He dropped his head to his hands and started rubbing his temples.

Without looking up he said: 'What's your connection in all of this? We've nine victims: five murdered in the first six months, Katya and Mihaela plus the left foot of another girl we've got to assume is dead – so that makes eight. And, of course, Connie makes nine.'

'She's not dead,' I shouted. 'She's not dead!'

'And the girl at the castle makes ten.'

'Have you identified her yet?'

Bancho nodded. 'Jade Wesson, aged eighteen. Went missing from Pilton last night.'

'She's not Eastern European and she wasn't a redhead. He's accelerating ... the Ripper's previously gone to the trouble of finding a particular shade of hair. I think that's why he shaved her head. And you can't deny that, last night, Thomas Foster was in jail,' I reminded him.

'I'm not overlooking that fact – whatever you think.' Bancho took a deep breath. He was tired, beaten, and his breathing had the sound of a death rattle.

'You still think he's guilty?' I asked.

'I *know* that he is. Let's assume that there are two killers and–'

'And what?' I interrupted him. 'That means

Thomas Foster's partner is still killing whilst he's in prison? You can't just bend the facts to suit yourself, you're not in China.'

'Put aside your prejudices and listen.' He scratched his head and walked up and down in front of the victims.

'I asked to be informed of any crimes that happened around houses you were connected with.' I stared at him blankly. Coughing, he reached into his drawer and pulled out a new picture. Taking Blu-Tack, he placed it on the wall.

'A cat ... violence to a cat?'

'Well, the pet owner was very upset. She made quite a fuss...'

I knew that serial killers often start out by being cruel to animals. I took the photograph from the wall, and stared at the dead cat. It was obvious what he was getting at, the animal's throat had been cut and torn – it was similar to the marks on the girls. He could see on my face that I understood his point.

'Was Thomas Foster in jail when this happened?' I asked, flapping the photograph in front of him. He nodded. 'Now, Brodie, I want you to tell me the truth ... is there anything else I should know?'

I stared at the dead girls. I wanted to snatch Connie's picture from the wall but I stopped myself. As long as she was there, Bancho had to look for her and that had to be good – right?

Taking a deep breath, I turned to face him. 'The Ripper sent me a text. He said it should have been me...What the fuck does that mean?' I took a cigarette out and lit up.

'You're not allowed to smoke in here.' He

259

pointed to a sign on the wall. I shrugged my shoulders and started pacing, all the better to think. 'So – arrest me.'

He reached over and took a cigarette out of my packet. 'I thought you'd stopped,' I sneered.

'I was under the same impression regarding you.'

Our bitchy sparring was just to buy us some time to come up with answers.

'What did the Ripper mean? That he meant to take me instead of Connie? Or he should have killed me and plucked my eyes out?'

I wandered over and switched the kettle on. I needed a serious caffeine fix to keep going. The burst of adrenalin during the night had depleted my energy; if I wasn't going to fall over, I needed help. Waiting for the kettle to boil, I pushed Bancho to one side.

'How do you get on the Internet – what's your password?'

He didn't tell me, frightened to give away too much personal information, but he did type it in himself. I Googled an assortment of words – nothing.

'The latest female he abducted was Connie. In what way is she the same as the rest of his victims?' I asked Bancho. He saw where I was going with this.

I carried on. 'She's a redhead – okay, let's think how we could classify redheads. Who are the most famous redheads? Where do you get more of us? Why would he dislike us?

'Here's something – *National Geographic* is warning that redheads could become extinct as soon as 2060.' I turned round to catch his eye.

He was making the coffee. 'I hope we catch the fucker before then.'

'Well that's nothing to do with the Ripper,' said Bancho. 'It's a recessive gene. Less than two per cent of the population have it.'

'True – it was a gene mutation in Northern Europe and Celts are traditionally redheads. Why would he dislike us?'

'Brodie – where would I start?' Bancho was pushing it but I accepted his coffee. He went on: 'Maybe his mother, lover, father, significant other was a redhead?'

'My clients' parents don't have red hair,' I pointed out.

Bancho pointed to his wall: 'Well, maybe we're overplaying the red hair. Maybe they were just accessible.'

I shook my head. 'No – he doesn't seem to have any trouble with access. He got into the Thistle Chapel and he made his way into the castle. You're the expert – you've been to Quantico, and for once I'm not knocking you, but what if he is smarter than that?'

Bancho's eyes had clouded over.

'The way he's acting, it's erratic – there's no real pattern. The tableau at the castle was complex and entirely different to the other scenes. What if he has no signature?' Bancho said.

There was a thought rattling around in my head that I didn't want to voice yet. The way he was toying with us reminded me of chess – in particular, a move known as 'the knight's move'. It's been around since the seventh century. It's illogical, and it's a phrase used to describe schizophrenic thinking. It's unusual among chess pieces – what if the Ripper was unusual amongst serial killers? If he was, we'd need to catch a lucky break.

'I've got something,' he said. All the while I had been talking and thinking, he had been researching

'Celtic Saint – so we presume she's a redhead – came to Scotland with nine maidens. Her beauty was unsurpassed. A knight fell in love with her but she rejected him and he accused her of casting a spell on him with her eyes. So he plucked her eyes out and hung them on a thorn bush. In the eleventh century, Edinburgh Castle was known as the castle of the maidens.'

'Well it's interesting,' I said. 'The castle's centre-stage with him, and removing or brutalizing eyes is part of his signature. But the changing m.o. doesn't fit.'

But then Bancho thought he'd found another similarity. 'A knight fell in love with her? Christ! Don't tell me the Ripper has developed a crush on you too.'

I bit my tongue, unsure of what to say. I didn't like that last link – I didn't like it at all.

Chapter Forty-Seven

Royal Mile, Edinburgh
Friday 28 December, 10.30 a.m.

After refusing Bancho's offer to phone a taxi for me, I had to walk. A warped part of my mind felt that, if I didn't suffer, some even greater tragedy would occur.

Connie was still missing. How the hell could it get worse? I knew how. She could be dead.

As I walked, the girls from the wall kept me company, their empty, dead eyes judging me. Head down against the prevailing wind, step by step, I made my way, reflecting on those previously pretty faces. Screwing my eyes, I endured a few long moments with each one in my head, their plump mouths warped by screaming, silenced forever. Katya Waleski lingered with me. I told her to go away – she didn't belong with the rest. I was sorry she was dead, but, nevertheless, she had presumably taken the drugs herself, so maybe she could shoulder some of the blame? Her death was misadventure, unfortunate, but shit happens, and I didn't really care, now that Connie was in danger.

Down at St Patrick's Church, the worshippers were arriving for eleven o'clock Mass. I envied them their faith At the great black wrought-iron gates to the church, I debated whether or not to go in and light a candle. On reflection I decided

263

against it. These girls were young and vibrant; to feel their presence I would need to walk in their steps, not dwell on their deaths. Surely, they were more likely to have partied in the Cowgate than knelt down in St Pat's. Typically, I ignored the voice that pointed out that the youth of Eastern European descent still attended church, unlike their UK counterparts.

In truth, I was searching for Connie. I wouldn't be closer to her in a church. Increasing my pace I marched to a landmark she loved. The mechanical cow's backside attached to the front of the Rowan Tree pub made her hoot with laughter. It lifts its tail and shoots out smoke at passers-by. Along with the one o'clock gun, the farting bovine helps the good citizens of Edinburgh keep track of time. The smile quickly left my face as I walked under South Bridge. It was once a fashionable place just outside the city gates; now it's a cheerless underpass into the Grassmarket.

Tourists are bringing the area up. The Edinburgh Vaults are a popular haunt; in fact I'd found out that Thomas Foster worked there. I was surprised. I didn't think sons of billionaires worked, but apparently his parents had seen what too much excess could do and they'd insisted on a touch of reality in his life. A laudable sentiment, especially if it didn't matter a toss what kind of degree he got, given that he wouldn't have to work a day in his life. My footsteps echoed off the moss covered walls. Water dripped incessantly and I was uncomfortably aware that the vaults were beneath the pavement. Foster worked there as a storyteller, explaining that the caverns were hewn from the rock, describing the businesses that existed in the nooks, the ghosts and the characters.

Where would the girls haunt, I asked myself? At the moment they were haunting me. A shadow crossed my path. I had heard that spirits could follow people – right now they were inside my head.

My mobile rang. The one I keep for important clients and friends. I was pleased to be disturbed, sure that it would be Joe. But the face of the phone showed 'caller unknown'. As the tremors began again, I stopped where I was. Turning away from the wind, looking back at the Rowan Tree, the cow's backside emitted a blast of dry ice 'smoke'. I forced myself to answer.

'Brodie.'

I just kept breathing – that was hard enough.

'Brodie. You look scared. You should be scared, Brodie. I thought you knew? What's good for me is good for you – and good for Connie.'

He didn't try to disguise his voice as much this time – accentless, educated - but the tone was guttural and throaty. There was no mistaking the aggression. Shrugging my shoulders, I searched for the right pitch – soft and low, a pretence at friendship. 'I did as I was told,' I said, copying Kailash's cajoling tones. Obviously, I wasn't an impersonator, because he barked straight back at me.

'Listen to me! What's the matter with you? Don't you want her back?'

Fighting the urge to swear, I opened my free palm and beseeched him. 'Please, let me speak to her.' I wouldn't be ashamed to beg if I had to. His answer wasn't exactly unexpected. A grunt. He

265

was posturing, threatening. I had lost nothing, but then he surprised me.

Her voice came.

It was a recording – maybe I deluded myself but I'd swear it was Connie.

'Look, it says Lucas Baroc has recovered from the metatarsal injury. Club doctors have declared him fit to play on New Year's Day! I WILL get to meet him.'

Connie was so excited. Baroc had been out for six weeks through injury, and Connie had suffered agonies over the tiny bone in his left foot. She'd been torn between wanting to meet him and hoping injury would keep him on the bench at the New Year's Day match. A businessman walked towards me, a *Scotsman* clutched under his arm. He looked astonished as I mumbled something about borrowing his paper and snatched it, turning to the sports pages.

There it was, today's lead story about Baroc's recovery. I thrust the paper back at him and felt myself knocked against the wall by the force of emotion. I whispered into the phone: 'She's alive.'

'Of course she's alive – but she won't be for much longer. You've been stupid, Brodie. You released Thomas Foster and that was a very naughty thing to do.'

'What the fuck are you talking about?' I gasped.

The line went dead. And my heart stopped. I didn't get the chance to tell him I hadn't released Thomas Foster. Some bastard had gone over my head.

Hunkered over a gutter in the Grassmarket, the sour taste burned the back of my throat. Wiping the snot and acid from my nose, I kept going until there was nothing left in my stomach to vomit. Bancho's text came in towards the end.

Qk wk on Foster

Quick work? Bancho hadn't released my client – so who had?

Chapter Forty-Eight

Kailash's home,
Ravelston Dykes, Edinburgh
Friday 28 December, 12.15 p.m.

'She's alive!'
They all stared at me. My eyes were locked with those of my mother. The clock on the fireplace mantel ticked loudly. Kailash cleared her throat but couldn't speak.
'I knew it... I knew if anything really bad had happened to her I'd be able to tell.' Malcolm collapsed against the cushions on the sofa, patting his heart.
'Connie's been gone over thirty-six hours – statistically she should be dead–' I stopped mid-sentence, afraid to say the words and afraid they would hurt Kailash even more if I did. Kailash was frightened to have faith like Malcolm, too many bad things had happened to her in the past.
'But,' I continued, 'I heard her voice... She

sounded...' Tongue-tied, I struggled to find the right words, '...alive and happy.' They were the best I could come up with.

'What do we do now? Did you consider she might just have been forced to repeat something after she was kidnapped?' Kailash eyed me doubtfully.

'I don't think she knew she was being taped,' I said. 'She was reading from today's newspaper. If it was a put-up job, then the Ripper's made her feel very relaxed; she was chattering on and on about Lucas Baroc's foot, the sort of nonsense she spouts at Joe and Eddie.'

'Did you think she sounded drugged?' Kailash asked, her voice cracked with nerves.

The possibility had crossed my mind. I knew it was more likely than not.

'I couldn't say,' I replied.

Kailash ran her fingers through her own hair, pulling at it until Malcolm laid his hand on hers. 'You'll have none left if you keep that up – it won't do Connie any good. What are we going to do, Brodie?' he asked me. They'd all gathered at Four Winds as I made my way there. As soon as I'd spoken to Kailash I'd phoned Bancho, and after several minutes he'd calmed down enough to listen.

Bancho had been labouring under the mis-apprehension that I already knew that Thomas Foster had been released. He didn't take the news well and was sulking, accusing me of attacking him behind his back, trying to make him look bad in front of the press because he'd believed that Thomas was the killer. I'd gone back to St Leonards and he'd rushed to meet me – ostensibly to drive me to Kailash's, but his initial reaction was to get his hands round my throat while screaming something about undermining police authority. He spewed expletives at me. The vomit stains on my jacket went some way to convincing him that I was telling the truth, and he was almost nice to me as he drove me to my mother's – if niceness could be measured by shutting the fuck up.

He was in the kitchen at Kailash's trying to find out who had authorized Thomas Foster's release – now was not the time to point out that neither of us had a legitimate complaint against the decision to release him from Saughton. Indeed, it could be argued we were both failing in our duties for not having done so earlier. For my part I found it disturbing that neither Thomas nor Adie had contacted me about Thomas's sudden release. I was certain they weren't leaving me alone out of concern for my family turmoil. If it hadn't been for Connie, I might even have given a damn.

Derek arrived with lunch, using Malcolm's hostess trolley. We all ignored it, except Bancho, who had followed Derek; grabbing five of the salmon sandwiches he stuffed them into his mouth. Coughing, he thumped his chest in an effort to force the sandwiches down his gullet into his stomach. Bancho's eyes watered until Joe relented and thumped him on the back.

'Thanks,' he rasped, pouring a cup of milk from the jug.

'You're standing there stuffing your face as if we've got all the time in the world – wait much longer and Connie could be dead,' I said.

269

'I wasn't aware the police were waiting,' Kailash said anxiously. 'What are they waiting for? What's happening with Foster? Is he behind this?'

'There's not much to tell, Kailash,' said Bancho, shaking his head and already regretting what he was about to say. 'I'm being forced to agree with Brodie about the Masonic connection. Chief Constable Nadler might be a Mason, and so is Adie Foster. What else would explain Nadler's interference in this case?'

'The chief constable should have been offering Adie Foster hush money for wrongful accusation,' I interjected. 'We've been over this so many times – there's no evidence against Thomas Foster.'

Bancho ignored me and spoke to everyone else. 'We're still waiting on the DNA.' Tightening his jaw he failed to speak calmly. 'The chief constable negotiated directly with the Crown Office without telling me.'

I eyed Bancho up and down, mulling everything over. 'And before you start considering my position, Brodie, what about your own? Adie Foster cut you out of the loop as well.'

'I know. Why?' I asked. 'Why would Adie Foster do that – he's not a stupid man?'

'Sometimes I think I must be very stupid,' Kailash said quietly. 'I don't care about any of this conspiracy shit... Find Connie.'

'Thomas Foster is important to the Ripper for some reason,' Joe said. 'He's the fall guy I reckon.'

'I think he is,' I agreed. 'Thomas Foster was only charged with the murder of Katya Waleski because of a tip-off and a photograph that showed him with Katya on the battlements.'

I licked my dry lips, all too aware that what I was about to say would lead to accusations that I was just trying to get my client off. I'd soon turn into the Girl Who Sets the Guilty Free.

'What if the Ripper called in the information?'

'Why would he want to stitch up Thomas Foster? The guy's a psycho – his thing is mutilating redheads.' Bancho reached for another fistful of sandwiches and we all stared at him. 'What?' he whined defensively. 'All this stress gives me an appetite.'

Shaking my head I continued, trying not to watch the nauseating sight of Bancho cramming more food into his mouth. 'Let's assume that the Ripper did set Thomas up – do they know one another? Does it matter? The next question that needs answered is why did Adie Foster cut me out of the loop – he must be hiding something.'

Lavender grabbed a mug and poured stewed tea into it. Clicking three sweeteners into it, she then took the largest scone. Eyeing us defiantly, she said: 'I'll need all the energy I can get. I'm going to nail that bastard Adie Foster even if I have to hack into the FBI itself. I'm a bit rusty, but–'

'How can she? How could she do that?' Bancho lifted his hand in Lavender's direction as she walked out of the room, noticing the shifty glances that passed between the rest of us. There was no way we could initiate Bancho into Lavender's secret. Lavender Ironside wasn't even her true name – she'd found it on a gravestone in Alvie, a churchyard in the Highlands. She needed a new identity and the real Lavender Ironside wasn't using hers any more. I'd known Lavender

271

for more than five years, yet I didn't know her real name. All she told me was she was on the run from the police, over some mistake regarding the Bank of England. Lavender had learned to be a computer hacker to keep an eye on her boyfriend at the time. She found she loved hacking computers more than she loved him and she was good at it – too good.

'I have to take this at face value. If Thomas Foster isn't the Ripper, he might know who is. It's worth chasing up; he needs to be interviewed.' Bancho wrote it down in his book as I sighed.

'Christ, Bancho – tell me that you can remember a straightforward detail like that?' I snapped. He raised his eyebrow and continued with his jotting, before meticulously folding his book and putting it in his pocket.

I hit on the only real plan I could think of. 'He's out there. The Ripper is still out there. He has Connie. People know him; they've looked into his eyes, eaten with him. We're having no luck with the photograph. Maybe it's a disguise. Whatever ... he has a mask of sanity, otherwise he wouldn't be able to get close to his victims. But that one girl escaped from him. We have to find her. It's Connie's only chance.'

Chapter Forty-Nine

Kailash's home, Ravelston Dykes, Edinburgh
Friday 28 December, 4 p.m.

Arms folded across his chest, he looked at Four Winds and cursed. He had been smug, over-confident, and now he was praying he wouldn't be asked to pay for his mistake.

Could he justify why he had let her believe Connie was alive? Weak. Weak. Did he expect her gratitude? The answer was 'yes'. Pity made him behave in such a foolish manner; stunned by her sunken eyes, her pale, drawn complexion. He'd knocked the fight out of her. That carcass was not the Brodie he knew and prized – the final confrontation would be no good if she didn't fight back.

Thirty-eight hours had passed – thirty-eight long hours in which he had practised patience. It had been difficult. He sighed, taking a moment to congratulate himself on his fortitude but also recognizing how hard it had been. The Watcher was doing everything in his power to make his plan work – nobody would get in his way. To the left of his foot, the snow was still stained red, a reminder to him of a time in the recent past when he had not shown such patience. He smiled and fingered his serrated blade: such a useful tool.

The media camp around the house had grown

273

even larger but he liked that. Crowds provided him with a cover to get close to her. He rolled his tongue around trying to think of an appropriate word to describe his relationship to Brodie – comrade. A self-satisfied smile crossed his lips. He was sure they would be very good friends – and soon.

In fact, he was making friends with the whole family.

He considered it an honour having Connie in his home. He'd followed Brodie's career closely through the Internet. He was her number one fan. It had been an ambition of his to study Scots law; however his other talents – privileges he might say – took him in another direction, so he was forced to follow the law vicariously. During his online research he'd come across Brodie McLennan. He needed an ally.

The front door suddenly opened and the press stirred, ready to record another minor moment in 'a parent's worst nightmare'. Their cameras panned the leafy streets of this exclusive suburb. Connie lived in the kind of house where these things just don't happen. The media was gearing up to ensure that the nation poured out its grief; after all, she was one of theirs.

His eyes flicked over the mawkish tributes left by strangers; cheap pink teddies with childish scrawls. Cameras clicked in the semi-darkness at Lavender Ironside and Jack Deans as they left the house. The flash startled Lavender; like a wary animal she searched the crowd. Her beady eyes stopped on him for a few long seconds before moving on.

He shrank back, frightened. He knew all about

the new Mrs Gibb – he'd even gone to her wedding. There was no end to the things she could find out online about him, given her talents – if she chose to do so.

They were getting close.

He would have to act fast.

Glasgow Joe pulled back a curtain in the living room and peered out, giving The Watcher an opportunity to spy on their conference. He had no doubt that Brodie was filling them in, telling them that good old Tom Foster was innocent. The Watcher was in a mood to excuse her; no one was perfect. *Well, almost no one.* He felt a little ashamed, though. He was acting like one of those sanctimonious vigilantes.

So, Ms McLennan – where are you off to tonight? he drooled, whispering the words as she stepped out onto the paved driveway. His pleasure in her appearance was short-lived; Glasgow Joe was hot on her heels – wasn't he always? Opening the top box on his trike, the big bastard pulled out a spare helmet and handed it to her. Colour had returned to her face a bit. The Watcher had given her hope – what had she done for him? Brodie McLennan was making him mad, and that wasn't a good idea – she wouldn't like to meet him then.

She needed him.

Brodie held Joe's shoulder, as she threw her leg over the trike. The machine roared into life, disturbing the neighbourhood. The Glaswegian drove at the reporters, scattering them like pigeons.

Bonnie and fucking Clyde, he muttered under his breath. He smiled to himself as he remembered how that scenario ended.

Chapter Fifty

Lothian and St Clair, Edinburgh
Friday 28 December, 8.30 p.m.

Night had fallen by the time we got to the office. Joe and I had to get petrol for the trike before meeting up with Jack and Lavender outside the offices. The computer equipment Lavender had insisted I install was second to none. Jack tried to switch on the overhead lights when they entered the office. Lavender switched them off. 'I work with just a desk light,' she told him, tapping her finger lightly off her temple. 'Helps the concentration.'

'How do you intend to find her?' Jack asked. Lavender did not look up at him.

'I'm not looking for Connie... I'm going to find the Ripper. These killings started in July. But his behaviour escalated too quickly for a novice. I think the bastard's done this before somewhere else. And, wherever he's been, there's a trail... I'll hunt him down with a little help from my friends.'

'Friends?' Jack asked. But Lavender was now engrossed as her fingers flew over the keyboard.

'You may have already guessed,' I told Jack, 'Lavender isn't referring to us. She belongs to a loose group of hackers who call themselves vengeance.org.'

'How did she join them?' Jack asked, probably

hunting for another story.

'Lav says if you have to ask how to join, you don't belong.'

Lavender's half-moon reading glasses, a recent necessity, were perched on the end of her nose; they kept sliding down and she kept pushing them up. It was the only time her hand left the keyboard. Three cups of cold coffee sat untouched by her right hand. She was a model of efficiency. Jack told me that, when they arrived, she'd assessed his hacking skills – then asked him to make coffee.

Suddenly, Joe cleared his throat purposefully, as if he was trying to call the room to order. It worked.

'Seeing as our efforts are moving online now, I have something I need to tell you,' he said, looking uncomfortable.

'Some time ago, Brodie's name cropped up on a perverts' website called The Hobbyist. There's been no recent mention but Bancho's monitoring it and he's pretty sure–'

I stopped his flow. 'Yes, yes... I know about that.' Joe stepped back in surprise. The smart-arse thought he'd kept it from me. I told the others: 'Look, this website stuff is just a waste of time. For a start it's an American site. That's obvious from the users, the spelling, the addresses and the references. It's a stretch to think the Brodie McLennan in question is me, "right here in li'l old Edinburgh".' For the last few words I affected a drawling, American accent. 'And anyway, it was posted six months ago. So let's move on shall we?'

'Brodie, I don't think you're seeing the full

picture here,' said Joe.

'Lucky I've got any picture at all,' I snapped. 'You obviously weren't going to tell me!'

Joe ignored that, took a deep breath, and continued. 'It's originally a US site, it's true. But the most recent links take you through to other sites. In mainland Europe,' he paused and then went on, 'and in Scotland.

'The post you saw was just under six months ago. Bancho's people were monitoring for further posts – but then they checked *back* the way through old threads.

'There was another post two weeks before the first, almost seven months ago...'

I knew he was about to drop a bombshell of some description. At least Lavender was still firing on all cylinders, her fingers tapping away again.

'Jack. Use Brodie's computer. "thehobbyist. com" all lower case, all one word,' she ordered.

She turned back to her screen. 'Demonika, one of the full-timers at vengeance, has just sent me some stuff on The Hobbyist,' said Lav. 'The site started in San Francisco and then other chapters opened across the US. I'm just printing off a list of chapters now. Whoever opened The Hobbyist chapter in Scotland has some connection with these places in America.'

She gave me a copy, although I wasn't sure what I could do with it. It was long, too long to help me out in the near future. I stuck it in my pocket.

Jack had found the site. He leaned forward on his seat, eyes wide, staring in disbelief at the screen.

'Shit, Brodie,' he said. 'Who the fuck is this guy? The Watcher? What sort of weirdo bastard is asking about you? The bastard wants your address!'

At Joe's command, he navigated back to earlier posts – and I read it over his shoulder.

It appears Catalina and Florenta are no longer available, my friends. Does anyone know where I can find Brodie McLennan?

In my mind's eye, a calendar flipped back six months ... to when the first two victims were found. My God. And I'd dismissed his later post out of hand. Even as I was petrified for myself, feeling as if every hair on my head and body was standing to attention, I was overwhelmed by feelings of guilt and stupidity as well. This was a lead to whoever had Connie – and I'd missed it. I felt the anger rise up, boil over and spew outwards. This was all Joe's fault.

'Why the hell didn't you tell me about it?' I shouted at him. 'Why did I have to find out by eavesdropping on you and your buddy Bancho? Even then I couldn't possibly know the relevance unless you two told me! Or are you really so conceited and macho that you thought you could *protect* me?'

Joe's face was white. I didn't get a chance to find out if he was equally angry with me, or just hurt, because while I was venting my spleen Lav had been concentrating on moving things on.

Ignoring my outburst completely, she said: 'I'll cross-reference the details of The Hobbyist with the rest of the information that's coming through. The first thing I need to do is see if Thomas Foster has a connection.'

Jack was still bug-eyed on the website. 'I thought you said the last entry was six months ago. There's a new one ... posted just hours ago!'

Joe and I shot across the room to peer over his shoulder. Lavender followed.

He placed his finger on the cursor; a deep groove had formed between his eyebrows as he saw Connie's picture posted on the site. I'd guess we all felt the same chill. It had been taken the day of the football match in the Meadows; she was lying on the ground after the illegal tackle, blood pouring from her nose.

'What kind of sick bastard would put a photograph of an injured child up on the web?' he asked, shaking his head.

Peering into the screen, I placed a finger on it. 'Follow that thread,' I commanded. The words were indistinct because I was biting my bottom lip as he scanned the messages.

'Stop! Open it up.'

Jack did as he was told.

'It's a photograph of Connie taken after she was kidnapped. Brodie, she's wearing the Roxy sweatshirt I gave her for Christmas,' he said, without meeting my eyes. I leaned forward, squashing him out of the way, as I printed the image. Watching the photograph roll out of the printer, I felt the life being squeezed out of me.

Chapter Fifty-One

Lothian and St Clair, Edinburgh
Friday 28 December, 9 p.m.

'What's she doing in that pic?' Jack asked as he squinted.

'She's playing her Xbox – she's online playing with other gamers; look at the headset.' We all stared at each other as Lavender spoke.

'So, if she's being held somewhere and is safe, then if she was online playing, could we contact her?' Jack asked, his voice hesitant as he recognized his technological limitations.

'We could log on and list her as a friend. If she confirmed that we were her friends, then we could search for her online any time she was playing and...' Lavender stopped.

'And? What are you thinking?' I asked.

'It couldn't be that easy – if she was online and we had a headset we could talk to her. It's a long shot but if there's anyone who can find her in that community its–'

'Moses!' we all said at the same time.

Moses was an avid online gamer; his saving grace was that his fear of poverty and his sense of responsibility prevented it from becoming an addiction. He was a true insomniac and whiled away the wee small hours playing with other sad bastards in different time zones. Unlike Connie, he enjoyed playing against Chinese people because he needed the challenge. Sexual abuse at the hands of a paedophile ring in childhood had left him with post-traumatic stress disorder; unable to endure the night sweats and flashbacks, he fuelled himself with caffeine and chocolate.

'Being an online gamer is part of the bond she shares with Moses,' I said. 'Connie doesn't have a lot of friends because Malcolm watches her like a hawk.'

Jack shook his head and gulped a large mouthful of cold coffee. 'Has he never heard the rule about talking to strangers?' he asked. 'Doesn't apply on Xbox live-gaming as far as I can see,' I replied. Jack scratched his head, his shoulders slumped. 'Christ, even Malcolm is more computer-literate than I am.'

'Yeah, well – he manages the girls' Internet bookings, so to that extent he has moved with the times,' I said.

'Brodie,' interrupted Lavender, 'this is a shot in the dark but predators do frequent these rooms and if she moved to another media with him – like email or webcam – then they could have arranged to meet up.'

She went silent, got up and stood by the window. It was freezing outside, a snow flurry was falling, and the coldness of the glass must have gone some way to stopping the hot flush she seemed to be experiencing. 'Bancho said there was no sign of a struggle in her bedroom. She went willingly or she was drugged, maybe both. If she met him on the net, then the chances are none of us will know him.' Lavender fanned her

282

face, which was the colour of putty. 'I should have checked the parental controls were in force in the games she was playing; I'm the one who knows how to do this stuff.'

'Moses should have checked,' Jack said, unconvincingly. The mere idea that Moses Tierney would be responsible enough to impose checks on a minor was laughable. Some of the Dark Angels were runaways barely a couple of years older than Connie. His business empire would grind to a halt if he did not recognize the autonomy of minors.

Lavender stared at the fluorescent clock on the wall as the seconds ticked away. Like an hourglass, it felt as if every falling grain of sand brought Connie closer to death. Even Lav had to admit she needed help in her quest to hunt down the killer online. She sighed and went against her nature; she was a control freak, and preferred to dictate to everything and everyone around her. Now, she had to let that go. Dialling his mobile she held her breath. Moses didn't always pick up, but this time he answered her on the second ring. She put him on loudspeaker.

'Please tell me you've found her. I'm sick with worry.' Moses could barely speak for the tightness in his throat. He knew first hand the suffering Connie would be experiencing at the hands of a paedophile if that was who had taken her; he seemed to be walking a thin line between sanity and a breakdown. I wondered whether it was possible for him to distinguish where his pain ended and Connie's began.

'There's a lead, Moses – I need you to follow it,'

Lavender told him.

'I'll do anything.'

'Get on Xbox live – see if you can find her; we think she might have met someone online.'

'Not a chance,' he replied immediately. 'I set the parental controls on the handset – she can't go anywhere dodgy without me knowing. In fact mostly she only played with me.'

It was a crushing blow. Lavender had tried to tell us at the outset that the chance of this working was remote, and it had seemed too easy; nonetheless, she had built her hopes up. Jack put his arm around her as her lips trembled.

'The other difficulty we have is that she'll be playing on his site using his name; it's too hard to change just for a short period. Unless I know who he is, or what game-tag he uses, I'm fucked on my controller,' said Moses.

'What about her controller?' Lavender asked. 'Surely that's with the police?'

'I'll contact Bancho and arrange for you to get it,' Joe intervened.

'I'll get hold of Connie's controller to find out who her friends are – it'll tell me if they're online or not,' Moses said.

'Will it also tell you the last time she played with them on her console?' asked Lavender.

'Lavender – if that bastard has contacted her online, believe me I'll find him.'

The phone went dead. Moses was always too busy to bother with social niceties – especially tonight.

Chapter Fifty-Two

Pilrig Street, Leith, Edinburgh
Friday 28 December, 10.30 p.m.

Lavender had struck gold. Grandspin, one of her associates in vengeance.org, had hacked into the Lothian and Borders police computers – and bingo, he'd come up with a list. It contained the names of girls, including the dead girls Katya, Bianca, Mihaela, Florenta. Glasgow Joe recognized some of the other names, so armed with only a scrap of paper, we set off in search of the girl who had survived the Ripper – even though in my heart I feared she was a phantom.

I jumped off the trike as it was slowing to a stop, and ran to the stairwell of the flats in Pilrig Street. The snow was coming down fast and furious; I pressed a buzzer at the side of the door and waited. My foot started tapping – not a good sign.

The names were all from Eastern Europe, picked up from Bancho's monitoring of The Hobbyist site. Joe had expected Bancho to share this information it was no surprise to me that the bastard hadn't. The girls had appeared, and then, for one reason or another, had disappeared from the street scene in Edinburgh. At least one girl was lying dead in some remote corner of Edinburgh, but the prostitute I was hoping to find tonight had escaped from the clutches of the Ripper early on in his career. One thing was certain: she wouldn't be a redhead by now. In hiding she would have done everything she could to change her appearance. I was praying she didn't dye or shave her pubic hair as well, otherwise identification would be difficult. I was assuming she wouldn't cooperate because if she existed she had gone to ground, become a ghost.

The stair door clicked open. Joe was at my back; holding on to my shoulder he pushed me behind him. 'It'll look less suspicious this way.' I didn't like to ask how you could look anything but suspicious at an illegal brothel.

He marched in, ignoring the crushing smell of cat's piss in the stairwell. He took the stairs three at a time. I ran to keep up. I pressed the front door bell but, when it opened, our way was barred; it would seem sex slaves, prostitutes and tennis stars are not the only thing Eastern Bloc countries export. The female bouncer was doing a good job of impersonating a brick shithouse – in a previous life she had definitely been an Olympic hammer thrower. Glasgow Joe has always had reservations about hitting women, especially ones who can match him pound for pound. Joe leaned forward and whispered in her ear; she smiled coquettishly and stepped aside. I shivered. 'Brodie, there's someone I'd like you to meet.' He pointed at the hammer thrower. 'Juliana.' He eyed me coldly, my distaste was obviously written all over my face. I stuck my hand out to introduce myself.

The hallway of the flat was pretty bare. The other doors were shut and, I assumed, occupied. Juliana led us into the kitchen. Cheap units lined the small room and its walls were marred by handprints and stains I didn't want to investigate. A calendar of Bucharest hung on a loose nail above the kettle, a red pen had marked crosses and someone was counting off the days until an event.

Juliana's nails were shell pink and clean, in stark contrast to her massive, sausage-like fingers. She retrieved cups from the cupboard and placed a teaspoon of instant coffee in each one. I pointed to the red crosses. 'Who made those?' I asked.

Juliana tapped her butcher's hands over her heart and tapped some more. I raised an eyebrow at Joe. 'What are you waiting for?' I asked her.

'In three weeks I get married – my fiancé will repay the loan to them as soon as it is through from building society.' Juliana smiled; it looked as if, inside, she was already doing a victory slide. My mind was doing cartwheels: I thought she was the hired muscle and now I'd discovered she'd been forced into prostitution too, which by her looks was surprising enough, but, to cap it all, she'd found a man amongst her customers.

'Erm, your fiancé? Is he from Edinburgh?' I asked.

'No – he from Musselburgh,' she replied.

There were so many things I wanted to ask, and I knew that I didn't have much time. Thankfully, Joe interrupted appropriately for once. 'Juliana – Brodie. Brodie – Juliana. Introductions over.' He took a sip of coffee. 'I've been keeping my eye on these brothels for some time – the lassies are frightened to open their mouths; through the grapevine I heard about Juliana.'

The big woman smiled, and like every newly en-

287

gaged woman I've ever met she kept flashing her ring about. The diamonds were little more than chips, but he was laying out a lot to her owners.

'Juliana's man,' continued Joe, 'is into cross dressing. He's straight but they often go for – no offence, doll – butch women, don't they? This guy heard about Juliana on The Hobbyist site and decided to check her out. The rest, as they say, is history.'

'My reputation spread once I came here – I appeal very much to a certain type of man. My man likes to dress as woman – sometimes – but he's no hobbyist!' Juliana spat into the sink. 'Joe met my man, Arthur.' She smiled again. 'Joe asked if he could meet up with me – maybe I could help him with some things. After my man says it's okay, I agree.'

Joe nodded and smiled throughout this conversation. 'Do you have anything for me?' he asked her.

Juliana reached down into her extensive bosom and pulled out a rumpled photograph taken from an Internet website. She slid it across to him. 'Sonia – she change her name, colour of hair, but she's the one you want. He put her in hospital for five weeks.' Juliana held up her hand and splayed her fingers, giving me another opportunity to admire her good fortune.

I looked at the photograph. A doe-eyed girl with elfin features and a sleek black bob stared warily out at us. Joe bit his tongue; we both knew that this girl had the fair skin of a redhead. So much depended upon her. Could she identify the Ripper? She'd kept silent for months – why should she

288

speak now? Joe took his mobile out of his pocket. Looking at Juliana, he spoke slowly: 'Arthur? He explained to you what I was going to do?' He nodded, encouraging her to agree, and even I was impressed by how much he had done on his own.

'Oh, yes. I said to him, time to get out of this business; they've had enough out of me,' Juliana said. The three of us stayed quiet. None of us really wanted to address the ways in which people got their money out of Juliana and others like her. The silence was awkward – but not for long.

Wham! Suddenly a sledgehammer started breaking through the front door. The first smash cracked it, the second and third took it off its hinges. A black jackboot from an intruder brought it crashing down in the small hallway, bringing down the coat stand. The sound of screeching filled the air as two underweight waifs ran screaming out of the front room. They clutched their scanty clothes to their chests; they looked frightened and ashamed at the same time. Close on the heels of the slaves, a man who had struggled into his boxer shorts came running into the melee, his flaccid penis poking through the opening, jiggling as he ran. An enormous hairy muffin top hung over his pants. I held his eye. I looked from him to the young girls and back again. I saw fear but no shame.

My right leg moved involuntarily back; it swung forward in an arc, connecting with the punter's wedding tackle. On the basis he wasn't using it in any marital bed, I figured no one would miss it, especially those young girls he'd just had a threesome with. The punter crashed at my feet, while the intruders stormed in over the top of him, sledgehammers held aloft. They herded us into the kitchen. It was a sickening crush; I like to choose the naked people I share epidermal surfaces with.

I sidled up to Joe. In a fight there was no one better. Using his body as a shield, I watched the action. Five men carrying weapons had burst into the flat and the occupants of the other rooms were now being frog-marched in beside us. One of the punters was at least ninety. It was sickening – they could at least have allowed him to put his knickers on; for my sake, not his.

Then I heard a voice I recognized and everything changed again.

'Police, you're all under arrest.'

Chapter Fifty-Three

St Leonards Police Station, Edinburgh
Friday 28 December, 11.35 p.m.

Bancho bundled us all into the back of a waiting paddy wagon; when I say 'all', Glasgow Joe was exempt. He was allowed to drive the trike to St Leonards. I was squashed between Juliana and a half-naked punter with the hairiest back I've ever seen. Juliana kept wriggling around to get more space, and I ended up the meat in a very unpleasant sandwich.

It was the first time I'd ever travelled in a police van, and I sincerely hoped it would be the last. It was a high-profile police raid; Joe and I had been caught in its net, and paperwork would have to be processed before we were allowed back on the street to hunt for Connie. I'd screamed in Bancho's face but his attitude implied Connie's abduction was a matter for the police. I didn't agree – I was sick of pointing out that they were no good at bringing children home alive.

Joe tried to get me to shut up; Bancho was very close to charging me with breach of the peace and resisting arrest. I calmed down when Joe pointed out that the fact he was allowed to drive the trike meant we would be able to start hunting for Sonia as soon as we were released and he was sure it wouldn't take us long, now we had a photograph to go on. She couldn't stay a spectre forever. I had started to believe she was flesh and blood, not some figment of an overactive imagination. I was excited; we were getting closer to the Ripper, and closer to Connie.

The paddy wagon drew to a jerky stop outside St Leonards, and the motley crew and I disembarked. I felt filthy, tired and just bloody desperate to be on my way. We were heading for the police cells; surely for Connie's sake if not mine, Bancho wouldn't make me languish there. The still, small voice of reason in my mind knew if the detective thought for one moment that I was interfering in his investigation he'd lock me up and throw away the key until the first court on 2 January – but that was way too late.

Desk Sergeant Munro walked towards me shaking his head. 'Lassie, will you never learn?' He smiled sadly and tapped me gently on the

291

head. 'You don't have the sense you were born with. As for Glasgow Joe, what was he thinking of, taking you to a joint like that?'

Sergeant Munro had separated me from the crowd. Presumably on Bancho's instruction, he took me into a private room and set about the paperwork to release me. He laid his pen back down on the desk and held my eyes.

'Brodie, do you have any idea what these animals who traffic in humans are like? They're not your junkie from Pilton: it's the Mafia, Russian and American. It's international organized crime … you're lucky you're still alive.'

'Lucky?' I shouted. He was trying to be kind but I didn't feel lucky when Connie was still missing. He raised his hand to quieten me. 'There's still hope for your sister; there's plenty of time for grieving if it doesn't have a happy ending. Those girls out there: what age do you think they are?'

'Fifteen,' I answered.

'Close. They're *fourteen* and the poor souls don't even know they're in Edinburgh. They can't speak English, and they've been kept inside for months being used by dirty old bastards like him.' Sergeant Munro jabbed his pen in the direction of the hairy, fat man.

'Imagine shagging something like that forty times a day.' He shivered and smiled at me as he pushed a form across for me to sign.

'It's a big deal rescuing these lassies... I'd bet my wages the poor wee souls will be caught again and on their backs in a Birmingham brothel before January is out.'

I handed him his form and pen back.

'You know where Bancho's room is... Oh, and Brodie, stop fighting with him and we'll all be better off.'

'Thanks.' My voice was cold. I didn't see much to be grateful for and, pushing the chair back, I left. The corridor to Bancho's room was empty, and I heard the noise long before I even saw the door to the operations room.

Thummp, thummp, thummp.

Banging. It sounded like he was being attacked but, in spite of the good sergeant's pep talk, I didn't feel like rushing in and saving him. The door was slightly ajar and a sliver of brighter light shone out. Warily, I edged the door open with my toe. The shouting and swearing was extreme, even to my accustomed ears, but there was only one voice.

My mouth went dry, and I stood in the doorway, mouth open, appalled, witnessing a man's complete meltdown. Bancho was banging his head off the wall; a shattered telephone lay in bits on the floor. I could only conclude that he'd received news he didn't want to hear, and I knew it was Connie. I put my hand on his forehead. It was cut and bleeding. I held him, I had to calm him down; I didn't want to discover the source of his pain but I had to.

Bancho needed to tell me what he knew, what had happened – I was bloody fed up with men keeping secrets from me.

'Tell me!'

He refused to answer, shaking his head violently from side to side, but his eyes drifted in the direction of a scrunched-up message. As I moved to pick it up, a shadow crossed his eyes whilst he debated whether or not to let me in on his secret and I quickly grabbed the message in case he changed his mind. The information was written on a yellow message pad. Patch had phoned two hours ago and left the results of the DNA test on Thomas Foster. I now understood why Bancho was in hell. Thomas Foster's results were negative; he was not the Ripper. Now there could be no dispute.

How many girls had died as a result of DI Bancho's narrow-mindedness?

Chapter Fifty-Four

St Leonards Police Station, Edinburgh
Friday 28 December, 11.55 p.m.

'Brodie, stop!'

Bancho was shouting at me, but I didn't have time to stand around and comfort him; he'd made a mistake that he would have to learn to live with. Maybe when I had Connie back home I'd take him out for a drink and let him cry on my shoulder. It was a big maybe.

'Brodie, you need to listen to me.'

Bancho shouted again, he wasn't giving up. Taking the stairs two at a time I was heading for the front door; nothing and no one was getting in my way. Surely Joe would be ready by now. Sonia was out there somewhere. She knew what the Ripper looked like; perhaps she had an address. I allowed myself to get carried away and I even imagined she knew his name. When Sonia was found, everything would be all right; Connie would be found and we'd have a good New Year. I tried to convince myself ... and I was succeeding until Bancho grabbed my arm.

'Didn't you hear me?' Bancho asked. He was breathless and, taking my arm, he tried to pull me back downstairs. I dug my heels in.

'Please, there's something you need to see.' His voice was horribly gentle and immediately I felt numb. I supposed I was going into shock. Bancho continued to pull me along the corridor and into his room.

'I got a phone call.'

'From the usual source?'

Bancho nodded, 'Yeah ... the one who sent Joe the photograph of Thomas Foster and Katya.'

'Why should we believe anything that bastard has to say? It's partly his fault; he was the one spending time on Foster when the real killer was out there.'

'No, what he sent was an accurate picture... I assumed Thomas Foster was the Ripper; I was wrong ... it's my fault.'

He pulled out his chair and refreshed the computer screen. He didn't warn me about what I was about to see, but I suppose no waiting would have prepared me. A picture of a Roxy hoody. Taking a deep breath, I pulled out my mobile and called up the image Lavender had downloaded from The Hobbyist site after Connie was kidnapped. My sister smiled out at me as she played Xbox live.

Holding the phone up to the screen, and viewing the images side by side, I still didn't want to commit myself. It was too dark to say for sure. I switched on Bancho's desk light, dithering back and forth until I could stand the uncertainty no more. Bancho scurried about at my side.

'It's hers, isn't it?' Bancho asked. He didn't want to hear my answer. I breathed in deeply through my nose; holding my breath, I nodded. The sweatshirts were one and the same, but on the PC screen, the quantity of blood on the ripped hoody – the one that Joe had given her for Christmas – left little room for hope.

Bancho held me; my pain was beyond tears.

Time seemed to stop; the realization of Connie's death went in like a bullet. After the initial jolt, it was as if someone had injected novocaine into my brain. Numbly, I pushed Bancho away, but he wouldn't let me go.

'Wait, Brodie. There was a message with the picture. It said we'd find "something of interest" in Niddry Street.'

I felt the breath being sucked out of me.

'No, it's not what you think. We didn't find ... Connie. DI Smith went straight there. She's still there but all she found was the hoody.'

'Who is he? Who is this fucking secret informant who knows so much? He's been in my flat, for God's sake! He chose clothes for me, he got things all laid out as if he was my fucking maid! Now, what does that say to you? It shouts pretty clearly to me that he's obsessed. What's he got to do with anything and why is he pulling our strings? What

296

else does he know? Why doesn't he just come out into the open?' These were my questions but I did not expect any answers. I knew I was wailing, my reasoning lost in a mire of confusion and pain.

Bancho paused, looked me straight in the eye and said: 'I think he's the Ripper and he's been laying a false trail of evidence against Thomas Foster.'

'We have to find her – we have to bring her home,' I said. I did not add that I could not stomach the thought of Connie lying cold, alone and naked.

I didn't need to.

Chapter Fifty-Five

The Shore, Leith, Edinburgh
Saturday 29 December, 1.35 a.m.

Somehow, the fact that she was dead made it even more urgent to find her. My mind wouldn't accept it until I touched her, stroked her face, and held her in my arms. How strange – I could understand those old men who refused to admit their wife was dead because they couldn't bear to be parted from the body. Of course, in my mind's eye, I saw Connie sleeping peacefully, not battered and bruised on Patch's table.

Since the first moment I saw the dead girls in Bancho's room, they walked before me, silently begging for their day in court, for justice; but

297

mostly they wanted retribution. Before Bancho had shown me the image of the sweatshirt, I'd taken this as a good sign. In my imagination at least, Connie had not joined them. Was it false hope, or did part of me really know she might still be alive?

Actually, I was disgusted with myself. It wasn't long since I'd been bitching about not being kept informed. Now I understood – ignorance is bliss. I dragged my feet along the icy cobbles of the Shore. How much easier it would have been to search for Sonia if I'd still had faith she could help me find Connie. Anger raged in my gut; if Sonia had spoken up, the police would have arrested the killer by now and Connie would be safe.

There was a little voice in my head – not so little actually – that was saying words I didn't want to hear. She wouldn't have been any safer if the killer had asked for me to represent him, it whispered – I'd have made sure he walked. Uncorroborated evidence from a known prostitute was a defence counsel's dream.

The girl we were searching for was easily spooked; to find her we had to employ subterfuge. Joe had left the trike in Constitution Street as part of the deception – no man goes kerb crawling on a motorbike; where would he do the business? If he was to be the presumed pimp or client, I was to be the prostitute. I plastered makeup on my face and borrowed some clothes a lap dancer had left at the Rag Doll. I teetered in ridiculously high heels and a crotch-covering mini. It was freezing, and each step I took hurt, but I found the physical pain comforting. It meant that I was doing something.

A gaggle of street girls huddled in a close, smoking and leaning into one another, trying to keep warm. If anything, they were even more scantily clad than me; at least I had a jacket on. The train tracks on their undernourished arms told me nothing I didn't already know. These girls were addicts doing anything and anyone to fund their habit. As they shivered it seemed more likely they would die of hypothermia than anything else.

They preened themselves as they saw Joe approach; one even went as far as to throw her fag away. She crushed it out with the ball of her foot, taking care to display a thin thigh and an emaciated calf. A gold chain encircled her ankle; it had caught on the ten-denier black tights and there was a run in them that reached her knee. Her face fell when I tottered up the rear.

'Oh, it's you.' She took another fag out of her pocket and stepped back into the close. Holding her hands around it, she got a light from a friend's cigarette end. 'What brings you down here?' she asked me. 'Business must be bad if lawyers are turning to this game.'

I stared into her face, a face much older than I had first thought, but the harder I tried the more her name escaped me; my amnesia was obvious. She tapped my shoulder as if the shove would help me remember. 'It's Senga – Senga Palmer.' Her voice was high and nasally. 'You act for my boy – wee Billy Palmer? He was lifted on Christmas Eve – silly wee bastard was on bail, so now he's in the poky till his trial.' Turning to the other girls, she explained, 'He's as guilty as fuckin' sin – still, it's best he does as many days as he can on remand

and hope the judge will backdate it. She smiled at me and said quite kindly, 'Penny dropped has it?'

I nodded like an automaton. 'I saw him a couple of days ago,' I smiled because it seemed more like a century ago. 'He asked me for a kiss.'

'Well, I hope you didnae gie him one – dirty wee bugger!' She smiled at her colleagues. She stopped smiling when my tears fell. I couldn't get the words out. It was hard enough to breathe. I was relieved that Joe ignored me and started asking for their help. He took the photograph of Sonia from his inside pocket. Senga Palmer responded by taking her mobile phone out and using it as a light. Then she bent down and rummaged in her handbag. I was ready to move if I saw smack – she needed a clear head to be of any use. I needn't have worried. She pulled her reading specs out and peered; Senga was every bit as old as she looked.

Her head was nodding like a little dog on the back shelf of a car. 'Aye. I know who she is. Even know where she stands.' She started to scratch the inside of her arms dramatically. 'Sorry though. I'd love to help but I cannae leave here until I've turned a trick.'

'How much?' Joe asked.

'Fiver for a hand job, six for a blow, tenner for the full Monty with a johnny, fifteen without.' Glasgow Joe took a wad of cash from his back pocket and handed her a twenty. She put her arm through his. 'I cannae really work the maths, son,' she said. 'What do you want?'

'Just tell me where Sonia is, that's all.' Joe's nerves were shredded, he was in no mood to be polite. Senga looked at the money and gave us what we needed.

It took us less than five minutes to get there, but it was a different world. The Shore, like most dockside areas throughout the world, has been redeveloped and is now home to trendy bars and Michelin-starred restaurants – but not everything has been pulled up to the same level. I had always called where we were heading 'the banana flats'. You can imagine their shape, a testimony to bad architecture, and as soon as Joe said where we were going, I felt sick. Suffice to say there was no way Gordon Ramsay would be opening his next restaurant on the ground floor of this development. Sonia had fallen far if she wasn't fit to stand with Senga Palmer and her crew. Joe ran into the dark recesses. He stopped and waited. Taking out his wallet he counted cash and I could hear the rustle of crisp, clean fifty-pound notes.

The million-dollar question, was it enough to tempt Sonia out of the shadows?

Chapter Fifty-Six

The Shore, Banana Flats
Saturday 29 December, 2 a.m.

'Where is she, Joe?' I hissed at him from the shadows. We thought it was unlikely Sonia would appear if another 'prostitute' was there; Senga Palmer and her gang defended their territory like

301

a pack of wild dogs and to survive Sonia had learned, early on, to stay away from them.

'She's here.' He was standing under a light patiently counting his money. 'I can't push her. We just have to wait until she's ready.'

'But we don't have time to wait,' I hissed again.

'What option do we have: everything rests on this damaged wee lassie?'

He was right about having no other cards to play; I pushed myself back into the darkness, leant against a huge concrete post and waited. It was a good thing I had work to do, and I could not afford to lose myself in grief. I thought of Sonia, how had she survived not only the horrific attack but this hostile environment as well? Her business must be bad if she left her punters waiting this long.

By the time Sonia stepped out, I had given up hope; the sight of her raised a twisted smile on my face that faded when I saw her face. I barely recognized her from the photograph. Her scars were as deep on the outside as I imagined they were inside. Her hair was dyed raven black but her milk-white complexion gave away the fact that she was naturally a redhead. The light showed tell-tale puckering around her eyelids: the bastard had sewn her eyes open, just as he had the others. Joe gently pulled her out into the open. She was trembling, desperately clutching a small golden crucifix that hung around her neck as if her life depended on it.

I smiled, and nodded at her as Joe placed a fifty-pound note in her quivering hands. He held up the photograph of the priest taken at Connie's football match.

'Is this the man who attacked you?' Sonia took the photograph, and her trembling stopped.

'He's not the man.'

Joe breathed in deeply, unwilling to take no for an answer – we were so sure we'd found him.

'Look again, doll... Come over here where the light's better.' He led her five feet away to an equally dim spot and handed her another fifty-pound note. Sonia refused to take the money, shaking her head. 'No, I already tell you it's not him.' Her voice had a conviction and strength that was at odds with her frail damaged body, and I knew she would keep this denial up for hours.

Hours that we just didn't have.

The phone rang; it was Lavender. She spoke in a monotone. The only way she could deal with this was to work.

'Another photograph has been posted on The Hobbyist website. I'm sending it to you now. Brodie, it appears to be a picture of the guy who was looking for you.'

'Send it direct to Joe's phone.' I was trying to save every second I could. 'Have you found out any more about Thomas Foster?' My client's DNA results proved his innocence, but he was connected to the Ripper whether he knew it or not.

'Remember the list of towns and cities where The Hobbyists had chapters?'

It was only a matter of hours ago that Lavender's friend Demonika had unearthed the places where The Hobbyists pursued their depraved pastime, but it seemed like months.

'Well, they have a chapter in New Haven, Connecticut.'

'New Haven ... that's the town where the University of Yale is based.'

'Mmmh ... that's right. I was wondering if the Ripper was setting up Thomas Foster as a fall guy for his murders,' Lavender said.

'The same thought's crossed my mind – and even Bancho's!' I told her. 'Who the hell is this guy who keeps posting photographs and messages on The Hobbyist?'

'Brodie, he *must* be the Ripper ... he's committing these murders.'

'Could it be a vendetta?' I asked. I didn't hear Lavender's reply; I was too busy listening to Sonia describe her attacker. Joe had shown her both photographs – the one just in from Lavender and the screen grab of the 'priest'. She was right – neither of them fitted her description.

Chapter Fifty-Seven

The Shore, Banana Flats
Saturday 29 December, 3 a.m.

'When I first saw him ... I thought it was my lucky night ... he was so young, so handsome, so clean.' Sonia's eyes were filling with tears, but as I reached out to touch her she flinched as if expecting a punch.

'He took me in his car; it was a rented one ... he

is an American, I think he is a tourist. At first he treated me like a lady. He said how pretty my hair was, he kept touching my hair and saying it was just perfect – why I dye it now.' She clutched her golden cross even more tightly, and spat on the ground beside me. Sonia was keeping away the devil.

'The man had champagne in the car... I thought very nice ... but it was drugged ... from the first sip it tasted odd... I felt my tongue swell... I couldn't breathe, or see straight, and I realized my luck was running out.'

I had a paper hanky in my pocket; it was crumpled, grubby but unused, and Sonia accepted it gratefully.

'I passed out ... when I woke up I was in a dark cellar, it smelt of cats' pee; the floor was dirt and a rat ran over my hand.' She showed me her finger: a chunk had been taken out of it, presumably the work of the rat.

'Did you find out where the cellar was?' I asked.

'No, I never found out and I never want to know, it is enough that I carry it around in here–' she tapped the side of her head – 'always.'

She nodded at me as if I would know, or could understand the hell where she had been. I didn't, and I prayed that neither did Connie.

'I felt the needle go into my eyelid, he pressed down on the eyeball and pulled ... like so.' She mimicked the action. My stomach was rebelling, to witness another human being in such pain and not be able to touch or comfort them was unnatural.

'My eyes became very dry... I kept trying to

blink … but it hurt.' She pointed to the red marks on her eyelids. 'The stitching.'

I offered her a cigarette and she smiled weakly. 'I came here to be secretary … who knew people could lie so much?' She laughed grimly at herself.

'He had a knife … a knife he loved … this knife was special to him … a pirate's knife.'

'I don't understand … what's a pirate's knife?'

'Here, I show you.' Sonia dragged me over to the wall, spat on the end of her index finger and drew a sign, which left a slimy trail. She was no artist and it meant nothing to me.

'He tied me like so.' She splayed her arms and legs out like Da Vinci's Vitruvian Man. He had secured her tightly, exposing her vital organs so he could inflict maximum pain.

'I was bound so tightly, I couldn't move. The ropes were tied very tight, the bindings cut into my wrists, blood dripped onto the cellar floor.' Sonia held her wrists up for me to inspect; the scar tissue was wide, deep and purple. None of the other girls had these marks because he cut their wrists off.

'I tried to get away, I pulled, tugged and jerked the ropes as he came at me with his pirate's knife, but I couldn't move. I couldn't close my eyes; I saw everything he did to me. When I tried to scream he put a cloth in my mouth … it was difficult to breathe.' Sonia closed her eyes against the horror. The night was cold but beads of sweat had broken out on her skin.

'He used his knife to slice through my ankles. It was like electric shock, and then exploding like a bomb. I fainted I think; when I wake up he was hacking at my leg using all his strength to sever my ankle.'

Sonia lifted up her right leg. Grabbing my hand she ran my fingers over her leg, and I could feel a chunk of skin missing. I could feel her chipped bone and some screws; surgeons had put a steel plate in her ankle to repair the damage.

'I prayed to die ... dear God end this now... End my life now, I begged. Then the Madonna, she heard my prayers. First footsteps, then voices in the dark... I didn't shout. He thought I was still unconscious or maybe dead. He was frightened and I was pleased. He dragged me like I was a sack of potatoes along the rough floor. It scraped and scratched my skin. I wanted to scream but if I wanted to live I could not. I discovered at that moment I wanted to live very much.'

I chose not to comment on the quality of her life. Whether this information led me to Connie or not I would help this girl.

'He pulled me up the stairs – many, many stairs; each rough step it chipped and cracked my bones.' Sonia touched her ribs, and placed a finger on her lips. 'But still I did not make a sound,' she whispered.

'He kicked me into the gutter, and left me like a dog. I was frightened to move ... many, many people walked past me thinking I was drunk ... what kind of man does this?'

Joe and I hung on every word as Sonia went on to describe the man in detail. As she spoke, the horrific realization came over me that I knew him – and I knew where to find him.

Chapter Fifty-Eight

'Bourich', Gamekeeper's Road, Cramond
Saturday 29 December, 3.30 a.m.

It came like a bolt from the blue; it was so unexpected I didn't have time to react. Glasgow Joe gave Sonia his house key; he told her to go there and when he returned he would make sure she was safe. Then he jumped on the trike and I was left standing and waiting; he had no intentions of taking me into the Ripper's lair, but I wasn't asking for anyone's permission.

Lights were being switched on in bedrooms as my screams of fury woke up the residents of the flats, but Joe was unmoved. In frustration and fury I grabbed my bike helmet and fired it at him. I caught him on the shoulder and he tried to massage it as he drove. I hoped it didn't ease the pain as I watched him drive into the darkness to Adie Foster's house.

The Fosters lived on the right side of the tracks. It was a world apart from the banana flats, but the taxi ride there gave me time to consider what to do next and make some calls. Luckily, the driver sensed my mood and merely grunted in my direction.

'Bancho.'

'I'm too busy just now, Brodie. I'll catch you later.'

308

'No, you need to listen to me... Glasgow Joe cannot be given another "five minutes" with Thomas Foster. He'll kill him this time – you're in charge so bloody well act like it. If anything untoward happens at the arrest it could lead to Thomas Foster walking – we don't know what his involvement is and you've just released him. The Fosters will claim it's police harassment ... with my client being a foreign national the embassy or the American government might get involved.'

'I've told you before, Brodie – don't tell me how to do my job.'

He hung up on me. I could tell Bancho was worried. That Glasgow Joe needed to be controlled, and he was enough of a man to admit he wasn't up to the task.

'I'm really in a hurry, could you step on it please?' I smiled at the driver. No doubt he was wondering what a tart was doing using the contract cab for the lawyers Lothian and St Clair. But the bald taxi driver said nothing as he pushed his foot to the floor like he was Lewis Hamilton.

I phoned Lavender for her to investigate.

'Lavender ... what does Niddry Street mean to you? Are there any buildings, churches, locations connected with that place?'

'Connie's sweatshirt was found there, nothing else.' A painful silence fell between us. The phone went dead. We were too busy to be polite.

Normally I would never cross the line and act against my client. And I was still Thomas Foster's lawyer. I would be until I withdrew from acting or he sacked me. But I believed Sonia. She had no reason to lie. And Connie's life was at stake.

No contest.

The roads were empty except for a few cabs and Tesco lorries coming back into the city. So why did I still feel like I was being watched? The fine hairs on my neck stood on end. My fears were dispelled as I drove into Gamekeeper's Road, Edinburgh's millionaire row. The house was named Bourich. At another time, in another place, it would have raised a smile. Bourich is a Gaelic word that loosely translated means chaos, confusion or a bloody mess. Just like the case against Thomas Foster.

The driver took me to the front door. I dived out and as soon as I gathered my wits together to sign the man's contract slip, he was gone. Bancho was waiting outside but I couldn't see Joe. I had a bad feeling about this and as I approached the front door it got worse, my stomach began to ache – a sure sign something was wrong.

Even from the front garden the house sounded like a venue for a World Wrestling Entertainment title fight.

'Didn't I tell you to control him?' I shouted at Bancho as I heard more glass smashing. Bancho looked like a man who had been vindicated: his chin was up, his shoulders were back and he was enjoying the sound of Joe at work – he wasn't about to listen to me.

'Get in there you idiot and stop this!'

I ran round the back to the French windows. Joe had thrown one of the granite boulders that lined the driveway through the glass, and it had shattered into what seemed like a million pieces. It was a good job that there were no neighbours nearby or their attention would surely have been attracted by the noise. We followed a trail of his blood. Bancho leant against the wall of what seemed to be Adie Foster's office. There were the usual family photographs and several showed Thomas at chess competitions – he was quite the little grandmaster. Bancho lit a cigarette and enjoyed the nicotine; he held it in his lungs. The noise suggested Joe was banging Thomas's head off the stairs.

Unconcerned, Bancho wandered round the office fingering the framed photographs. He was particularly interested in the image of Thomas Foster taken in Revolution Square, Bucharest; Thomas was pointing out the bullet holes that led to the end of communist rule in Romania.

'Brodie, what was it about those women that angered him ... was it unrequited love?'

'Oh, Bancho, we don't have time ... this case is a tangled mess ... and we're not going to get any answers if Thomas Foster is dead.'

He followed me into the hallway, just as Glasgow Joe was thrown from the top landing. Joe wasn't fighting Thomas Foster, he was wrestling with the Sumo bodyguard I'd met on Christmas Eve. Blood poured from Joe's nose as he lay winded on the floor. He didn't look like a bookie's favourite as the Sumo came hurtling down the stairs after him. I took the pepper spray I always carry out of my bag and, turning, sprayed it into the Sumo's eyes. The fat man was blinded and covered his face, staggering backwards.

I helped Joe to his feet. Bancho radioed for the two constables guarding the perimeter to come in and clear up the mess. I didn't need Joe to tell me that the Foster family were not at home.

'You ran this by the chief constable?' I accused. 'The chief constable who happens to be a Mason in cahoots with Adie Foster?'

'I had to... I didn't think the bastard would tell them,' said Bancho apologetically.

I was furious. But I had to choose my battles carefully. 'The chief's got a lot of explaining to do, but right now we'd better get to Edinburgh Airport – it's common knowledge the Fosters have a private jet. How fast can you drive?'

Chapter Fifty-Nine

Edinburgh Airport
Saturday 29 December, 4.45 a.m.

Sonia's story changed everything but it didn't make anything any clearer. She claimed to have been attacked by a man answering to Thomas Foster's description. The detail of her evidence could only have been given by someone who had experienced it; the press did not know that the victims were alive when their ankles and hands were hacked off – yet Thomas Foster's DNA did not match the Ripper's.

Bancho had radioed the control tower and the Foster plane had been refused permission to take off. The light in the Edinburgh Airport terminal was harsh, but even in a dim light Bancho would have looked rough. This case had aged him more than was fair, and I couldn't see a happy ending. Glasgow Joe stumbled into the empty concourse, even worse for wear than DI Bancho.

'You have enough to arrest him, and question him for six hours, but I think you'll get enough evidence to charge him with Sonia's assault ... provided she'll give you a statement. Sonia is in the flat at the Rag Doll pub. Even if she does cooperate, this time he'll get bail,' I warned.

'Of course ... so then he'll be free to walk the streets and kill at will,' Bancho snarled, as he reached for his phone and called for a squad car to collect Sonia.

'There's only Sonia's eyewitness account,' I said. 'And there's also DNA evidence it wasn't him. But maybe Thomas will tell us the identity of the real Ripper before his father takes him out of Scotland to a country that doesn't have an extradition treaty.'

'Breach of bail,' Bancho fired at me.

Bancho was wrong again. I bit my tongue. I was not yet strong enough to point out all the weaknesses of his case. We walked together down the open space of the hall; DI Bancho was in the middle, separating Joe and me. It wasn't necessary. We were too broken to fight. The check-in desks for Air France and Virgin were black and silent – they matched my mood.

I dug my hands deep into my pockets. I could keep going if I focused on just one step at a time; I knew I would lose it if for one moment I considered the bigger picture. Connie was something I needed to deal with, but not right now.

313

The dead girls walked before us. I was sure Bancho was talking to them – he kept patting the pocket by his heart where he kept their photographs. His nails were bitten to the quick and several of them had red, open wounds where skin had been ripped away.

Will he ever recover from this case – will any of us?

I turned to Bancho and a small moan escaped my lips. I shook my head; I didn't want to point out the obvious. *I didn't want them to mistake my motive.* 'Thomas Foster is not on bail. When I asked for bail it was refused. The chief constable had him released without any conditions. Unless you have anything else on him, he can fly off into the sunrise.'

'Sonia – she identified him.' Joe was looking round and Bancho tried to eyeball me into pulling a legal rabbit from a hat. But I couldn't oblige.

'The attack was more than six months ago – it wasn't witnessed. Any DNA that could have pointed to Thomas Foster being her attacker has been washed away in a thousand hot showers ... and I think Sonia's a runner,' I said.

A couple of Edinburgh Airport police were waiting to escort us through the door marked 'private'. They were both in late middle age, and the spread of their waists indicated it was a long time since they had graced the rugby field. The officers paraded proudly in front of us, like Tweedledee and Tweedledum holding open every door. As soon as we were through they rushed onto the next set; it was vaguely distracting. Especially since DI Bancho had confirmed he didn't have a plan for holding my client. I was in new territory; very good at getting scumbags out, no practice in keeping them behind bars.

Bancho was running his hands through his thinning hair, obviously racking his brains for a plan.

We were getting nearer to the plane but Bancho was no nearer to finding a solution to his problem of keeping Thomas Foster within the jurisdiction of Scots law. He'd been working the case for months, destroying himself through overwork; was it likely the solution could be with us before midday? I thought not. The final door pushed out onto the runway, the morning sun just a couple of hours away from breaking through. The cold wind assaulted my face.

'I think it's best if I don't go any further. After all, I am his lawyer – no doubt he'll ask for me when you arrest him.'

I stopped dead. Joe continued moving apace with DI Bancho.

'I'll give you one piece of advice, Bancho,' I said. The runway was wet and shiny; he turned around and cupped his ear, he wanted to hear what I said. I knew he needed to take this advice.

'Before you get on the plane, speak to Lavender – she's expecting your call... Put it on loudspeaker,' I whispered.

He stopped just within earshot; he understood my difficulties. I was still Thomas Foster's lawyer, there was a limit – in fact there were many – as to what I should be doing.

For once he did exactly as he was told.

'Lavender, I understand you have something for me.' He scratched his head and waited whilst she brought up her screen.

'DI Bancho, The Hobbyist website has a chapter in New Haven, Connecticut. After Thomas Foster joined the Yale student body, murders started happening ... four girls found over a period of nine months and the same m.o. as the Edinburgh murders, all corresponding with Thomas Foster's term.'

'Lavender, was he charged?'

'No ... he wasn't even a suspect ... his red-headed friend was ... but here's the funny thing – the guy's details have all been wiped from the FBI computers.'

'So Foster's not the killer ... his friend is?'

'I dunno ... you tell me, but the main suspect would be more likely to have a redheaded relative who had tipped him over the edge.'

Bancho closed his phone and continued walking towards the plane. All we knew was that Thomas Foster might be an accessory to murder. But where did that leave Sonia's story?

Chapter Sixty

Edinburgh Airport
Saturday 29 December, 4.30 a.m.

The Watcher's night had just got better. It was delightful giving Brodie a lift out to Thomas Foster's house. Of course he'd been with her all night, applauding their progress. When the big oaf drove off without her, The Watcher clapped his hands. It was really very careless of Joe – he could have been anyone. The Watcher had many disguises; he liked to hide in plain sight, so he affected the disguise of ordinary people who no one would question. Cabbies can go anywhere. He could almost smell victory. All that he wanted now was to see Thomas Foster marched off the plane and taken into police custody. But perhaps that would be foolhardy. Thomas Foster was the only person who knew his true identity and his role in the Ripper case. Maybe freedom was necessary for him too.

Just thinking of Foster made The Watcher press himself back into his car seat, into the shadows. He gave himself a quick lecture. He had to exert patience and control himself. The many months of work he had put in were coming to fruition. He had come so far, he could bide his time. After all, Thomas was a formidable opponent.

The battle of wills between himself and Foster had started on another continent; their enmity had spread to Scotland. The Watcher was not a cold man – he sighed, regretting the necessity of so many lost lives. Indiscriminate murder was not elegant and The Watcher admired finesse. He sighed again and closed his eyes for a moment's quiet reflection.

To be honest, Brodie McLennan had disappointed him. To begin with, he'd had high hopes for her, he'd even hoped that they could be allies, but sadly it had been proven that her intellect simply was not up to it. Besides, she'd looked rather tatty and torn leaning up against the pillar in the airport terminal, not quite what she was a

317

few weeks ago.

He got out of his vehicle and marched adjacent to them. He sniggered – they were, of course, marching to a different drummer. The Watcher liked the military analogy. He had been a keen member of the Officers' Training Corps at school. Using the night-vision goggles, he watched them stand on the tarmac with that stupid detective. He wondered whether Brodie had given Bancho the information he'd fed to Lavender Ironside? Now she was quite a surprise! A revelation; a bonus. The Watcher stopped for a moment to consider how Lavender had acquired the skills to hack into the FBI computer – he was right to fear her, and even more right to involve her. Hopefully, they were on to Thomas Foster by now.

Time was running out.

Didn't she understand the concept of delegation? Bancho would arrest and detain Foster using the information he had fed to Lavender Ironside. He needed Brodie back in Edinburgh, ready to pick up the rest of the trail he'd laid for them. He drummed his fingers impatiently off the goggles. Dear God. Would they ever shut up and get a move on? He had plans for Brodie McLennan, even if they were not quite as satisfying as he had initially fantasized. Call him an old romantic, but he still had high hopes for her.

The sight through the night glasses was truly remarkable; there was such detail that he could even see the tired rings around Brodie's eyes. She zipped up her jacket and pulled the collar up against the wind. Her fingernails were torn and dirty. No lady had hands like that. He wondered

318

if the blackness under her nails was bike oil; for some reason he found that possibility exciting.

Finally they were on the move – how chivalrous of that big bastard to put his arm around her to shelter her from the gathering storm. Glasgow Joe seemed to be searching the skies again, scanning the perimeter of the fences ... searching for *him*, no doubt. Trying to keep her safe. It was laughable. The Watcher sniggered on his way back to his vehicle. They hadn't caught on to him by now and they never would. Once Thomas Foster was safely contained behind bars he would go back to his old life, which was markedly more comfortable than this one.

He wondered if they'd discovered the secrets of Connie's sweatshirt yet.

He shivered – it had nothing to do with the cold and everything to do with anticipation.

Chapter Sixty-One

St Leonards Police Station, Edinburgh
Saturday 29 December, 7.15 a.m.

The taxi headed to St Leonards. He had a clear run with the roads devoid of traffic. The citizens of Edinburgh appeared to be taking the whole two-week period of Christmas and New Year off. Glasgow Joe was twitching about in the back seat. It bothered me – it seemed more than his usual reluctance at being a passenger.

The Sheriff Court was quiet but today was a working day; we had a few custodies, but they were being covered by Eddie, and Louisa was going with him in case he needed help.

There were no trials or deferred sentences: even the judges were on vacation.

The taxi driver was chatty, cheery in spite of the time. I was worried, and when I worry I chatter like a budgerigar. Glasgow Joe was too busy staring out of the windows to notice my discomfort. I didn't want the cabbie asking me where I'd been last night. What I'd been up to over the Christmas season. What was on the cards for today.

And so I succumbed to asking him the usual questions: what time had he come on, when would he finish, had he been busy? As if I was at all interested in his answers. He served his purpose well. His mundane small talk anchored me in the present, so I could consider my next step.

As the cab drew up outside the police station, dawn had not yet broken; the reception desk was empty, and the Christmas tree still twinkled pathetically. Nothing had changed. The driver handed me a contract slip to sign; as I handed him back the paper and his pen he caught my hand and held it, his eyes dug into mine.

'I hope you get her back.' His eyes shone. 'My grand-daughter played against her at football, just before Christmas – she's very upset; well, we all are.' He nodded and turned back to his steering wheel. I clamped my lips together and nodded back. Malcolm was so much better at graciously receiving people's sympathy than I was.

Two teams of detectives were working on this;

Connie's case was being treated as child abduction, separate although linked to the Ripper murders. Kailash, Malcolm and Moses were at Four Winds with the second team and Moses was playing Xbox Live, still searching the gaming community for her. He would not give up until we had her back – dead or alive.

Sergeant Munro was still on the front desk – he must be working a twelve-hour shift. All overtime had been cancelled and officers from other forces had been drafted in to patrol the streets. The streets were filled with the type of girls the Ripper loved so much. Sergeant Munro was busy – I could tell he'd seen us but he kept his head down working on a piece of paper. I waited, every bone in my body ached, I wanted to fall into a deep sleep and never wake up – I couldn't be bothered playing games with him.

'You'll be here, to see Thomas Foster,' he said curtly. 'Well, he's being held for six hours and, as you well know, under Scots law you've no right to see him during that time.' Sergeant Munro opened up the reception desk and walked through; he held the large bunch of keys that were attached to his trousers in his hand. He walked slowly, fingering the individual keys in silent contemplation. Glasgow Joe was leaning against the wall staring out at the street, lost in his own hell. Sergeant Munro shouted twice before Joe heard him.

'Oi! Big man – you'd better come too.' Sergeant Munro held the door open for Joe, who was doing a fair impersonation of a somnambulist. I reached for his hand. I had a feeling Sergeant Munro was not taking me to see Thomas Foster but rather to give us news about Connie. He showed us into a dreary interview room. Joe and I have both been in these rooms before, and never have I wanted to be in a place less than I did now.

I slumped down on the table and watched the clock's big black second hand tick away the time. Joe and I were beyond speech but we continued to squeeze each other's hands. The door squeaked open and a young white-blonde WPC, who was MTV pretty, looked at us, then anxiously laid down two mugs of strong sweet tea – which we had not asked for.

'Sergeant Munro thought you could do with some of this.' She placed the tea and Rich Tea biscuits on the table and left. I gave her six months on the force. It was no reflection on her, but if she couldn't bear to be in the presence of people whose lives had been ripped apart, she wouldn't last long. The mugs lay untouched in front of us as we continued to watch the seconds tick away.

At 7.56 a.m. the door opened again and Detective Smith entered the room. Her hands were behind her back, poorly concealing a large evidence bag. In spite of her best attempts to break this to us gently, I could see it was Connie's sweatshirt.

I caught her eye; she knew she'd been rumbled so Detective Smith tossed the evidence bag down on the table in front of us. We both shrank back. I inhaled deeply and held my breath. Staring at the thing was horrible; the pale pink Roxy sweatshirt was covered in dried blood. My heart raced at sprinting pace, a hot flush ran through my body, sweat appeared on the small hairs at the back of my neck and slowly trickled down.

Detective Smith had not yet deigned to speak. Reaching down she picked up the evidence bag and threw it against the wall. Joe and I glanced at each other.

'It's fake!' she screamed. 'Fake fucking blood – the kind of shit you buy at Hallowe'en from joke shops. The Addams family – quite a joke, Ms Mc-Lennan.' She leant over and sneered into my face – I could smell last night's whisky on her breath. 'I want the truth – or you'll see in the bells in jail.'

Her words went over my head as, pushing back the chair, I ran to the evidence bag and held it to my heart. There was a chance, a small glimmer, that Connie was alive. The next problem was how to get out of here and find her – by the look on Detective Smith's face we were going nowhere. She was playing the golden rule of child abduction over and over in her head. 'It's the family, stupid, it's always the family.'

Chapter Sixty-Two

St Leonards Police Station, Edinburgh
Saturday 29 December, 8.30 a.m.

I sat there and said nothing as she snatched the sweatshirt out of my hands; Joe had already been led to another interview room for questioning. It was the first rule of interrogation – divide and conquer. It was my intention to say nothing; Detective Smith believed my silence inferred guilt, although the law said otherwise.

Detective Smith strutted about the room. It was tiring just watching her, and I wanted to be left alone with my private thoughts. Connie was still out there – that's why I didn't see her with the dead girls yet. I just had to get out of here and find her before she *did* join them. Detective Smith could keep me in this room for six hours but my time started after Thomas Foster's so he would be on a plane before I was released.

'Nancy Drew, that's you,' said Detective Smith. She pointed her finger in my face then she pulled out her detective's badge and threw it down on the table. 'Is it worthless?' She paused. 'D'you think I got it by collecting tokens off crisp packets?'

Dutifully, I shook my head. 'If a tiny part of your ego could acknowledge the fact I earned it,' she said, hitting her badge off the table again, 'then let me help you find Connie.'

If I wanted to get out of here, now was not the time to point out my concerns over her track record. Fifteen child abduction cases and not one found alive.

Detective Smith threw herself down on the chair opposite me after delivering what she thought was a good 'help me to help you' speech. I made no reply and, rubbing her face vigorously, she tried to dry wash away the tiredness and frustration.

She allowed a minute to pass in silence. I know exactly how long it was. I watched the hands on the clock and counted down the seconds. Finally, she looked up at me with a mixture of anger and disappointment.

'How will you live with yourself when I find her broken, naked body? I'll find her – she might be dead but I'll bring her home – lay her at your feet and we'll both know you could have saved her.'

Her guilt trip didn't work on me. I didn't have time for it. And I knew she was only having a go at me because of her own abysmal record in bringing home abducted children alive. She was also pissed off at my involvement in 'her' case.

Detective Smith stood up and pushed back her chair. It squeaked as it moved along the floor. 'You're free to go. I'm going back to my office – go over what scanty leads I have for the thousandth time and see if something jumps out at me. If you change your mind, stop by for coffee.'

I didn't have time to waste so, thirty seconds after she left, I found myself asking for directions to her room.

It was smaller than Bancho's but location is everything. Situated right next to the water fountain, she was bound to be up on all the latest station gossip. It was tidier, and the victim's wall was smaller – it ripped my heart to look at it. Malcolm had fallen into the trap of most parents when asked for a photograph. There were at least ten different photographs on the wall. Detective Smith reached into her bottom drawer, and pulled out another bundle.

'Malcolm,' I said.

She nodded. 'He insisted.'

'It's crazy – it'll make no difference.' I spoke softly.

'Do you have any idea what's going on?'

I shook my head. 'But I know someone who might.'

She sat on the edge of her chair, mouth open like a fish ready to take the bait. I didn't keep her waiting.

'Thomas Foster.'

'He's your client and his DNA doesn't match,' she said.

'I know. I still think he's connected.'

'Well, this has a different feel to other child abduction cases I've worked.' I bit my lip – don't mention her track record, I said to myself.

I wandered over to Connie's wall. There was bugger all on it. I raked in my pockets and laid out what I had on Detective Smith's desk: two photographs of suspects, a piece of paper and silver foil filled with a ball of used chewing gum. I put the gum back in my pocket.

I smoothed out the note.

'Active evil is better than passive good,' she read.

'He left that note in my room.'

'What does it mean?' She looked to me for information.

'William Blake – annotations to Lavater.'

'Brodie, what's he trying to tell us?'

'He's a pretentious prick?'

'Well, he might be – but in his mind, what does it mean?' Detective Smith knew enough about me to be certain I'd researched the hell out of this quote – I'd chosen not to discuss it with anyone because it showed what we were up against.

I blew loudly through pursed lips; the act of

getting inside the madman's mind was tiring.

'The moral difference is not between good and evil, it is between action and inaction. Moral virtue cannot produce an act because it is restrained by rules.'

'What does that mean?' she asked, handing me my cup of coffee.

'It means that in his mind he has done the right thing. In legal terms he has no *mens rea* – no guilty mind. If there is no *mens rea*, he cannot be found guilty.'

'He left evidence in your bedroom that he is insane.' Detective Smith swallowed the hot coffee too quickly. She put the mug down, spilling coffee on the desk, and then began to thump her burnt oesophagus. At least she understood what we were up against.

'Clever bastard, isn't he?'

I nodded. 'Or maybe he is just plain mad.'

Chapter Sixty-Three

Bancho's Operations Room, St Leonards Police Station Saturday 29 December, 9 a.m.

Joe was waiting for me when I came out. His arms were outstretched and he pulled me close. Holding me tight, he gave me strength – I hoped I gave him some too.

'It's the first time I've been in here,' he said, still

cradling me. 'All my conversations with Bancho have taken place over the phone ... these photographs...' Joe was wrestling with his emotions; we needed cool, clear heads if we were going to find my sister.

'By my watch, Bancho arrested Thomas Foster at five thirty a.m. It's now nine o'clock, so we only have another two and a half hours to get information that will lead us to Connie... Bancho's just fishing with him and my client is too smart to fall for it.'

'You're not entitled to see him until eleven thirty. so if he's released he takes any information he has about Connie with him.' Joe stiffened with frustration.

'I have to convince Bancho to let me see him ... it's our only chance.'

'Do you think he's questioned him about the New Haven murders?' Joe whispered into my hair. Holding each other we could pretend, just for a second, that nothing was wrong. For Connie's sake we had to hold it together.

'You're the one who keeps telling me he's not an idiot. The American murders match Sonia's description of what happened to her.'

'He's not likely to confess ... and Lavender said it was his ginger friend who was the suspect ... it seems to me that he cooperated with the FBI ... he tried a citizen's arrest, led them to evidence that incriminated his friend. They don't think it was his fault that the serial killer got away.'

'So the only mention Thomas Foster got in the FBI files was a ... commendation?' I was finding it difficult to breathe; I stepped away from Joe. 'It doesn't seem right... Sonia wasn't lying and I know that the man who attacked her is my client.'

'I thought you weren't supposed to judge whether clients were innocent or guilty ... you're just there to represent them.'

I tapped the pictures. 'Memento mori ... the Victorians loved them, pictures of the dead. They made them quite an art form.'

'Brodie, I didn't take Latin at school.'

'Remember you must die ... the English translation is ... "Remembered you must die,"' I said looking at him.

'But not like that ... no one deserves to die like that – those girls deserve retribution. How did the American suspect escape?'

'Friends in high places tipped him off. Jack reckons that Thomas Foster is a Bonesman. I think it's likely that the New Haven killer is a Bonesman too.'

'You're going too fast...' He put his arm around me, and we stared at the girls, both trying not to look at Connie.

'Yale University is the home of one of the world's most influential secret societies,' I explained. 'Interestingly, it was once known as the Brotherhood of Death ... they meet in the "Tomb" every Thursday and Sunday and one of the most important rituals is that they have to share a personal history.'

Joe frowned: 'So they tell each other their deepest, darkest secrets and leave themselves wide open to be controlled by blackmail ... is that what's happening here? Thomas Foster didn't come forward with the goods when his ginger pal started taking the game too far... Why did they let the

329

other guy off?' Joe was edgy, and time was running out.

'The Skull and Bones is tiny, only fifteen members are tapped a year. That's why it's extraordinary they're so influential ... at one time you couldn't get into the upper echelons of the CIA unless you were a Bonesman, so it wouldn't be hard to get a Bonesman out of trouble.'

'So, the ginger killer got out of the country. They could still have put him on the FBI's most wanted list – extradited him,' Joe said. I didn't answer immediately.

'On every section the US would have been granted extradition; the crime is sufficiently serious, there exists a prima facie case, he would get a fair trial, murder is a crime in both countries, and the penalty would fit the crime,' I said.

'So why didn't they do that?' he asked.

'They didn't ask. Someone buried the evidence – they've buried the killer's identity so deep Lavender can't even find a nickname for him ... and he's walking about Edinburgh getting ready to strike again,' I said.

'Why ... would people hide a killer? It doesn't make sense.'

'Bit of mutual backscratching – get him out of here and we'll look the other way,' I said. 'As you know, I raised this point when I asked the judge and the police officers if they were Masons – when people in power owe their loyalty to a secret brotherhood, the law is inevitably bent...'

'But they're not Masons,' he said.

'No, they're Bonesmen – and until the seventies the Skull and Bones didn't keep their membership list secret, but they did keep their ritual secret. As G.W. Bush said, *It's so secret we can't talk about it.* John Kerry refused to answer questions on it *because it's secret.* Secrets and lies lead to getting away with murder.'

'Soon after Foster arrived in Edinburgh, the murders started. I think his American friend set up The Hobbyist site here.' Joe still looked embarrassed for having kept it a secret from me.

'The Hobbyist website deals with sex slaves... the US doesn't have a law against human trafficking. G.W. Bush, aka the Bonesman, promised zero tolerance, but Congress said it was too hard to impose so they just didn't bother,' I said, pulling a cup from the dispenser. The water was cold and refreshing.

'Brodie, are you telling me our hands are tied? It's up to the United States to give us the identity of the killer and they're not going to? For some reason Thomas Foster doesn't want to help the police here so he'll walk out of here a free man at eleven-thirty, taking the Ripper's identity with him? We've got fuck-all chance of finding Connie then.' I grabbed his arm; he looked as if he was going to storm the room where Bancho was interviewing Thomas Foster.

We walked along the corridor towards the interview room. Bancho was out having a drink – Joe and I could see that he was having no success.

As he caught sight of us approaching, his grip on the cup tightened.

'How did Sonia's statement go?' Joe asked. Bancho threw the cup in the bin and snarled, 'What statement? You idiots ... she's done a runner. She wasn't there. We're searching Leith again for her now, but I'm not holding my breath.'

'I want to see my client,' I said.

'You know you don't have any right...' He eyed me up and down, suspicious of my motives. If I murdered him in jail, would Bancho be an accessory to the fact?

'What's your answer?' I held his eyes. 'Have you questioned him about Connie?' I asked. Glasgow Joe growled in the background.

Shamefacedly he shook his head. 'It's not my investigation – I've only been quizzing him about the redheads.'

'So ... he has no reason to believe we suspect him of having anything to do with Connie's kidnap?' I said.

'Well, we are both agreed, he's not a fucking idiot. He took her – she's a redhead. Of course he knows we suspect him.'

'I don't agree. He's an arrogant bastard, and if he thinks he's walking out of here with the Ripper's name, he's mistaken,' I said. 'I think he's part of a killing team – that explains the DNA. He doesn't have to kill – he's doing this for some motive of his own,' I said. 'And I think his partner has Connie.'

I took a deep breath. 'Thomas Foster isn't the only one who knows the Ripper. We all do. Connie went *willingly* with her abductor. She knows him ... we all know him.'

Chapter Sixty-Four

**The Operations Room,
St Leonards Police Station
Saturday 29 December, 9.30 a.m.**

'If we know him, where is he hiding? I'm a pretty good judge of character. I'm sure I would have spotted something dodgy; my senses have been on red alert. How could I have looked into this man's eye and not known?' Glasgow Joe shook his head, disgusted with himself.

'It might be someone she's met on Xbox Live,' I said. The problem we had was that every one of us from Kailash to Moses prided ourselves on being a good judge of character, and I was all too aware of what they said about pride coming before a fall.

'Maybe it's a woman? Things aren't always what they seem.' Bancho's train of thought was interrupted when his phone rang. He listened in silence, nodding deferentially.

'No, sir, I wasn't aware the US embassy was involved,' he lied. 'Yes, sir, I understand the difficulties with the press. But, sir, I have new evidence. An eyewitness. The victim ... it was an assault on a prostitute.'

The conversation was obviously concluded by the other party and Bancho put the phone down.

'That was the chief constable. Adie Foster's in

reception – he's filed a complaint with the chief and I've been told I have to speak to him ... to calm the bastard down – avoid a diplomatic fucking incident.' He fired his mug off the wall next to the dead girls and it shattered.

'Calm down man,' Glasgow Joe eyeballed him. 'We don't have enough time for you to lose it.'

'Bancho,' I said. 'You've got two hours left to hold Thomas Foster. His father is gonna wait upstairs to whisk him somewhere, anywhere there are no extradition treaties,' I said.

'Really!' he replied sarcastically. 'You think I wasn't aware of that?'

'You go and continue your interrogation of Thomas Foster. I'll speak to his father; I'll calm him down and find out what he knows.' I tried to make it sound like I was doing him a favour, but there's no such thing as a free lunch. No one was going to stop me seeing Thomas Foster before the six-hour deadline ran out.

'Bancho, you will let Brodie speak to Thomas Foster before eleven thirty.' Glasgow Joe was not asking, he was telling the detective inspector what was going to happen. Bancho walked out of the room.

'He'll let you in to see Thomas Foster,' Glasgow Joe nodded at me.

'Are you sure?'

'Brodie, I'm positive ... what are you going to do in the meantime?'

'Adie Foster's upstairs. He knows more than he's letting on ... but I gave DI Smith the photographs of the two men and I want to show them to him.'

'You don't have a lot of time. Set the alarm on your watch. How long do you think you'll need?'

'Fifteen minutes is all I've got.'

By the time I got to Detective Smith's room I had already lost six minutes. Mercifully, the room was empty and, due to the tidier nature of the female detective, the photographs and the note were already pinned on the wall. I kissed my finger and laid it on my sister's picture.

With my free hand I shoved the evidence in my pocket and ran upstairs, not easy in the high heels and pelmet skirt I was wearing. Desk Sergeant Munro had put Adie Foster in a side office. It was a utilitarian, easily scrubbed-down type of room; no fabrics in which germs or lice could linger. The grey linoleum smelt of industrial disinfectant. Mr Foster was about to have an apoplectic fit, and it couldn't come soon enough as far as I was concerned.

Adie Foster was a man used to negotiating. He had instinctively moved round to the side of the Formica desk that the interviewer would occupy – the position of power.

'Don't you think you're a little ... casual?' he drawled, looking at the tart's outfit that I was still wearing. He looked like a CNN anchorman, his glossy grey hair unnaturally thick for a man of his age, his Botoxed forehead showing no emotion.

'I'm sorry, it's been a hard few days trying to prove your son's innocence. In spite of the fact that my sister's missing, I've trawled every cathouse in Leith and stood on street corners. You may have heard – I don't like to lose,' I said.

His eyes widened with surprise; he wanted to

buy into my story so I gave him more. Unsmiling, he stared at me. His nod of approval was barely discernible but I was watching for it.

'My grandfather, Lord MacGregor, and the Enlightenment Society were delighted when you instructed me. By the way, it was a stroke of PR genius to make your son work at the City Vaults ... it goes some way to dispelling the spoilt little rich kid image.' I kept nodding, reeling him in, even managing a smile, although without showing my teeth – it was more of a grimace.

'If it's such a good idea I wish I had thought of it – but I've never made Thomas go out to work.'

'Oh...' I paused, to better let my next line sink in. 'A member of the Enlightenment Society must have got that out to the press.'

My eyes read his every movement. He was buying it – not because I was good, but because he wanted to believe there was an easy way out of this.

'Well, I knew your ... "connections" ... were the reason you got Lucas Baroc such an excellent result. Lucas merely thought you were brilliant.' He laughed. *Arrogant bastard – he was relaxing, things were under his control again.*

'You were right of course. I understand you couldn't keep me fully apprised of the situation, but the Enlightenment Society did,' I said, slowing down enough to note the surprise in his eyes.

'I met with them on Boxing Day – we were gathered in the WS library for a function to honour my grandfather.' I spoke in a slow, measured tone, the rate of a human heartbeat, until he began to make those reassuring little nods again.

336

'I know about his misunderstanding with the FBI. In spite of what the chief constable may think, the US government will not get involved.'

I thought they would but I needed to see his reactions. Nothing. I mimicked the tone of voice, even matching his breathing; Machiavelli would have been proud. *Keep your friends close and your enemies closer. Adie Foster was a sly bastard. He was giving nothing away, forcing me to do all the talking. Truthfully this wasn't going to plan – so far I had learned nothing.*

'Thomas just has to keep his mouth shut for a couple more hours and he'll be home and dry... There is, however, one difficulty we have...' I said.

Adie Foster froze. This wasn't what he wanted to hear. It was not my job to point out problems – I was there to find solutions. I took the photographs of the priest and the man from The Hobbyist site out of my pocket and tried to slide them across the desk to him. The desk was sticky with spilt Irn Bru and the pictures got stuck. I waited to see if he would examine them.

'Do you know him?' I asked. But I already knew the answer from his rapid blinking and the way every facial muscle froze as he recoiled from the six-by-ten images. I was enjoying pushing the image in front of him. Whoever this man was, he certainly knew how to get under Adie Foster's skin.

A sweet paper lying on the floor crackled beneath his handmade shoes – he was backing away from the photograph. Mouth closed, I ran my tongue along the bottom edge of my teeth. I had him.

'Your son has an enemy. Care to tell me about it?' I slapped the photographs noisily down on the desk. He shook his head still backing away, ghostly white beneath the tan. *Was he going to vomit?*

I waited, counting my heartbeats; they were loud enough for Adie Foster to bear. He was lost in the silence of private thoughts; Detective Smith's help-me-to-help-you speech came to mind.

'I can't do this on my fucking own.' My voice was harsh and aggressive and shocked him out of his trance. I had once read a book on *How to Marry a Millionaire*. Apparently they are so rich everyone agrees with them, so they find difficult, high-maintenance women irresistible. I wasn't hitting on Adie Foster but I'd tried everything else – wasn't he the type of man who made up Kailash's clientele?

Adie Foster hated women, especially women who swore. He stood to his full height, and as an ex-linebacker for the Bulldogs, his physique was still impressive. Not missing a breath, I picked the photographs up and slapped them off his chest. I pounded them off his pectorals and shouted at him. Surely somewhere way back he was used to obeying a woman; his mother, a nanny, even a schoolteacher? I tried to claw the memory back to the surface of his mind.

'Adie Foster,' I pronounced each syllable. 'Tell me now – who is this man? What does he have to do with your son?'

I had backed him into a corner, and he seemed to have shrunk. 'It's a secret,' he whispered.

'Tell me about it.'

'I can't talk about it – it's secret.'

'Tell me NOW... I'm used to keeping secrets.' I slapped the photographs into his face.

'It's his *Anam Cara* from Yale.' He dropped his head, his words were barely audible.

Anam Cara: *soul friend. This friendship was based on an oath; it linked them in blood, a bond more enduring than brothers. This was the man Thomas Foster had confessed to during his initiation. Was he blackmailing Thomas Foster – was that why Foster was protecting him?*

The alarm on my watch buzzed and I had to leave the room.

Chapter Sixty-Five

St Leonards Police Station, Edinburgh
Saturday 29 December, 10.03 a.m.

We had less than eighty-seven minutes to break Thomas Foster and find Connie; weariness and Bancho's demeanour told me it wasn't going to happen. We reached the door of the interview room. Bancho stopped. He wasn't going any further. I needed to speak to Thomas alone.

The air left my lungs as Bancho threw me against the wall. My forehead rested on the flimsy stud partition. Kicking my legs apart he nearly knocked me through it. He forced my arms above my head; he didn't have time to wait for political correctness and a WPC to do a full body search.

'What the hell are you doing?' I screamed at him.

His hands gripped me through the leather jacket, squeezing every wrinkle in the hard fabric. He probed. It was obvious his intention was to check out every nook, cranny and cavity in my body. I felt his hands on my torso, his fingers climbed my ribs, searching my bra for concealed blades. DI Bancho was not enjoying his work; in fact he seemed to find it even more distasteful than I did.

'Glasgow Joe is within screaming distance!' I hissed.

My legs needed shaving but he didn't notice, his hands kept slapping them looking for something. Up the inside of my legs. I bit my tongue as he checked my panties. The man was nothing if not thorough and the bastard knew me too well.

'Stop it ... what are you doing?'

He ignored me, continuing with his search, prodding, poking, and finally his hands reached into my pocket and pulled out the backup plan – a Swiss army knife.

'What am I doing? I'm saving you from yourself. I hope you'll return the favour.' He pocketed the knife I always carried on the Fat Boy. I could write a book on the uses I have found for it – none would have been more satisfying than gutting Thomas Foster. Maybe then he would give me the Ripper's name. If Bancho felt the urge to take police brutality too far today, I promised myself I wouldn't stop him.

'You've got half an hour,' he said, scratching his head.

'You promised me longer.' I pulled him round to face me. He stepped back, the last few minutes was enough contact with me to last a lifetime.

'No, you promised yourself! Now you're lucky I'm giving you this … don't waste it,' he said. I knew he would be waiting just outside the door; he didn't trust me even with my bare hands.

I wasn't going to do anything foolish. I grabbed his lapel and whispered in his ear – I needed to get rid of him. 'A search warrant … we need a search warrant. Ask Detective Smith to get one for the City Vaults and as many bodies as she can muster … you know my family will help.'

'Why?'

'I'm looking for the smoking gun that will nail the Ripper and his associate,' I told him.

'Give me more than that.'

'Niddry Street appears once too often in this case for it to be a coincidence. Niddry Street where Connie's sweatshirt was found, Niddry Street where Sonia was discovered after the assault. What made Niddry Street so special? The City Vaults, where Burke and Hare, Edinburgh's first serial killers, hunted their victims, and where Thomas Foster said he had a part-time job.'

'Okay,' said Bancho with a note of resignation that suggested he might finally be coming on board.

'It's about domination and control,' I said. 'The Ripper takes sexual pleasure in having the power of life or death over his victims. He keeps trophies, I'd lay my life on it, and if he does they're in the vaults. We're going to get him.'

Chapter Sixty-Six

St Leonards Police Station, Edinburgh
Saturday 29 December, 10.10 a.m.

The door slammed behind me, the key turned in the lock. Christ, here I am looking like a red-headed tart throwing myself at a beast who feeds off my kind. The beast in question continued to do a fine impersonation of a Calvin Klein underwear model, his pale blue Oxford cotton shirt from Savile Row freshly laundered, his light beige chinos and tan loafers continuing the yachting theme.

He smiled but there was no warmth. He extended his hand and said, 'So good of you to come, ma'am.' His palm was cool and dry. His heart rate never reached above forty-five. His eyes flicked over me, taking in the cheap high heels, the torn black tights, a push-up bra barely hidden behind a supermarket scoop-top tee shirt.

'I gave you advice once before, ma'am – d'you regret not taking it?' he asked.

'You told me not to take your case – you were right, too, you didn't need me.'

I leant against the door, our eyes locked. I could feel him winning as the faces of the dead girls swam before me. I couldn't let him beat me. What was it Lavender said? Oh yes, I did remember.

I fitted the Ripper's signature – although I was

342

a little on the old side, and not quite the job description he was after. Would Thomas Foster fall for human bait? Sonia was clear Foster had attacked her, but the DNA was unequivocal. My best hope was he would attack me, buy me some time to find the Ripper.

Reaching up, I took the pen that held my hair in a French knot out, and my hair tumbled around my shoulders in a mass of red curls. As per normal I didn't have a comb so I used my fingers, teasing out each strand of hair. I was engrossed in this and could see him gulping. He tried to ignore me but I wouldn't stop. I wound strands of hair around my index finger and, perfecting the curl, I let it bounce free.

I looked up at him. He was on his feet, his hands were in his pockets and he was pacing. I took a cigarette out and lit it. I knew he was the evangelical type of non-smoker, anything to piss him off and rile him. I drew hard and swallowed the smoke, releasing rings of noxious fumes in his direction. He waved the smoke rings away.

'Those cancer sticks will kill you,' the little prick moralized at me.

'Another piece of advice, Thomas,' I said. 'We are full of it today, aren't we?'

I walked over to him and blew smoke in his face. I had made up my mind he wasn't walking out of here in seventy-six minutes, even if I had to punch myself in the face and claim rape – that little bastard was staying put.

'Anyway, Mr Genius, you should be delighted I didn't take your advice. Because I am your legal counsel–'

'–anything I tell you is confidential ... more hush-hush than the secrets of the confessional,' he mocked.

'Exactly,' I said, deciding the hair play was more effective than the cigarette smoke in unbalancing him. I took my jacket off; perhaps the sight of my neck would spur him on to spontaneous violence. He laughed.

'You just don't get it, do you?' he said.

'Sure I do, Thomas. You and your friend have got away with murder on two continents, but that's not satisfying enough for you, is it? The pleasure's spoiled because no one knows how clever you really are – even I think you're going to walk because of Daddy's connections.'

He closed his eyes, and for a moment I thought he was preparing an attack. Adrenalin pumped through my system, a trickle of sweat ran down my left arm and his eyes opened like a reptile's. He smelt my fear and it excited him. I had to get the balance of power back in my direction.

'Connections – that's the real reason you didn't want me, isn't it? You knew who I was, and my Grandaddy's connected. Did you get scared – is that why you changed your mind?' I mocked him.

His eyes closed again. He was meditating, trying to regain composure, a technique no doubt picked up during his chess tournaments. His breathing steadied and I watched a prominent vein in his neck bob up and down – his heart rate was slowing. He was winning again. Thomas looked up and smiled at me. Clasping his hands together he steepled his index fingers and tapped them off his lips. I couldn't let this happen; I didn't like to lose either.

I kicked him hard in the groin but his reactions were fast. He held my calf in the air and I hopped on one leg but I would not cry out. I could feel the frustration building. My throat was tight; it was hard to breathe. He sniggered, I flailed my arms about but he would not release me. In desperation I tore at his shirt and threw the photographs at him; they missed ... flying through the air and landing near the corner.

Luck was on my side, though, they landed picture side up. Thomas Foster froze as he stared at the man in the photograph. He dropped my leg. I stumbled, placing my hand on the desk to prevent a fall. He clasped his Breitling watch and ran to pick the images up. Holding the photographs aloft he started to laugh. He laughed like a maniac.

'Tell me who he is!' I demanded.

'No.'

'Don't tell me it's a fucking secret,' I said.

He snapped at me. I had touched a button. 'I don't follow their code.'

'If you don't tell me who he is, you're just like your father. He wouldn't speak either,' I said.

Thomas Foster's eyes slid from side to side in his head, weighing things up. For the first time I saw his ugliness. His shirt was open to the waist, exposing his chest. I clutched my throat to stop the vomit.

And that's when I knew I had him.

Chapter Sixty-Seven

St Leonards Police Station, Edinburgh
Saturday 29 December, 10.17 a.m.

Things started to go haywire again when I looked at the clock. I had less than fifteen minutes to get the information I needed from him. He was still holding the photographs and laughing – and he didn't give the impression of stopping any time soon.

I ran my fingers through my hair, though not to get his attention. Frustration made me want to pull each strand out by the root.

'Your father is the winner – you're going to walk free from here, and it's all thanks to him!' I lied, watching him to see if it would get through. His laughter slowed; he buttoned up his shirt, but I had seen all I needed to.

'That night after they arrested me at my parents' house, I was scared out of my wits,' he said.

'No wonder – your father couldn't pull the strings quite so easily in Edinburgh.' He looked at me doubtfully.

'From the first time we met I knew, I knew I was going to win ... no matter what.' He came close in to my face and sniggered.

'How'd you work that one out?'

'Just your attitude ... you'd do anything to win ... that's your weakness ... your Achilles heel.'

346

'Let's not talk about me – let's get on to your favourite subject. You owe your father big time: is that why you won't tell me who this is?' I tapped the photograph.

'I have science on my side, ma'am. It's irrefutable – that bastion of forensic science, DNA... Ha, it's not my DNA, ma'am, it says I didn't rape them and I didn't kill them, ha ... how about that?'

'I've spoken to Sonia–'

He interrupted me. 'You need to win this more than me; if you want it so bad, let's play Ulam's game.' He sniggered, not expecting me to know what he was talking about, arrogant little bastard. He was almost right, but something nagged at the back of my mind.

'Ulam's pathological liars' game.' I said it slowly; necessity was pulling it from the dark and dusty recesses of my mind.

'Very good!' he said, walking around the room clapping his hands. He was careful not to destroy the photographs.

Ulam's game was described as a well-known game semantic for mathematical probability – Lukasiewicz logic and product logic. Well known to nerds! To win the information I needed to beat a chess grandmaster who had a higher IQ than Einstein in less than – I looked at my watch – eleven minutes.

'Do you want to play?' he asked, raising his left eyebrow and staring me down.

'Why not? I always liked the YES/NO guessing game. Shall we start at the beginning?' I pulled the photograph from his hand.

'Did you meet him at university – yes or no?'

347

I asked.

'I'm not going to play if you're not going to be specific. You're not very good at this, ma'am,' he drawled.

'Did you meet him at Yale University?' I asked.

'No.' His smile was chilling; he was right, I wasn't very good at this. I sat down opposite him. I had to take this seriously. It was my one chance. My last chance. We faced each other like a couple of grandmasters. Only one of us was pretending.

'Did you meet him on The Hobbyist website?' He laughed again, like it was some great secret joke.

'Hell, no.'

I didn't care how it looked. I put my head down on the table. It was too heavy to hold up; I only just stopped myself banging it off the melamine top.

'Did you meet him at the Skull and Bones Society?' I snapped.

His lips pursed into a thin line, the muscle in his jaw twitched and tightened – he was under pressure. Thin beads of sweat formed on his forehead, a furrow appeared between his brows. Something had happened at Yale that Thomas Foster didn't like. I could hear the seconds ticking down in my head. I had to ask the questions even if they were way off the mark – and I had to speed up. Feeling the pressure, my brain function seemed to slow down.

'Did the Ripper kill at Yale?' I asked.

'Yes.'

'Did you kill?'

'Yes.'

'Did he know you were a murderer?' I asked.

'I object to that term,' he said.

'Not a valid objection – you have to play by the rules,' I said, knowing this was the only thing that would get through to Thomas Foster. He played by rules, used them – that's what a grandmaster did.

'Did he know you were a killer?'

'Yes.'

'Did he guess?' I asked.

'No.'

I wanted to know how the man who called himself 'The Watcher' had discovered Thomas Foster's secret but, according to the rules of Ulam's game, I couldn't ask. Perhaps they were a killing team.

'Did he follow you to Scotland?'

'Yes.'

'To join you?' I asked.

He shrugged his shoulders.

'To kill you?' I asked again.

'Yes.'

I was beginning to see the limitations of this game. It would give me information but no clues that would help me.

DI Bancho knocked on the door.

'Two more minutes,' I shouted.

'Did you take Connie?'

'No,' he whispered and began to laugh again. 'He beat me to it.' He giggled.

The chill knifed through me, my mouth was parched. I glowered at him for several moments, then I stood up unexpectedly and made for the door.

'Hold up a minute, Brodie. Don't be irrational.

349

Don't you want to finish our game?'

'The police have to release you in ten minutes,' I lied. 'There isn't enough time for them to pin anything on you – what do I care about some redheaded whores? You didn't take my sister.'

My fingers were already on the handle. I turned to face him.

'By the way – I still think your dad won,' I said. The hair on my arms and the back of my neck were electrified.

'You're the winner, Brodie. You won – you got the Ripper off – how good does that feel?' he asked.

Fury bubbled inside me but I remained utterly still.

Thomas Foster tittered, a soft, joyless giggle.

'I sold you a lie about Katya Waleski and you made it work – you even thought it was Moses Tierney's fault. Anyone was to blame except the prettiest boy in town.' He fluttered his eyelashes like a Disney character, mocking me. I knew about the halo effect and I had fallen for it.

I held my thumb and forefinger up, giving him the Loser sign.

'LOSER,' I mouthed.

'Oh hell, I've gotta tell somebody. Look at them ... the whole of Lothian and Borders police force have been scouring for evidence. He's the only adversary I respect,' he said.

Thomas Foster waved the image of The Watcher in my face.

'He's had backup – he's been feeding inform-ation to Bancho. Even together they still couldn't catch me.' Thomas was gleeful, it all spilled out of him, he'd been dying to boast.

I looked up at him and said callously: 'Okay, what's the twist? Why redheads?'

'Well, I'll give you a clue, ma'am. The man you call The Watcher – he likes redheads ... you could even say he loves them. But that's his private business; we respect a man's secrets. If you want to know more, you're gonna have to ask him yourself.' He nodded at me, as if he was about to tell me to 'have a good day'.

'I know you didn't pick on Eastern European girls because they were sex slaves – that must have made it hard for you. It was too easy ... just cattle. No one even missed the bitches,' I said.

'That depends,' he said in a slow, cold drawl. 'Maybe someone else was afraid when these girls went missing. It might draw the authorities' eyes elsewhere.'

'More secrets,' I said.

He made his thumb and forefinger into a gun, he pointed it and clicked. Winking his left eye he said 'Gotcha', and his laugh filled the room.

Bancho knocked impatiently on the door. I opened the door. His hand went up and closed it; leaning against it he whispered in my ear.

'It's gonna be fun watching you ... when they open up my cell and give me a fiver for the taxi home.'

'One last chance – tell me who he is!' I snatched the photographs from his hand.

'See, that's the funny thing. You already know.' He fell against the wall and started to laugh. He was still laughing as I walked down the hallway, laughter that would disturb me in the stillness of the night for years to come. Bancho was waiting; I stopped and whispered in his ear.

'Before you release Thomas Foster, you are going to receive an anonymous phone call. Take the information you'll be given seriously.'

Chapter Sixty-Eight

City Vaults, Niddry Street, Edinburgh
Saturday 29 December, 10.45 a.m.

'Detective Bancho...'

I was making the phone call in the back of a police car on my way to the vaults. The most fundamental ethic a lawyer has is client confidentiality. As Foster remarked, it's more sacred than the secrets of a confessional, and I was about to breach it. Bancho played his part. He pretended he didn't recognize my voice, and he ignored the fact that my name came up on his mobile.

'I have information which will lead to the arrest and conviction of Thomas Foster. Tell Patch that Thomas Foster has Blaschko's lines.'

'Blaschko's lines?'

'The lines of Blaschko ... it's an extremely rare unexplained phenomenon of human anatomy. Tell Patch that Thomas Foster's chest is covered with the S-shaped pigmentation patterns. Blaschko's lines are an invisible pattern built into human DNA... When a layman sees them it looks like stripes.'

I'd learned about Blaschko's lines many years before, when Patch was lecturing us as law students. He had been involved in a case where DNA evidence had been proved to be fallible.

'Are you telling me that Thomas Foster's a zebra?' Bancho sounded disappointed.

'No, I'm telling you that Thomas Foster is a chimera ... he has more than one type of DNA in his body. Patch needs to look at all his samples again ... retest Thomas Foster: one will match with the semen.'

'Bollocks – DNA is unique to each person, the samples show the semen in the girls could not have belonged to Foster – DNA can never be wrong.'

'That's the lie they sold us for a century about fingerprints ... how many were hung on the back of that belief? We're still learning about DNA. Trust me: Chimera Syndrome exists!'

'What the hell's a chimera?' Bancho asked.

'In Greek mythology, a chimera was a beast made up of a lion, a goat and a dragon. Human chimeras aren't as drastic as that, but within the last few years we've discovered they do exist – no one knows what percentage of the population might be chimeras.'

'So he could have at least two different sets of DNA in him?'

'Correct!'

'Holy shit – I'll get Patch on to it.'

I hung up before he used my name, and just as the car pulled up outside the City Vaults in Niddry Street. I mentally kicked myself for not having worked this out sooner. What Sonia could tell us about the place where she was held and what we knew about where she was found: this had to be the place. The vaults are a series of rooms under the South Bridge in Edinburgh. Work was started in 1785, to span the Cowgate gorge and meet up with the growing Edinburgh University. There are nineteen arches but only one is visible. The Ripper had hidden his trophies somewhere inside these eighteen hidden crypts. So many people have reported sightings of ghosts in the vaults that they are a big draw to believers in the paranormal – which was why Sonia was still alive. Thomas Foster attacked her on Hallowe'en – the only night the vaults are open to the public.

The Dark Angels were already there, looking at home in these subterranean catacombs.

'We've got forty-five minutes to find what we need – is everyone clear what we're looking for?' I said. 'Somewhere in these vaults is the room the Ripper used to torture his victims – I'm certain he's the type of killer who likes to keep trophies to prolong his pleasure.'

Kailash stared at me sadly through eyes so swollen with crying she could barely open them. Her skin was free of makeup and deep lines of mourning had been etched around her mouth. She was defeated, and for the first time she looked older than her years. Glasgow Joe put his arm around her and held the torch as they set off to search.

'Tick-tock, tick-tock – let's get a move on,' said Cal, looking at his Brietling watch. He was the Dark Angel I had seen in George Street selling drugs with Blind Bruce. My eyes widened in surprise as I recognized him as the priest from the Meadows. He stiffened. Our eyes locked.

'Cal's right. He was her favourite Xbox friend. We don't have all day,' Moses shouted, clapping his hands and shooing us off. We switched our torches on; they flickered over the floors and ceilings like World War II searchlights. What we sought was carefully hidden in plain sight ... the Masonic way, the way of every secret society from the Illuminati to the quilts that detailed the underground maps for runaway slaves.

What we really needed was someone schooled in the ways of secrets – my grandfather. Unfortunately, he had been sedated by his doctor and Malcolm had remained behind to care for him.

The vaults were freezing. There was no sunlight or ventilation, water ran down the stone walls; originally the vaults were mainly used as storage facilities but they were never waterproofed and eventually the merchants moved their goods elsewhere. The slum dwellers then moved in. The area became a notorious red-light district with as many as ten families occupying one room. There was no sanitation. Even today the atmosphere is oppressive.

This was the first police search carried out within the vaults. Connie's sweatshirt and Sonia had been found outside in Niddry Street. There was no reason to connect them – no reason unless you knew of Thomas Foster's obsession with the place. And I wasn't the only one who knew.

A rat scuttled by my foot. I was on my own. I leant against the dank wall, the damp chill seeping into my bones. Tick-tock, tick-tock. Cal's phrase would not leave my mind. Every sinew and fibre in my body locked.

I held my breath as the damp smell of cats' pee threatened to overwhelm me.

I continued to walk forward. The ground was uneven and the darkness became my friend – no one could see my tremors. I followed the scratching of the rats. How could there be so many when there was nothing to eat? I forced myself on, wishing I had on my heavy bike boots instead of the stiletto sandals. My toes poked through holes in my tights and I could feel the claws of the rats as they ran across my foot.

I found Cal, the Dark Angels' chemist, quickly enough. Just as I expected, he was prodding the girl with him to make the discovery. Like the Pied Piper, he was surrounded by rats as he stood in the shadows doing what he did best – watching.

'Cal, are we close to finding something?' I asked, struggling to keep my voice calm. I listened, the echoes from the other search parties sounding very far away. The smell of damp decay hung heavy in the air like a wet blanket.

'Yes, I can almost guarantee it.' His voice was cold; he knew I had unearthed his secret and a sad smile crossed his face.

The scratching of the rats was very close, every scrape of their claws on the dirt sent goose pimples up my arms. Fear-induced sweat trickled down my spine, a painful water torture I was desperate to wipe away, but the nibbling, foraging sound of the rats kept me frozen and spellbound.

Slowly, carefully, I placed my hand inside my right jacket pocket, my fingers searching for salvation. It was empty. Nervously I rummaged around in my left pocket, but it was futile. There was nothing I could do with an empty cigarette packet and a box of matches. The stupid bastard Bancho had forgotten to give me my Swiss Army knife back.

I was unarmed and about to confront The Watcher. He observed my every movement, including the way my face fell when I realized I was defenceless. I pulled the cuff of my jacket over my hand to pretend I had a weapon.

He put the flashlight into my eyes, blinding me, and he slowly tilted his head to one side and smiled. A menacing chuckle escaped from his lips; he was enjoying this. The pretty Dark Angel scrambled about in the dirt struggling to move an eighteenth-century whisky barrel. Crimes of robbery and murders are not new in the vaults.

'Just lift it up – and be careful,' he hissed.

'Well, shine the bloody light down here so I can see!' she snapped back.

I felt him falter, should he stay or go? In that moment he made his first mistake. He shone the light down into the recessed archway. The whisky butt was made in the eighteenth century from oak to hold over five hundred litres. The girl tried to lift it up. But then she hesitated for a split second. She could already smell the death and decay. She dropped her corner down onto the packed earth with a thud; shaking her head from side to side she backed away from the cask, standing on my toes in the process.

None too gently I threw her aside. Lifting up the oak cask was no easy job. My silent mantra was repeated over and over: I hate this, I hate this. It was no good; it was too heavy. I needed his help but the question was, would he give it? He placed the torch down on the floor. The girl had already run away and we were alone in the shadows as we lifted the giant whisky butt up and threw it into the back of the recess.

It bounced and rolled against a wall. I screamed ... and screamed. The rats were undisturbed by my shrieks and happily continued to gnaw on the feet of the dead girls. Some of the toes were still painted pink with pearl nail polish. I don't know how many bodies we still hadn't found, but I knew from this putrid pile that it was a hell of a lot.

I didn't stand a chance. Hypnotized by the horror of the scene before me, the first I knew of the attack was the prick of the needle. Even in my terror, unconsciousness was not welcome.

Chapter Sixty-Nine

**Mayfield Private Clinic, Edinburgh
Tuesday 1 January, 2.45 p.m.**

'I'm Dr Watchman. You're in the Mayfield Clinic. Do you know what happened?'

'I was hit. Just once – but once was enough.'

'No, you were drugged. You hit your head on the way down,' he corrected.

'What is your name, Ms?' he asked.

'Brodie, Brodie McLennan.'

'How many fingers am I holding up?' He shone

a light in my eyes as he fired these questions at me. All I could see were toes with pink nail varnish and all I could hear was the sound of rats gnawing. I fought back the hot bile that rushed into my throat.

'Four. No, wait ... two fingers. You're holding up two fingers.'

'Are you experiencing any pain?'

'Is the Pope a Catholic?'

'Are you experiencing any pain?' he asked again.

'My head feels as if it has a troupe of dancing elephants on it. Oh, and I want to vomit ... real bad.'

An Irish nurse handed me a grey papier-mâché bowl that looked like a top hat, and when I held the sick bowl out in front of me, I noticed I was hooked up to an IV. *How long had I been out?* I couldn't wait for the answer to come to me. Hot green bile came rushing from my gut; I didn't remember eating since Christmas Day so where did it all come from?

Nurse Boyle wiped my mouth and handed me chips of ice to suck. I leant back against the pillows. Reaching under my arm she hauled me to a sitting position and she switched on the television set.

'Turn it off!' I groaned as the noise split my skull in two.

'Doctor's orders – it stays on,' he said, smiling. He had a nauseatingly cheerful bedside manner under the circumstances, and a fatherly but prematurely grey beard that padded his cheeks and made him look like a hamster. That reminded me once more of the rats. At least the television gave me something else to focus on, but the volume was unbearable.

The Hibs anthem 'Sunshine on Leith' rang out around Easter Road. It was a capacity crowd. The green Santa hats were out in force for the Edinburgh Derby. Good God, the Derby!

'How long have I been out?' I asked.

The doctor smiled reassuringly. 'Three days, I'm afraid. We were concerned about possible spinal injuries so we kept you sedated to minimize further complication.'

I closed my eyes tightly, screwing them shut so firmly it was painful. I couldn't keep it up. The home crowd had now started up a rendition of 'Glory, Glory to the Hibees' as the teams came onto the pitch. Lucas Baroc ran out holding the hand of a boy who looked as if he was eight. I swallowed hard – life goes on. The crowd cheered loudly as the Hibees took to the pitch; the announcer could hardly be heard above the roar but I didn't need to hear him. The crowd was chanting.

'Connie–Connie–Connie...'

She was holding the hand of Joe Stanley, the Hibs captain. A dyed-in-the-wool Hibee, she was never going to be happy about holding Lucas Baroc's hand. He was the striker for the enemy. No wonder she hadn't been overjoyed at my present. The camera was all too aware of who she was and, as the crowd continued to bellow her name over and over, the camera cut to the directors' box to show all the family – except me. Kailash, Grandad, Malcolm, Derek, Joe, Moses, Lavender and

360

Eddie, all there with wet faces. She turned and waved up to them. She even blew them kisses. Then – little show-off – she blew a kiss to the camera. Foolishly, I tried to catch it, regardless of what the doctor would think of my concussion.

'I said if you did as you were told she'd be returned to you.' My heart stopped, every cell in my body froze as it recognized his voice. I scrambled to get out of bed but my legs and arms wouldn't work properly. The nurse had left the room and we were alone.

'Diazepam,' he explained. 'I wanted to tell you how I did all this for you ... but you wouldn't understand, you'd try to run away ... unless I took precautions ... that's all it is ... a precaution.'

'Why did you take Connie?' I hissed at him. I could feel the drugs working their way through my system, numbing my muscles as I struggled, once more, to retain consciousness.

'We'll get to that... Well done for figuring out Thomas's secret. You went up in my estimation again...'

'What's the link between you and Thomas Foster?'

'You're disappointing me; I thought you had all that figured out,' he said, settling into a chair beside the bed.

'Call it a last request, tell me everything.'

His smile was like the Angel of Death's. He'd fill the IV with some poison so it would look like an accident. He could give me an overdose of insulin and Patch would think it was a complication from the head injury. Lying on Patch's table... I'd always feared that would happen. Somehow facing the inevitable made me relax – it was either that or the effects of the diazepam.

'I won a scholarship to Yale,' he said. He sounded strangely regretful about it. 'In my last year I was tapped to be a Bonesman. Oh, like you I thought it was a foolish society. But it had the potential to advance my career. At the initiation ceremony–'

'You're given an *Anam Cara* – and yours was Thomas Foster.'

'Correct... Also at the ceremony we were locked in a pit for twelve hours and we had to confess everything to our soul brother... Thomas's confession shocked me. I tried to go to the authorities but he knows the president and there is the small fact he's a chimera.'

'So what did you do?'

'I thought I'd done all I could...' There was a wistful tone in his voice that even I, in my weakened state, picked up. 'It was my intention to keep my head down and get through it. But my opposition to him excited Thomas and he started to kill even more frequently.'

'Soul mates, soul brothers, whatever... I thought the whole point was that you supported each other, kept each other's secrets no matter what. Isn't that how you got away with so much?'

He was quiet for a moment. Was he toying with me again, even at this stage?

'Ah well. Part of the rite, of course, is that I also had to confess everything to Thomas. Unfortunately that included my own proclivities, functions and dysfunctions, the main one being a complete inability on my part to have sexual

362

relationships with anyone.' He shrugged. 'It's personality disorder. Treatment has been futile. I have lurid fantasies ... most of which would make your hair curl even more, Brodie.' He looked at my hair. His eyes bottomless, like a shark's. I felt the menace and feared it.

'There's not much point in being anything but honest with you. You'll never tell anyone now,' he went on in a chillingly casual tone.

'My tastes are ... extreme. Violent and brutal, yet filled with longing. If you could see into my mind, well ... you would have nightmares forever. Call it a curse or a blessing. It can be both. But the fact is I will never know the satisfaction of physically realizing them ... except alone. I've learned to apply my own ... controls, over myself and others.

'That information could be as damaging to my career as the society is advantageous. You can imagine how complex my relationship with Foster became. It was as if with every victim he felt he was taunting me more. We alone knew the full extent of each other's secrets. I was his only audience. He was showing off how he could manipulate women sexually, physically, fatally. Every performance was for me.

'The extra twist being that he laid my DNA at the scene ... it's ridiculously easy. Drop a few stray hairs here and there ... bingo! I was now the main suspect in the New Haven killings. Actually I hate killing. Recently I had to kill a cat. It was distressing and revolting but, alas, necessary. Thomas, on the other hand, is a psychopath.'

'Your name has been scrubbed from the FBI record.'

'True … people within the Skull and Bones knew what Thomas was like. They protect their own … up to a point. He went past that point and was becoming an embarrassment.'

'So you were sent across to Scotland to keep an eye on him.'

The Watcher nodded.

'His choice of victims changed. Before, he had chosen redheads because of me. Typical pop psychology … a man targeting redheads must have a redheaded mother?' He shook his head disdainfully. At the same time, he peeled off the gray beard, wincing and revealing 'Cal's' chin underneath.

'I noticed your ginger roots. Real Dark Angels never let their roots grow in. Your Breitling watch was obviously genuine, and the handmade brogues gave you away in George Street when you were selling drugs with Blind Bruce.'

'Well … whoop-de-doo… It's all very well being wise after the event, Ms McLennan.' He sounded annoyed.

'The peroxide burnt my scalp; it was horrible.' He sat down on the edge of the bed. 'I followed him the night he murdered Katya.'

I opened my mouth to speak.

'He got lucky… I made a mistake.' A tinge of red coloured his pale complexion.

'What did you do?'

'I didn't watch him properly; Katya had her dress and bag on the cannon. She went into her bag – I thought she was getting a condom. She wasn't. It was lipstick … he wrote a message on her… Katya couldn't see or understand what he

364

had written ... to her it was a mild fetish.'

'That explains the message "more will die".' I pushed myself back against the pillows, and allowed the drugs to wash over me. I felt the slow relaxed smile fill my face; everything seemed marvellous.

'I took the photograph of Thomas and Katya but I didn't catch the moment of him writing the message or him throwing the handbag after the body.' He smiled apologetically.

'What about The Hobbyist site?' I asked.

'That was a genuine site. But Thomas found a better use for it. He used it to incriminate me, to send me warnings or leave clues.'

'Why did I appear on it?'

'Thomas knew me like no other person. I went to boarding school in Perthshire and I was aware of you ... very aware. I wanted to follow you in studying law but I won a scholarship to Yale. He knows I like older women...'

He could not meet my eye.

'It was because of you I thought of joining the Dark Angels. It provided a perfect cover ... and if you ever want to punish me, believe me the time I spent with them was more than enough retribution.'

'Why couldn't Patch categorize the knife Thomas used?'

The Watcher went into his trouser pocket and pulled out a round disc. He pressed a button and three serrated blades popped out.

'A custom-made bear claw, serrated titanium edges – we were given it at the initiation ceremony.' I heard the same awe in The Watcher's voice that Sonia described in Thomas Foster's.

'Why would someone describe that as a pirate's knife?' I slurred. The drugs were fuddling my brain now.

He chuckled and held the bear claw in front of my face: the skull and crossbones, the sign of the Bonesmen. But Sonia knew it from the pirate's flag.

'I'm sorry, Thomas Foster wanted you to suffer because of me. I knew it wouldn't be long before he attacked Connie ... that's why I took her.'

'You evil fucker–'

'I kidnapped her and saved her life ... do you still think I was wrong? Active evil is better than passive good: I left you a note.'

'Did you hurt her?'

'No, I gave her a sedative and then I took her up to Perthshire to my mother's. Connie knows me and likes me; she's clever and funny. We played on the Internet every day. She kept me sane. My mother knew what Thomas was capable of ... and I had to watch him so I took Connie out of Edinburgh. I explained it to her. It wasn't difficult. She trusts me and she was willing to do anything to save you. Her upbringing has, shall we say, made her more willing to accept dramatic turns in life.'

'So what was the link between the Bonesmen and the Enlightenment Society?'

'The head of the Enlightenment knew that Thomas was a menace. He was supposed to tell you to keep him in jail until we could get more evidence on him.'

Of course, that was exactly what Lord Port Soy

had tried to do at the function.

'Why did Thomas Foster choose these locations? They weren't random.'

'He was firing a shot across the bows of the Bonesmen – threatening to expose them.'

'Who was he trying to expose when he picked on Eastern European sex slaves?'

The Watcher raised his eyebrow.

'Why, his father. Thomas hates his all-controlling, untouchable father. Didn't you know Adie Foster was one of the eight American defence contractors hauled before a Senate committee hearing for running sex slaves in Bosnia? Nothing happened, of course. He used his connections to ensure the US did nothing significant to stop sex trafficking. It's the new slave trade.'

'No. I didn't know any of that. But if you're not involved, that explains why no murders were committed while Thomas was in prison. All the bodies we found had been killed before he was locked up behind bars.'

'If you're wondering why you're alone ... I spoke to your family and said you needed complete rest.'

Didn't they watch *The Godfather?* I wanted to scream. He saw the terror on my face.

'It's only diazepam – it will wear off,' he said as he rose from the chair and towered over me.

He bent down. 'I'm hard to find, Brodie ... don't come looking for me,' he rasped in my ear. Then he planted a kiss on my forehead and turned the television up.

'I don't make promises I can't keep.'

The door slammed and he left me watching the

367

match; the TV cameras kept panning to Connie and her family. It was one-nil to Hibs at half time. The commentators were discussing the play when the announcer at Easter Road said they had a request for Connie Coutts's big sister. I smiled until the song started playing. He was letting me know he would be 'watching me'. It was The Police: 'Every Breath You Take'.

BOOT.